P9-DGX-608

# PARADISE DOGS

**Also by Man Martin**

*Days of the Endless Corvette*

# PARADISE DOGS

Man Martin

Thomas Dunne Books
St. Martin's Press New York

This is a work of fiction. All of the characters, organizations, and events portrayed in this novel are either products of the author's imagination or are used fictitiously.

THOMAS DUNNE BOOKS.
An imprint of St. Martin's Press.



www.thomasdunnebooks.com
www.stmartins.com

ISBN 978-0-312-66256-1

First Edition: June 2011

10 9 8 7 6 5 4 3 2 1

For Dad

# PARADISE DOGS

# Paradise

Adam Newman and Evelyn Winston fell in love over a plate of cold chili dogs and limp onion rings.

After her husband Vince's ship went down in the Pacific, Evelyn realized that if she didn't plan to sit around in Green Cove and mildew, she needed to create herself a life. There was still war work to be had, but Germany had surrendered, and she foresaw Japan wouldn't hold out much longer, so she mailed out teaching applications to every county in Florida: Orange County wanted her.

With the insurance money from her husband's death for a down payment, she and a remarkably charming and remarkably ugly realtor looked at potential houses all one day in late June, finally stopping at a diner for a late lunch.

When the realtor, whose name Evelyn kept forgetting, picked her and Kean up in his truck at the motor court, he recited a snatch of poetry for her, "It takes a heap o' livin' in a house t' make it home. A heap o' sun an' shadder, and ye sometime have t' roam. Afore you really 'preciate the things ye lef' behind, and hunger fer 'em somehow with 'em allus on your mind."

After this unexpected font of cornpone sentiment, Evelyn sat and stared uncomfortably out the window and said nothing. It was only later she realized he'd been joking, and the funniest part of it was she hadn't realized it was a joke.

The day was already unforgivingly hot. They cranked the truck windows down of course, but they weren't driving fast enough to stir much breeze, so they only managed to let in gnats by the armload. In the seat between them little Kean was sweaty and irritable. Evelyn took off her wide-brimmed Spanish hat and gave it to Kean to fan himself. They turned off a brick street and onto a dirt road shouldered on one side by marsh and on the other by pinewoods. A heron waited like a question mark in the reeds.

When Evelyn got out to look at a bungalow, her damp blouse peeled from the seat and then clung to her back like wallpaper. Sweat darkened the armpits of the ugly realtor, whose name Evelyn kept trying to recall. Gordon? Henry? Charlie?

The bungalow disappointed even the realtor. Black ovals under the sinks warned of faulty plumbing; gobbling white termites infested a nearby woodpile; the whole place reeked of dank. The ugly realtor shook his head grimly: not much to choose from in central Florida. He explained apologetically that he normally dealt with commercial real estate, orange groves and Brahma bull ranches mostly. Something caught his eye and he left Evelyn and Kean standing by the truck to investigate a tangle of green vines by the woodpile. For a moment, aware he was being watched, he struck a comic pose of exaggerated discovery and declaimed, "Stout Cortez with eagle eyes stared at the Pacific." From a distance, in his white shirt and light tan fedora, he wasn't that bad-looking. He came back through the tall grass and sandspurs, kicking sand from his loafers and bringing blackberries in his hat; that they stained the crown purple seemed of no consequence to him. Evelyn ate some and gave some to Kean.

He was good company at any rate. Most men were still overseas, and those that were in the States seemed put off by a widow with a small son, but Gordon, Henry, or Charlie was only eager to please, and his eagerness pleased Evelyn. Kean got carsick, and they pulled over so he could upchuck, but the realtor was unfazed. After patting Kean's back and giving him a mint, he stood stock-still and pointed at a brown something lumbering in the saw palmetto in the pinewoods beside the road. When she saw it was a wild boar, Evelyn had the all-overs, but whether from joy, fear, or just excitement, she couldn't say. Feral hogs had been hunted to the point they'd almost given out, but it seemed there was still at least one left.

The realtor was gallant; he always opened the car door for her without making a scene of rushing around the front of the car. When they stopped at a diner, he held her chair.

Their waitress apologized for sitting as she took their orders, but explained she had arthritis. She'd tied copper wire around her ankle, she told them, but it hadn't done any good. Adam—which was the ugly realtor's name—asked to inspect the wire. He knelt at the waitress's ankle, and Evelyn found herself admiring the muscles along his back.

"Are you a root doctor?" the waitress asked. "My mama was a root doctor, and I got some leaning that way myself. I'm always first to know when a woman's going to have a baby."

Adam did not confirm or deny that he was a root doctor, but merely said, "Yes, I thought so. You have this wire twisted right-over-left. You have to twist it left-over-right. One second." He untwisted the wire and then retwisted it and took his seat. "See if that doesn't help."

Adam ordered them chili dogs—the menu was very limited—and a beer for himself, which Evelyn thought a very urbane and sophisticated thing to do in the middle of the day. When the waitress left, Evelyn whispered conspiratorially, "She actually thinks you're a root doctor."

"You actually think I'm a real estate man," Adam said. Evelyn laughed at that. "Actually I just like helping out." Then he told her a joke.

"In the middle of a play, this actor grabs his chest and falls to the floor." Adam clapped the table to demonstrate. "The other actors gather around in panic, and then one of them says, 'Is there a doctor in the house?'

"For a second no one says a thing, then in the back row a man stands up and says, 'I'm a doctor.' So he goes up onstage and loosens the actor's collar and palpitates his chest and whatnot until an ambulance gets there.

"So the ambulance driver says, 'Thank God you were here, Doc, you probably saved his life.'

" 'Well, the truth is,' the man says, 'I'm not really a doctor, I'm a bookkeeper.'

" 'My God,' says the ambulance driver, 'you had this man's life in your hands! Why did you tell these people you were a doctor?'

" 'Well,' says the man, scratching his chin and thinking about it, 'nobody else stood up.' "

The joke didn't strike Evelyn as particularly funny, but she laughed anyway. She had resigned herself to going back to her room at the motor court and spending the night convincing herself by heroic self-assurances that the bungalow was not so bad after all, and that if nothing else was to be had, she and Kean could make do. But as they ate, Adam described a house that would be just perfect for them: a three-bedroom, two-bath stucco that backed up onto an orange grove. When the blooms came in, they perfumed the place up something fierce. There was a live oak from which, if she wished, they could hang a swing for Kean. The best place in the world to raise a family.

He took a shiny brass key from his back pocket and pushed it across the table toward her, and Evelyn realized that Adam was describing his own house, and that he was flirting with her, had in fact been flirting with her all day. She knew then that she was going to marry him—red face, flattened nose, cauliflower ear and all—that marriage was as certain as the cooling summer squall promised by the distant thunder.

The rain began, and Evelyn pulled Kean's chair to hers so he could sleep, his sweaty head in her lap. Outside, hailstones cracked and popped against the diner's roof and windows. Adam gave her a cigarette, first making it disappear into his mouth, and then extracting it from his ear. She laughed at this sleight of hand, and he lit it for her with a flick of his Zippo lighter. Vincent had not smoked nor approved of her smoking, so lighting up now seemed gloriously devil-may-care.

"We could have a hot dog restaurant. People will come from miles around, and we'll make so much money, we won't be able to count it, You can make better hot dogs than this, I bet," Adam said.

"I sure can. I'd fry them. Of course, we'd need special casings."

"Now we're going to keep it simple. Simplify, simplify, simplify. Simplify. We won't sell hamburgers, fried chicken, or barbecue. Just hot dogs."

"But the very best hot dogs."

They came back after their wedding, and the waitress told Adam her arthritis was much better, thank you. She also told them Evelyn was pregnant, and that she was surprised that Adam, as a root doctor, hadn't guessed.

# ONE

# Adam, in Perfect Health, Begins

Ernie Costa buzzed the door to let Adam out, and it clicked locked behind him. Eight A.M. on a peaceful downtown sidewalk with two hundred fifty thousand dollars' worth of stones in a purple bag in his jacket pocket. A cool breeze stirred the collar of his favorite blue windbreaker, but the December sun was bright in the cloudless sky.

The lark was on the wing, the snail was on the thorn, LBJ was in his White House, and all was right with the world.

In the three years, two months, and eight days since Adam had been separated from the only precious things in the world—his wife and son—he never once stopped hoping to be reunited with them. At last he figured he would unbungle all his previous bungles. At last he could be happy again. In his excitement about reuniting with Evelyn, even his anxiety over the Cross-Florida Barge Canal receded. He recalled some lines they had taught him at Sisters of Mercy Academy: "I, now forty-seven years old in perfect health, begin."

Honeysuckle grew from an asphalt crack and pulled

chunks of paint and stucco from the wall of Costa's Diamonds, but it was winter, and there were no blooms on the vine. Morning was the best time of day. He wished it were earlier, while sunrise still pinked the sky between the telephone wires on East Central and the air was not yet spoiled by exhaust. Still, better than half the day remained to change his life and outrun disappointment.

Two hours before it opened to the public, Costa's Diamonds had held just Adam Newman, Ernie Costa, and Ernie's teenage daughter, Rachel, who sat behind the counter sullenly watching a transistor TV with an orange-capped antenna, a screen the size of an index card, and a handle like a lunch box.

On the snowy screen, the Cheerios Kid—"He's got Go-Power!"—mounted and armored, rescued Girlfriend Sue from a dragon's clutches. To be fair, the dragon was not actually clutching Sue at that moment, but sitting close enough that he might clutch her any second if he hadn't already. If the dragon thought his fiery breath would avail him, however, he soon learned otherwise because the smoke rings merely recalled to the Kid those tasty O's. Pausing only to guzzle a stream of Cheerios straight from the box, our hero charged stage left—legs whirling like a rotary saw. A sound effect like dishes thrown downstairs indicated he had landed a punch, and in the next scene the Kid flexed an outsized bicep, his other arm protectively around Sue, as the chastened dragon woozily watched the stars orbiting his field of vision.

Meanwhile, Ernie had arranged the diamonds on a black velvet square.

"So, boss, what do you think?"

Adam picked one and let it fall into his palm; with his thumb he push-broomed the others into a pile and then swept them all up in one pass. Misgivings about this exchange mounted in Ernie's chest like a wave, and he stiffened slightly, his hands raised in front of his white shirt. Adam pressed the diamonds into his lifeline a moment, then let them rain through his fingers. They fell into casual groupings—most of them gregarious, two slightly aloof. "What size are they?"

"Two and a half to four carats. I mixed them up—there's a couple of emerald cuts and a princess cut in there." Ernie bent behind the counter and retrieved a sheaf of twenty-four papers, two for each diamond in Adam's hand. "I'll need you to sign these papers before you can take them out of the store."

"That's right," Adam said. "I guess it wouldn't do for me to go losing these, would it? Ha-ha."

"Ha-ha." Foreboding swelled in Ernie again, and a serious look fell over his face like a damp rag. "I want you to be careful out there, boss."

"I'll be careful."

"I mean, you're one of the nicest people I know, boss, but sometimes you trust people too much. There's some bad people out there." Mr. Newman was a good man; Ernie hated thinking of his friend getting taken in. "The fact is," Ernie added, "I'm kind of in a tight spot myself right now. I owe some money. If anything happened to these—"

"I'd make it good," Adam finished.

"What I'm saying is I'm really out on a limb here."

"Nothing's going to happen to them." Adam applied the Newman autograph on the indicated spaces. "This is going to thrill her," Adam said.

"It sure will."

Driving around all day in scalding sunshine looking at investment properties had blistered Adam's puffy face into a calico of reds, browns, and pinks, which never healed even in winter. His peeling scalp clung to a few strands of red hair as fine as cornsilk floating up from his head; his nose had been mashed out of shape and one ear slightly cauliflowered from fistfights at Sisters of Mercy Academy where his mother had sent him after the Old Man's accident; his head looked like a beach ball someone had partially inflated before giving up. In sum, his appearance was not likely to cheer love's lingering gaze, yet he possessed a near genius when it came to women. He often thought of writing a book on courtship secrets; it was certain to be a best seller. Of course, it didn't hurt to know a jeweler who was willing to let you walk out of his shop with a couple of hundred grand or so worth of diamonds.

What woman could resist the thing with the diamonds? When Evelyn had accepted him the first time, he'd poured a sparkling handful in her lap and said, *Take your pick, darling, any one you want. We'll set it into a ring later.* He'd asked her to marry him several times before then, but each time she'd put him off. They had known each other a very short time, she was in no specific hurry to remarry, and she judged him as the type to propose as many times as it took. But when a dozen diamonds lay in her lap, shining against her dark skirt like a starry sky, there was simply no way to refuse.

It had worked once. It had to work again.

"Rachel, you need to witness these," Ernie said, holding out the sheaf and a pen for his daughter. She ignored him. "Rachel!" She complied without taking her eyes from the tiny screen.

"Does Uncle Bert know about this? He's not going to like it."

"My brother-in-law," Ernie explained, lifting his eyebrows. "He's the one I owe."

"A rough customer?" Adam asked.

"You wouldn't want to meet him in a dark alley," Ernie confirmed. Discussing his brother-in-law made him uncomfortable, and he looked away. "I'll put the diamonds in a case for you."

"Oh, don't bother," Adam said. Ernie raised an eyebrow when Adam scooped them into his bag. Ernie had a box ready in his hands, but the purple velveteen bag seemed more opulent; Adam would have to keep it turned when he poured the diamonds out for Evelyn, so she wouldn't see the Akron Marbles label.

Standing outside Ernie's shop with the bag of diamonds in his pocket, Adam did not kid himself that the second proposal would go as smoothly as the first. This time there were new challenges to be overcome: getting out of his engagement with Lily Manzana for openers. Then there was the whole history of the french fry incident.

A squirrel scouted the curb for orphaned potato chips. It popped upright in a moment of routine panic, but no cars were coming, and it lingered erect to savor the cool air and quiet of its surroundings. Costa's location could hardly be called a chichi district, but then, downtown had no chichi districts. Past the city limits lay the lush hardwood hammock—cabbage palms, loblolly bays, oaks—and skirting that, orange groves that were now in full fruit, but here, in spite of the tinsel Christmas decorations overhanging the street and the reminders that there were only Four More Shopping Days, the city wore the joyless face of many a town in central Florida.

Interstate 4 had come through, but the region still fairly trembled in anticipation of the next big thing, the thing that would lift it from being a largely rural cracker town into something like modern glory, as had happened in Palm Springs and Miami. Adam had been only a child during the 1920s boom, when you could hustle Detroit and St. Paul rubes into shelling out their life's savings for vacant lots with sinkholes, and by the end of the day, those same rubes could unload those same sinkholes on still other rubes from Newark and

Chicago at a healthy profit. But the land craze had receded, leaving central Florida largely unchanged.

Adam looked left and saw the steeple of First Presbyterian, once the tallest structure on the skyline. Now the town was warted with buildings, a few as tall as ten stories. The city's quest to modernize resulted, however, as if by design, only in raising the general squalor. The courthouse annex, a turquoise-colored concrete waffle that stood beside the Greek Revival courthouse like an ugly stepsister, necessitated not only closing Court Street to make a parking lot, but demolishing the "old" courthouse, a redbrick Victorian with a clock tower to one side that had been a fixture of the landscape even before the Old Man himself was born. Stately emperor palms had been brought in for the new courthouse, which made the place look a good deal more tropical than the uprooted oaks they replaced, but offered neither acorns for squirrels, climbing places for children, or shade for anyone. Adam had cheered with the rest of the town when street pavers came in after the last world war. *It's about time*, the citizens had told one another approvingly, but now, although he scarcely would have credited that a street could be pretty, he realized that the old brick streets *had* been pretty, and he regretted thinking of them hidden under coats of black asphalt.

Looking at the brown brick tiers on the storefronts across the street filled Adam with an unexpected sadness. He smacked his lips and tasted the dry air. He took a Pall Mall from his shirt pocket, lit it with his trusty Zippo, and turned his thoughts to Evelyn.

Naturally Evelyn would be hard to convince—once she made up her mind there was little chance of unmaking it—but the impending marriage to Lily would put a point on the matter. He would tell her he loved her and couldn't live without her. *If you don't take me now, darling, I'll be gone forever,* he imagined himself saying. *Gone.* There could be no arguing with such patient love as he had. She would relent.

"You certainly appear incited this morning," Lily said when he returned to the jeep.

Adam had long since learned to accept his fiancée's peculiar mode of expression without comment. "She walks in beauty, like the night," he quoted for her, "of cloudless climes and starry skies, and all that's best of dark and bright, meet in her aspect and her eyes." Just about the only thing he'd gotten from Sisters of Mercy Academy besides an ability to hold his liquor and a well-earned reputation as a fighter was the facility of quoting poetry by the yard.

Lily looked at her *Reader's Digest,* a feeling in her stomach as if she were the winner on the TV show *Queen for a Day* with host Jack Bailey; once upon a time there was a gallant business owner who quoted his wife poetry as a shy waitress wiped his tables and bussed his trays, watching and dreaming that someday maybe someone would recite for her.

Adam backed out of the parking space. "We're off to Evelyn's," he said.

"To pronounce our engagement," Lily said complacently. At his side, she tucked the collar of his handsome starched shirt under his windbreaker.

Adam said nothing but took a drink of beer.

Lily could not restrain her sigh.

"What?"

"Maybe we should postpone until later to celebrate," she suggested in a voice she tried to make cheerful—he hated being mothered, she knew—and patted his chest.

Lily's insinuation that because Adam was frugal, he was some kind of a lush irked him; 8:00 A.M. was early to have a beer, he knew, but he had pulled the tab on the way to Costa's without thinking, and now that it was open, there was no point letting it go to waste.

"There is an open container law," Lily said. A black and white squad car passed in the rearview mirror. "Are you aware of that?"

Adam was aware. "So?" She was always trying to work him—never telling him directly what he should do, but always dancing around with sly hints, queries, and insinuations. He took a defiant swallow. "You'd like to get a law enforcement officer involved in this, is that it?"

She looked at her magazine, studying Liz Taylor's photo with the intensity of a spurned Debbie Reynolds. "I am only remarking." Her eyes stung, but she would die before she let him see. He always took care of her; just once, couldn't he let her take care of him? "I do not desire you to get a citation." Lily turned a page. "Did you make a note? Dr. Bateman says you are supposed to make a note."

Adam gripped his filter tip in his teeth and slipped a notepad from his back pocket. Holding the notepad against the steering wheel as he drove, he wrote, *Monday: A couple of beers.*

The other week, Lily had made him an appointment with Dr. Bateman, which Adam had assumed was for a blood test, but in reality was so they could gang up on him about his "drinking."

*You've got to face it, Adam,* the doctor had said. *You have a drinking problem.*

*What else can I do, Doc? I practice every chance I get.*

Lily and Dr. Bateman were not amused. Dr. Bateman had looked stern and concerned, and Lily had looked worried but also satisfied—like someone's damn mother who's been vindicated by the headmistress. *I told you what would happen if you picked fights.* Adam sat on the chilly examination table, stripped to his striped boxers, on that white paper they roll out so you won't have to think about the diseased half-naked person who'd been there before you. Adam was the only one not fully dressed. There was no way you could tell him that wasn't a deliberate tactic: get someone to take his pants off before you negotiate with him. Adam would have to try that the next time he closed a deal, but how to get the other guy naked?

*It is not just his drinking*, he'd overheard Lily whisper to the doctor outside the examination room. *It is also his impersonations.*

Adam could have told him that his "impersonations," as Lily called them, had nothing to do with drinking. He never planned to pass himself off as other people; he simply wanted to help. Girlfriend Sue never objected to the Cheerios Kid, *Hey, you're not really a knight!* When dragons were involved, the man for the job stepped up, and that was that.

After the examination, Dr. Bateman suggested Adam check into Chattahoochee *for a few days*. Adam had been to Chattahoochee once before—he'd gone out of love for Evelyn, that reason and no other, surrendering his shoelaces and painting those damn therapeutic ceramic alligators—but he didn't care to repeat the experiment.

Dr. Bateman had finally wrung a concession from Adam that he would keep a daily record of how much he drank; thus far, the record confirmed his so-called drinking problem was all in Lily's head. The entry for each day read the same, *A couple of beers.*

While he was thinking about it, though, the mini-cooler did need a refill. "Tank's nearly empty," Adam said. "I'm stopping at the Sinclair on Eola."

As the gas pump announced each gallon with a ding, and the attendant sponged water onto the windshield and began to squeegee it away, Adam got out and spread his arms. The cool air was refreshing after sharing a ride with Lily.

"I need to go over and make a call," Adam said, pointing a thumb at the phone booth.

"You have to monitor your business concerns," Lily said eagerly, and Adam said, yes, it was business. The mention of Adam's investments always made Lily feel like a schoolgirl getting to meet an astronaut. Adam had a hand in everything, and glamorous artifacts of his enterprises graced his home, such as the mysterious map of land purchases hanging over his office desk. She knew he wasn't *just* going to monitor his business concerns, but her eyes followed him with prideful ownership.

She had worked so hard to be worthy of him, starting years ago when she had told him, *There is a snake in your garden.* He took a hoe out to kill it, but he never guessed what loving pains that information had cost her: practicing over and over, until she could pronounce it properly, *snake*—hours scraping greasy Spanish from her speech, all those vowels with never enough consonants to go around, starving for an *hache* or *erre. Snake:* she'd learned to say it precise and clean, like sophisticated Aunt Esperanza who married the Greek doctor, not flabby, silly *es-nake*, like Lily's fat cubaña mother—*I'm es-cared of es-nakes!*—and far from the Spanish *culebra*, coiling and stretching in the mouth like a muscle.

She had come a long way.

Adam made a mental note before going into the Little General next to the Sinclair to donate to the bell-ringing Santa Claus on his way back out. Paying for his tallboys, Adam studied the palm tree display at the register. XMAS SPECIAL, said the sign, BUY TWO OR MORE FOR ADDED TROPICAL AMBIANCE. The sign explained that the palm trees stood five feet tall when fully inflated and came with Christmas lights attached. He fingered the vinyl fronds of a tree that had been inflated as part of the display.

"Is it Ex-mas already?" Adam asked. "Seems like only yesterday it was just Ex-giving."

"Haw," laughed the fat girl behind the register. "You want a receipt with that, sugar?" The farther south you went in Florida, the more high-toned people tried to act; at the Palm Springs Stuckey's, the waitresses smoked nothing but Benson & Hedges, but here in central Florida, thank the Lord, you could still find a few genuine crackers—good-hearted Southern girls who could chew Fruit-Stripe Gum, smoke a Lucky Strike, and make small talk all at once.

"You sell many of these?" Adam asked.

"Not really," she admitted. She sucked the cigarette between her plump red fingernails. "People want something more traditional."

"What aspect exactly of an inflatable light-up palm tree could be considered untraditional?" Adam asked, and then, without waiting for an answer, "Can you break a quarter so I can make a phone call, dear?" He needed to get his business out of the way so he could speak to Evelyn with a clear head.

On the way to the phone booth, he dropped a dollar fifteen into the red bucket and was acknowledged with a "Merry Christmas" from Santa. Adam didn't consult the phone book hanging from its chain, but looked through the business cards in his wallet—as always, at the sight of General Potter's card (*U.S. Army, Retired*) Adam's heart momentarily beat faster, but he continued flipping through cards until he found one with an oily stain along its crease from sitting in his wallet. He dialed the number and stared through the glass wall.

Farther south, Eola led to the neighborhood he'd lived in before his temporary divorce—sweet bungalows shaded by live oaks and, below that, orange groves with bright fruit hanging like ornaments this time of year among dark shiny leaves. A right and a dogleg would take you to the Wigwam Motel, where Adam had once spent the night in an authentic concrete Indian teepee, but here it was sandy vacant lots and sad cinder-block buildings as widely spaced as a hobo's teeth. A sign with Winged Justice holding a flaming sword—GABRIEL ANGELO, BAIL BONDS—swayed and creaked on rusty links, and chilly sunlight scraped through green bristles of the scrawny pines between the single-wides across the street. Poor central Florida. Who would come to redeem her?

A familiar voice answered the phone, and Adam said, "Hello, Randal. How are you, you old rascal? Adam Newman here."

"Hello, big'un. Just fine. You?"

"Fair to middling. Fair to middling. How's that pretty wife of yours?"

"Fine as frog's hair. She was just asking about you the other day. She says maybe we could have you out for supper. We could fry you up some catfish."

"I'd love that," Adam said. "Maybe I could bring," the next word had a knob that caught in his throat, "Evelyn. If I can talk her into it."

Randal's response was solemn, "What about Lily?"

"She doesn't understand me the way Evelyn does. I wish she did, but she doesn't. Lily's kind of narrow. I'm working on a deal right now to get me and Evelyn back together."

There was a silence at the other end before Randal said prayerfully, "Oh, Adam, I hope so. Me and Sarah keep hoping y'all two'll get back together. We're pulling for you."

"You take care of Sarah," Adam said. "Don't you let a good woman like her go. 'A man who finds a wife, finds a good thing.'"

"Yes, sir."

"Anyhoo, the reason I called is I was wondering if you'd

given any more thought to that matter we discussed. Those five acres near the interstate."

"Listen, about that. I'm sorry, Adam." Randal hesitated. Hearing the pause, Adam already knew what Randal was going to say next. "This other outfit showed up and made an offer. Right out of the blue."

"Another outfit." This was not unexpected, and yet blood rushed to Adam's head. The telephone booth seemed to sway, and he put his hand against the smeary glass to brace himself.

"Yeah, I'm sorry I didn't let you know first. But it was right out of the blue. And it was such a good offer—and they didn't just want the five acres, but the whole ranch. The offer was so good, I couldn't pass on it."

"This other outfit. Ayefour or Compass East?"

"Ayefour, that's the name of it. You heard of them?"

Adam exhaled from his nose. A rust-and-primer-covered Belair came gunning from the trailer park.

"Ain't these Ayefour people on the up-and-up?" Randal asked.

The Belair hopped the curb, and with a dry, flapping pop like a fat man's fart, its tire burst.

"No, nothing like that," Adam said. The driver had gotten out and was staring in mute consternation at his lopsided car. Someone was in trouble, and Adam was the man for the job; this trumped even the Cross-Florida Barge Canal and the mysterious Ayefour Corporation. "I wish I could talk, Randal, but I've got to hang up now. There's a situation here." Adam imagined Evelyn watching from above, seeing him discuss the most important land deal in Florida's history and then coolly proceeding to help a fellow mortal in distress. The Amazing Adam Newman. "Just keep an eye out and let me know if you hear about Ayefour buying up any more land in your area." He hung up and hurriedly scribbled on the back of the card,

*A4 purch: 12/21/65.* He ran out. "I can help, I'm really experienced in these things."

"You're a doctor?" came a feminine voice from the car. "Praise Jesus!"

"Jesus!" Adam echoed.

Now his angle of vision allowed him to see that a woman, a girl really, lay in the front seat. Her chest rose in rapid, desperate huffs, and her damp face shone with exertion.

"Praise Jesus," the girl said.

"Praise Jesus," Adam repeated automatically, crossing himself.

"She ain't religious," the young man told Adam. "She figures it's better to say 'praise Jesus' than 'fuck.' "

Adam nodded at the wisdom of this.

"Help me get her to your car, and we can drive her to the hospital," the young man said. Though probably no more than nineteen, he already had the calloused hands and leathery tan of an orange picker.

"Had we but world enough and time," Adam said, "that plan would work out fine. But your baby's on its way right now."

"Look—" the boy began in a truculent tone.

"Jesus, Johnny, he's a doctor, just let him do it!" the girl said through clenched teeth and emphasized her point with a protracted grunt.

"Are you really a doctor?" Johnny asked suspiciously. He had unruly dark hair and suspicious-looking eyes.

"Have you heard of Dr. Bateman?" Adam had a vague notion he could get them to his own physician.

"We need to get her to the hospital," the boy said.

"We don't have time for that," Adam said. He could already see the protruding crown of the baby's head—a small furry coconut.

"You're not really a doctor," the boy said.

"Jesus, will you quit talking and let Dr. Bateman work?" the girl said.

What should Adam do? This sort of thing always seemed to happen to him. Telling them at this juncture he wasn't a doctor would do none of them any good. Childbirth wasn't such a big deal, was it? Women had been delivering babies since forever with no help at all; Seminole Indians used to give birth in the middle of the field and go right back to hoeing potatoes. Or was that the Irish? He wiped his stubbly chin. In an instant he made his choice. He slung off his blue windbreaker and rolled up his sleeves. "You start on that tire," he told the boy, "and I'll start on your wife."

"You're not a real doctor," the boy repeated.

"Jesus, Johnny, Jesus," the girl said. "Just let Dr. Bateman do his job!"

Adam Newman always stood ready to offer himself when needed, and if he wasn't needed—for example, if Adam Newman, Real Estate Speculator and erstwhile Restaurateur wasn't required, but Adam Newman, Veterinarian, or Adam Newman, Attorney-at-Law—he stood ready to offer that too. Once in a summer squall, he stepped in as Adam Newman, Traffic Cop and directed cars through a broken stoplight until a genuine patrolman arrived to replace him and quiz him suspiciously about his qualifications. The officer had looked less than convinced by Adam's explanation that he was a plainclothes traffic cop, but no one could fault the judicious efficiency or the graceful, almost balletic élan with which he'd waved the cars safely past.

Adam knelt beside the rust-scabbed car. The girl's dress, the color of dry palmetto fronds, looked as if it should belong to a much older woman. The sodden panties rolled to her ankles, dusty black loafers, and white socks made Adam sad.

The upholstery was old and full of holes, and Adam imagined springs must be poking her back.

The main thing, he thought, was to be a reassuring presence; he needed to *sound* medical. "I want you to make yourself as comfortable as possible, dear," he said tenderly. What else? "With your knees bent at forty-five degrees and shoulder-width apart. Take light tiny breaths as if you were trying to whistle but don't know how." Adam demonstrated—"Whhh! Whhh! Whhh!"—before he got light-headed and rocked back on his heels. He lifted a Schlitz from its carton, pulled off the tab, and took a steadying sip. "The head is coming first, which is good," he said diagnostically. "I don't want us to go for anything fancy today—just the basics. Some people ask me, 'Doc, can we have a breech delivery?' but personally I like to keep things simple. Like Thoreau said, 'Simplify, simplify, simplify.' And if I might add, simplify."

"Praise Jesus! Praise Jesus! Praise Jesus!" She craned her neck and pushed.

"You're not really a doctor," Johnny repeated obdurately. He frowned, and Adam realized he'd cupped his hands as if he had on a catcher's mitt, as if he expected the baby to shoot out like a fastball. Adam rubbed his hands together and rested them on the door jamb in a more relaxed posture, and after another moment of regarding Adam distrustfully, the boy sullenly put the jack beneath the car and began to crank it.

"Now, miss, whenever you're ready, I want you to push." The coconut top came forward; now it was clearly a head. "Push. That's it. . . . No, no, no! Loosen the lug nuts before you jack up the car. You'll never get the tire off that way."

"What's going on?" The cashier and Santa had come out to see the commotion. "Oh, my God!" Aware she had stepped into a medical environment the cashier spat out her cigarette and crushed it under the toe of her shoe. Her gum she swallowed.

"Jesus! Is it out yet! Jesus!"

"Please give us room," Adam said over his shoulder. "This is a delicate business. You're doing fine, miss. We'll have that baby out in a jiffy."

"Do you need us to boil water or something?" Santa asked.

"That is a myth, sir. Like painting alligators." Adam did not want to sound brusque, but he wished the cashier and Santa Claus would go mind their own business. These situations always drew well-meaning meddlers.

The top of the head had emerged.

"On second thought, do you have bags of ice? Get one for me." The cashier trotted away on heavy thighs and Santa followed, unsure what else he could do.

"Do you need towels?" Johnny asked, thinking of a delivery he'd seen on *I Love Lucy* or else *Bonanza*.

The baby was coming, coming. "It's not a bad idea," Adam admitted. "But there won't be towels around here. Go to the men's room and grab as many paper towels as you can. They should be sanitary enough."

As soon as Johnny left, the head passed through, and then the whole baby from shoulders to feet slipped steaming into sunlight as smoothly as a trout sliding down a hull into the water. "There it is! There it is!" Adam said triumphantly. He wrapped it in his blue windbreaker to keep it warm.

"Oh, Jesus," the girl said. She laid her sweaty head back on the upholstery, her knees trembling. The miracle of childbirth operated like a magnetic field; in short order the boy, the cashier, Santa, and Lily all converged on the spot.

"What's happened? Is it—" The boy ran up with two fat fistfuls of brown paper towels.

"It's a beautiful baby boy!" Adam said. "Oh, wait a minute. Excuse me. Baby girl. Euggh. And there's the placenta." The kinked purple cable leading from the baby trailed a magenta pillow. "In olden days the mother cooked and ate the placenta for nourishment," Adam informed them, "but that is not something I would recommend." Adam lifted the baby up to her father. "You can take it from here, son," he said. "I'll take a look at this flat." He offered the new mother a clump of paper towels. "Press these against your . . ." What was Latin for pussy? "Hold these against your*self*," he told the girl. "There's a certain amount of bleeding."

Adam knelt beside the tire, and Santa helped him slide it off the bolts and replace it with the spare. After Adam released a mechanism on the jack, he and Santa began finger-tightening the bolts, one with each hand as the car lowered. Adam did not mind that grease from the tire and bloody mucus from the birth coated his fingers in a sludgy mixture; this was the witness of a man who was master of all situations. "I, now forty-seven and in perfect health," he said lightly to Santa, "begin." Then he addressed the new parents, "Now you two need to get to the hospital as soon as possible. And then get a new tire. This one's almost as bald as the flat one."

Lily's red capris and high heels appeared by Adam's elbow. "Oh, Adam, you wonderful man, I saw!" She knelt and put her arms around his neck as he worked on the tire. She kissed the back of his head. "Is there anything you can't do?" Adam felt some trepidation lest she broach the topic of his nonexistent medical training, but he couldn't help feeling pleasure at her praise.

The cashier came galumphing back with a sack of ice. "What do you want me to do with this?" Sweat pasted her black curls to her forehead.

"Excellent, you're just in time. Take those beers there and that ice to my jeep. You'll find a mini-cooler in the backseat sitting on a case of sparkling Burgundy. Put the beer in the cooler and pour the ice over it."

# TWO

# Adam Proposes a Toast

The Little General restroom where Adam and Santa washed up boasted an old-fashioned cake of soap inlaid with a single coiled black hair.

"Hell of a way to start a Monday," Santa said. The tile walls of the little restroom echoed with his comradely laughter. His beard was off, and he was grinning from ear to ear. Grease stained his white fur cuffs.

No morning is more joyous than one spent helping others. Adam imagined Lancelot scrubbing up after slaying a particularly pesky ogre or restoring a maiden to her father. Miles from Camelot, he had done it to prove himself worthy of Guinevere. Adam always jumped at any opportunity to make himself wonderful in Evelyn's eyes. In the bathroom mirror his face glowed.

Adam returned to his jeep, and for a while following this deed, he drove in silence that fell on his heart like a song. Evelyn would have been proud at the way he'd handled the baby and the tire jack. All too soon, though, Adam felt the airy lightness of being competent, on-the-spot Dr. Bateman evanesce, and the burden of being plain Adam Newman returned to his shoulders like a leaden blanket.

"You were wonderful back there," Lily said. Then she added in a small voice, "You weren't impersonating someone, were you? You didn't tell them you were a doctor? It wasn't like the previous incident, was it, when you volunteered to take part in that play?"

In a community theater production of *Oklahoma!* as Adam and Lily listened to the anticipatory cacophony of the orchestra tuning up, a tearful stage manager stepped before the purple curtains to say that Curly, who had no understudy, had ruptured his appendix, and the show was canceled. Disappointment welled from the audience like water from a hidden spring. People had dressed up and put on perfume and cologne for an evening at the theater and perhaps a good restaurant later, and now they'd have to go back home to leftovers and *Walt Disney's Wonderful World of Color.* Adam rose. It so happened that he'd starred in that very role in an off-Broadway production, he said, knew all the lines by heart, and could fill in if they wished.

They wished.

Luckily Curly's costume fit. Adam saw no reason to inform the cast that he hadn't really been off-Broadway but at Sisters of Mercy Academy, and he hadn't been Curly, but Macduff, and it wasn't *Oklahoma!* but *Macbeth.* He had, however, listened to the LP enough to know most of it by heart, and songs he didn't know he filled in by repeating words from ones he did. Besides, Macduff's lines added an unexpected frisson to the Rodgers and Hammerstein script; when Adam, rakishly pushing his cowboy hat back, murmured to his sweetheart Laurey, "Let that dark angel thou still hast served tell thee Curly was from his mother's womb untimely ripped!"

or "Turn, hellhound, turn!" it drew gasps that would have delighted Shakespeare himself.

As they drove into the old neighborhood, Lily held a page open to show Adam an ad. "Look at this."

Adam looked. "Uh-huh."

"Vinyl slipcovers," she explained. This way he could smoke his cigarettes if he wanted, and when he forgot to put the butts in the ashtray, it wouldn't hurt the furniture. Adam pulled his wallet from his back pocket with one hand and thumbed out several twenties. "Do you think that's enough?" With Adam, Lily never had to ask; he took care of her slightest desire without a second thought.

He finished his beer. He was bursting to tell Evelyn about the Cross-Florida Barge Canal—a matter that in the interest of national security he must conceal for the time being—but once their temporary divorce was over, he would naturally confide in her. He imagined explaining the map—the cryptic map on his office wall, the significance of which even Lily had not divined: blue and red pushpins marking the purchases of Ayefour and its shadowy nemesis Compass East, describing an area bigger than Manhattan. He imagined Evelyn asking questions: at first, short, almost monosyllabic queries to clarify a point, concentration burning in her beautiful heavy-lidded eyes. Evelyn would nod thoughtfully, soaking it in. Finally she would begin filling in gaps herself, seeing the implications, offering new insights, speaking with the same soft-voiced intensity she'd had when they planned their restaurant.

Adam turned into the Lake Cherokee subdivision and onto Ponce de Leon Place, where he'd lived and once been happy; even the thought of the Cross-Florida Barge Canal failed to banish his gloom—so much had come between them! If only he could go back in time and start over. Not all the way, just two years ago—as far as the french fries.

Perhaps because his head was filled with these painful recollections he hit the mailbox.

"Stop—" Lily began, but too late. The sideview mirror had already hooked the mailbox. Adam twisted the steering wheel sharply, but in the urgency of the moment, turned toward the box instead of away from it.

Having just turned a shovelful of earth to inspect the chubby worms roiling in contentment among some cantaloupe, Evelyn heard a sound like iron fingernails on blackboard. She looked serenely from her shovel and announced to herself, "That must be Adam."

Adam's son, Addison, and stepson, Kean, along with Kean's girlfriend, Kathleen, were also home for Christmas break. Addison had been trying to come up with a plot for his yet untitled story, but hearing Adam hit the mailbox dragged him from his thoughts, and he joined the others outside.

"The mailbox appears to have been struck," Adam explained. It lay under the jeep as if it had crawled there to change the oil.

Relieved, Adam saw no anger flash in Evelyn's dark eyes; a twist to her perfect lips said she chose not to be annoyed but amused. From the mailbox's nose she took a handful of letters. "Bills," she said. "Oh," holding up a glossy envelope, "the Mortons sent us a Christmas card."

Lily and Evelyn bore a strong if superficial resemblance; both wore their dark hair in a bouffant and were about the same height although Evelyn was the heavier of the two. Lily was younger by nearly two decades and was by most standards prettier, but Evelyn's large lids drooped languidly over dark eyes like half-drawn shades, in a way that spoke of wry amusement at everything she saw. Adam could never resist that look.

Adam's arrival hadn't gone as planned, but it did not do to

be disturbed at trifles or accidents common or unavoidable. The mailbox thing could happen to anyone. Still—why did these things always happen to him, and why did it have to happen today? But as Disraeli said, never complain, never explain; the best thing at an awkward moment was to pretend it hadn't happened. In any case, Adam was home! Home! He belonged to this scrubby Saint Augustine growing in balding patches; that live oak spreading low arms draped with Spanish moss like the ghost of a loving father; the live Christmas tree he'd bought at a school fund-raiser, its chewed-up side hidden from this angle. Behind the house, bright oranges hung in the trees.

Adam dabbled in the orange grove business, which he hated for its never-ending battles with medflies and the toil of smudge pots when frosts came, but he loved the fruit itself—and when the blossoms came in, and groves all along the road were in bloom, the fragrance spoke to the soul like the promise of forgiveness.

"Hi, I'm Adam Newman," he said, extending his hand to the pretty brunette beside his stepson.

"I'm Kathleen," she said. "Actually, we've met."

"Oh, right," Adam said. "You're Addison's girlfriend, aren't you, dear?"

"No, I'm—" She cast her eyes down, discomfited. "We were never—"

She and Addison had never been more than almost-dating back in Advanced Brit Lit. Then Addison had introduced her to Kean, and the rest, as they say, was history.

Adam knew none of this, so the matter was opaque to him, but he decided not to pursue it. Adam only felt comfortable pretending to be someone he was not: Adam Newman, CPA, or Adam Newman, DDS; around the people he loved, plain Adam Newman found himself behind an invisible wall that no amount of cheer or goodwill allowed him to break through.

"I've got a present, son," Adam announced. Presents made everything better. "You'll have to help me carry this in," he said. "It's pretty heavy."

"You didn't have to, Dad," Addison said. Addison hugged him—dutifully, Adam thought—but a hug was a hug, and Adam resisted the urge to hold on after his son let go.

Kean bit his tongue. There was no point being jealous over something so absurd, but the pressure to remark was too great. "Of course he got *you* something," he muttered.

"It's weights," Adam explained. Adam and Addison hefted the present from the backseat; Adam let his son take the stern and he himself steered from the front, walking backward into the house and taking an exaggerated step over the threshold to show how careful he could be. "I read your column every day, son," Adam said. "I show it to everyone."

"It's just a part-time job writing obituaries, Dad. I only write what they tell me."

"It's the *way* you write them."

Addison's face heated. The way he wrote the obituaries was a matter of discontent with his editor. Just yesterday Addison had recorded the oddly Druidic notice that Mrs. Jomef was survived by tree children.

Adam and Addison lugged the weights to the Christmas tree in the living room, where Adam said, "Perfect, let's set it down."

"Wait," Addison said, "not yet, be caref—" Adam did not hear the muted sound of glass crunching inside cardboard. A dark stain reeking of alcohol and gardenias spread over the smashed present and up the box of weights: the perfume Addison had bought Kathleen.

Adam got the barbell, which was boxed separately. Exclamations of surprise and fear attended his putting it under the tree. "Watch out for—" Adam heard a clonk and felt a vibration along the box. He turned to see a lamp reclining on its dented shade. "No! No!" The barbell swept the lower branches; red and silver balls exploded in splinters on the floor. The next swing would have infallibly dispatched the aquarium. Not daring to approach her fiancée head-on, Lily laid her hands on Adam's shoulders from behind, and like a well-behaved child surrendering a firearm he has unwittingly brought into the family room, Adam yielded the package to Evelyn, who placed it behind the tree. They did not let him get the case of sparkling Burgundy he had for Evelyn but sent Kean to fetch it.

Evelyn picked up the smashed present and examined the card. "What a shame," she said to Kathleen. "It's for you,"

Broken glass rattled wetly as Kathleen took it. "Sweet," she said, but whether she was commenting on Addison's thoughtfulness or the fragrance that cloaked the package like fog, Addison couldn't tell. "I'll throw it away in the kitchen trash can."

"Actually, could you put it in the garbage outside? It's pretty overpowering."

When Adam looked at the people around him, pale and skittish though they appeared, he could imagine his life was back as it had been. "So everybody's home for the holidays. Home for the holidays." His beautiful wife, Evelyn, talented son, Addison, and stepson, Kean—coming in just now with the cardboard box, clinking with bottles and promise. Together. Even their waitress Lily was there. Surely the calendar had been turned back. Surely they were about to begin the shift at Paradise Dogs, but just now were discussing some aspect of hot dog making.

*You can't put raisins and sunflower seeds in the coleslaw.—We said when we opened this restaurant, we would serve only the very best, and the best coleslaw has raisins and sunflower seeds.—But this coleslaw is going on hot dogs. No one wants raisins and sunflower seeds on a hot dog!*

Ultimately Evelyn's raisins and sunflower seeds prevailed, and as it turned out, Adam was the first to admit, customers loved them and would cross town for one of their slaw dogs. That had been the secret of their success—a simple menu: nothing but hot dogs and the trimmings. Simplify, simplify, simplify. And, Adam always added, simplify. But every ingredient, every detail, was the very best. Paradise Dogs had made them both wealthy, and even, for a time, happy. He recalled Sundays, lying naked with Evelyn: tangled sheets and new-made sunlight, his head resting between her breasts while she ran her fingers lightly over his ribs and belly. She whispered to him, or blew soft, soundless whistles through the fine hairs on his bald spot. They ate breakfast in bed and their dachshund, Charley—or was it a beagle?—licked the plates.

The memory made everything glow and sweetened the air as if with some floral bouquet.

"So how's the compost doing?" Adam asked once they were seated.

"Wonderfully." Evelyn was an avid composter. "If the worms had their way, they'd get nothing but apple cores and banana peels. But I figure they'll eat the onion skins when they realize there's nothing else." Evelyn took her earthworms' welfare to heart, but she didn't believe in coddling them.

"We have something exciting to tell everyone," Lily said, changing the subject.

The baby. Adam raised his hand in acknowledgment and ducked his head with a grin. Pleasure warmed his face. He would have preferred to keep that a secret, hoping one day he and Evelyn would run into the couple by accident. The boy and his bride would be effusive over Adam's deed, and Adam would gallantly accept the praise he never sought. All the more to win Evelyn's heart. Lancelot never ran back to Guinevere saying, "Did you hear how I handled that ogre?" He let the news drift back on its own. But, if Lily would tell it now, let her.

"We are engaged to be married," Lily said, and waited as if she were about to receive a trophy. The air in the room was as still as the inside of a glass paperweight. Don't be disappointed, Lily assured herself, refusing to let her smile fall. You knew they would not embrace you or something. It's not like *Queen for a Day*.

"Well, that is good news," Evelyn said finally. "Congratulations."

There was a chorus of congratulations. Addison and Kean shook Adam's hand. How would Lily's announcement affect his negotiations with Evelyn? In the long run it probably helped; buyers get more eager when someone else shows interest. The time had come to squeeze all his strength and sweetness in a ball and roll it toward the gates of life.

"Hey, Evelyn, I heard a great joke." He paused. "It's not really appropriate for the children; let me tell you in the kitchen."

"Okay," Evelyn said.

Addison, Kean, and Kathleen looked taken aback to be called children. Lily maintained a fixed smile; she had more than a suspicion what would transpire in the next room, but she could also predict how it would turn out.

Adam followed Evelyn to the kitchen. This did not feel right. It was not romantic, traipsing behind her like a nervous boy about to show his mother his report card. *How did you do this semester? Did you study like I told you?* Still, the die was cast. All would change when he poured the diamonds in her lap.

"Do you want a seat?" he asked. Standing face-to-face was no good; telling her he loved her couldn't be broached standing, especially in the kitchen, of all places, as if they'd come to get a Coke. Besides, he needed her seated to pour diamonds in her lap—but wait—she was wearing slacks. Slacks. She needed a skirt to make a hammock for the diamonds; with slacks they would spill through her thighs.

"No, I'm good standing," she said pleasantly. "So tell me the joke."

"I love you. I have always loved you. I want you back." He should at least say this kneeling. He crouched toward the floor.

"Ha-ha-ha," Evelyn laughed and turned away. "That sure was a funny joke all right," she called loudly enough to be heard in the living room.

She was lovely in her refusal and elegant as ever. Evelyn left him wavering in his crouch. The trash can in the corner gaped at him. His feet tingled with the sudden awareness of the terrazzo under his soles, and under that, miles and miles of rock and sand, and under that, horrible black emptiness. He saw it now; the proposal had been a joke. All along he'd been coming here to make a joke, and he hadn't known. Not knowing had been the biggest joke. Now he knew. He would need a drink, something more than a couple of beers.

"Yes," he said. "I thought it was funny too. That's why I told it to you." Profound ugliness rose in him. He followed her out.

Back in the living room, Adam opened the sparkling Burgundy. There was a bang like a gunshot, and Kean ducked the flying cork.

"Adam, watch out," Kean said.

"Sorry, I'm sorry," Adam said with genuine regret. "Get the glasses, Evelyn. We are celebrating my engagement to—"

"Adam," Lily said, "we need to go. I'm sure they want to get back to—"

"It's pretty early for a drink, Adam," Evelyn said.

"Get the glasses, Addison," Adam said. Evelyn had not stirred. "I got to make a toast." Evelyn would have thrown her arms around and lavished kisses on him if she'd known the secrets he was keeping: the Canal, Ayefour, Compass East. Adam managed a grim smile at the thought.

Addison brought everyone wineglasses. Adam circulated, topping off each glass with bubbling purple and occasionally refilling his own.

"So, when is the wedding?" Kathleen asked.

"Soon as possible," Adam said grimly. "Sooner. Addison can be best man, Kean can be groomsman, and you—my dear," to Kathleen, "can be maid of honor. Would you like that?"

"Well, sure," Kathleen said uncertainly.

"And after the wedding, maybe, there'll be a surprise for all of you." Adam looked meaningfully at Evelyn. "Big. Bigger than the wedding. Big as Florida. Or as *wide* anyway." He laughed at how close he'd come to spilling the beans about the canal.

"Okay, dear, just one drink," Lily said. She touched his shoulder gently. "And then we'll go."

"Durn it, bottle's empty," Adam said. He worked the foil and wire cage off the next bottle. Another bang and a cork ricocheted against the wall, narrowly missing Kean's ear.

"Adam, are you *aiming* for me?"

"No, I'm just a good shot. I'm sorry. I can't help it." The sound of the popping cork and the near mishap lowered him into a slough of despond. He filled his glass again. "A toast," he said, lifting his spirits.

"Adam, the carpet!"

Bending to see where he'd sloshed Burgundy, Adam's rump bumped the tree off plumb, sending a few more glass ornaments to oblivion.

"I'll get a wet rag to clean that up," Kathleen offered.

"I'll help," said Addison.

"Start with a dry cloth," Lily advised. "That's more exorbitant."

Adam drained his glass and set it and the bottle carefully on the TV. He attempted to right the crooked tree, but was impeded by an ottoman placed in such a way as to be always underfoot.

"Adam, leave that alone," Lily said, patting a couch cushion beside her at a far remove from the tree. "Come sit over here."

Taking his glass and bottle, Adam complied like a boy called from a fight and forced to apologize to his opponent. "Something's going to happen soon," Adam said. "I wish I could tell you all about it, but I can't because—there are other forces in play." He mind turned to the canal, and in his agitation, he miscalculated the number of foot-pounds of force required to set his glass on the coffee table. The stem snapped, and Burgundy drenched the tabletop.

Addison caught his mother's eyes. Their expression seemed to say, *Here we go.* He briefly saw Kathleen's stunned expression and looked away, mortified.

"Oh, Adam," Lily said. To say this was not the wedding announcement a girl dreams of was understating the matter by a wide margin. An angry needle bored between her brows. Why did his family have to make him so nervous? He drank more when he was nervous.

Addison and Kathleen returned and scrubbed the carpet. Lily and Evelyn got more dishcloths from the kitchen. Adam went to the bathroom down the hall.

As the four of them sopped Burgundy with purple-stained rags, Lily said to Kean, who observed the scene with detachment, "So, a little bird informs me you are going to medical school." Kean confirmed the little bird's data. "You are going to be a physician just like your father," Lily said. "Your first husband was a physician, wasn't he, Ev?"

Adam, passing through from the bathroom to the kitchen, grimaced at the mention of this impossible rival: the handsome war hero who died young and left a widow to love him and a son to worship him forever.

"After you won that championship, Kean," Lily said, "we all expected you would be a karate instructor, and Addison," turning to Addison, "you're in school too. An English major." The unspoken comparison swelled until it filled the room.

"Journalism minor."

"What?"

"I'm also minoring in journalism," Addison said, head down, furiously scrubbing the carpet.

Adam returned with a fresh helping of Burgundy, this time in a sturdy jelly glass without one of those fragile stems so prone to breaking. Nothing anyone could say or do could persuade him to surrender his drink—after all, he'd barely drunk it below Donald's sailor hat.

"Okay, dear," Lily said. "Let's hear the toast."

"The toast?"

"You said you wanted to make a toast."

Adam raised his glass. " 'In Savannah's sunny clime, where I used to spend my time—' " He paused and said, "But before that, I have to get something from the car."

He left, and those assembled waited apprehensively for

whatever new surprise he had in store. Lily sat straight, her feet on the floor and knees together. "Adam did something quite remarkable this morning," she said, trying to sound conversational. No one asked what. They listened for Adam.

Lily sat, her face growing hotter by the second. Jack Bailey didn't drape red velvet on your shoulders, and there was no applause from the studio audience—*what that poor woman suffered!*

"He delivered a baby," she was saying. "This was an actual occurrence—I am often amazed at his many accomplishments." The wreckage Adam had wrought made his many accomplishments seem the stuff of fantasy, but no one was listening; they were too busy staring at the door for Adam to return.

She'd won; she was about to be one of them, but Evelyn and the boys weren't going to suddenly respect her. Nothing really alters how people treat you. Instead there's only a brief respite among strangers, which, if you know what's good for you, you'll accept for what it's worth, and then dig your toes in for the next long weary, uphill push.

Adam did not return. They waited. He still did not return. Finally, Evelyn said, "Addison, got outside and see what's keeping your father."

The fallen mailbox lay on the ground, no longer covered by the jeep. Adam had left without his fiancée.

# THREE

## Adam Bungles

Addison spent a few minutes the next morning as he did most mornings: lying in the dark with a comforting daydream of hanging himself. The stiff bristles of a fat hemp rope cinched under his chin, the moment of decision before kicking the chair, a short, sharp shock, and then nothing. Normally the thought of showing up for his part-time job at *The Sentinel* was enough to inspire this fantasy, but today his customary workday dread was augmented by mortification over his father's performance in front of Kathleen.

Addison rose, and after sitting motionless before his typewriter in the wan hope that words would come, he ate a light breakfast: grapefruit half, toast with butter. His mother gave him the cadre of vitamin pills she'd taken to dosing the household with—desiccated shark liver, B complex, E, C, and garlic. He dressed in the button-down white shirt and narrow black tie that he had recently adopted as his wardrobe. The finishing touch was two black ballpoints in his shirt pocket to make him appear the earnest, professional intellectual he wished to seem.

In spite of these preparations, Addison did not go to work in high spirits, but then he never went to work in high spirits. Coming through the composing room, he forced a smile and, as cheerily as he could manage, greeted the paste-up artists hunched over tables with X-Acto knives and waxy strips of text. No one's gaze lifted, and he went to the newsroom, where the Royal Selectric crouched in wait and a black telephone nested in its coiled cord.

"They wouldn't call it work if people liked doing it," Addison reminded himself.

Seeing Addison, Mortimer the Rat stuck his head into Mr. Beasley's office and said something. An informer. Beasley came to the door and bid Addison approach with a crooked finger and a dark look. Unsteadily, Addison rose and walked.

Addison entertained no misconceptions as to what this interview concerned; he did not, for example, imagine that he was about to win the coveted Gold Pen Award or be promoted to features writer. He'd known the moment he saw it irrevocably in print that "Mrs. Jomef" was a hideous bungle; the "tree children" was a simple oversight, a garden-variety typo—but "Jomef" he had let through after cool deliberation. What had he been thinking?

That was the very question Mr. Beasley kept posing: What had he been thinking? Never, before coming to work at *The Sentinel,* had Addison experienced being yelled at so loudly, so long, and at such close range. Was it only his imagination, or did Beasley's hot breath, humidified by a fine mist of saliva, actually ruffle Addison's hair? Beasley paused only for Addison to insert an occasional "Yes, sir" and "No, sir" and "I understand, sir. It's not a funny thing, sir." Beasley interspersed his theme on the tremendous importance of accurate obituaries to bereaved families with rhetorical questions such as, "Are you insane?" and "Are you smoking reefers?"

The tree children of Mrs. Jomef would not soon be forgotten, nor was it the first time that this had happened. In the month Addison had worked at *The Sentinel*, days had gone by with only minor errors here and there, and then for some reason, the column erupted in an absolute plethora of misspellings and transpositions. The way Rhonda talked, *n* sounded so much like *m* and *s* like *f*; *h. a.* was indistinguishable from *a. j.* It hadn't occurred to Addison to question the surname Jomef; he'd assumed it was Middle Eastern; although, to be honest, there were times he should have wondered how it was possible for so many people with unheard-of names—Snith, Ajll, Sreenam—to die in the space of one day in a small Floridian city.

After swearing never to commit such an atrocity again, Addison slunk to his desk. His colleagues avoided eye contact; Addison could not decide if this came as a relief or an additional burden of disgrace. Hot shame pressing his face like a towel, Addison sat at the desk, called Rhonda at the funeral home, and identified himself.

"Well, Addison—*smack*, *smack*—are we going to get it right today?"

For some reason Rhonda Peterson was always noisily chewing gum when he called. Although Addison had never met her, he imagined her as petite with rhinestone-covered cat's-eye glasses and red hair with brown roots. "Yes, ma'am," Addison said with a confidence he was far from feeling. "But let's take it slow."

"We'll take it as slow as you like, dearie. *Smack*, *smack*. You ready? *B*. Got it?"

Addison and Rhonda were the slowest—and least accurate—obituary-writing team in *The Sentinel*'s history. Rhonda always spelled out the obituaries one letter at a time, and for some reason—terror of past failures, perhaps—Addison never thought of asking her just to read the whole notice to him.

"Got it. *B* as in bog."

"Right," Rhonda said. "*D* as in dog. *Smack, smack.* The next letter is *A*."

A long and sweaty session of obituary writing later, Addison drove home simmering in a hum of self-recrimination. He would do better, he *would*. There was no question of ever being promoted to features writer; the best Addison could hope was to keep his job long enough for Beasley's white-hot contempt to cool to a bearable level.

Had Addison ever had any real writing talent, or had he deluded himself? Once—his bright past filled him with wild regret—there had been no doubt of the promise of Addison's prose. After his first story, "The Softly Trembling Darkness," in which a young man copes with his wife's unexpected death, some in freshman English class, while acknowledging its undisputed strength, whispered darkly that it had been a mere fluke, and that Addison would never be able to equal it. These whispers were dispelled when he came out with "The Gently Hovering Shadow," revealing how the sudden death of a child causes the protagonist to take stock of his life. For a time after that, Addison could write nothing else, and an unvoiced fear settled like morning dampness over the English Department. The Milton of U.F. had lost the gift! But just when everyone thought the AM signal of his inspiration had gone under a bridge, Addison produced "The Tenderly Wavering Twilight." But was it good? Could it match his earlier work? On reading it, the intelligentsia of the Humanities Building agreed with one voice that it was a breakthrough: the story of a young man who must deal with the sudden and unexpected deaths of his wife *and* his child.

He had set himself on his next work, "The *Somethingly Something* Dusk," but the missing adverb-participial combination felled him. A sheet of paper, blank save for the definite article "The," had sat curled under the roller of his dusty Underwood typewriter for so long, if he took it out now, no doubt it would be permanently fishhook shaped.

Popping noises. Adam Newman needed to get up. He had to warn the Old Man that he'd touched the gun. He'd been repeatedly told not to, but he had.

He opened his eyes. A beer can's teardrop-shaped mouth gaped at him. A crumpled can slouched beside it. Beneath a partially drawn shade, dew valleys lay in brightening panes. From the hallway, the black grate of the floor furnace provided the popping sounds.

He slipped his hand from the covers and laid it on the pillow beside him, squinting to make out his Timex. The time didn't seem right. Adam shook his wrist and checked again, but the second hand didn't move; he'd forgotten to wind it. He checked the electric clock radio behind the beer cans.

Morning. Eight A.M.

Adam swung his feet out of bed and put them on the floor. There was something he was supposed to remember, but for the life of him he couldn't recall what. He took a sip of warm beer and discovered too late he'd put out a cigarette in it. His dirty clothes were scattered on the floor, and as he made his way to the bathroom, he scooped them up and put them in the hamper.

As he stood waiting for the pee to come, Adam lifted the cover from the toilet tank and removed a bottle of Jack. He took a sip of this, screwed the cap back on, returned it to the tank, and replaced the toilet lid. The throbbing in his head subsided slightly, and Adam congratulated himself on his foresight in keeping bottles of booze hidden in various handy places throughout his house.

Outside in his bathrobe in the too bright sun, Adam was momentarily alarmed to see no jeep in the driveway, but a brief reflection consoled him that he must have prudently left it somewhere and taken a cab home. He picked up *The Sentinel*, and as he returned to the house, waved at Mrs. Sykes, who was engaged in one of her endless gardening projects.

"It worked," Mrs. Sykes informed him cheerfully over the hedge.

"Ah," Adam said. He had no idea what she was talking about.

"Wrapping my hand in a red towel for an hour. It worked. A week later, the warts were gone."

"That's superlative," Adam said in the heartiest voice he could manage in his condition. "I told you so."

"That doctor didn't know what he was talking about."

"Judge him not too harshly," Adam recommended, and returned to the house, flipping *The Sentinel* to the obituary page.

He set up the percolator and adjourned to his office, where on the wall a map showed the purchases of Ayefour and Compass East. Sitting in his comfortable swivel chair, feet on the desk, absorbed in prose, he felt his headache recede. Peace fell over him like a sunrise. Adam was content. Every time he read the obituaries, he marveled how his son could bring such spark to a column that from a less visionary writer must be tedium itself. He took red-handled scissors from the drawer of his rolltop desk and began to cut out the column.

The phone rang. It was Lily.

"Adam, thank goodness. Are you well? I have been agitated ill about you. I haven't seen you since nine o'clock on yesterday."

The angel of compulsory alligator painting had fanned Adam's face with her powdery wings, but spared him for another day. Adam had dodged a bullet, law-enforcement-officer-wise; twenty-four hours was the minimum time for filing a missing persons report.

"Sorry, darling, I didn't mean to worry you. I'm fine."

"Horace called," Lily continued. "He said your jeep is parked at the Fish Camp." She said the name as if it left a greasy spot on her tongue.

"That's good. It's just where I left it, then."

"And someone by the name of Mr. Adder called about a real estate transaction."

"Adder?" The name was unfamiliar.

"He said he'd call back. He was from Compass East."

Compass East! A knot rose in Adam's throat. It had only been a matter of time, he supposed.

"Also Ernie Costa called," Lily said on the other end of the line. "He sounded very immersed. He said you need to get in touch with him immediately. He said you would know why."

# FOUR

# Adam Looks Around

As Addison pulled into Ponce de Leon Place, the radio interrupted its string of holiday favorites to play "Mrs. Brown You've Got a Lovely Daughter," a song he associated with Kathleen. The upbeat melody of happier times—*Walkin' about, even in a crowd, well, you'll pick her out, makes a bloke feel* (half beat pause) *so proud*—dropped into a slower, sadder tune of love lost: *If she finds that I've been round to see you (round to see you) tell her that I'm well and feelin' fine . . .*" The nobility of this became excruciating with a plaintive, *Don't let aw-on, don't say she's broke my heart/I'd go down on my knees but it's no good to pine.*

On top of everything else, Addison was in love with his brother's girlfriend.

No, he didn't love her, Addison corrected himself. And it was stupid getting worked up over a corny song. He rubbed the moisture from his eye with the heel of one hand. He merely felt great, great personal respect and fondness for Kathleen and wished only for her good regard in return. In fact, although he would never tell her so, she was not even attractive; she was too skinny, her forehead too high, and her nose was crooked. He felt no desire, for instance, to tilt her chin upward with his fingers and brush her lips with his.

He hated his life. When had things turned so rotten? He did not blame Kathleen for ignoring him.

He didn't see her car. She wasn't there. Good. No, not good. Not bad either, neither bad nor good. Just a statement: Kathleen wasn't there. He didn't feel one way or the other about it. Wait a minute—her car was parked across the street. Addison's spirits lifted. Dang.

Addison parked the Volkswagen and got out. From the backyard Addison's mother saw him and waved him over.

"Could you help dig this?" she asked, leaning on her shovel. "The ground's pretty hard here where I've been pouring out grease."

Throwing his necktie over his shoulder to keep it clean, Addison dug through a waxy shield of congealed grease. Evelyn Newman's composting efforts yielded mixed results in the landscaping department. In spite of—or perhaps because of—the regular internment of coffee grounds, banana peels, grapefruit rinds, eggshells, and knobby cabbage cores, the backyard was almost entirely foliage free. Few experiences are less appetizing than unearthing last week's leftover chicken perleu, so Evelyn's constant search for fresh burial spots meant nothing—with a few notable exceptions—was permitted to grow; a volunteer vine from a smashed jack o'-lantern grew into the lower branches of a lemon tree, and late-season pumpkins stretched oblong by gravity hung improbably amid the yellow lemons.

"Where's Kean and Kathleen?" Addison asked. The daily addition of hot bacon grease had solidified the soil to the consistency of licorice.

"They're riding his motorcycle. Kean wants another book to study for the MCAT. He's finished with the first ones." She studied the hole's growth as Addison dug. In some spots earthworms coiled in gay profusion, and in others they showed neither hide nor hair. "They didn't care for that hot grease," Addison's mother diagnosed. "I knew it'd scald them, but I figured they'd put up with the burns once they tasted how good it was. But I guess it ran them off. I'm going to put in some other stuff and see if that doesn't bring them back." At her heel was a white plastic bucket of green pepper stems, carrot butts, and fat trimmed from a pot roast. "The soil's pretty compacted," she observed, as she poured the bucket into Addison's hole. "I wish I had some excelsior, that fluffs the soil up some." Addison's mother lived by the theory that Styrofoam was as good as perlite for aerating the soil. "Thanks for doing this." Evelyn sighed. "Now I have to go out and buy new ornaments. Your dad laid waste to the old ones."

A motorcycle engine made them look down the street; Kean was coming back with Kathleen snug behind him, her arms around his waist, her nose buried in his black leather jacket.

Addison focused on tamping down the soil. He dreaded facing Kathleen after his father had made such a fool of himself. To have something to say as much as out of genuine curiosity he asked, "Why did you ever marry Dad in the first place?"

"Because he adored me," Evelyn said. Sensing this didn't satisfy Addison, she added, "In every romance there's an adorer and an adored. Your father is very good at adoring, and I like being adored, and there's something about your father that draws people to him. It's hard to explain—people like him and trust him. He's able to make things happen." While they were opening Paradise Dogs, after Evelyn had called everywhere without avail for someone to make frank casings strong enough to withstand frying, Adam sealed a bargain in just one visit. A local butcher somehow mistook him for a health inspector and offered to make hot dogs to Adam's specifications at a sweetheart price. "And he made me laugh."

Addison shook his head as he put his tie back in place and laid the shovel over his shoulder like a rifle. Now there was something he truly did not understand. Supposedly his father had this legendary sense of humor, but Addison couldn't see why anyone would find him funny who would not find dental surgery equally funny.

"Your father loves you, you know," Evelyn said. "He thinks the world of you." Evelyn never regretted leaving Adam; she feared what he was turning into and what she had begun turning into when she was with him. But nor had she ever doubted that he loved her and Addison. Addison needed a father, and even more than that, Adam needed a son. Carrying the empty compost bucket, she walked alongside her son back to the house as Kean turned off his rumbling bike and he and Kathleen got off.

"Hey, kiddo," Kean said. Addison had never told Kean this, but he hated being called kiddo. Kean slung a backpack off his shoulders and took out a blue and red glossy-covered book, *Preparing for the MCAT.*

"Are you about to study?" Addison asked, and then, "Hi, Kathleen." Addison had a private rule that it was okay to speak to Kathleen as long as he greeted his brother first.

"Yeah, I'm going to, but I've got to get some kicks in first," Kean said. "I promised Sensei I'd keep in shape." No doubt it broke Sensei Heshiki's heart to lose his prize pupil to the field of medicine. Kean's gleaming three-decker tristate karate trophy would gather dust alongside mementoes of his other triumphs: his trophies, rock collection, visible man doll, ham radio, and slide rules. By contrast, Addison had an Underwood typewriter, a Magic 8-Ball wearily leaking blue juice from having been shaken too many times asking the same question, an incongruous statue of a golfer breaking a club over his knee with the legend *World's Worst Golfer* that Addison had wasted his money on at the Woolworth's because it reminded him of a character from *Fractured Fairy Tales*, and a troll doll with greasy green acrylic hair. Kean's modus operandi was to excel and move on, bored by anything once he mastered it, unlike Addison, who preferred screwing things up and sticking with them, exploring new and unheard-of ways to screw up while finely honing the old ones.

While Addison's mother left to buy ornaments and Kean changed into his karate uniform, Kathleen sat in the swing under the live oak with Addison at her feet. Addison plucked a spear of Saint Augustine and twirled it in his fingers. He wished Kathleen would ask him about himself, and was glad she didn't. "How's school going?"

"It's not going at all, not next semester, unless I can get my hands on about six hundred dollars before classes start."

Addison automatically reached for his back pocket as if the money might be there. He knew he was unimportant—less important than a tennis game, less important than a seminar on semantics, and that only the presence of his brother kicking a metal pole nearby kept her from one of these other activities. "What about your fellowship?"

"I've definitely lost it for good," she said. "Technically the philosophy department meets Saturday to discuss renewing me, but it's over. I have an aunt in Arkansas who says there's an office job for me in a bauxite mine, so that's probably where I'll wind up. Without Dr. Buskirk on my side, there is no fellowship." Kathleen sighed and stared into the distance. "They all think he's insane. Buskirk, insane! He's the most brilliant man I've ever met," she said. "Even smarter than Kean."

Thanks for that, Addison thought.

Kathleen liked Addison more than he knew. He reminded her of a fairy-tale frog, the sort that, once kissed, turns into a prince. There is no mistaking such a frog; he is always twenty times bigger than a regular frog, sometimes he wears a crown, and he talks. And when he talks, he promises to turn into a prince, and why would a frog lie about a thing like that? But once you kiss a magic frog, you fall in love with him, and there you are. Sure, he'd be a prince, but traits from his formative years would be bound to linger. He'd keep jars of flies around the house, for instance; he'd be very discreet about it, and dreadfully apologetic whenever any got loose. But still. You'd love him anyway, as the saying goes, warts and all. But every summer vacation he'd insist on going to the lake. Always the lake.

Besides, Addison was a writer, thoughtlessly pumping more words into the Opoyo, like a man bailing water *into* a sinking boat. No, it was better to keep her distance, enjoy his company, and pretend not to notice the gleam of froggy longing in his eyes.

"It wasn't even really a commitment," she went on. "Dr. Buskirk just couldn't explain to anyone why he *shouldn't* be committed. He had already dropped the adjectives and adverbs from his lectures. By the time they came for him, he was down to interjections, the only part of speech he thought could penetrate Opoyo."

"I never understood this Opoyo thing," Addison said truthfully, although he wanted less to hear about Opoyo than just to hear Kathleen talk. "Isn't he the monster that spells himself backward and forward?"

Kean came out and kicked the metal post supporting the carport. *Whang! Whang!*

"That's Ogopogo," Kathleen said. She leaned toward Addison, sitting Indian-style on the ground, conscious of the need to explain herself very clearly. During her time with Dr. Buskirk, neither of them had been able to make another living soul understand Opoyo, which only confirmed their hypothesis. Kean kicked harder; the metal post rang. "Opoyo is why the harder you try to communicate, the less you do. Opoyo's everywhere, but you can't weigh it, touch it, or smell it, but when words travel through it, it distorts them, like looking at a pencil in a glass of water. So when you speak," Kean's kicks rang quite loudly now, but Kathleen didn't raise her voice; shouting in the Opoyo was the mistake of tourists and parents of small children, "your meaning gets refracted. Nothing you say is understood the way you mean it. Dr. Buskirk says the only thing to do is express yourself slightly off," she pointed her hands at each other, her right hand tilted to demonstrate the angle that communication must be skewed, "so as it crosses the Opoyo, it's refracted the proper degree." She brought her hands together, adjusting the angle to align her fingertips. "That's the purpose of metaphors, parables, everything."

"Uh-huh, uh-huh," Addison said and nodded. But in truth he could hear only his brother's kicks. It was lovely, though, to watch her speak and see the ineffable charm that high forehead gave to her crooked-nosed face.

In fact, though, Kathleen had begun to believe that Dr. Buskirk was wrong—Opoyo did not fill space evenly; it was left there, a residue of words. Words themselves might be Opoyo, though perhaps with a nugget of non-Opoyo meaning at the core, like a grain of sand in a pearl. In any case, through the friction of transmission, a slug-trail Opoyo sloughed off. To compensate for the slimy accumulation, people resorted to ever thicker coatings of Opoyo. For a time this might work. Fat layers of verbiage guaranteed at least some of the speaker's intention penetrated, but consequently yet more Opoyo was left behind.

How else to explain the way Opoyo behaved? If Mission Control radioed John Glenn thousands of miles above in his Mercury capsule, with complicated instructions to adjust his altitude by so many degrees, Glenn had no difficulty understanding exactly what was expected and doing it, but for married couples with decades of Opoyo hanging between them like a mucus curtain, the simplest statement traveling the shortest distance reached its hearer if at all only as a dull red vibration. *Here's your coffee* turned into *Where were you last night?* and *Is there any cream?* became *Nag, nag, nag.* After a semester of twice-weekly lectures, you could barely make out the blackboard through the sticky Opoyo fogging the classroom.

Kathleen was on the brink of something major, if only the committee would renew her fellowship. Dr. Russell could be counted on to side with Dr. Buskirk, but in Buskirk's absence, Dr. Russell would go with the majority. Dr. Holman would be little help at best, and Dr. Joseph was dead set against her. It looked as if the only alternative was the bauxite mine.

Adam looked around the room as if he suspected a squirrel were loose in the house. Where were those diamonds?

"What is your opinion of my suggestion?" Lily asked over the phone.

"Well, I think it's super-duper. You should definitely do it." Adam opened and closed drawers in his rolltop desk. Nothing. Nothing.

"Your presence is also required," Lily said.

"Well, of course. Without me, that defeats the purpose of the whole thing. That goes without saying." Adam swiveled in his chair, hoping to see an unaccustomed purple bag sitting somewhere. Could he have possibly left them in his pants?

"I have called Father Peel to arrange an eleven o'clock appointment."

"Father Peel?"

"The priest, Adam. St. George's has a strict provision against performing marriages without a counseling session with the priest. It's very mandatory."

"Wonderful." Where were they? The zebra-striped ceramic alligator that served as a doorstop offered no clues in its yellow-pupiled eyes. The framed black-and-white photos of Adam shaking the hands of governors and celebrities were similarly unhelpful.

"We have to meet today if we are going to have the ceremony as soon as you say."

Adam made a nonverbal grunt of inquiry, reaching down the front of his pants. Could the diamonds be in his boxers?

"You said you wanted to get married as expeditiously as possible," Lily said.

"Right, right, right, right, right, right." The diamonds didn't seem to be anywhere. The map on the wall caught his eye, and a dark thought popped into his head—could General Potter (U.S. Army, Ret.) have arranged this? Could it even be that Compass East was behind it?

Adam had exhausted the possible hiding places in his own house. He asked himself when was the last time he remembered seeing the diamonds. He had asked himself, if he were a bag of diamonds, where would he be? He asked had he searched under the bed and in the dresser drawers—the answer came back that yes, he had, but he would search again to make sure.

All of this with no result.

He had bungled well and thoroughly this time. This might be the one even he could not unbungle. He would not have borrowed the diamonds in the first place if it hadn't been for the terrible french fry incident, which culminated in his temporary divorce. Every loose thread of his bungled life led to another thread, and still another thread before that. When had things begun turning bad? Back when his mother decided to send him to Sisters of Mercy in Savannah? But his mother wouldn't have done that if it weren't for the Old Man's accident. And the accident . . .

Adam bit his lip against a sudden welling of tears and for some reason thought of the brick streets of his childhood now covered in black asphalt.

At last he decided he must have left them at Evelyn's house. He showered, changed, and called a taxi.

When the cab, weighted with Adam and he with his meditations, motored up to the house on Ponce de Leon Place, Addison, Kean, and that young lady were sitting in the swing that hung in the shade of the live oak. More accurately, Kean and that young lady were sitting in the glider while Addison stood awkwardly nearby, trying to look nonchalant and failing in his white button-down shirt and skinny black tie. She was definitely Kean's girlfriend. What had ever given Adam the impression she was Addison's?

Adam needed to find Addison a girlfriend. Adam, already feeling more confident about finding the diamonds, made a mental note to take care of that as soon as he got back the jewels and remarried Evelyn.

The girl could use more meat on her and had a crooked nose, but she was pretty enough if you liked the type. She really looked much more suitable as Addison's girlfriend. Next to Kean in his karate uniform, who had a tad too much meat on him, she looked like a rail.

Adam approached the trio. Some careless lout had destroyed the mailbox that Adam had planted; it sat leaning propped in the hole of a cinder block. What was the neighborhood coming to?

"Is your mother here?" Adam asked. The answer was negative. "The other day, when I was here, did I leave something?"

"Like what?" Addison asked.

"You left a mess. You just about destroyed half the furniture," Kean said, "and then you got into the sparkling Burgundy and destroyed the other half celebrating your engagement."

Even in his predicament, Adam couldn't resist a smile. Warmth crept over his face. He foresaw years ahead, sleeping late on Sundays with Evelyn, a schipperke or Scottie dog at the foot of their bed. "Engagement?"

"To Lily."

"Oh." His smile fled like frost from a teakettle. "Where's your mother?"

"She's shopping."

Adam pursed his lips and nodded judiciously, as if approving this activity. "Did I leave a little purple bag here yesterday?"

"A shopping bag?"

"No, smaller." Adam used his hands to demonstrate its size.

"A Christmas present?"

"Maybe. Did you see it?" None of them had. "It's really important that I find it. I can't tell you how important it is. Do you mind if I look inside?"

Kean shrugged in reply. It irked Adam to address this question to his stepson as the oldest male. After all, it was really Adam's house; he had repaired that stoop and planted that gnawed Christmas tree and that uprooted mailbox. Nevertheless, Adam nodded his head in gratitude and began retracing his steps from the other day.

"What was he talking about?" Kathleen whispered. Her legs crossed, she tapped the air with one sneakered foot. A cardinal hopped across the lawn. If Addison could have touched the skin along the underside of that perfect Achilles tendon, he imagined it would be as smooth and cool as he imagined the skin inside her thigh.

"He's got d.t.'s," Kean said. "He needs to dry out."

"What is he *doing*?" Kathleen asked.

Adam performed an unsteady knee bend in the driveway.

"Dad, can I help?" Addison asked.

Adam straightened. "Yes, son, you can. That would be spectacular."

Reluctantly Addison left Kathleen's feet and joined his father in the driveway.

"The key thing is," Adam said, "to reenact every single step I took when I arrived. I will begin with emerging from the jeep." Now Addison realized his father was doing an elaborate pantomime of opening the back door of the jeep and hefting out a box of weights. It was so convincing Addison felt obliged to close the invisible jeep door after him. "No, no, I don't need help carrying the weights," Adam explained, "these are wholly imaginary, but notice how my pants pockets bulge open when I squat. Follow along as I go and look for any place the dia—purple bag might have dropped. In those liriope lining the driveway, for example." Addison did as he was asked. What a wonderful son, Adam thought. They should have spent more time together when Addison was little, but it was not too late; things could be restored. He would find a way to break off his engagement to Lily Manzana, then propose to Evelyn. Soon all this would be forgotten in her arms, but first to find the diamonds. Being with his son, Adam felt more certain than ever he would recover them soon.

Kean's voice floated through the air as Addison parted the green fingers of liriope, looking for a purple bag.

"The Y chromosome doesn't combine with another," Kean was telling Kathleen. As a premed student, he was filled with fascinating information such as this and was always glad to share it. "Well, it does a little, but hardly at all. Now keep in mind, the Y is what makes someone a male instead of a female. This means I have virtually the identical Y as my father." The slight emphasis on the word *my* made Addison's face heat with the unspoken implication about his own Y chromosome. Adam took one ponderous backward step, fingers curled around the corners of his imaginary box, and then another. Addison searched among the liriope for his father's bag and dully wished to insert something in Kean's conversation. "And my father had almost the identical Y as *his* father. My Y chromosome has been virtually unchanged for thousands of years—right back to my remotest ancestor."

In the oak tree's shadow Kathleen pretended to listen but lost Kean's words in the ooze thickening around his head. Lately she'd gotten so she could not only recognize but almost *see* the Opoyo. Whatever Addison and his father were doing—and it was incomprehensible—made more sense than Kean's voice: Mr. Newman, knees bent, walking slowly backward toward the house, hands poised as if carrying a glass cube, astoundingly heavy but perfectly invisible, while Addison, weaving back and forth to either side of the driveway, combed the monkey grass.

The mail truck came. A moment of puzzlement crossed the mailman's face to see the mailbox propped up in a cinder block; Kathleen could tell he wanted to ask what had happened, but reconsidered interrupting Adam's and Addison's backward parade, and left his burden of bills.

Adam and Addison went inside. "The secret," said Adam, who'd had a lot of practice losing things, "is to search each place thoroughly before moving on to the next. Your amateur searcher darts room to room looking in isolated places. 'Maybe it's under the couch cushions in the living room.' 'No?' 'Maybe on the bedroom dresser?' 'No?' 'The silverware drawer.' And they waste all their time charging around the house and never find what they're looking for because they're not methodical. From this point on, I want you to imagine we're Scotland Yard detectives; we must search this room entirely before moving on. Thoroughness is our watchword."

They searched the living room thoroughly indeed. It was not under the wounded ficus plant. Or at the base of the dented floor lamp. Or behind the fish tank. Adam spent some time contemplating the perfumed Christmas tree. The lower branches looked as if a swarm of ornament-eating locusts had attacked. The presents, too, had obviously undergone rough treatment; some were trapezoids, some accordion shaped.

"What happened here?" Adam asked. "All these presents reek of perfume."

Addison started to explain but said nothing. He silently bet his father never even lost a purple bag in the first place. That would be just like him.

They split up; Addison started in the bathroom—he remembered his father taking a lengthy pee the other day—and Adam took the kitchen. "I was standing here," Adam said to himself, "and she was—" He pointed where Evelyn must have been. How far had he gotten in his proposal? Obviously he hadn't brought out the diamonds, or they'd be engaged right now. Was it possible they actually were engaged, and Evelyn was just keeping it a secret? He started to kneel, but his knees buckled, and he nearly fell. Whoa—he needed some sustenance.

Could he have left the diamonds on the counter? Jeweled crystals of a plate of Christmas cookies sparkled beneath Saran wrap. Not here. He sandwiched two cookies around a third and ate them as he looked behind the toaster and the knife rack: no luck. Maybe the silverware drawer? He found no diamonds, but crumbs dropped among the knives and spoons. Evelyn would not like that—he licked his finger and meticulously dabbed up each flake and ate it. Better eat the rest of the cookies and prevent mishap—eating cookies made him thirsty.

Was it remotely possible he'd put the diamonds in the refrigerator? He decided it was. The bottom shelf held a ham, which he tore a piece from and ate as he searched the other shelves: no purple bags, just a six-pack of Coke. Cola, cola everywhere, nor any drop to drink. Soft drinks reminded him how thirsty he was. Maybe he should try the spice cabinet.

Although everyone agrees it is quite tasty in a Christmas cookie, few are willing to drink vanilla extract straight from the bottle; those who have tried it, however, would assure you that while unlikely to replace Dom Pérignon at the dinner table, its concentrated, oddly metallic flavor is not unpalatable once you get used to it, and the natural caffeine of the vanilla bean coupled with alcohol (35 percent by volume) make it a beverage that leaves one calm yet alert.

Adam drained the bottle and thus fortified was calm yet alert indeed when his son reported his lack of success. "I'm ninety-nine percent certain now it must be in my jeep," Adam said, "but let's do one more look round. You take the kitchen and living room, and I'll take the other rooms in case there's somewhere one of us missed."

After completing his search, Addison rejoined his father.

"I still haven't seen—are you looking through Mother's drawers?"

"Of course not," Adam said and slammed it.

"What are you doing in Mother's room?"

Adam sidestepped this question. "I don't think we're going to find them here. I'm certain now I dropped them in my jeep. Get some paper, and I'll write your mother a note." Addison left, and Adam refolded his ex-wife's panties, having pressed them once more to his face, and replaced them once more in the drawer. This room had many memories. He rested his hand on the cypress carving he'd bought Evelyn a decade ago. The mountains of the world sat on an elephant, and the elephant stood on a turtle. It had been polished to a dark glow and smelled of lemon oil. Beside it stood a silver-framed picture of Evelyn's first husband in his navy whites; the Distinguished Service Medal hung on its blue and gold ribbon on the corner of the frame. Vince. The doctor.

What did a doctor know about fighting? True, Adam had never entered the boxing ring, and being small-framed, he lost twice as many fights as he won, but for sheer willingness to fight, for deep down dogged determination to come up swinging no matter how many times he got knocked down, for pure spunk, no one held a candle to Adam Newman. And yet the draft board refused him, as if fallen arches had anything to do with holding a gun. The thought of touching another gun made Adam shudder, but he would have done even that if his country asked him.

Adam wondered if his mother, in her unyielding determination to save him from himself, had pulled strings with the draft board to have him declared unfit for service. *Thank you, Mother dear, thank you, thank you, thank you. You always found just the perfect way to make my life hell, like putting me on the train to Sisters of Mercy in those damn blue shorts you picked out.*

Addison returned with notebook paper and a pen, and Adam wrote, first sticking the pen tip in his mouth as he mentally composed his letter. Ironically, the one person he wanted to confide in about the diamonds—Evelyn—he couldn't tell. Evelyn would understand and feel the right blend of compassion, anger, and disappointment. Lily would never get angry or disappointed. Lily always believed Adam was on top of things and knew what he was doing. Evelyn knew him better than that.

*D*

He nearly wrote "Darling" but thought better of it.

*ear Ev,*

Addison and I are looking for something I lost. It is a small purple bag. I can't tell you what it is because it's a surprise, but it's very, very, very important that we find it. If you come across it, please call me at once. If I'm not there, leave a message with my service. Do not tell Lily. I cannot stress this enough; do not tell Lily.

Adam

XXX OOO

The *x*'s and *o*'s were a nice touch. Evelyn couldn't take offense because they were merely playful, yet Adam had squeezed his whole soul into each of those *o*'s. Those *x*'s held little drops of his heart's blood. He weighted the corner of the note under Evelyn's lacquered jewelry box with its inlay of elephants crossing a bridge, each one holding the tail of the next. Accidentally he knocked Vincent's picture facedown, but did not trouble to right it. "Like I said, it's probably in my jeep anyway," Adam said as he rejoined his son in the living room. "I bet I dropped it in there. Maybe I put it in my glove compartment."

"Well, good," Addison said. "I bet that's it." The pause it

took Addison to gather the implication of this exchange could scarcely have been timed on a Swiss watch. "Do you want me to drive you to your jeep?"

"That'd be magnificent, son. I'd appreciate it. I can give you directions."

"I'm a little low on gas."

"We'll get some."

"I'm taking Dad to get his jeep," Addison yelled as he left the house with his father. Kean and Kathleen were still sitting in the swing. Had they been kissing? "Don't do anything I wouldn't do," he added in his best lighthearted voice. "Ha-ha." The laugh was so forced, he actually enunciated the syllables, *ha-ha.*

They jolted into reverse in Addison's Beetle.

Adam rolled down the window in spite of the temperature and rested his arm on the door. He turned on the radio and heard "Jingle Bell Rock." Adam shook his head. What kind of song was that? No one took pride in lyrics anymore. He twisted the knob through an interval of static and found Dean Martin's silvery voice in the middle of "That's Amore," a song Adam would always associate with Paradise Dogs. Combining the twin themes of love and food, it had been a hit when their restaurant's success was at its apex. *When the stars make you drool, just like pasta fazool, that's amore.* They'd sing along as Evelyn kneaded dough and Adam browned ground beef for chili. Their waitress would look up from wiping tables and smile uncertainly.

Being with his son, his spirits lifted. At Chattahoochee, Dr. Dewberry labeled Adam's temperament, buoyant as a rubber duck in a bathtub, "emotionally labile." Adam and Addison would find the diamonds; he would break it off with Lily Manzana and be reunited with Evelyn. "Do you ever have déjà vu?"

"Didn't you just ask me that?"

"What?"

His father hadn't gotten the joke. "Nothing," Addison said. Addison loved his father, but found it hard making conversation with him.

Adam shifted uncomfortably in the vinyl seat; his knees felt jammed against his chest in the Volkswagen. "You and I are always thinking, we're a lot alike."

In spite of himself, this comment pleased Addison.

Adam tapped his sweat-greased brow. "Always thinking, that's how I make my money." Awkward silence followed. "Do you ever have déjà vu?"

"Didn't you just ask me that?"

"What?"

"Nothing."

"I have the strangest feeling of déjà vu," Adam said quietly. They pulled into the Sinclair on South Eola. "Fill 'er up," Adam told the attendant. "I may go across the way and buy myself a ginger ale. I'm a mite parched," he said. "You want anything?"

"No thanks."

As the attendant pumped the gas, it occurred to Addison that it might be a good idea to call home. He didn't need to speak to anyone, but he had a strong urge to interrupt Kean and Kathleen's conversation. Maybe through some happy coincidence Kean would be locked in the bathroom or something and Kathleen herself would answer.

Addison walked to the phone booth, plunked his dime in the slot, and dialed. The phone burred twice, and Addison surveyed his surroundings. In one direction lay a trailer park. In the other stood a tall white rust-flecked pole that held the Sinclair sign.

"Newman residence," the voice on the other end said. It was his mother.

"Hello, Mother," Addison said.

"I just got home. Kean said you're with your father?"

"Yes," Addison said.

"You aren't letting him drive, are you?"

"No, Mother. I'm just taking him to his car." Cold wind stirred the scrawny pines in the trailer park across the street.

Evelyn Newman didn't believe in smothering her sons by being overprotective. She didn't pry into their activities or, for example, try to dissuade Kean from karate or motorcycle riding. But being in her ex-husband's company entailed an entirely different degree of risk; it was as if her son had set off across the moors companioned by a charming and lovely associate who just so happened to be a known werewolf and on a night that promised a full moon.

"Don't let him drive." "No, Mother."

"Don't take him to a bar." "No, Mother."

"Don't let him drink." "No, Mother."

"Don't let him out of your sight." "No, Mother."

"Don't forget what happened the time he told those people he was a fireman."

A creased and dirty business card on the floor bore the unmistakable scrawl of Adam Newman: *A4 purch: 12/21/65.* Addison picked it up. "No, Mother."

There was a sigh on the other end of the line. "Okay, just get him to his car and get back as soon as you can."

At the door, a Santa Claus with grimy fur cuffs winked at Adam and intoned "Ho-ho-ho," in a way that seemed fraught with private meaning. When Adam went to the register, the cashier took her Lucky Strike from her mouth with painted fingernails and said, "For you that tallboy is free."

"You don't say," Adam said, gratified. "That's mighty kind."

He pointed at a display of inflatable palm trees by the counter. "Hard to believe it's Ex-mas already."

"Seems like just yesterday it was Ex-giving," the cashier quipped.

"You know," Adam said, "I have the strangest feeling of déjà vu."

"No fooling."

"It's him!" Everyone in this place seemed to know him.

A young couple stood behind him. The girl held up a newborn in a pink blanket for Adam's inspection. The baby, in one of those soft snug knit hats they put on newborns, pressed a tiny fist to a red face that looked like a squashed apple. The baby looked very fresh, Adam thought, to be out of the hospital. How long had Evelyn stayed in with Addison? Surely Addison hadn't been *this* new. The poor were not welcome to stay as long as people with money.

"Now that's what I call a baby," Adam said pleasantly.

"We're naming her Bateman. Johnny was against it, but I said."

On the whole, Adam was inclined to agree with Johnny, but it seemed impolite to say so. Besides, Adam had taken an instant liking to the young mother with her scrubbed face, too thin red cotton dress, and heavy men's shoes—in fact, he was already halfway in love with her. His was a heart that fell in love easily. He didn't know why this delightful young woman had addressed him, but he played along. Frequently people Adam didn't know came up to him, recalling friendships struck up, promises made, or fights provoked, of which Adam had no recollection.

"Ah, Bateman. A lovely name."

"After you."

They'd named her Bateman after him. Didn't make sense. Nevertheless, the gesture touched Adam to his heart. He spoke to them with sudden sweet earnestness, "Promise me one thing. Promise me you won't send little Bateman off to a boarding school. Believe me, dear, whatever she might have done, she'll already be sorry for it, and it will only make things worse. Later I can give you a comprehensive list of boarding schools not to send her to, but for now, just remember Sisters of Mercy Academy in Savannah."

"We live right across the street in Cypress Park," the girl said. "Maybe sometime you could—"

"He's not a real doctor, Jane," Johnny said with the petulant certainty of a first grader announcing there is no Santa Claus. "I don't know what he is, but he's not a real doctor."

"Of course I'm a real doctor," Adam said. For some reason it seemed essential to maintain this.

"Real doctors don't have—" Johnny did not finish his sentence, and so Adam did not learn what he had that real doctors did not.

"Don't listen to him, Dr. Bateman," Jane said. She placed her hand lightly on his wrist. She had fingers as long and delicate as a Raphael Madonna, but her nails were split and uneven, and her cuticles were red. "I'm so glad we ran into you and got to thank you." She smelled of innocence and Ivory soap.

"Me too."

"So long, Dr. Bateman."

"So long, Jane. So long, Johnny. So long, little Bateman."

As he walked with his tallboy back to his son's car, the joy of meeting his namesake evaporated, and a sense of discontent weighed on him.

Adam gave the attendant two wadded green bills for the gas, Addison put the car into gear, and they jerked into the boulevard. "I found this in the phone booth while I was making a call," Addison said, handing his father the card. "It looks like something of yours."

Seeing his handwriting on the back of the creased, grease-stained card, the notation of Ayefour's latest purchase, made the small hairs on Adam's neck stand up. Perhaps it was only a coincidence, but was anything ever really a coincidence? Were Ayefour and Compass East mixed up in this diamond business? Were they trying to send him a message?

"You probably want me to tell you what this card means," Adam said.

"Well—"

"But don't ask me because I can't tell you."

"Okay."

"I'd like to, but I can't."

"Okay."

Adam stared at the handwriting on the card with a noisy sigh. Nothing would please him more than sharing the secret of Ayefour, Compass East, and the Cross-Florida Barge Canal with his son; only with the greatest personal effort could he restrain himself from doing so. "I'll tell you if you swear to keep it to yourself, if you really want to know."

"No, maybe you'd better not."

"Right. You're a journalist. I was forgetting."

"Right."

"In the fullness of time, perhaps I can let you in on this, and then maybe you could use it in one of those stories you write."

"That'd be great," Addison said, nodding and smiling as if he'd just filled his mouth with some delicious food.

Adam imagined a story about himself filled with action, hairsbreadth escapes, code names, assumed identities, and a final confrontation with a shadowy nemesis bent on world domination, like in *Dr. No.*

Adam stared out the window. Surely Potter, the Ayefour representative whom Adam had turned down at their meeting, would not go so far as that? Still, Adam knew what a serious game Potter was playing; with stakes as high as this, laws were made to be broken. Adam had spotted William Potter as military as soon as he saw him; that cool gaze, those squared shoulders, the long assurance of being top dog.

*Navy?* Adam had asked.

*Army*, Potter replied. *Major General. Retired. You?*

*Four-F*, Adam admitted, too proud to drop his gaze. *Fallen arches.*

Because Adam had been willing albeit unfit to serve, he'd gotten the Honorable Service Pin—honorable! A plastic eagle, wings spread but feet planted—fallen arches, no doubt—signifying that this bird wasn't no way doing no fighting for nobody nohow. No one called it the Honorable Service Pin, and no one used the nickname to Adam's face, but he knew what it was: the Ruptured Duck. You had to wear your Ruptured Duck to keep from getting questioned by MPs or hearing dark mutters of passersby: *What's wrong with him? Why isn't he doing his bit?* It was a choice between the humiliation of facing the world with the pin or without it.

Adam would have happily sold Ayefour his land, but he felt entitled to be admitted to the inner circle about the so-called Venezuela Project—the code name assigned the Cross-Florida Barge Canal. After thirty minutes of having all his questions parried by bland nonresponses, Adam had begun to grow exasperated. *I know what this is for*, he said, *but you're buying up too much land—and in the wrong directions. You're going north and south and you should go east and west. I need to see your engineers.* General Potter turned up his powerful but manicured hands as if to show he hadn't brought any engineers with him. *I've done my research*, Adam said, *I know what this is for. Will you at least admit you still work for Uncle Sam?*

*No*, Potter said, with a wry smile, his voice as velvety and self-satisfied as if he'd spent the afternoon inspecting troops, *not Uncle Sam*.

"Dang it," Adam told his son, catching his breath, "I just remembered. I have to meet Lily at St. George for marital counseling. We'll have to stop off there and go by the Fish Camp later." Adam lifted a trembling Pall Mall to his lips and lit it with his trusty Zippo.

"Dad, what is in that bag you're looking for?"

"As a matter of fact, it's about a quarter million dollars' worth of diamonds," Adam said. He threw his hand out to brace himself against the dashboard. "You'll want to keep your eyes on the road, son. It's bad for the tires to run up on the median that way."

Addison recovered himself and said, "Have you considered calling the po—?"

"No law enforcement officers!" Adam said.

"What were you doing with a bag of diamonds anyway?" Addison asked.

"Well, it's sort of a secret, but your mother and I may be getting back together. I'm not kidding myself. I know it probably won't be easy."

Getting Mother to take back a dangerous, drunk-driving, precancerous, ugly, irresponsible, diamond-losing lunatic. No, it would probably not be easy.

"There's Lily," Adam said. "I'll have to break it off with her. But first, we have to find the diamonds."

# FIVE

# Adam Gives Advice

"Of course, we have yet to see if there'll be a happy ending," Adam said. The car jolted as Addison shifted from second into third.

"What?"

"The story you wanted to write. About me." In Adam's mind Addison's story would feature someone just like Adam himself, only younger, better-looking, and more physically active. "I'm ninety-nine percent certain everything will turn out fine—with the diamonds, your mother, and the Cross-Flor—that is, everything, but we really won't know for sure until everything is said and done." Adam sighed and looked at the passing scenery. "Of course, I guess suspense is the part that makes it interesting. That makes it a surprise when everything turns out right."

"Well . . ." Addison said. He had no more intention of writing a story about his father than building a toothpick tower to the moon, but he could never resist talking about his craft. "Stories don't have to have happy endings, Dad. My stories, for example." Addison thought of his earlier triumphs, "The Gently Hovering Shadow" and "The Tenderly Wavering Twilight." Where could he go from there? How about a young man coming to terms with the death of his *son*? No—that was too much like "The Tenderly Wavering Twilight," in which the daughter died; besides, in "The Gently Hovering Shadow," the protagonist's wife *and* daughter had died. Reducing the death toll to a mere son would seem like retreating. "I really don't like happy endings."

"Why not?" asked Adam, who adored happy endings.

"It's deus ex machina, God from the machine," Addison said. "In Greek theater when they wanted to lug in a happy ending, a crane would lower an actor playing Zeus onto the stage."

"And Zeus would tie up all the loose ends?"

"Exactly," Addison said. "But the world isn't that way. Someone doesn't just show up out of the blue to straighten everything out. The truth is things almost never work out for the best. There's really only one true ending to any story: everybody dies."

Adam nodded in unhappy acceptance of this. He decided he didn't care for stories with true endings; he had grown up on uplifting books that the Old Man had read when *he* was a boy. His favorite was about an orphan who shines shoes by day and studies accountancy at night, salting away pennies in a savings account.

The part that used to bring tears of outrage to Adam's eyes was when someone steals the shoeshine boy's bankbook! But trying to withdraw the funds, the culprit exposes himself with clumsy lies as the shoeshine boy watches from a place of concealment. The shoeshine boy wants to let him off with a warning, but the policeman on the scene is adamant: the culprit is a no-good with a long and villainous history. He takes the would-be thief away, never again to darken the book's pages.

Riding a ferryboat in the last chapter, the shoeshine boy hears an affrighted shout, "Child overboard!" Not thinking for his own safety, he leaps to the rescue. He is an expert swimmer, the narrator now reveals. The relieved father, a gentleman of business, immediately offers the shoeshine boy a position at ten dollars a week. The shoeshine boy demurs, but the child's father insists, for he has recognized the boy's hidden but unmistakable qualities of character; moreover, promises his new employer, there will be increases as he should merit them.

Adam knew real life never worked out that way—that life did not provide happy endings, but this was exactly why stories had to. Adam's earliest ambition was to be a shoeshine boy and then to grow up like his Old Man.

Adam loved his Old Man as he dreamed Addison might one day love him. The Old Man had faced German gas and charged a machine gun nest. He owned a pearl-handled revolver, *which Adam was not allowed to touch.* The Old Man was afraid of nothing except thunder. He wasn't really afraid of that, but after the boom before a summer squall, he might spend days brooding in his study over dark concerns. When the Old Man was pleased, he'd come out, his roar rattling plates in their cupboards: *My boy and I want some bacon, fry us some bacon!* Adam's mother would let Hassie fry up a pound of bacon, even though she hated any greasy thing in her immaculate kitchen.

The day before his accident, the Old Man emerged buoyant from one of his brown moods, his big shiny keys jangling from a ring in his hand, and took Adam to see his friends the Dreggors. Things would have been perfect if only Adam hadn't gone exploring in the Old Man's study later that day.

But surely it wasn't too late to unbungle his other bungles.

They turned from Livingston onto Main. Merchants had frosted their windows with fake snow. From somewhere a bell choir jangled its way through "The First Noel."

"So is there a girl in the picture?"

"What?"

"Do you have a girlfriend?"

"No. Sort of. Actually, no."

"But there's a girl you have your eye on."

"Yes. Sort of." He'd nearly made a fool of himself over her. Thank goodness she never saw the letter he'd composed one feverish night. He could never find it later, but consoled himself that under the influence of better judgment, he must've thrown it in the trash without thinking. But now he only wanted her friendship. And maybe to do one amazing thing to make himself wonderful in her eyes.

"Attaboy! The secret to getting a girl is simple," Adam said, pressing his palms against his knees as he tried to think what that secret might be. "You have to give her everything. Lay the world at her feet. Nothing's too good for her. Other men try to play it cool, and that may work for them, but you and me, we're romantics. We fall in love all the way, and we fall hard. We're willing to die for love if need be. We're like modern-day knights. Like the man who threw his cloak over the mud puddle for the lady."

"Sir Walter Raleigh."

"That's the man! And the woman ended up marrying him, too, didn't she?"

"Actually, I think she had him imprisoned."

"Well, that's the sort of thing we have to put up with sometimes. They're not always reasonable," Adam said. "Like your mother. Nothing against her. But she would get worked up over the dangedest things. French fries, for example. But the key is letting them know you love them and can't live without them. I made a point of telling your mother every day, 'I love you.' Just like that. Did it first thing in the morning so I wouldn't have to worry about it for the rest of the day. That's the secret of a successful marriage."

"And a fine marriage it is."

"What?"

"Nothing." Addison pulled to a stop at a red light. A woman crossed with a large bag in each hand, her face pink from exertion in the chilly air. "Dad, have you thought it might be better just to go ahead and marry Lily?"

"Lily doesn't understand me like your mother does." Adam was stern. "When you have a wife, you can't just replace her with someone else. It's not like backing over a dog, where you can just run to the pound for a new one and hope no one notices. When you meet someone like your mother, you know it's for keeps, that she's the only woman you'll ever love. Besides," Adam added darkly, "she wants to check me into Chattahoochee."

"Chattahoochee?"

"I went once, out of love for your mother and no other reason. It is not an experiment I care to repeat. First they make you surrender any possession with which you might unknowingly endanger yourself—your belt, shoelaces, and aftershave. Then they sit you down to paint one goddamn therapeutic ceramic alligator after another." Adam mentioned the alligators with special vehemence. They seemed to be the greatest affront of all. "And have daily chats with sundry pill poppers and drunks, and—if you are really, really lucky—a complete stranger who smells like cumin breaks down and throws his arms around you, and soaks you with what you can only hope are tears and not, which is more likely, slobber. In the bad old days they could lock me away willy-nilly, but now they need the testimony of a law enforcement officer, three affidavits, and a judge's approval to compel me to hand over my shoelaces and start painting alligators.

"Ah, and here we are—St. George's," Adam said, brightening.

The mousy blonde secretary at St. George's, who was just stepping out, told Adam and Addison to make themselves comfortable in the rector's office. Father Peel was giving Lily a tour of the chapel, and if they ran into the organist, they might even discuss musical selections. "I don't think they'll be back right away," the secretary said, "the lady was very talkative." The last word came out in a whisper.

Adam and Addison sat on a couch in front of the rector's desk. The room had the faint indefinable smell of priests—unleavened bread, perhaps. There was little for the eye to rest on in Father Peel's office: an oak desk with a matching cabinet behind it, a coffee cup with the motto *Father Knows Best*, a yellow legal pad, an ashtray full of colorful golf tees, and a golf ball. A putter leaned in the corner. There ought to be Muzak while you're waiting for a priest, Adam reflected. He experimentally hummed a few bars of "The Girl from Ipanema" before giving it up and lapsing into silence.

Exactly when had things gone so wrong? There had been a time—hadn't there?—when things were perfect. He and Evelyn had been happy. Business had been good. The boys respected him—or were capable of respecting him eventually. Addison and Kean helped out after school, Addison splitting the fresh buns, dotting on butter, and setting them on the conveyor-belt toaster as Kean dropped dogs in the grease to fry. No trendy vegetable oil for Paradise Dogs! They fried everything, including onion rings, in a secret mixture of lard and butter flavored with seared country ham. Each hot dog was plucked from the sizzling grease just as a bun emerged, brown on the edges with yellow suns of melted butter in the center. From an aluminum pot simmering behind the counter, Adam ladled on chili good enough to eat on its own. Theirs were expensive dogs, but that did not deter the throngs of customers.

*We don't serve chicken, hamburgers, or pizza*, Adam always said, *no doughnuts, barbecue, or spaghetti. No salad. No noodles. No rock lobster or Cornish game hen. Just hot dogs.*

*But the very best hot dogs*, Evelyn always added.

You couldn't buy kraut good enough for these hot dogs; you had to make it fresh, and there was no question of making such transcendent kraut from cabbages lying out in the A&P for just anyone to handle; you had to grow them yourself, and don't even get the Newmans started on the subject of relish.

They sold the restaurant, but the new owners lacked the mania to seek such perfection. They added vegetarian hot dogs and chicken franks, and closed in a year. Paradise Dogs was now a dry cleaner's. Sometimes, it's true, the awful burden of creating the perfect hot dog had lain on Adam's shoulders like a mountain range, but Lily Manzana—back when she was still a waitress—flattered him when they were alone, using the precise English she had mastered with "It Pays to Increase Your Word Power." *You are so perspicacious and have such acumen*, she told him when they took beer to refill the pie tins in the garden out back. The only thing slugs love more than a good head of cabbage is a nice pie tin of beer. *Mrs. Newman is so auspicious to have you.* Adam would tell Lily he wished Evelyn understood him as well as she did. That conversation would have taken place about this time of year—cabbages are winter vegetables—but Adam recalled it as being blistering hot. He remembered sweat prickling under his shirt and how he'd squinted against the sun to fill the pie tin, first taking an experimental sip. Adam smiled at the memory. Dang, Evelyn *had* been auspicious. He'd been auspicious too, only he hadn't realized.

But things would be better now. As soon as he got the diamonds back, he and Evelyn could be reunited, and the diamonds were in his jeep; he was sure of it. In fact, he seemed to recall deliberately tucking them under the driver's seat for safekeeping.

"Dad?" Addison said. "I was thinking about those diamonds."

"Yes, son?" said Adam.

"Maybe we could offer a five percent reward."

"What?"

"For the diamonds. Maybe we could offer a reward."

"Uh-huh."

"There's a girl who lost her funding for college, see," Addison said.

A tumbler fell in Adam's mind. "And you want to help her out."

"Yes."

"Naturally," Adam said. "Never miss a chance to do a good deed. I think a reward is a colossal idea. Now, I couldn't just give you the money. It ruins a boy to just give him money," he said, trying to sound severe. He would have gladly just given Addison the money for the asking, but this way was better. "You have to earn it. But as soon as we get the diamonds from the jeep, and they're definitely there, of course I'll give you a ten percent finder's fee. Fair is fair." They shook hands to close the deal. "So," Adam said, patting his thighs. "There's a girl. A girl? A girl? Who is the girl?"

"I really can't say," Addison said. Addison almost hugged him for delight. He wondered why he'd never noticed how handsome his father was before—how his blistered bald head perfectly set off his distinguished round, ruddy face with its elegant cauliflower ear, and that exquisitely flattened nose. If he had known it would be this easy getting money out of his father, he'd have done it days ago. Unlike his mother, who had conservatively parked her share of the restaurant proceeds in a CD and returned to teaching, Adam's father went into speculation. At any given time it was impossible to guess Adam's financial condition because whatever he didn't spend, he was forever leveraging into bigger investments; he was hocked to the teeth to buy land and margined stocks—his wealth poised on a tightrope over a deep abyss of financial ruin. From one moment to the next Adam might be rolling in loot or digging under the couch cushions for grocery money. Addison had approached his father at the ideal time.

"Oh, son, I just hope you find half the happiness your mother and I have." Adam sighed in contentment. "Well," he checked his watch, which was not running—a clock on the wall said the market was still open. He had to monitor his portfolio. "I don't expect the padre will mind if I use his phone."

Adam sat in the leather chair behind the desk and took the phone from its cradle to dial his broker. "Sam! How are you, you old rascal? Adam Newman here." Adam paused, an open-mouthed grin as he listened to whatever chummy insult Sam the broker made in return. "Ha-ha. Fair to middling, Sam, fair to middling. Now here's what. I want to close out of eLoye—right, all of it, cut my losses. And I want two and a half blocks of Moore Locks—Yes, put it on my margin—No, no limit—Right—Let me know, and I'll put a check in the mail." Adam listened to Sam's reply and laughed. From outside the office two voices—a man's and a woman's—rose in noisy disagreement. Their words were indistinguishable except as a tuneless series of blahs and blatts. Adam drummed a few bars of "The William Tell Overture" on the desktop. "And I'll still respect you in the morning, and no, that dress doesn't make you look fat, and I'm from the government and I'm here to help. Ah-ha-ha-ha-ha."

It dimly occurred to Adam that perhaps he shouldn't commit to such a large stock purchase until he knew for absolute certain he wouldn't have to reimburse Ernie Costa, but the diamonds were in his jeep for sure; they had to be. Besides, investing in this particular company was sure fire. He could see now that the flyer he had taken on eLoye had been ill advised. It was too speculative, too blue sky, but Moore Locks was old-fashioned and rock-bottom solid. Adam couldn't imagine what could possibly go wrong. He could never imagine what could possibly go wrong, a weakness that was to have unfortunate consequences at intervals throughout his life.

Whatever the disagreement outside had been, it stopped and the door opened. A couple stood on the other side. Adam looked up at them from the priest's desk and gave a half wave. He was nodding and smiling as if Sam on the other end of the phone line could see. "Ha-ha-ha. Okay then. Bye, Sam." Adam hung up. "Hello, can I help you?" he asked.

"We're here for marital counseling?" the woman asked shyly. "We're Betty and Jeff."

"You came to the right place, dear," Adam said. Betty was a no-longer-young blonde with the wide blue-eyed stare of a woman who has found life a disappointment but is determined to make the best of it. Jeff had the fleshy face of a man in transition from trim youth to doughy middle age.

"Where's Father Peel?" Jeff asked. "You're not Father Peel."

"No, not Father Peel," Adam said. "What can I do for you?" He picked up the golf ball and tossed and caught it nonchalantly with one hand. He tossed it three times, but only managed to catch it twice. The third throw sent a hail of golf spikes from the ashtray. Reaching for the ball, Adam overturned the coffee cup, spilling room-temperature Maxwell House over the yellow legal pad that bore the notes for a sermon.

"You're not the priest," Jeff said.

"I bet it's one of those exchange deals," Betty said. "Ecuminimalism. I heard about it in *Newsweek.* You're a Baptist, aren't you?"

"Well, sort of," Adam temporized, unwilling to say an outright no. He realized that when he said he wasn't *Father* Peel, he'd inadvertently implied he might be Pastor Peel or else possibly Rabbi Peel. He set the coffee cup back upright.

"He's not a minister," Jeff told Betty. "You don't know what you're talking about."

If there was one thing Adam resented, it was being called a liar. "Of course I'm a minister," he retorted. "It's just what Betty said. It's an exchange deal." He rested his hand on the sodden legal pad and pulled it back with a surprised grunt.

"And who's he?" Jeff asked, regarding Addison. "A missionary?"

Adam decided he did not care for Jeff's tone. "Yes, as a matter of fact he is," he said. "Was. He's just returned."

Addison swallowed as if he'd been force-fed a pocket watch, but dutifully nodded. "It was just a small mission," he mumbled, answering Jeff's disbelieving stare. "Fort Lauderdale."

"Praise Jesus," Adam added, feeling additional corroboration was needed. It was a phrase he believed frequently employed by Baptist ministers.

"Praise Jesus," Addison echoed softly.

"Well, maybe we can just talk to this guy," Jeff said. "I don't want to wait around here all day."

"It really isn't my place," Adam demurred. "Father Peel will be back shortly."

"Yeah, we ought to wait for the regular priest," Betty agreed.

Adam realized that when Father Peel did show up, there would be an inevitable awkwardness as it was disclosed Adam was not, as he had allowed Betty and Jeff to believe, a minister, but just another supplicant for counseling. At the time he couldn't come up with a graceful way to disabuse them of their misconception. "Maybe you two could come back tomorrow," he suggested.

"I'm not wasting another day on this," Jeff said.

"See," Betty said, "there you go again."

"I'm sure this guy is just as good," Jeff said. "Aren't you?"

"Well," Adam said. There seemed no way to dislodge this couple until they got their counseling, and the longer Adam put off revealing he was a mere civilian, the more embarrassing the eventual revelation would be for everyone. What should he do? Could he really pass himself off as a minister? Of course, he *did* have an opportunity to help a couple struggling in love's stormy sea, and he happened to possess a wealth of knowledge on the subject.

"Well, maybe I could do a little something," Adam said. "As you embark upon married life," Adam told Jeff, leaning back and steepling his fingers, "remember that women want things a certain way. Take, for example, french fries. If you make yourself french fries, and frankly I suggest you avoid them altogether, you must remember to pour the Crisco out—never, never leave it in the skillet. Women do not like waking up and finding a mess in the kitchen." Their stares were as blank as a chalkboard before the first day of school. "But when you do pour it out," Adam dropped his head to look at the desk; his posture and voice spoke of one who wrestled with a painful memory, "you must make absolutely certain you do not pour it in the silverware drawer. I know you'll say that's an easy mistake to make, coming home late at night and sleepy, like peeing in the laundry hamper thinking it's the toilet, but—"

"That's not our problem," Betty said.

"What?" With difficulty Adam cleared his head of the ghastly image: Evelyn's livid face in the morning light—a few forlorn salted french fries lying on a ketchup-encrusted plate—fork tines barely protruding from a frozen lake of gray lard in an open drawer. There were many things she could forgive—had forgiven—but that had not been one of them.

"We don't have a problem with french fries," Betty said.

"Will you let the man speak?" Jeff said.

"See?" Betty said. "That's the problem. He's always making me feel stupid."

"Please, have a seat." Adam gestured toward the couch. Addison rose to make room. Betty and Jeff sat, but they didn't touch shoulders. Before their temporary divorce three years, two months, and nine days ago, Adam and Evelyn had always sat with shoulders and hips touching, feeling each other's reassuring warmth. Oft times would he clasp her hand in his, but these two sat with a strip of daylight between. Still less did Jeff clasp Betty's hand. It would take all Adam's ministerial expertise to heal this breach. "You say he makes you feel stupid."

"I never said she was stupid," Jeff said.

"You don't have to say it. Everything you do says it." To show what she meant, Betty folded her arms, looked at the corner of the ceiling, and sniffed in exasperation—giving what a fair-minded observer would say was an excellent impression of Jeff.

"And what about you?" Jeff challenged her. He addressed himself to Adam, "The other day I'm changing out a wall outlet, and she keeps asking these nagging little questions. 'Is that the right kind of screwdriver?' " he asked, imitating his wife, who evidently made such inquiries in a high, nasal voice. " 'Don't you need electrical tape?' 'Shouldn't you turn the power off?' "

"I see, I see," Adam said. "I see this sort of thing all the time at our church. It's the number-one complaint right behind french fries, isn't that so, son?"

Addison nodded. "You probably just need to communicate more," he offered weakly.

"You're exactly right, son," Adam said. "I was about to say the same thing myself." Adam noted his son's wide-eyed expression and feared Addison was about to overelaborate, a classic mistake of amateurs posing as Baptist ministers. Adam decided to get him out of the way before he tried speaking in tongues or looking for some snakes to handle. "Son, why don't you run out and see if you can get something to wipe up this coffee?" Adam shook a few drops from his fingertips.

"Sure, Dad," Addison said gratefully and slipped from the room like a freed hostage.

"He's a fine boy," Adam said once he heard Addison's footsteps heading down the hall. "But nervous. Life in the mission," Adam said impressively and fell into silence, as if dwelling on some unspeakable ordeal in Fort Lauderdale.

This additional information didn't instill any great confidence in Betty. "I think we'll just wait for the priest," she said.

"Please forget what my son was saying about communication," Adam said, ignoring her. He had to wrap this up before Father Peel and Lily arrived and disaster ensued. "Communication is the worst possible thing you can do. I can't tell you how many marriages I've seen ruined by communication. Did you hear footsteps?" Adam asked in sudden alarm. He went to the door and cracked it to make sure no one was coming. The coast was clear. "Fortunately the real solution to your problem is very simple." Adam paused to think up a solution. As an ad hoc representative of the Southern Baptist Convention, he felt a fiduciary obligation to push the product. "Any time he makes you feel stupid—"

"I never said she was stupid," Jeff said with an angry furrow between his brows.

"I want you to say 'praise Jesus.'"

"'Praise Jesus'?" Betty said.

The logic of this remedy was not readily obvious to either of them, and in fact, Adam himself didn't know quite where he was heading. "And Jeff, naturally, if she says 'praise Jesus,' you've got to say 'praise Jesus' too. And Jeff, whenever she starts to nag you about something—for example, the way you're putting in an electric outlet—"

"I just didn't want him getting electro—"

"Praise Jesus," Jeff interrupted.

"And if he says that," Adam told Betty, "you must also say 'praise Jesus.'"

"Praise Jesus?" Betty said.

"So let us recap," Adam said. He returned to his seat, steepled his fingers again, and leaned back in the chair a bit too far, losing his balance and thumping his head on the cabinet behind him before righting himself. "Any time anger's wind lays its chilly touch upon the bloom of love, you must say 'praise Jesus.' And anytime you hear your mate say 'praise Jesus,' you must also say 'praise Jesus.'"

"Praise Jesus," Betty said.

"Praise Jesus," Jeff said.

"I really don't think this will solve our—" Betty began.

"Praise Jesus," Adam said.

"Praise Jesus," Betty said.

"Praise Jesus," Jeff said.

Betty and Jeff laughed and leaned against each other.

Adam noted with satisfaction that they touched shoulders at last. When they did, they seemed gloriously natural and in love, and Adam loved them for being in love.

"I feel like an idiot," Jeff said.

"Praise Jesus," Betty said.

"Praise Jesus," Jeff said.

"The Good Book tells us we are all idiots in the sight of God," Adam said. "I may be paraphrasing somewhat. Clasp her in your arms. Tell her you adore her and place love's tender kiss upon her lips. I will avert my gaze." They kissed. "Now go forth. Be fruitful and multiply. After—of course—you get home and a decent interval."

When Addison emerged from the bathroom, he met Father Peel and Lily in the hall.

"This is Adam's son by his first marriage, Addison," Lily said with her characteristic exactitude.

"Hello," Father Peel said. Addison's face heated as the priest shook his hand. Although it would have been impossible not to notice the roll of church toilet paper in Addison's other hand, the priest did not allude to it. This lack of comment made Addison feel as conspicuous as if he'd been caught transporting a dead armadillo. The bathrooms at St. George's did not have paper towels, but a single cloth towel on a conveyor-belt-like roll, so Addison had improvised; naturally he planned on returning the unused portion once he attended to the spilled coffee, but at the moment explaining this flummoxed him. In any case, Addison knew he must stall the priest and his future stepmother until his dad finished what he was doing in the office.

"I was admiring your beautiful church," Addison said. "It's quite old, isn't it?"

"Not as old as all that," said Father Peel. "But the parishioners know St. George's is their church. We like to think it is a source of joy and inspiration to—"

"Where are you taking the church's bathroom tissue?" Lily asked. There was little she noticed that escaped comment and she noticed everything.

Before Addison could frame a response, Jeff and Betty came down the hall laughing and holding hands.

"Are you here for counseling?" Father Peel asked. "Because I—"

"No, we're good," Betty said. "We're good."

"Praise Jesus." Jeff laughed.

"Praise Jesus." Betty laughed.

And without further explanation the two were gone.

"Adam must be waiting for us in your office," Lily deduced from this otherwise inexplicable exchange.

SIX

# Adam Selects a Hymn

"It wasn't necessary to bring your son," Father Peel said when the three of them rejoined Adam in the office. Adam explained that he wanted Addison as his best man.

"Did you hear that, Addison? You are designated the best man!" Lily poked Addison's chest with a bright red fingernail as if she'd made a wicked double entendre. At close range the sweet cedar reek filled his nostrils. Addison could have forgiven his future stepmother for laughing at her own jokes and even for making jokes that weren't funny—it was doing both at the same time he found hard to take.

"Actually," Addison said, nervously passing the unneeded roll of toilet paper from hand to hand, "I need to step out for a second anyway, but I'll be back in a little bit, Dad, and we'll—"

"Yes, we will," Adam said.

Addison took a chair outside Father Peel's office. Soon they would retrieve his father's diamonds, and Addison would get his reward. He envisioned presenting Kathleen with her tuition. He imagined her uncharacteristically inarticulate as she counted the bills he'd stuffed into a crisp white envelope. *How did you—? How—?* she would stumble through the words. *It's nothing*, Addison would say nonchalantly, *don't give it a thought. That's enough, isn't it?* He would lift her chin in his fingers to examine her grateful, tear-filled eyes. And then, on an impulse they both knew was right, he would lean in, but just a hairsbreadth before their lips met, he would pause. His face flushed at the thought.

The first day in Brit Lit, Addison had kept his sight trained on Geoffrey Chaucer's improbably small horse in the textbook, stealing sideways peeks to confirm the incredible fact that the prettiest girl in the school, if not the city, sat next to him. He reasoned she couldn't possibly be as pretty as all that, and if he thought her inexpressibly lovely, it was only in comparison with ordinary girls. If she ever smiled at him, a chorus of hidden violins wouldn't *really* swell into melody, and it was silly to imagine it would. After all, even from this angle he could tell her nose was crooked, and her forehead too high. Moreover, he consoled himself, if she's half as pretty as all that, she can't be very bright; pretty girls never are, certainly not girls whose slightest glance calls up string symphonies from invisible orchestras.

But then Mrs. Turner was stuck for a historic date, and Kathleen supplied it: 1564, the year of Shakespeare's birth. With that, Kathleen Neligan sank her hook deep in Addison's heart.

Against all odds, Kathleen became his friend, and when she looked up with glowing eyes from a piece he'd written to say, "Addison, this is good," it really was exactly like hearing an orchestra. This was before "The Softly Trembling Darkness," but his work already bore the unmistakable Newman touch. Not so much a story as a sketch, it was a tender untitled piece about a basset hound named Charley, the boy who adored him, and the Buick that separated them forever. In Kathleen's eyes he had been transformed—at least briefly—into something marvelous. He would do anything to feel the way he did that day, like a balloon that she had suddenly inflated.

Once, he and Kathleen had taken the long way around to Woolworth's, coming down Rosalind by Lake Eola, and met a gray-haired woman staring in consternation at a live oak in her front yard. *Oh, young man, can you help me? I was beating out this rug.* She pointed to a green throw rug lying on the fence. *I swung back to give it a good thump, and I must've let go.* She pointed at the tree. A broom hung by its head in a crook amid the Spanish moss in the upper boughs. *Don't I just feel like the biggest fool.*

Live oaks are easy climbers, and Addison had the broom down in a jiffy. He offered to beat out the rug for her, and thoroughly whacked it, raising puffs of gray dust to the appreciative *My, you're so strong* of the woman.

After they helped spread the carpet back down in the woman's foyer, Kathleen squeezed Addison's arm and briefly pressed her face into his neck. *You are so sweet, the way you helped out that lady!* After that Addison was filled with ambition to help out as many old ladies as possible. In fact, he could think of nothing he'd like better than to write stories for Kathleen and help out old ladies.

Maybe things would have gone differently if he had never introduced her to his brother. Addison had many things to regret, and he regretted each of them with great thoroughness and tenacity.

The first time Kean met Kathleen, his wet black leather jacket had shrunk to him from rain and sunshine, and he had to strip it from his body like a lemon peel. *I just drove my motorcycle straight here from Gainesville. I ran into a cloudburst, but I didn't pull over.* He rolled up his sleeve to show them his upper arm. *My arms are still all tensed up from holding the handlebars so long. Feel that.* Kean had not yet decided he wanted to be a doctor, but he already had considerable interest in anatomy. Addison felt, and his brother's bicep was indeed rock-hard. Kathleen, even though she had no particular interest in medicine, also felt Kean's muscle to test its hardness.

If Addison had worried he would need to make small talk to shore up the flagging conversation between Kean and Kathleen, he needn't have. They found each other so interesting, they scarcely paid Addison any attention. It turned out the university was holding a series of evening lectures open to the public, and that Kean would be happy to take Kathleen on his motorcycle if she thought she'd be interested. She thought she would be.

Addison felt petty about his reaction, but he couldn't help it. It was stupid being disgruntled if his brother and Kathleen liked each other—if anything he should feel just the opposite, but no matter how he thought about it, nothing in the situation gruntled him in the least. The three of them continued meeting in the Woolworth's until Kean's break ended and he returned to the university, and after that Kathleen stopped coming to Woolworth's also.

Finally Addison passed her a note in lit class: *We haven't gotten to talk in awhile. Want to go to Woolworth's after school?*

He spent all day in pleasant anticipation of enjoying Kathleen's company without Kean around, but when he went to sixth period, he found she'd left his note on his desk, having written her reply on the back.

*If you don't mind, since Kean won't be there, I'd rather not come. I skipped tennis Tuesday because Kean got me back so late from Dr. Buskirk's lecture Monday night, so I'd like to get to the court today.*

After several rereadings, Addison realized Kathleen had left him not one note, but two. One written and the other unwritten. Put together, the written and unwritten parts went like this:

*If you don't mind*—and even if you do, I'm sure you'll be too polite to mention it—*since Kean won't be there*—and Kean is the only reason I show up—*I'd rather not come*—and what would be the point of having me there if I'd rather be somewhere else?—*I skipped tennis Tuesday because Kean got me back so late from Dr. Buskirk's lecture Monday night*—because I'd rather see a lecture with Kean than play tennis—*so I'd like to get to the court today*—because I'd rather play tennis than see you.

The anguished night after receiving this letter, he wrote her his own letter, which he later—mercifully—lost.

Now sitting outside the priest's office, he imagined doing some deed of derring-do so she might admire him again. Being with his dad when they found the diamonds didn't seem enough, somehow. Addison would have retrieved any number of brooms and diamonds; he would have faced dragons, submitted to durance vile, and outwitted evildoers to win her favor.

After Addison left, the priest said, "Now you two wanted to have the wedding—"

"At the earliest expedient time," Lily supplied. Adam started as if he'd sat on a joy buzzer. "Adam says he wishes to get married as soon as possible," Lily said, squeezing Adam's hand and nuzzling his shoulder.

"Well, I don't think the padre here will be able to arrange—" Adam began.

"Do you want a big wedding?" the priest asked.

"No!" Adam said.

"Just something intimate, a few friends and family," Lily concurred. She snaked her arm under Adam's and snuggled up.

"It's a tricky time, of course." Father Peel got out a desk calendar and studied the grids, clicking his teeth together in thought. "Christmas is Friday, and that's a busy time for us because it's, you know, Christmas and all. If you want to do it right away, we could squeeze you in Tuesday morning—say, ten-thirty. We could have rehearsal on Monday."

"What if we had the rehearsal Saturday after Christmas, and then have the wedding on Sunday?" Lily suggested. "The church should be pretty vacuous the Sunday after Christmas."

"Well, that might work," Father Peel said. "We could squeeze you in after the ten o'clock service. Say, eleven-thirty."

Adam felt like a prisoner who's just been asked to eat his last meal a little more quickly, and in fact would he mind skipping the dessert, because *we're on sort of a tight schedule here.*

"We also need to discuss—" Father Peel trailed off. Things in his office were not as they had been. Three golf tees lay underfoot. His legal pad was dark-stained and moist.

"The readings," Lily supplied. "Perhaps we should consult a Bible to select them."

"No, we don't need to bother with that," Father Peel said. The truth was he never had felt entirely at ease around Bibles. He had graduated near the bottom of his class in seminary, and since then, had felt a growing apathy toward his faith. Fortunately, he'd discovered that all most people required in a priest was a clerical collar and a benign smile. "In any case, for the first reading, many people like First Corinthians, thirteen, 'Though I speak with the tongues of men and angels and have not love—' "

"'Have not charity,'" Lily corrected, "'I am become as sounding brass.'" There was a pause, but before Father Peel could rush to fill it, Lily went on, "'And though I have the gift of prophecy, and understand all mysteries—'"

Adam sat transfixed as chilly dread stole over him, but Lily continued reciting with that careful enunciation, as if each word were a splinter she was tweezing out of her palm. She came to an end. Father Peel's eyes unglazed, and he said, "Well, good. First Corinthians it is, then. Now, for the second reading, many people like the Beatitudes, 'Blessed are the poor in spirit—'"

"'For theirs is the kingdom of heaven,'" Lily finished for him. Why did she always do this shit? Who was she trying to impress? Or, as Lily would have insisted on putting it, *whom*? "'Blessed are they that mourn, for they shall be comforted.'" Lily had powers of recall fearsome to behold. "'Blessed are the meek, for they shall inherit the earth. Blessed are the peacemakers, for theirs is the kingdom of heaven.'" Adam wasn't sure, but hadn't someone inherited the kingdom of heaven already? Lily was starting to falter. Adam found himself listening with some slight relish. "'Blessed are they that hunger and thirst,'" she said, but couldn't remember what made hunger and thirst blessed, and lapsed into silence. Blessed silence.

"I was really hoping for something from the Book of Hank," Adam said. Father Peel looked at him in perplexity. "*'I'm gonna find me a river, and then I'm gonna pay the price/I'm going down in it three times, but, Lord, I'm only coming up twice.'*"

Father Peel laughed.

"That is not in the Bible," Lily said. "He is being facetious," she explained. "He is always very facetious." She laughed, to show she enjoyed a good joke as much as anyone, but her face heated, and she looked away. She had wanted

Adam to be proud of her, and for a while there, she had convinced herself he was.

The rest of the session at St. George's held little to delight and much to appall. They discussed many hymns, several of which Lily insisted on singing verses from, waving her hands in the air as if she were conducting herself. Adam's suggestion to incorporate the Navy Hymn, *O, hear us when we cry to Thee for those in peril on the sea*, was ignored. The rest of the Episcopalian hymnal was notorious for its dirgelike melodies yoked to unsingable lyrics: *Jesus, grant us, through thy merit to inherit thy salvation, hear, O hear our supplication.*

At last Adam rejoined his son.

In silence, Addison and Adam drove down Jefferson, turned right on North Orange and left on Livingston, across the tracks, and under the overpass. The air was growing cooler. The last vestige of civilization dropped behind, a muffler on a metal pole advertising an auto parts store. Dark green vegetation made darker by the failing light lined the road.

Soon, Adam told himself, ignoring the weight gathering in his gut, I'll have the diamonds and Evelyn and I can be reunited. This would make the third engagement ring he had given her. The first she banged up with a hammer and threw out the kitchen window. Maybe one day someone would unearth it planting petunias and think he'd stumbled on a diamond mine in central Florida. Evelyn, having seen the folly of dramatic gestures, held on to the second one, even through their temporary divorce.

When Adam went to Evelyn with the second ring, he declared, "I love you and I can't live without you," over and over until she relented. As his penance, he had to check into

Chattahoochee. He'd known it would be a slice of humiliating hell, and it had been, but he'd endured it all—painting alligators and giving up his belt and shoelaces for her.

It showed there were some things you could still unbungle.

Had not Adam and Addison been so intent on finding lost diamonds, they might have stopped at a bridge to admire a scene of brief and heartbreaking beauty. A red sunset lit the lake like a mirror; cackling Bonnet Runners scooted over lily pads chasing bugs, and bass churned the surface as they rose for a final snack before settling against the murky bottom. These had been here first, before the armadillos and mimosas had been brought in and made themselves at home, before railroads and orange growers and cane growers, before Creek and Choctaw joined up with runaway slaves to make the Seminoles, before the crackers from their exhausted farms in Georgia and the Carolinas, before Ponce de León and the Spanish, and even before the original Saturiwa and Timucua, who had never seen a white man and knew no better than to think the whole world was like this and always had been and always would be.

The day of the accident the Old Man emerged from a brown mood and took Adam to the Dreggors. The Old Man and Mr. Dreggor sat on the deep front porch, their feet on an unpainted rail, fanning flies with palmetto fronds. The Old Man said some armadillos had gotten loose in Hialeah, and now folks were catching them all the way down to Miami. Mr. Dreggor said he'd never laid eyes on an armadillo and wouldn't mind seeing one. He understood they had shells like cooters, but were in actuality some kind of possum.

They talked about the Old Anchises Boar, a legendary one-eyed boar that had lived in those parts as long as anyone could recall and was rumored to be immortal. They swapped tales of Bone Mizell, King of the Crackers, who with a whip and a cowcatcher dog-hunted wild cattle, the rangy, gaunt descendants of the Spanish cows Ponce de León set loose in St. Augustine. Bone died in 1921, a few days after Adam's third birthday, and it gave Adam the all-overs to think he'd once shared the earth with this giant. Bone spent money fast as he made it, and he made it faster than anyone. He would ride a horse into a bar and order whiskey right from the saddle. At the mention of this, Mr. Dreggor passed the jug, and the Old Man took a long, reverent pull before handing it back.

Adam knew about shine; even his mother kept it, and had it on offer for anyone who stopped by, be it the sheriff himself, but his mother aged hers in an oak cask with charred peaches thrown in for flavor. She never had it "raw," like Mr. Dreggor and the Old Man.

Mrs. Dreggor let Adam make cornmeal. *Grind me this much*, she said, handing him a mug with rust flecks breaking through its white enamel. She didn't keep store-bought meal like his mother, but had dried corn in a burlap sack by a grinder in the kitchen. *Run it through once for grits, three times for meal.* Adam scooped a mug, dropped it in the hopper, and turned the heavy iron crank with one hand, holding a Murphy bowl with the other to catch the shower of crushed meal. Mrs. Dreggor didn't fix cornbread the way Hassie did either; she fried it instead of baked it, and there were no eggs, milk, or white flour mixed in. Just water and salt.

For dinner they ate cornpone, greens, and a perleu with something called swamp chicken, which Adam couldn't identify, except to know it wasn't chicken. He ate a big plateful, happily self-conscious that the Old Man had an eye on him.

Driving home in the Model A, the Old Man asked Adam, *You know what swamp chicken is?* When Adam didn't reply, he said, *Snapping turtle.* Adam's chest swelled as if a gentleman of business had offered him a position at ten dollars a week. Everything the Dreggors put on the table carried the glamour of personal danger. Mrs. Dreggor plucked needles off prickly pears to make jelly, you had to pick poke greens at a certain time or they weren't fit to eat, and coontie was downright dangerous if you didn't do it right. A few moments later, when the Old Man said, *You and I are a lot alike*, Adam turned his head because he couldn't keep down his proud smile. Cumulous clouds towered above the moss-draped oaks, threatening a thunderstorm that afternoon. *Me, the Old Man, and Bone Mizell.*

Adam pointed to a building that at one time had been a farmhouse. "Here's the place."

A yellow reader board identified it as the Fish Camp. Adam's jeep was parked alongside a few other cars in the sand-and-gravel parking lot beside a green Dumpster.

At the sight of their destination, Adam's remaining faith that they would find the diamonds left him, and his chest felt scraped hollow as a dug-out canoe. He'd thought he remembered leaving the diamonds in his jeep, but his memory often played tricks on him, as he now remembered.

"That's a bar, Dad."

"It's really more of a dance club. The sign says LI E MUSIC."

"It also says DRINK SPECAIL5."

"We're just going to search the jeep," Adam said.

Adam unlocked the jeep, and while he looked under the driver's seat, Addison checked the passenger side. Adam reached under the front seat and said with a hope he did not feel, "I think I know just where it is. I'm sure I dropped it here when—" But instead of bringing out a bag of diamonds, he found only a notebook that read, *Monday: A Couple of Beers.* In real life, Adam realized, shoeshine boys rarely arrive in the nick of time to catch culprits as they try to withdraw the funds.

Addison opened the glove compartment and slammed it shut.

Vanilla-flavored gorge rose in Adam's throat. Where were those damn diamonds? Why did these things always have to happen? Dread sank in his stomach, like the feeling when you wait and wait for your mother to find and punish you after the shot declaring your guilt. *What have I told you?* "Maybe it's in the backseat," Adam said, looking at the Fish Camp. "I could have dropped it when I was getting out your weights."

"Maybe," Addison said. He crawled in the back and ran his hands between the cushions. He imagined finding the diamonds and instantly being in a position to endear himself to Kathleen.

Adam looked also, but without hope. "Do you know I've barely eaten anything all day?" he said, and licked his salty lips. "I could really use a bite. You know what I think? I think I might have left them in there. You keep searching; I'll be right back."

Addison didn't hear him with his head down as he felt along between the cushions, imagining the look on Kathleen's face. When he didn't find anything, he looked up. The jeep's back door yawned at the parking lot. An evening breeze started up. His father was not in the picture.

# SEVEN

# Adam Gets a Drink

Adam stopped at the cigarette machine inside the door, dropped in two quarters and pulled the plunger below the Pall Malls. He flicked his trusty Zippo and let three long draws of comforting smoke swirl around his face like the edge of a fleece blanket. A neon sign at the left of the bar indicated a men's room was to be had. A three-foot-tall aluminum tree hung with red balls offered Christmas cheer to the right.

To the roughnecks, rednecks, and crackers who frequented it, the Fish Camp provided a base of operations for the four f's of their leisure activities: fighting, fucking, and fixing flats. To Adam, the semidarkness and beer smell of the Fish Camp were home when home itself was bitter. It was where he went after Evelyn threw her ring out the kitchen window, and where he'd taken Lily following the french fry incident.

The Fish Camp's name was no flight of fancy; it had once been a fish camp in deed as well as name, but even then, visitors did more drinking than fishing, so the owner bowed to popular opinion and made it a bar outright. He was just one melee away from losing his liquor license and shutting down, but he managed to stay on good terms with local law enforcement by reporting bar fights promptly, thereby helping them reach their arrest quota.

A tight red dress caught Adam's eye. He sauntered over. Horace the bartender acted quickly to clear room for his friend—getting an empty glass off the bar and out of harm's way—but not quickly enough. As Adam took a stool, his casual elbow landed on the peanut bowl's lip, catapulting goobers into the air.

Ignoring the pitter-pat of legumes raining upon the bar, Adam nodded to the woman in the red dress, whom he recognized as Chastity Spratt, a lass whose checkered career, stormy love life with Jerry—the smartest and best-looking of the McIntyre brothers—and eventual engagement to the biggest and ugliest of them—Strawberry—had provided the Fish Camp with much conversational fodder.

"Here you go, Adam," said Horace, setting down a Jack and Coke. From his scowling jowls and single bushy eyebrow, you might have expected Horace to be an insensitive, callous lout who kept a set of brass knuckles behind the counter. As it turned out, he did keep a set of brass knuckles, but what he lacked in eyebrows, he more than made up for in thoughtfulness. Horace dropped ice in a glass when Adam came in and had the drink mixed before he crossed the room. Horace knew what Adam wanted before he asked and was only too happy to provide.

Behind the bar lay a red Santa cap, which Horace had worn to work in an ill-advised gesture of holiday jollity. The cap had fallen in a puddle of beer, and Horace yielded to the fait accompli and drafted it into service as a bar rag. Beside the rag Bing Crosby, salted with a little static, crooned "White Christmas" on a transistor radio.

Adam took a vivifying drink and nodded to Horace that he would need another. He hunkered so that his red windbreaker bunched up nearly to his ears. "When I was here last night, did I leave anything?"

Horace shrugged. "Your jeep."

Adam rubbed his neck. Losing the diamonds clung to him like a noose. It was not a good time to have his money tied up in real estate and margined securities. As much as Adam hated to consider the possibility, he had to wonder if one of his Fish Camp buddies had taken the diamonds. The thought darkened the room.

The phone behind the bar rang, and Horace picked it up. "He ain't here," he said and hung up. The Fish Camp protected its patrons' privacy as jealously as a Swiss bank.

"If you came across someone's personal property that wasn't yours," Adam introduced a hypothetical dilemma, "you'd return it, wouldn't you? You'd try to find the rightful owner?"

Chastity snorted derisively; some questions didn't need answering.

"White Christmas" ended, and an announcer came on to read the headlines.

"Well, that depends," said Horace, who was as candid as he was considerate, "on what it was and who lost it in the first place. Finders keepers. Have you lost something?"

"Have I lost something?" Adam repeated from a depth of loss so deep it defied expression. What had he ever had that he hadn't lost? "Have I lost something?" Then he quoted Kipling, " 'If you can make one heap of all your winnings, and risk it all on one turn of pitch and toss. And lose . . .' " Adam paused. The pause was his favorite part of the line.

"'And start at your beginnings, and never breathe a word about your loss.'"

"You sure know a lot of poetry," Horace said with the same expression someone else might say, "You ought to let a doctor look at that."

"Sisters of Mercy Academy, where my mother sent me after the Old Man's accident," Adam explained, "was very big on poetry. In fact, I myself wrote a poem about it. 'You can talk of John Donne's sonnet, if you've read a little on it . . .' It's called 'The Rime of Sisters of Mercy Academy.' Would you care to hear it?"

"No, thank y—"

*"The Rime of Sisters of Mercy Academy:*
"'You can talk of John Donne's sonnet, if you've read a
little on it,
"And those metaphysic thoughts are what you're thinking.
"But when you read Augustine, you'll find it quite disgustin',
"And the time will come for you to go out drinking.
"In Savannah's sunny clime, where I used to spend my time,
"A'reading about Hamlet and King Lear,
"I'd go with a friend or two from the sordid crew I knew,
"And we'd hie us down to Blackie's for a beer.
"For it's beer, beer, beer!
"The cashier got our order loud and clear!
"And we'd drink to Milton's verse, and to Kipling's, which
is worse,
"And quaff great flagons brimming full of beer.

"I was tested on Monet, and Degas, Renoir, Manet,
"Wrote essays on the rise and fall of Crete.
"My knowledge of Rosetti made my brains feel like
spaghetti

"And knocked Sister Eglantina off her feet.
"But at length our tests were done, we'd sneak out and
have some fun
"Down the street, to Blackie's Package for a beer.
"For it's beer! Beer! Beer!
"We'd drink until our vision wasn't clear!
"And we'd laugh and sing till dawn, and we'd wake up on
the lawn
"With headaches and a ringing in our ears.
"My paper on Aquinas got a jolly good A minus,
"But I'd trade off all my learning for a beer."

Horace had already turned his back and was occupied with bartenderly duties. Adam took a drink and cracked the skull of a meditative peanut lying on the bar. He sighed. It was late; Ernie was probably closing. Might as well get this over with. "Can I borrow the phone, Horace?" Horace passed Adam the phone, and Adam dialed with a reluctant finger. "Hello, Ernie? Adam Newman here—she told me—yes, yes—about that, there may be some slight de—I—the fact is, I thought I had them in my jeep, bu—uh-huh—yes—Now, I don't, not right now—I—mm-hm—mm-hm—mm-hm—yes—not a hundred percent certain, no—yes—I understand, er—I—yes, I under—I understand this isn't a good time for you to—yeh—Don't wor—Er—Ernie, I'm going to take care of—I'm going to take care of it—Ernie, you need to calm down, I'm going to take care of it—well, so long, now. Thank you, Ernie.

"He took that pretty well," Adam told the air as he replaced the phone in its cradle. "He's a good friend." Where had things started going so bad? Where could you go to begin retracing your steps and unbungle all your previous bungles?

Actually, though, as he considered it, Adam felt almost grateful not to be burdened by the hope of finding the diamonds. The certainty that he would have to make good their loss to Ernie was something to be grateful for in such an uncertain world. And really, a quarter of a million dollars would hobble Adam, but he could start over. Forty-seven is not as old as all that. Letting go of hope was like ungrasping a thorny stem. It was astonishing how painful it was, pretending that maybe that he hadn't bungled after all—it made things much simpler to own up to it: he'd bungled it as always—catastrophically this time—now he could relax and be himself.

A sense of profound ugliness stole over him.

"So how are you, Chastity?" he asked.

"I've been better," she admitted. "I messed up, Mr. Newman. Have you seen Strawberry around?"

"No. Maybe he's with Jerry or Larry."

Chastity shuddered at the mention of her fiancé's brothers, and without knowing the source of her sadness, Adam felt a wave of compassion. He had messed up good himself on occasion and knew what it was like. "What's wrong?"

"I messed up good."

"We have established that," Adam said firmly but not unkindly. "How precisely did you mess up?" When she did not reply, Adam laid a hand on hers. "Feel free to confide in me, dear," he told her in a voice misery rendered as smooth as hand lotion. "Earlier today I was able to help out a lovely couple over at St. George's."

Her head lifted. "You're a minister? Like with a church?" Nothing in Adam's résumé suggested he was a candidate to receive the call, but among the orange pickers and their retinue who knew his many accomplishments, Adam's abilities were so legendary it would not have surprised her much if he'd claimed to be a brain surgeon.

"Well, I don't have a church," Adam admitted. "But to return to our theme. How have you messed up?"

Chastity Spratt was alluring in the way of slightly unwashed women. Only nineteen, she had long dark hair parted down the middle, a heart-shaped face, and liquid eyes that had a way of looking up through slightly lowered lashes guaranteed to raise a healthy man's heart rate. Tonight, however, her head sank like a heavy blossom on a wilting stem. She took a final draw on her cigarette and stumped it in the ashtray. "I did it with his brother."

Adam let out a low, slow whistle. When Chastity messed up, she did not do so by half measures—her messing up was broad, deep, and wide.

Adam asked, "Jerry?" Chastity's former lover. She said nothing. "Larry?"

"Both of them."

Adam slipped from the stool, and it was a moment before he recovered. "When?"

"Friday."

Adam waited for her to mention another day, and when she didn't, he whistled again. There was something almost sublime about the scope of Chastity's catastrophe.

"How did this happen?"

"Mr. Tucker give them a hundred dollars cash money each for working smudge pots the night the temperature got so low, so naturally they wanted to get drunk. Only Jerry told Strawberry to go into Gainesville and get a new rim because that back tire wasn't never going to keep no air with the old rim burred out the way it was." She sighed. "And Jerry had a new color TV, and he said me and Larry could come over and watch Walt Disney."

Adam nodded in commiseration. He could well imagine the scene: two amorous swains, Pabst Blue Ribbon flowing like wine, *Walt Disney's Wonderful World of Color* on TV. It would be enough to turn the head of many a girl. Unable to think what to say or do, Adam offered her a cigarette, first making it disappear into his mouth and then pulling it out of his ear. He was adroit, among other things, at on-the-spot magic. He then lit a cigarette for himself.

"Oh, yeah, there's a fellow been looking for you," Horace told Adam, snapping him out of his reverie.

"Ah!" Adam's heartfelt concern for Chastity did not dampen the hope that flickered like the coal on the end of his cigarette. Maybe whoever was looking for him had the diamonds. Maybe Adam had given them to someone for safekeeping. Maybe his luck had turned.

Evelyn did not allow herself to become immediately alarmed when Addison did not return from taking Adam to his jeep. She distributed the surviving ornaments evenly over the tree and filled in the most glaring gaps with the new ones she'd bought. There were few decorations to choose from less than a week before Christmas, so she'd settled for plastic cartoon-themed ornaments: Hanna-Barbera figures dressed as elves with wire hangers in their heads and marked "slightly irregular" because the manufacturer had given Yogi Bear and George Jetson startling cherry red lips and staring almond-shaped eyes like Egyptian tomb figures.

Then she went in the backyard and turned a few black earth clods to inspect her worms; on the whole they seemed in good spirits, but the addition of carrot butts had been insufficient temptation to draw them back to the grease spot.

Contemplating her earthworms, however, failed to soothe, and she went inside. Kean was reading his new MCAT book and Kathleen a text on semantics. Kean and Kathleen never seemed to do anything with each other, just next to each other. Evelyn put on a pot and brewed herself some Orange Pekoe.

She tried a murder mystery, but domestic homicide and English countryside did not gratify. She put her book down and looked at the clock. Entirely too much time had gone by since Addison had left, she decided, and she gave herself permission to worry.

Oh, Jesus, she thought, please, I hope nothing has happened to them.

She realized she had included her ex-husband in this silent prayer, and went into the kitchen to call Lily.

Evelyn had always been grateful for Lily's precision. Even during her days as a waitress, Lily never said "chili-slaw-dog," but always specified "hot dog with chili sauce and cole slaw." Lily informed her that, yes, she had seen Addison with Adam when she'd met them at St. George's for marriage counseling, but they'd gone to retrieve Adam's jeep and she hadn't seen either of them since.

"Marriage counseling?" Evelyn asked. "You're still going through with it, aren't you?"

"Of course we are," Lily said.

Lily heard Evelyn's release of breath on the other end, and that was all it took. The two women knew each other's thoughts as thoroughly as if they'd spoken them aloud.

*So you won't back out—you're definitely going to marry my ex-husband?*

*Yes, and I couldn't be more delighted.*

*You and me both.*

*I'll do my best to look after Adam for you.*

*I appreciate it. Good luck.*

Evelyn pulled the Yellow Pages from the kitchen drawer and dialed the Fish Camp.

"He ain't here," was the bartender's response. No surprise there.

She stepped into the living room. "Kean," she said, "I

need you to drive out to the Fish Camp and tell Addison to come home."

Kean looked up, not sullenly—he was too well-mannered for that—but nor did his face dance with boyish delight. "I'm not his keeper," he said.

"He needs a father figure," Evelyn said.

"He has a father," Kean said.

"It has been a long time since he left," Kathleen said. "Maybe we should really go get him."

It had taken but a twinkling to surmise where his father had gone; the remainder of the time since then Addison spent wondering whether to go in after him. Waiting for Adam Newman to come out of a bar was like waiting for the pimento to come out of an olive, but the question remained: Should he just leave or was there an obligation to at least notify his father he was leaving?

Addison imagined explaining the inevitable disaster to his mother later: *Well, I followed Dad into this bar, see, and . . .*

He sat on his haunches in the backseat, visually measuring the distance from the jeep to the door of the Fish Camp. He became aware that as he was staring at the Fish Camp, someone else was staring at him. A not unpleasant-looking man with a neat mustache and dark slicked-back hair watched him with mild curiosity from a green Pontiac. His red bow tie and the shoulders of his herringbone jacket were lit by the dashboard light. The stranger's hands rested on the wheel as if he were considering driving off, or maybe that was just the most comfortable place to put his hands. It was definitely odd to be watched this way, and yet Addison didn't feel particularly threatened. When the stranger saw Addison staring back, his expression didn't change; he nodded benignly, got out and walked over, a leather attaché in his hand.

"Do you know the owner?" the stranger asked.

"Of the jeep? My father. He's inside."

"You certainly resemble him. I can see that now. My name's Wrigley Adder." His breath smelled of mint. Wrigley's handshake was firm, but the skin itself was loose and crepey. Addison discovered Wrigley was one of those people whose age is impossible to guess—his eyes shone with youthful vigor, but amid a complex crosshatch of wrinkles that resembled the delicate scoring of lizard skin. "I actually came here looking for your father. Let's go see him."

They found Adam Newman inside pulling a cigarette from his ear for a woman in a red dress.

"You're a hard man to track down, Mr. Newman, but I knew you had to show up sooner or later. As long as your jeep was outside." Wrigley clearly knew Addison's father, at any rate. Where had Addison seen that waxy black hair and that dapper mustache before?

"You're the one who's been looking for me," Adam deduced. "Perhaps you'll join us in a drink. If you think we'll fit. Ah-ha-ha-ha-ha." Before Addison could bid farewell and leave, Adam took his elbow and breathed a whiskey whisper into his ear, "He's got the diamonds."

They sat—Wrigley, Adam, and Addison—beside the woman in the red dress where the thoughtful Horace had already set fresh drinks.

Adam raised his in a toast to Wrigley and Addison. "No moaning of the bar," he said.

"What'll you have?" the bartender asked Addison.

"Just water, I guess," Addison answered.

The bartender shrugged at this inexplicable request. He poured a glass from a rusty faucet and dropped in three ice cubes with fat fingers before handing it to Addison. The bartender returned to cleaning glassware with a sodden Santa hat.

Addison contemplated the filmy glass in his hand. The Fish Camp smelled of cigarettes, stale beer, and the faint sweet reek of urinal cakes wafting from the men's room nearby. The bartender had graciously gone to some small trouble to fill an unheard-of request, a request that, moreover, would be free of charge and therefore receive no tip. Addison wondered if it would be consistent with human decency to leave the water untasted nonetheless.

"My name is Wrigley Adder. My friends call me Wrigley."

"Wrigley," Adam repeated.

"Yes, I've been trying to get in touch with you about some property you own. I'm with Compass East."

The stranger could scarcely have stunned Adam more if he had introduced himself as Nikita Khrushchev. It was all he could do to remain upright. "I know who you are," Adam said.

Horace grunted and stopped wiping a highball glass to listen to the radio. "Johnson's not going to make the same mistake like Roosevelt did with the Nazis. Them commies will learn not to mess with the U.S. of A."

How could Adam signal Horace not to talk about the Communists just now? But Wrigley merely permitted the faintest vapor of a smile to pass his lips and said to Adam, "In that case you know my client would like to make a very generous offer for some acreage of yours." Wrigley put his attaché on the bar and took out some papers.

Adam took a slow drink and let the Jack and Coke warm in his mouth before swallowing. How should he handle this? Was Wrigley intimating he had the diamonds and was prepared to deal?

With his face turned from Wrigley, Adam grimaced at Addison in a way meant to convey an urgent message. "This is Mr. Adder, Addison. He is from Compass East. Realty."

Obviously these words were fraught with meaning for Addison's father, but Addison could not for the life of him guess what that meaning was. "We've met," Addison said blankly.

"So you're Addison," the bartender said. He gestured with his thumb. To Addison's astonishment, hanging behind the bar was an obituary that had been découpaged and varnished to a black cypress plaque. "My name is Horace. I own the place."

At Addison's side, the woman in the red dress looked at him with a flicker of interest. "You're the writer?" she asked.

Addison asked Horace, "Dad mounted one of my obituaries?"

"Your daddy mounts *all* your obituaries," Horace answered. "He gives them to everyone. I've got another one too. 'Ajrold Nartin, loving father of sex.' "

Addison cringed.

"Your father thinks you hung the moon," Horace said. He continued smearing a glass with his Santa hat.

At Addison's back, Adam said to Wrigley, "Well, I don't think we have to—The time isn't right to—" Something in the way Wrigley kept a hand on his briefcase suggested it contained something more valuable than just a real estate offer. "But what I want to know is what *form* would the payment take?"

"Form?"

"I could be a writer," the woman in the red dress said. "I got a story that'd curl your hair, only I got to wait till everyone's dead first." Then she stiffened like a golden retriever going on point. Addison followed her gaze.

Three men had entered the bar, all with weathered orange-picker's skin and reddish blond hair. The shortest wore a sporty green plaid cap and a neatly trimmed chin-strip beard that was barely visible against his sunburned skin. The middle, who had sideburns, wore a white blazer for his night out at the Fish Camp. The tallest, a giant with a red birthmark that eclipsed the side of his face, looked their way, turned contemptuously, looked again, and walked up, his jaw set and his gaze lowered. His companions followed. The tall one squeezed between Addison and Adam and waited for the bartender's attention.

The Fish Camp was crowding up. Farmworkers had claimed the tables near the stage. Occasional loud laughter or a shouted greeting rose above the rhubarb of ambient talk. Over the heads of the seated customers, Addison was startled to see a girl who looked almost exactly like Kathleen. The guy with her was a dead ringer for Kean.

"Addison!" the young man called out, raising his hand.

It was Kean.

Kean and Kathleen came over. "Mother sent us here to tell you to come home, kiddo," Kean explained. "She called Lily to find out where you were."

Addison turned his back to the bar to face them; Adam, Wrigley, and the giant flanked him on one side, and the woman in red flanked him on the other. Words of three conversations danced around Addison's head like gnats.

"Strawberry," the woman said. Addison felt her arm brush his back as she reached behind him to touch the tall man's hand.

Strawberry flinched, pulling his arm from under her fingers. "PBR's," he told Horace, holding up three fingers.

There were three soft clonks as Horace set down the drinks.

"Actually," Addison found himself telling Kean, "Dad and I are in the middle of something kind of important." Why was he saying this? Had he lost his mind?

"Don't worry about him," Kean said. "He'll be fine."

Something in the slight contemptuous topspin Kean gave the word *him* grieved Addison. A few moments ago he would have been grateful for any opportunity to escape, but now he said, "I'm helping him with something really important, and," he looked at Kathleen, "it might be something that would help you out." He hoped an intrigued expression might cross Kathleen's face, but she seemed merely apprehensive.

"What I'm trying to say," Adam told Wrigley, trying not to stare at the attaché, "what would you be prepared to give in *addition* to cash?"

"Addison," Kathleen said, "you really need to go." Addison was torn between pleasure at Kathleen's concern and pain that she was taking Kean's side.

"I've been waiting here," the woman in red said. "You need to listen to me."

"Leave me be, Chastity," Strawberry said. "I ain't interested." He took his beer too quickly from the bar and wet Addison's shoulder.

"So are you coming?" Kean asked.

"I am not," Addison said, taking a decisive drink of water to dramatize his mood. He regretted the gesture instantly and wished he had something to rinse the sand flavor out of his mouth. He turned his head as if he needed more than anything in the world to find out what would happen between Chastity and Strawberry.

"I know I messed up, Strawberry," Chastity said, "but it was partly your fault."

"Leave him be," said the dapper one with the chin-strip beard. "He told you he ain't interested."

"Jerry, you cocksucker," she said.

There's no nice way of calling someone a cocksucker, and Chastity wasn't trying to be nice. But Jerry laughed it off. "Look who's calling *me* a cocksucker," he said to his companions.

Having grown up with three brothers forbidden under any circumstances to strike a woman, Chastity had developed a regrettable habit of slapping men. Not so much slapping, really, as patting, no harder than a kitten slaps a familiar bloodhound who regards her with a patient and indulgent eye; nonetheless, in moments of extreme dudgeon, Chastity was a known man-slapper. She could have stopped herself, perhaps, but she lacked willpower. It was a weakness that was to have unfortunate consequences at intervals throughout her life.

She slapped Jerry now, a tap across his forehead that Jerry would have scarcely noticed except for the indignity of seeing his sporty plaid cap hit the floor, promptly to be trodden on by a customer en route to the bathroom. Jerry huffed and seized Chastity's wrist, making her hand fly back and knuckle Addison's lip. Strawberry and the third person, whose name Addison later learned was Larry, gathered like storm clouds.

Adam, seeing his son in peril, went into action. Wrigley and the missing diamonds could wait. He turned on his stool and took Strawberry's shoulder, attempting to pull him from the scene. "Strawberry, hey," he began. Adam had once pulled a cigarette from his ear for Strawberry, and he hoped that this had forged a bond between them strong enough to soothe an orange-picker's stormy heart, but if Strawberry recalled the cigarette trick, it did not mollify him. He didn't turn but shot an elbow into Adam's ribs, knocking him nearly into Wrigley's lap.

There are those who with a soft word can turn away

wrath, who can crack a few jokes and defuse an ugly situation. Adam Newman was not one of those people. A fighter is sometimes described as a whirling dervish, and indeed, only the fiercest and most tenacious of dervishes, and even then only one whirling at maximum velocity, could have matched Adam's performance. Strawberry landed more punches and punches of better quality, but unfazed by the uppercut that loosened a crown and filled his mouth with salty blood, Adam, even as he fell, clutched for Strawberry's family jewels with both hands, a ploy that failed but resulted in tugging down Strawberry's pants, exposing his once-white cotton briefs.

Strawberry made the tactical error of reaching for his trousers, and Adam stood, butting his head into Strawberry's stomach and turning the big man in a perfect flip to the floor. Gratified at this coup, Adam paused and looked around, preparing to acknowledge the applause he half expected from the spectators. This gave Strawberry, again upright, time to clap fists on both sides of Adam's ears, temporarily deafening him. Strawberry hefted Adam from the floor for a maneuver that in the pro-wrestling circuit is called a pile driver. Adam kicked air and groped for eyes to gouge, hair to pull, or ears to tear—snapping his jaws the whole time in case some portion of Strawberry should find its way between his teeth.

Adam's intervention provided a clarity the conflict had thitherto lacked. Like the opening stages of many a scuffle, who was fighting whom had been hard to determine, but whatever had been the battle lines before, it became clear to the McIntyre brothers that this was to be a fight between them on one side and everyone else on the other.

Chastity kicked Jerry's knee with her sharp-toed pump, which was astonishingly painful, and nor was Addison idle. He rose to the fray, not to fight, but to extract his father; however, Larry immediately pinned him, circling an arm around his neck from behind, and attempted to wail on him with his free fist. This, fortunately for Addison, was difficult to do effectively from his position, but the tussle cracked Addison's ballpoints and stained his white shirt with blue ink.

Kathleen touched her boyfriend's bicep. "Kean, Addison's getting beat up." She did not need to tell him this, of course; Kean had been observing developments with the cool, practiced eye of a tournament fighter. He stepped forward like a surgeon, knowing exactly what to do.

It took him precisely three hits to settle the matter.

The first was for Addison's attacker: a single jab to the kidneys, not with a balled fist, but a fist shaped like a snake head as Sensei had taught him, and Addison was free. Without hurry, but not leisurely either, Kean turned to his next objective. A blow to the side of Jerry's head, and down he went, unhanding the gratified Chastity.

Last, Kean went to Adam's rescue. Strawberry was still holding Kean's stepfather aloft; he didn't really think he'd be able to throw the old man hard enough to make him bounce, but he intended to try his best. Kean punched Strawberry squarely in his Adam's apple, at which Strawberry remarked, "Guh." As he buckled and fell, he unloaded Adam into Kean's waiting arms like a bag of soggy laundry.

Kean had bested better fighters than these. In the fight that had won him the three-foot-tall triple-decker tristate karate trophy surmounted by a golden fighter poised midkick, Kean had broken three fingers, but so great was his concentration, he hadn't realized it until after the fight. Kean was a superlative fighter, an expert one, but he wasn't prepared for someone coming up from behind and coldcocking him with brass knuckles. It was Horace's policy after a brawl to ensure none of the combatants was in any condition to cause more disturbance.

"Are you okay, Mr. Newman?" Horace asked solicitously. Having done his bartenderly duty, he bore no one ill-will.

"Super-fantastic, Horace. Thank you for asking." Adam touched his lip gingerly as he rose from his seated position on Kean's belly.

It took Kathleen and Chastity to help Kean to his feet. He touched the back of his head and looked at his bloody fingers. "This is going to need stitches," he said. "I probably have a concussion."

Horace took Jerry by the shirt collar and belt and escorted him to the door; presumably he had already made his phone call to the police. It would not do, Adam realized, to be on hand when law enforcement officers arrived.

Adam stretched his belly over the bar to retrieve Horace's Santa hat and press it against his throbbing lip. "It has been my experience," Adam said with a sidelong glance at Wrigley, "that police usually show up pretty quick after these things. I'd clear out if I were you."

Wrigley's eyes could not have opened any wider if toothpicks had been inserted vertically under his eyelids. He did not need to be told twice.

Horace returned to help Larry to the door in the same fashion as he had his brother, pausing to glance at Strawberry, who sat choking and gagging on the floor. "I'm going to need help with that one," Horace predicted.

"Dad, I think we need to get Kean to a hospital," Addison said.

"That is a superb idea, son," Adam said. "And we'll take along this." He stood up to reveal the attaché Wrigley had left behind in his haste, partly because Adam had cleverly concealed it by lying on it as he reached across the bar. Adam was adroit at, among other things, on-the-spot magic.

# EIGHT

## Adam Goes to the Hospital

They left Addison's Volkswagen and Kean's motorcycle and drove to Florida Hospital in Adam's jeep. Still officially named Florida Sanitarium, it was called Florida Hospital by everyone because the word "sanitarium" was too redolent of Thorazine and shock treatments, and for Adam personally, of giving up one's belt and painting ceramic alligators. Chastity, Kean, and Kathleen crowded in the back and Addison drove. Adam would never have surrendered his keys under other circumstances, but he was eager to rifle through Wrigley's attaché.

"What is she doing with us?" Addison asked in a whisper. "What was that fight about?" The jeep was marvelously noisy and effectively muffled conversation from the backseat.

"Chastity is what the French call a *file de joy*," Adam said sotto voce, "or at least she was. I believe she has left that behind her." Adam summarized Chastity's vita for Addison—how she had once been Jerry's consort before becoming affianced to his brother Strawberry. Adam concluded with the tale of her titanic messing up. He held the attaché on his knees; he hesitated at the momentousness of opening it. He slid his hand inside. There was no velvetine bag, but against all expectations, his fingertips encountered a loose diamond! In a flash he saw his entire life restored: happy as he once had been, reunited with Evelyn—but no, it was only a paper clip.

"In any case," Adam said, "we have bigger fish to fry just now." He took all the contents out of the attaché: only papers and nothing more. "The dia—" He bit his tongue; in his excitement, he couldn't afford to raise his voice. He craned his neck to see if they were listening in the backseat. They didn't seem to be. "The dee-eye-ay-em-oh-en-dee-esses aren't in here," he went on, as if he hoped that even if the other passengers could hear him, they couldn't ess-pee-ee-el-el. "I didn't really expect they'd be, but these papers should be ve-ry interesting. Old Wrigley's wishing he hadn't left in such a hurry, I'll bet."

"What are you talking about?" Addison asked.

Adam double-checked the backseat passengers, and Addison followed his gaze. Chastity and Kathleen were sitting on either side of Kean, each holding a bicep.

Kean had the Santa hat pressed to the back of his head. "The third man's chin was up," Kean said, "so his Adam's apple was a perfect target, but I didn't see—" The aftermath of the fight had left him unusually garrulous. He seemed under a compulsion to narrate the evening's events over and over again with as much detail as he could muster.

The ladies were too intent on Kean to eavesdrop. It stung Addison to see Kathleen and Kean squeezed together. Addison wanted to do some great thing for Kathleen, but as always it ended up with Kean the hero and Addison the goat. Kathleen held Kean's bicep with a worried look. Addison wished he could take Kean's place. Even Chastity seemed absorbed in the responsibility of touching Kean's muscle while she studied his face.

"I first caught wind of the Venezuela Project about two years ago," Adam went on quietly. Interstate 4 between the Fish Camp and Florida Hospital was long and empty. The night was "south moon under," meaning it was moonless, and to practiced nostrils a faint cool smell foretold a fog rolling in. Through the windshield there was only the play of headlights on asphalt. The Shoeshine Boy book described a particularly clear night as awash with glittering stars, which fit the bill as far as the sky that night was concerned; Adam didn't think a sky could've gotten any more awash if its life depended on it. "Someone was buying up all this land along Interstate Four. Orange groves, mostly. One or two Brahma bull ranches, but this wasn't an ordinary investor. He was buying huge lots, and paying a hundred dollars an acre. No one could find out who the investor was, but the company representing him was called Ayefour. I tried to track them down." Adam shrugged at the memory of a futile effort. "I put a private investigator on it and everything, but they covered their tracks pretty well. Their mailing address is in Baltimore, but that's just a front. I kept my ears to the ground and heard about something called the Venezuela Project. They kept pushing me to sell my land, so I pushed back. I held out until they let me meet the top dog with Ayefour. I did: General William Potter himself."

"I never heard of him," Addison admitted.

"You wouldn't have," Adam said. "I had to do some research on him myself. He was in the big war, but he wasn't one of the glory boys like Ike or Patton. He was with the engineers. Then up to a few years ago he was governor of the Panama Canal. One of his responsibilities was widening it."

Addison's brow furrowed as he stared at the road ahead of him; he had no idea where his father was heading with this.

"I had to ask myself," Adam went on, "why an army general, retired supposedly, an engineer who still hasn't shook the sand off his boots from Panama, is overseeing land purchases in Florida. Finally I figured it out." Adam's heart beat against his ribs; he was about to share the secret. "This next part I'm going to tell you has to be strictly off the record."

"Okay."

"I mean it can't find its way into the newspaper."

"It won't."

Adam drew a noisy breath. The night air tasted sweetly of marsh. Father and son on the case—they were Holmes and Watson, putting their heads together over the mystery of the Red-Headed League or the Speckled Band. If only Evelyn could see them like this: on the trail of stolen diamonds and the shadowy Compass East.

"It's for the Cross-Florida Barge Canal." Adam waited for a puzzled exclamation from Addison, a "huh?" or "what?" There was none, so he continued, "Barges coming from the Mississippi have to go all the way around the tip of Florida to go up the coast. The government's going to dig a canal straight across to shorten the trip."

"I know, I know, like with Panama," Addison said. Even now an unfinished lock was slowly crumbling into rust and rubble over in Palatka. "Everyone knows about that, but they stopped the project. And anyway, the canal wasn't going to be anywhere near here."

"That's what they want you to believe. You have to understand the history of the whole thing," Adam said. "There was a proposal to dig it back in Double-You Double-You Two, and the Secretary of Defense said it was a great idea, only the war ended before they got started. Now it's back on the table, thanks to Castro. He can play hell with ships going around the tip if he wants to. If a shooting war starts, transportation will be paramount—moving troops, supplies. They're going to dredge the canal from lake to lake right through here up to the St. John's. See, it all ties together—the interstates, the railroads, the canal."

"How do you know it's a canal and not something else?" Addison asked.

"It's code-named the Venezuela Project," Adam explained, "like with Panama."

"But then shouldn't they code-name it the *Panama* Project?"

"They got to throw people off track," Adam explained. He had to forgive his son for not understanding the ways of the State Department. "Only a couple of other outfits got in the act," Adam went on. The strain of keeping his voice at a whisper made his hands shake. "Buying up land that Ayefour was after. There were two of them, one of them the Latin American Development Corporation, and the other one Compass East. *Compass East.*" Addison didn't respond to the name's sinister implication, so Adam clarified, "It's the Reds. The Communists are buying up the land before the government can. Get it? Compass *East.*"

Addison studied his father's stubbled face in the darkness. It made sense. The Cold War had been heating up ever since Russia captured an American spy plane four years earlier. Some people criticized the pilot for allowing this. What good is a cyanide pill in a fake silver dollar if you're not going to use it? they wanted to know. Then Kennedy invaded Cuba, which hadn't worked out so well. After that came a military exercise deposing an imaginary Caribbean dictator named Ortsac. The State Department maintained it was coincidence that Ortsac was Castro spelled backward, but Castro remained peeved nonetheless. Maybe Kennedy should have done the exercise first and *then* the invasion, but we'll never know. In any case, Castro put Soviet missiles in Cuba and brought the world to the brink of Armageddon.

It had been one of those decades.

Adam's face heated as he unburdened himself of his information on the Venezuela Project. He felt like he had touched the loose thread in the world, and if he tugged, it would lead to the original flaw that had spoiled everything: the Reds were a threat because at Yalta, chickenshit Roosevelt had signed over half of Europe, but he did that because we had to make nice with our Russian allies for defeating Hitler, but we had to do that because in Munich chickenshit Chamberlain knuckled under to Germany, but Hitler annexed the Sudetenland because the Allies had been too lenient—or was it too harsh?—on Germany after the First World War, and that wouldn't have happened except a crazy Serb killed an archduke, and that wouldn't have happened except . . . the rest was lost to Adam in the mists of time, but he knew if one could only follow them, those events would guide him back to the wellspring of all conflict, but now the U.S. of A. was on the cusp, the very cusp, of setting everything right, unbungling all previous bungles, starting by digging the Cross-Florida Barge Canal if only Ayefour could outdo Compass East!

"Why doesn't the government just—don't they have imminent domain?" Addison asked.

Adam shook his head. "They can't. Not in this case. 'The best laid schemes o' mice an' men,' as Robert Burns put it, 'gang aft a-gley.' Well, the original barge canal ganged a-gley so fast, it'd make your head spin. All these people got worked up about what it'd do to the alligators and manatees. They got in a wad and wrote their senator, and the project is officially on hold. Officially. That's why the government is doing it this way. Now you can't go reporting this," Adam said solemnly, "I know you have a journalistic duty and everything, but you can't go reporting this."

Addison thought it hardly likely that news of an international conspiracy would show up in the obituary column, but he only said, "Yes, sir."

Although brightly lit, Florida Hospital was nearly vacant; at first, except for the faint dinging of coded messages, they found no sign of the staff. When they located the admitting nurse, Kean offered his diagnosis: he would need stitches and he might have a concussion. The nurse said, "We'll see," then added, "Was this assault? Because we have to—"

"No law enforcement officers!" Adam shouted.

The nurse took Kean into the bowels of the hospital, and the rest of them waited in lumpy vinyl chairs by a big glass window that looked into the blackness. An elementary school had sponsored a coloring contest, and thirty pictures of Jolly Saint Nick adorned the walls, some done with the diligence of would-be Rembrandts and some with the scrawling enthusiasm of Jackson Pollack—swarms of subatomic particles orbiting Santa, leaving hot red trails. A glass table displayed *Life*, *Look*, and *Reader's Digest*. Adam dragged a trash can with a sand-filled ashtray on top across the floor to his chair, so he could have it at his elbow while he smoked and studied the contents of Wrigley's attaché.

"You need to call your mother," Adam advised Addison. He knew Evelyn wouldn't welcome news that Kean was in the hospital, but she would be more incensed to find it out later.

"I probably do need to call Mother," Addison agreed, looking at Kathleen hopefully. "Anyone want to help me find a pay phone?"

"I'm good," Kathleen said.

"I'm going to look at these papers, son," Adam said. "You go ahead."

"I'll go with you," Chastity said.

Finding he was to be accompanied by Chastity Spratt instead of Kathleen was like trick-or-treating and getting rocks instead of candy, but Addison set off anyway. As they went down the hallway, Chastity said, "You're sweet on her."

Addison was tempted to deny it, but only said, "How do you know?"

Chastity shrugged. At the end of a hallway they found a pay phone next to a snack machine. Addison dropped a dime in the slot and dialed.

"Newman residence," said his mother's anxious voice. Addison told her where they were and what had happened. She said calmly and without alarm that she would be right over. Addison assured her that Kean was fine and that they could take care of everything. She repeated calmly and without alarm that she would be right over.

Chastity stood visualizing trajectories of falling cracker packs in the snack machine's glass window. "We ought to get something to eat," she said, tapping the toe of her high heel. "We're likely to be here awhile. Give me some change."

Addison gave her a quarter and she dropped it in the machine and pulled the plunger under the cheese crackers. Nothing happened. She mashed the coin return button without result. "Stupid cocksucker," she said. The word set her off, and she pounded the glass.

"I have some gum," Addison offered by way of consolation.

"I don't want gum," Chastity said. "Gimme some more money."

"I don't think it'll take pennies," Addison said.

"Gimme."

He gave them to her, but the pennies only clattered uselessly in the machine's guts, and this time when Chastity tried the plunger, she couldn't even pull it out. "Cocksucker!" She slapped and kicked the machine. Then she turned her back and slid to the floor. She wiped her face with the back of her hand, smearing her mascara.

Chastity Spratt had known Strawberry McIntyre as long as she'd known his brother Jerry. At first Strawberry's spaniel-like adulation struck her as irritating, then contemptible, but lately she'd come to see it as useful if not downright neccessary. In exchange for Strawberry attending to her every wish, she condescended to let him worship her and even allowed him to believe that one day she would marry him. In the preceding days and weeks, however, she'd developed a taste for Strawberry's wholehearted adoration and begun to view him with an unfamiliar emotion her vocabulary did not have a word for.

But that was over. She'd messed up beyond redemption. Strawberry would never take her back. She wore the expression of one who has always had a Plan B ready in case Plan A failed, but having just seen the collapse of Plan Z, realized the supply of letters had given out along with the last available plan.

Addison said the only thing he could think of: "I'm really over her now anyway." Kathleen's concerns, in order of importance, were Kean, Dr. Buskirk, tennis, and somewhere below that, himself.

Chastity stared as if she'd just awakened from a dream. "No, you're not," she said. "You won't get over it. You ain't smart enough." She wrapped her knees in her arms and stared down the hall, dark eyes glowing. "You'll hang on and wait, and no matter what she does, you'll treat her kind. You won't brag on yourself. You won't try to be in charge or get your own way. You ain't in it for yourself. Anyone with sense would run off, but you stick around. And you'll put up with almost anything and still won't complain." Still sitting, she knocked the machine with her head. "Stupid." Behind the glass, yellow crackers hung over her like a regret.

Meanwhile Adam put on his reading glasses and looked through Wrigley's papers. At first glance, they contained nothing exceptional: the contract Wrigley had been prepared to offer with a description of the land and Adam's name already typed on the appropriate lines, a few business cards, a yellow legal pad with the phrase "Venezuela Project," some doodles of Donald Duck and Mickey Mouse, and some jottings someone had written in the neat, practiced lettering of an architect or engineer. Adam looked through the contract without much curiosity; it was in no way unusual except that Compass East's client was unnamed, and had the astounding price of a hundred dollars an acre. That was the modus operandi for Compass East and Ayefour; they came with a fabulous offer, but it was take it or leave it. Thus far, everyone but Adam had taken it.

"So," Adam said as he studied the contract. Preoccupied though he was with missing diamonds and the Cross-Florida Barge Canal, he would not miss an opportunity to talk to a pretty girl. "Addison says you're studying something at the university." In fact, Addison had told him no such thing, but Adam had just then formulated a hypothesis about the identity of the girl his son wanted to help out. He took a drag of smoke and tapped ash into the ashtray.

Kathleen had been looking at "It Pays to Increase Your Word Power" in *Reader's Digest*, pretending she hadn't felt a prickling of protective jealousy when Addison left with Chastity. Improving your vocabulary in the face of Opoyo was like putting up a struggle in a pool of quicksand: worse than useless. "I'm researching Opoyo," she said.

"Walk the dog? Around the world?"

"No, that's Duncan YoYo." She went on to explain as clearly and succinctly as possible how communication left behind a glutinous waste that made subsequent communication increasingly difficult. She did not hold out much hope that Adam would understand her.

"So nothing we ever say comes across quite the way we mean it," Adam said. His swollen lip made the words hard to pronounce.

"Yes," Kathleen said, "yes. That's it." No one but Dr. Buskirk himself had ever grasped the idea, and he was locked away, unwilling or unable to mutter more than "oh!" and "gee!" But this unlikely person, three sheets to the wind and preoccupied with the contents of someone's briefcase, had gotten it.

"Like how do we know we're even using the right words for things," Adam said. The jottings on the legal pad revealed someone had been noodling out the name for a project. There were series of words, written over and over, in different combinations: *Experimental prototype. Future city. Experimental prototype.*

Adam's heart began beating so hard that Kathleen's voice, "No, that's not quite it," registered only as a gnatlike hum.

"Like when we say, 'I'd like a cigarette,'" Adam said, "how do we know 'cigarette' is what it's really called?" He spoke automatically, barely registering his own words. *Experimental prototype. Experimental prototype.* "Maybe the real name for 'cigarette' is *xylophone*, or *alligator*, or *Katmandu*."

"No, that's not what I mean." Mr. Newman had come so close to understanding the Opoyo, but with every word, he seemed to drift farther away. Kathleen felt as if she were watching from the banks as a baby in a paddle-less canoe floated farther and farther downstream.

"Exactly, how do we know what we mean? Maybe when we say 'gopher turtle,' we really mean 'liriope.' Maybe we mean something else when we say—Oh, my God! Get Addison! I've got to go," he told Kathleen. "I'm sorry, but I need to find my son."

Adam jumped up and went to look for Addison, the attaché under his arm.

*Experimental prototype.*

He walked down an empty hall, took a turn, walked down another hall, took a turn, walked down another hall, his footsteps reverberating around him. The fact that every hallway in Florida Hospital looked exactly like every other hallway did little to reassure him. "Addison's got himself good and lost this time," he muttered. "I hope I can find him." He took yet another turn and found himself in a waiting room just like the one he'd come from, down to the Santa drawings and the row of lumpy chairs with green vinyl cushions. There was even someone who looked like Kean's girlfriend, the one that Addison was so smitten with.

Adam realized with mingled relief and disappointment that it actually was Kean's girlfriend. He'd returned to his point of origin. He set off again.

Before he got to the end of the first hallway, a groan coming from a partially open door made him look inside.

A white-haired woman lay in bed; in the half-light the white sheets gathered up in waves under her chin were almost blue. The room smelled faintly of medicine and maybe a little urine. "Are you okay, dear?" he asked.

"Is that you, Willie?" the woman asked.

"Are you okay, dear?" Adam repeated. "Do you want me to fetch the nurse?"

"Am I going to die, Willie?" she asked.

Adam stuffed the papers back in the attaché case and picked up the clipboard hanging on the foot of her bed. If he hoped to find the memo *going to live* or *going to die*, or a jagged line like a Dow Jones graph showing a trend either up or down, he was to be disappointed. Instead, boxes showed someone had been bringing medication on a regular basis. "Everything seems to be as it should be," he said.

"I'm sorry about Richard," she said. Adam had no idea who Richard was, but he didn't know who Willie was, either. "I love you, Willie."

"Same back at you," Adam said. There didn't seem to be much else to say.

Then she asked, as if afraid her slip might be showing, "Are the radio waves visible?"

"No, they are quite invisible," Adam reassured her truthfully. "So that's one thing at least we don't have to worry about. Do you want me to get a nurse, sweetheart?"

"I'm sorry, Willie," the woman said. "I'm sorry I hurt you. Can you forgive me?"

"Of course I forgive you, dear. There's nothing to forgive. Do you want a nurse?"

"No, feel better, Willie. Thank you."

"You're welcome. Go to sleep now."

Soon she was snoring softly. Adam closed the door soundlessly and walked down another corridor until he found himself at the hospital's front door. In the parking lot he saw neither pay phone nor Addison. Instead he saw a pair of car lights coming down the road. The mist was rising quickly and the headlights sent out two fuzzy beams. The sight of a lone car arriving at the hospital late at night transfixed Adam's attention. Evelyn's car turned into the parking lot and pulled up beside his jeep.

"Kean's going to be just fine, Evelyn," he told her. "They're taking expert care of him." He made a little circle with his thumb and forefinger, like a chef saying, "Bon appetit." He strode across the blacktop to meet her. "I don't want you getting on to him about getting in a fight," Adam told her somewhat peremptorily. He did not wish to be huffy with her, but the subject of getting into fights was one on which he had strong opinions—that Kean was only a stepson did not affect his views one iota. Adam's own mother had frequently gotten on to him about starting fights at Sisters of Mercy. *But I didn't start it—he started it by looking at me funny. You started it by making me wear those funny-looking shorts on the train.* He intended to shield Kean from a mother's wrath if he could. "Naturally, Addison and I did everything we could to look out for him, but these things happen, and—"

"I don't blame Kean, Adam," Evelyn said simply, without heat or anger.

This response, though it was exactly what Adam wished for, did not please him, and he took a step back, as if at an unspoken rebuke. "Well, good," he said, nodding his head approvingly, but Evelyn, waiting neither for Adam's approval nor disapproval, had already said something about checking on Kean and was heading to the front door.

"Anyway," Adam said, trailing behind her, "I don't want this to affect your decision in any way. About me." Evelyn looked over her shoulder for a chilly glance without slowing and entered the hospital. Her shoes slapped the floor. "I don't know if I ever told you," he said, "how dreadfully, dreadfully sorry I am about the french fries." The words, after being long withheld, came fast, and with giddy relief. Approaching the front desk, Adam softened his voice. "I know it must've been a terrible shock for you, waking up that morning to find that awful mess. If there were any way to make it up to you—I just wanted you to know I was sorry." They reached the front desk, and Adam stood beside her, resting his knuckles on the polished Formica top. Evelyn patted his hand. Adam said, "And could you ever forgive me and take me back?"

"I'm Kean Winston's mother," she told the nurse who finally appeared. The nurse explained Kean's condition; he needed some stitches and might have a mild concussion. He was in X-ray now, but the doctor was confident he would be just fine.

Satisfied, Evelyn turned and spoke in a calm, although not cheerful voice. "You already apologized for the french fries, Adam. It wasn't the french fries. It wasn't that you went around behind my back telling everyone that I didn't understand you. It wasn't even the drinking. After the french fries we had a fight, and you checked into the Wigwam Hotel. Do you remember this part, Adam? I visited you the next morning. I felt bad about the fight." Evelyn slowed down her words, but not so slow as a crawl. She wanted above all else to have a calm, steady voice. She did. It chilled him how little emotion she had; whatever fire had been in these memories had long since burned out. "Lily was in your room, Adam." The nurse gaped; all this was said at the same volume she might have discussed an oil change. "You don't have to ask my forgiveness. I'm over it now, and I forgive you. But I can never take you back, Adam. I never will."

She walked away from him toward the waiting room.

He asked her retreating back, "How could you?"

Adam stepped into the washroom. He splashed his hot face with cold water, then dried himself with the roller towel hanging on the wall. In the mirror Adam assured himself that his eyes' customary bloodshot-red looked just fine. What could he say at a time like this? *Okay, Evelyn, if that's the way you want it. We'll say no more about it. But I just want you to know that I love you and I've never stopped loving you. I'll always love you.* Good: simple, direct, sincere. He would say that.

He rejoined the others, putting on a brave face. His life seemed largely composed of rejoining others with a brave face. Addison and Chastity had returned and stared out the windows into black night. Kathleen stared at the *Reader's Digest*, pointedly not looking at anyone. Adam sat beside Evelyn and said in a voice he let tremble a little, "Okay, Evelyn, if that's the way you want it." Evelyn had picked up a *Look* and did not raise her eyes from it. "Okay, Evelyn," he repeated. "If that's the way you want it."

She looked up as if only just then she'd become aware of his presence. "What?"

"I said, okay, if that's the way you want it."

Spoken this way, Adam's words didn't make any sense, even to himself, but Evelyn tilted her chin slightly, said, "Ah," as if in comprehension, and returned her gaze to her magazine. Inside a Gemini astronaut was communicating with Mission Control a thousand miles below.

"We'll say no more about it," Adam said. He couldn't decide if her lack of response signified assent or that she just wasn't listening. He swallowed to clear his throat of something salty and burning. "Evelyn," he said. She looked up again, vaguely. "I was just saying we won't say any more about it.

"Thank you, Adam," Evelyn told him, "but you don't have to wait."

The flanking maneuver put Adam on different terrain; he found himself discussing driving arrangements instead of the implication of saying no more about his love for Evelyn. "But Addison's car is at the Fish Camp."

"We'll take care of it."

"And Kean's motorcycle."

"It'll just have to wait until he can drive it back himself."

"Well, I can drive everyone home."

"I'll take them."

"Well, there's Kathleen."

When his father said this, Addison looked to see Kathleen's answer. If against all odds she'd have said yes, he'd have taken a ride too, but it didn't take Kathleen a second to assess the safety of getting in a car with Adam. "I'll just ride with Mrs. Newman," she said.

"Can I show something to Addison?" Adam asked Evelyn. "Can I just show something to Addison?"

"I don't mind," Evelyn said.

"Look, Addison, come here." Addison responded with something less than eagerness. They stood in the threshold of the waiting room with their backs to the others. Adam held Wrigley's attaché in one hand and put his free arm around Addison's shoulders. "I don't think this has to do with the barge canal anymore," Adam confided. He tried to enunciate as clearly as possible, but with his lip, the words came out slightly slurred.

The whiskey on Adam's breath was dizzying. Addison kept his head back as far as he could manage. "You don't?" Addison said.

"It's bigger than that." With an unsteady voice Adam told about the mysterious repeating phrase jotted on the documents. "Compass East isn't just trying to block Ayefour. They're cooking up something of their own, I don't know what. An invasion, a secret weapon. I don't like the sound of this experimental prototype thing. They might be planning a whole city of robots or something. Replace human beings." A note in Adam's voice said he wasn't joking. "We need to track down Wrigley. He's the only one who can give us some answers."

Adam's face was flushed and blotchy. Addison looked at the floor. "There's a letterhead," Adam said. "The corner of Hanover and Washington. That must be Wrigley's in-town address. Compass East Headquarters. Please come with me."

"I think I'll just wait here with Mother," Addison said. Red, blue, and yellow lines led to various regions of the hospital. Instead of toe molding, a metal strip ran next to the floor like a baseboard. Easier to clean, Addison supposed. There was a smell of pine-scented disinfectant.

Adam had lost Evelyn, and now he was losing Addison. "I need you."

Addison looked up. There was absolutely no reasonable pretext for leaving the hospital, and Addison knew this. All responsibility, common sense, and self-preservation were on the side of staying. On the side of going was only his father's request.

"Okay," he said. The air pressure seemed to drop. Addison's mother had watched the exchange from the waiting room. "Mother, I'm going with Dad."

Evelyn could not have been more surprised—or displeased—if Addison had proposed eating a bucket of carpet tacks.

"You need to see how your brother is," she said. She held the glossy magazine as if it were a subpoena.

"He'll be okay," Addison said helplessly. "Dad needs me."

"Addison, you need to wait here," Evelyn repeated. She was not the sort of person to employ the phrase "*I forbid you,*" but she wished she were. It would have been a handy phrase to employ just then.

"Don't worry about Addison," Adam advised, putting an arm around his son and patting Addison's chest with his free hand. "He'll be perfectly fine. He'll be with me." These were not the words to calm a mother's anxious heart.

"Addison, you need to stay," Kathleen seconded, and for a moment Addison wavered, "for Kean."

"For Kean," Addison repeated dourly. "Kean's going to be okay. Dad wants me to go with him."

Addison and Adam left the hospital into the cool foggy darkness. Adam raised his arms forty-five degrees and quoted to the night air, " 'Out of the night that covers me, black as a pit from pole to pole . . .' " A paper fell twirling from the attaché. Adam knelt to retrieve it from the shiny asphalt; it shocked him how hard it had gotten to bend his knees.

Addison, still brooding over how Kathleen had said "for Kean," waited for his father to stand.

"She said she's not taking me back," Adam muttered. "She's not ever taking me back." He couldn't believe it. He felt dull and hollow as if waiting in the garden for Mother to come punish him. At the bang from the Old Man's study, he'd dropped a mimosa blossom and let it twirl like a pink and white parasol onto the wet paving stones.

*What have we told you?* In spite of their warnings, giddy from the triumph of eating swamp chicken and being just like the Old Man, Adam had taken it out to marvel over its gleaming barrel, milky handle, and astonishing heaviness. Now there was no way to take it back.

But surely it wasn't too late to unbungle his other bungles.

"She's not taking me back," Adam said. He didn't believe it. Then he decided he really didn't believe it. "She's going to take me back," he said. And then with more conviction, looking at Addison, "She's going to take me back."

In the jeep Adam slid the attaché under the seat and sat behind the wheel, but moments went by before he summoned strength to put in the key. "I know it won't be easy," he said, "but she is going to take me back." He started the jeep and turned on the radio. A shadowy hiss answered him: not even the national anthem at this hour. "I'm going to get the diamonds, and she's going to take me back."

Someone tapped on Addison's window. Chastity stood outside.

"I've decided I'm going with you," she said. "Those people don't want me."

A knot in Adam's throat made it difficult to say, "Get in." Addison moved to the backseat and let her in. Adam put the jeep into drive.

"Where do you live?" Addison asked.

Chastity said nothing.

"Where do you live?" Adam asked. Then, "We're sure not taking you to Strawberry's."

"I don't want to go there," she retorted.

They were already pulling out of the parking lot. "So where do you live?"

"I'm coming with you."

Adam shook his cigarette pack and pulled one out between his lips to light it. "This, in chess," he told Addison, "is called a zugzwang. Everything we can do is bad, and we have to do *something.* There's nothing for it but to take her along until she tells us where she lives."

En route to Hanover and Washington, Adam imagined taking a fork in the road that had never been there before and ending up, like in *The Twilight Zone*, back in time, just slightly, before he'd spoken to Evelyn at the hospital. He was convinced he could have won her back tonight if he had taken a different approach. If he could find the secret road that led back in time, he could unbungle the bungle. He had bungled so often before and she had always taken him back.

The address on the letterhead—Adam already mentally referred to the paper as Exhibit A—turned out to be a cinder block building under a lone streetlight. Across the street lay a grassy prairie that had once been a marsh before the Army Corps drained it. Now it was home to snakes and armadillos. The snakes hunted mice by day, and the armadillos hunted worms and insects at night. In spite of having poor eyesight, sometimes an armadillo crossed the road to forage. Sometimes this resulted in one less armadillo.

The streetlight hazily illuminated a pie slice of cinder block; the rising fog blurred the building's contours, making it look like a scene in a Bogart movie; all that was missing was a faintly groaning foghorn and Addison might have been in *Key Largo.* No signage identified the building as the secret headquarters of a Communist conspiracy.

They pulled to the shoulder beside the prairie. Addison followed his father across the street. Adam tried the glass door—locked, of course. He banged his first on it and then the plate-glass window with the flat of his hand, but with neither result nor any real expectation of result. Meanwhile Addison reconnoitered the perimeter and checked the windows. No light shone through the cracks of the lowered venetian blinds. No one lurked inside cowering behind the desk for them to give up and go away.

Addison shrugged. "We might as well go home, Dad. No one's here." Even the sleepless agents of Compass East were snugly tucked away at this hour, as visions of prototypes danced in their heads.

"Not just yet," Adam said. "We'll write him a little note, see if we can't flush him out." Adam went to the jeep and came back with a ballpoint pen. He emptied the cigarette pack and tucked the cigarettes into his shirt pocket for later. He tore the packet inside out and began to write on the inside, composing aloud as he went: "Wrigley," he said, "we know what you're up to."

"Don't say that," Addison said. Adam raised an eyebrow.

"We don't know what he's up to," Addison pointed out reasonably, "and if we tell him we do, we won't find out."

"Right," Adam said. "Wrigley, we *need* to know what you're up to." He wrote this and touched the pen to his lip as he considered the next line.

"We'll be in touch," Addison suggested.

Adam nodded and wrote this also, then added, *We have your attaché—Experimental Prototype.* He underlined the last two words several times and signed it *Adam Newman and Son.* Adam had no idea how he would extract the diamonds from Wrigley without selling his acreage, but that was a secondary concern. Adam Newman had never been on a battleship like Vince Winston, nor faced a machine-gun nest like the Old Man. The nefarious enemies of freedom had come to his hometown and this was his chance to do his bit against them. "I'm glad you're with me on this, son," Adam said.

He jammed the note—white side up, green side down—as far as he could under the aluminum frame of the glass door, leaving the better part to flap over the concrete like a dog tongue. His face felt stretched over his skull, and bending made it worse. "And now, if you'll excuse me, son, I have something to attend to." Adam stepped out of the yellow circle under the streetlight; his knees buckled, and he stuck his finger down his throat. He was rewarded with about three-quarters of a cup flecked with red pimento; he did not feel much better, though. He was strangely relieved to realize Lily was not there to see him like this.

"Dad, are you okay?" Addison asked when Adam rejoined him. Adam nodded and wiped the corners of his mouth. "I have some gum," Addison offered, taking out a pack.

"Gum would be splendid," Adam said and accepted a stick.

Back to the jeep they went, Adam's knees trembling, and he collapsed in the front seat.

"What are we doing?" Chastity asked.

"Stakeout," was Adam's answer. A word he'd learned watching *Dragnet.* Maybe Wrigley would show up after all. He'd have to show up eventually.

"Are you hoping your wife is going to take you back?" Chastity asked. "Does this have something to do with that? I heard what she said. She doesn't want anything to do with you."

Addison suggested they go home and get a good night's sleep, and Chastity said that if Adam thought this was going to get his wife back, he had another think coming. Adam told them that they weren't supposed to talk on a stakeout. Adam looked in the mini-cooler. Empty. He lit himself another cigarette.

"Trailing after someone like a puppy dog when they don't love you just makes you look pathetic," Chastity said.

"I'm not listening to you—dang!" Adam dropped a lighted cigarette in his crotch, and had to shuffle in his seat to retrieve it. Now there'd be a burn mark on his fly.

Addison had resigned himself to the idea that they weren't headed home anytime soon, and he needed to get Chastity off this topic. "At least we can get to see the sunrise," he observed.

"Sunrise?" Chastity asked, contemptuously looking out of the windows into the blackness. "What sun?"

"If you can already see the sun, it's not sunrise," Adam told her, and Addison was glad the change of subject had worked. "That's sun*risen.*"

"Everyone always talks about watching the sunrise, but they usually mean watching it after it's already up. Sunrise is before the sun comes up," Addison said. When he was little, Addison and his father had become something of sunrise connoisseurs. Adam would wake him early-early and they'd be out in the boat with their lines already wet while it was still dark. While they fished, Adam would tell stories of the Knights of the Round Table, who always seemed to get up to some adventure or other to impress the ladies back at Camelot. Adam and Addison had frequent occasion to discuss the phenomenon of daybreak. "Sunrise starts at the darkest part of the night," Addison said.

"In a textbook case," Adam confirmed, "a breeze starts up, and there's a cold snap."

"Then the sky over the treeline goes pink."

"But not one of your sissy pinks," Adam clarified, lest Chastity misunderstand, "it's like the silvery pink on a trout's belly. It's kind of subtle, and it changes pretty quick. You got to be on your toes to catch it. Before you know what color you're seeing, it's already different."

Addison sat forward, resting his chin on his hands on the back of the seat between Chastity and his father. Like oak trees, diamonds, and fingerprints, no two sunrises are exactly alike. "Sometimes red spreads like it was seeping into a blue curtain; sometimes there's layers of colors—red, yellow, and blue—like layered rocks in a postcard picture of the Grand Canyon, and everything above turns purple, but there're still stars in the west." Addison remembered how color came into the world those mornings on Crystal Lake. "That's sunrise," he said. "Once the sun cracks the horizon, it's pretty much over."

"Sunrise is the best part of the day," Adam said. "If you look at the sun once it's past the horizon, what's that? A circle next to a straight line. You can get pretty much the same effect putting a half dollar next to a yardstick."

Chastity said nothing, but nodded in comprehension. And so the three of them settled into their seats and waited for sunrise. And dozed.

A beam of light shone on Adam, waking him from a dream that the Old Man had a foolproof plan to foil Compass East, recover the diamonds, and win back Evelyn. A man's voice at his shoulder said, "Sir?"

Behind the glare of the flashlight stood the silhouette of a law enforcement officer. The hairs bristling on the back of his neck, Adam could fairly smell the ceramic glaze of a therapeutic painted alligator.

# NINE

# Adam Goes to Jail

"I need to see your license and registration," the officer said. Light scoped inside the jeep and rested on Chastity in her tight red dress and bandit mask of mascara. The significance of the pause was more articulate than words could have been. "Who are you?" he asked.

"She's my daughter," Adam supplied without thinking.

"Are you over eighteen, miss?" The officer apparently didn't believe Adam. He wore the wide-brimmed hat of the sheriff's department.

"The fact is—" Adam began.

"Way over," Chastity said.

"Do you have any ID, miss?" the deputy asked. Chastity folded her arms and looked out the opposite window in an attitude that did not suggest ready compliance.

"Officer," Adam said, "the fact is we're on a stakeout."

"You're what?"

Adam found himself staring directly into the flashlight's glowing eye. At any rate, he had the officer's attention again.

Addison sat up in the backseat, roused from a dream that he and Kathleen had gone fishing on Crystal Lake. The officer gagged. Believing mistakenly that there were only two people in the car, he swallowed a little tobacco juice at the discovery of a third.

With one hand Addison shielded his eyes from the flashlight. "What's going on?"

"Who else is in there?" the officer asked. If people started popping out of nowhere, who knew where it would end? In the next moment a swarm of malefactors might pour out like clowns from a circus car.

"Who are you?"

"Addison Newman. I'm his son. I'm a student at UF. Sophomore." Addison, who had lived a quiet life thitherto, had never been questioned by the police, so his answer was more thorough than strictly required. Had the officer waited long enough, he probably could have ascertained Addison's birthday and phone number. The officer didn't wait.

"Is she your sister?"

"No."

"I need y'all to step from the car." The deputy had recovered his wits from Addison's materialization in the backseat. "You too, miss. Keep your hands where I can see them."

As Adam stepped into the cool, luminous fog, he noticed the officer hadn't switched on the twirling red light. And shouldn't there be another car around, or at least another cop? Law enforcement officers, ducks, and nuns always travel in pairs. This one's being alone struck Adam as a potential breech of protocol, and he wondered if there wasn't some way to wedge leverage by threatening to report it. His mind was racing neck-and-neck with his heart. Which version of Adam Newman could get him out of this scrape?

Addison worried his father would make a bad impression

with his swollen lip and vomit-smelling breath. Was there any blood on his shirt? Addison's own shirt was missing buttons and had an ink stain on the pocket from the fight at the Fish Camp. "Dad," Addison whispered as he joined his father on the grassy verge of the prairie, "let me handle this."

They stood in a small circle in front of the jeep as the officer's flashlight selected a face at a time from the darkness. Addison's toes touched the blacktop, and tall grass prickled his Achilles tendons.

The officer asked Adam, "Have you been drinking?"

"Of course not," Addison responded.

"Yes sir, I have," Adam said. "I was a little bit tipsy, so I thought the most responsible thing to do under the circumstances was pull over and sleep it off a little."

"Oh, yes, actually he had been drinking," Addison concurred belatedly. "A little."

"And as I said," Adam said with a sheepish shrug and a grin, "I was a little tipsy. So I pulled over to sleep it off." Adam chose his words as if navigating a field of sandspurs and cow patties barefoot. Amateurs overelaborate; Adam kept his stories simple and fluid.

Adam fondled the keys in his pocket; he was convinced that one more moment and the officer would let him get back in his jeep and drive off, but Chastity said, "He was telling the truth the first time. We're on a stakeout. That's what he said when he brought me here."

This brought the flashlight to Chastity's face. "Are you his daughter?" the officer asked her.

"No," said Addison.

"Yes," said Adam.

The flashlight trained on one face and then another as Adam and Addison improvised a fable consistent with both

statements. Addison's skin prickled in shame, fear, and the sense of justice outraged. His father had done nothing wrong—not this time—and here they were the sport of this fat—even in the darkness and fog Addison could see the deputy was fat—this fat fool someone had given a badge, probably whose only qualification was being a bully like Nelson, the thrice-held-back hick who'd made it his personal duty to knuckle-punch Addison's left shoulder every two minutes in Coach Braddy's third-period social studies class.

In fact, the more Addison thought about it, the more the deputy reminded him of Nelson. He had the same incongruous, high-pitched raspy voice that always made Addison think of paprika, and Addison was certain that if there were light, he would see the two buttons above the belt buckle were undone, exposing a hairy navel, Nelson's personal sartorial trademark. Addison had fondly imagined avenging himself on this cretin by moving on to higher education while Nelson sank into well-deserved penury, but the Nelsons of the world, it seemed, all got jobs as sheriff's deputies where they continued terrorizing unoffending Adams and Addisons unfettered.

Even as Addison stumbled with his father toward the story that Chastity was Adam's daughter by a previous or else subsequent marriage, he knew he ought to object to their treatment. This was exactly the sort of scene he imagined one day Kathleen would witness, in which Addison calmly dispatched some swaggering bully who foolishly underestimated him, but each passing second made it more painfully clear that Addison wasn't about to dispatch anybody. Addison saw his chance to make an impassioned speech like Jimmy Stewart in that movie, employing phrases like "we the people" or "a more perfect union." Instead, he acted like he'd swallowed a lead sinker, stammering alongside his father, submitting to this lout like a coward. Addison's sense of failure might have become unendurable had not Chastity taken matters into her own hands.

Chastity, as has been noted before, had a weakness for slapping men. *I can take it or leave it alone,* is probably what she told herself about her habit, but the truth is whenever she was riled, she couldn't help herself. Whether because of the dispute over her identity or the feeling she was being ignored, Chastity was riled now, and she slapped the officer—not hard, she never slapped anyone hard, just a pat on the face to get his attention.

Sheriff's deputies, however, make no such distinctions; to them a slap is a slap and they act accordingly. His arm shot out for Chastity, but she was too fast; she ran a little way past the patrol car and stopped. The officer took a deep, exasperated breath. He shone the light on her, and she stepped to one side, although her silhouette was still visible in the mist.

Adam wondered how the officer would handle this. Chastity showed no inclination to run far, and in heels she couldn't run fast, but if the deputy pursued her, then Adam and Addison might get away. It was like a variation of the riddle in which you have to transport a chicken, a fox, and a bag of corn one at a time safely across a river. The deputy's solution, evidently, would be to lock the fox and the corn in his squad car while he ran down the chicken. He opened the back door and pushed Adam's head down, meanwhile twisting one wrist behind his back, roughly assisting him into the backseat. Addison received similar treatment.

Adam couldn't get a good lungful; he groped for a crank to lower the window or a handle to open the door, but discovered the back of a patrol car has neither.

After a minute, the door opened and Chastity was shoved in alongside. The officer got in the front seat and said tersely,

"License, please." He had swallowed tobacco juice, been slapped by a girl and compelled to chase her down. He had been in better moods.

Adam meekly passed it through a little cage door separating the front seat from the back. An identifying badge hung from the rearview: *Dooley*. Adam did not scrabble, claw, or chew the cage bars like a panicky squirrel in a trap, but no one who has seen a squirrel in such a predicament could fail to recognize the squirrelish quality of words that came from Adam's mouth as the deputy examined the license and began writing his report.

"The thing is, Deputy Dooley, frankly, I was just a little bit tipsy. We were just about to leave, really." Adam spoke to drown out that horrid clunk of the door of Chattahoochee's sixth floor closing and locking in his mind's ear.

Dooley spat into a paper cup and swallowed Coca-Cola from a green bottle. He took a can labeled *Snack Mate* and squirted an orange swirl on a Ritz cracker. This he munched thoughtfully while he wrote in a notepad. The action seemed to restore his equanimity somewhat, for his shoulders, hunched up after facing down magically appearing third passengers and runaway girls, relaxed. After finishing another cheese-topped cracker, he spoke into his microphone as he read from the license, a series of codes like "ten-four" and "Delta Parker Charley five niner niner" that ended with the words, "Adam Newman."

The staticky feminine voice on the other side said, "Adam Newman? The guy who ran Paradise Dogs?"

"Is that him?" Dooley asked. He turned his head and asked Adam, "Is that you?" Adam said it was. The news instantly transformed Dooley's demeanor. "Oh, man!" He broke into a smile. "Those were the best hot dogs ever. I used to go there every day after school."

"Ask him whatever happened to that restaurant," said the radio voice. "It was fabulous."

"New owners. It closed," Adam explained.

"We used to cross town just to get a bowl of your chili," the radio voice said.

"Well, the chili was really for chili dogs," Adam said. He had to put his face to the wire mesh to make sure the radio lady heard him. "We didn't really intend—"

"And the buns!" Officer Dooley said. "My word, you couldn't believe an ordinary hot dog bun could be so delicious."

"We set them out to rise every night at closing and baked them fresh the next day. We used our own sourdough starter. We never put in store-bought yeast."

"And I bet you ground your own wheat, too," Dooley joked.

"That would be silly," Adam said defensively. There was no point getting ridiculous about it. "We had a mill in Wichita grind to spec and ship it to us."

"So what have you been doing with yourself?" Officer Dooley asked.

Adam felt the tide turning, and the dreadful waters, dark and chill, of Chattahoochee's sixth floor receded slightly in his imagination. "Well, you know—skinning gators in the summer, and in the winter skinning Yankees."

"Ha-ha," the officer said.

"What's he say?" said the radio voice. "What's he say?"

"He said he skins gators in the summer and Yankees in the winter."

"Ha-ha."

"Well, ha-ha-ha-ha-ha," Adam said. "I'm glad that's all straightened out. Don't worry, Deputy, it was a natural mistake. I don't blame you one bit." Adam reached for the door as if, hearing his identity, it would have sprouted handles. It hadn't. He waited for the deputy to come around and release him. He didn't.

"Just because I like hot dogs doesn't mean I'm stupid," Officer Dooley said.

"But they were great hot dogs," the radio voice said.

"The best," admitted Officer Dooley.

"Thanks," Adam acknowledged numbly.

Now was Addison's chance to be Jimmy Stewart, the common man who stands up to injustice; all Addison could manage, however, was a meek squeak, "What's the charge?"

Dooley's mood had brightened at the memory of those delicious hot dogs, and he was inclined to be conciliatory. "Don't worry," Dooley said. "We're just talking public drunkenness here. Worst thing can happen is we keep you in the cooler overnight." Dooley's behavior was not untypical of the era before *Miranda vs. Arizona*, when law enforcement still maintained an attitude of breezy nonchalance when it came to taking people in. Earlier that year Bobby Kennedy had exhorted the Kern County sheriff to reread the Constitution, but no one had gotten around to suggesting the same thing to folks in central Florida. "She assaulted an officer, which I'm probably going to let slide, but y'all told me this cock-and-bull story about a stakeout, and I don't know who this girl is, whether she's your sister or not your sister, and on top of that it's clear all three of you are plastered."

Addison chose not to protest being lumped in as plastered alongside Chastity and his father. "But Dad admitted he was tipsy. He said he pulled over to sleep it off," Addison said.

"Okay, score one for him." Dooley licked his fingertip and tallied an invisible mark in the air. "Look, they probably won't do nothing but let you sleep this off, and you can be on your way first thing in the morning."

"What about my jeep?" Adam asked.

"It'll be fine," Dooley said. "We'll send someone for it." He took a pinch of ragged tobacco from a bag and placed it under his lip before starting the car. "Don't worry, we're going to take care of you," he assured them.

Few experiences are better calculated to overbrim the soul with leaden grief than riding a patrol car to jail. Adam and Chastity looked out opposite windows. Addison sat squeezed in the middle with only enough room to rest his hands on his knees with his elbows by his sides.

An eerie calm settled upon Adam. It was odd, wasn't it, he reflected, to be picked up this way? By a patrolman who didn't use his twirling light or travel with a partner? Right in front of Compass East headquarters, just after obtaining Exhibit A with its telling references to experimental prototypes? Adam replayed the events of the last twenty-four hours: Wrigley had contacted him at the precise moment he was most financially vulnerable, and then Adam had been picked up by this random law enforcement officer at the exact spot Wrigley would have known that Adam was bound to show up sooner or later. Could all that be just a coincidence?

"There's supposed to be a charge," Addison muttered. "They aren't supposed to take you in without a charge."

The revelation dawned on Adam like an old fluorescent bulb flickering into life: Dooley had promised to *take care* of them. "Are you really a law enforcement officer?" Adam asked.

There was a pause, a pregnant pause, Adam decided, before Dooley said, "Yes, I really am a law enforcement officer."

The dashboard lights picked out Dooley's contours in unearthly lurid tones. "Good Lord," he whispered to Addison, "how could we have been such fools?" The oldest trick in the book—and the incriminating attaché left back at the jeep! Adam twisted to see the streetlight and glowing cinder block triangle vanish in the fog. He gritted his teeth; he wished he could see Evelyn again, not that he wanted her exposed to such a dangerous situation, but to enfold her in his arms and tell her he loved her. What he would give to hear her talk just once more about the preference of night crawlers for apple cores over orange peels. With a pang, he realized he also realized he had not told Lily good-bye.

"We have to think what to do," Adam told Addison. The knights of old rarely found themselves locked in patrol cars—tactics employed against ogres and giants would be of little avail, nor did the adventures of shoeshine boys offer a helpful precedent. Adam would have to think. "I know about the Experimental Prototype," he told the driver.

"What?"

"I know about the Experimental Prototype."

"Then you know one more thing than I do."

"I don't know what they've told you, or how much you know, Deputy Dooley," Adam said in a voice he meant to sound cool and sardonic. "I call you Deputy Dooley because, of course, I have no way of knowing what your real name is, but there are some diamonds mixed up in this. If you were prepared to—come over—there might be a reward in it for you."

There was another pause in which Adam imagined the driver was considering the offer. Then, "Mr. Newman, I think the less you say right now, the better."

"We might as well be frank with each other. You managed things pretty slick, I got to hand it to you. You have us right where you want us, I suppose. There's no point pretending you're a sheriff's officer now. You can drop the act. You work for the Cubans?" Silence. Vague shapes of buildings and light poles moved past the windows. Fear prickled in his nostrils as Adam realized he had not been paying attention to where they were going and now had no idea where they were. "The Russians? The Chinese?"

"You're only making it worse for yourself, Mr. Newman."

"Where are you taking us?" Adam asked. "Where are you really taking us?"

"Mr. Newman, I don't know what you're talking about," their driver said sternly, "but whatever it is, you better quit talking about it."

"Dad, what are you talking about?" asked Addison, who still did not seem to grasp the outlines of their predicament.

"It won't do any good to offer him money," Adam spoke softly. "I'm afraid our 'deputy' is a True Believer. And we don't have time to talk him around—show him the fallacy of collectivism." Adam sighed and leaned back in his seat. He took their abductor's advice and kept silent. What did anything matter now: losing the diamonds, falling into the clutches of Compass East? Evelyn had said she would never take him back. He laid his forehead against the cool window and pressed the back of his hand to his mouth.

Addison stared out the opposite window and thought of Kathleen.

To Adam, it came as an enormous relief—and something of a letdown—to end up at the jail and not to be brought before Mr. Big or whatever sinister figure headed up Compass East's Experimental Prototype Division. Deputy Dooley really was Deputy Dooley then, although it was not unlikely he was a stooge, unknowingly at the bidding of Compass East; nevertheless, Adam's spirits rose slightly. Perhaps his luck was turning after all.

Adam could see, however, from Addison's ashen face that his son was taking it hard. He put a hand on his shoulder and said, "Buck up, son. It really isn't as bad as all that." He tried to sound cheerful and hearty. "Maybe you'll be able to write a story about this later."

They were offered phone calls, but Chastity said she didn't have anyone to call, and Adam said that although it was technically morning, he'd prefer to give Lily a chance to wake up before asking her to come get him. Adam, who had one eye on Dooley, was concerned about an eager look in the deputy's eye as he studied the notes in a manila folder, and was waiting to see if he might not need to call his lawyer rather than his fiancée. Addison accepted a dime to make his phone call while Dooley and the jailer discussed Adam's record. Reluctantly, Addison called home. He surmised correctly that by this time Kean would be done in the hospital.

Hearing her son's voice did not please Evelyn. This was Addison's third call in twenty-four hours, and none of them had been an improvement on the others; the first had been from a gas station, the second from the hospital, and the third from jail. As she told him that she would drive over and pick him up, there was something in her voice that said three phone calls in this series were her personal limit, and under no circumstances would she tolerate a fourth.

Adam and Addison were given fold-up cots, which they rolled in front of them as Timothy Moreland, the night jailer, took them to their cells. The city jail had only two cells, "One for the girls and one for the boys," Timothy explained as he followed them down the hall. Adam knew that Timothy intended the lighthearted remark to lessen the shame of being locked up by a friend.

"You know each other," Addison said.

"Oh, yes," Timothy said. "Me and your daddy go way back."

Adam's Old Man had known everyone, and at one time Adam had too, but families had grown, and the new air conditioners brought outsiders to the little town the way rainy springs bring mosquitoes, but Timothy Moreland and Adam had known each other for ages—even before the Old Man's accident.

The boys' cell already had occupants, and one of them paced, ducked his head, and called out, "You got some new prisoners for us, Officer Tiddler? You got some new prisoners?"

It was Jerry McIntyre.

Timothy ducked his head, lost his smile and regained it, but otherwise ignored this.

Timothy Moreland was an unlikely candidate to be a jailer. Raised by a spare-the-back-of-the-hand-spoil-the-child sort of mother, Timothy started at sudden movements and wore the desperate, flinching smile of a mouse determined to ingratiate himself to a roomful of cats. Jerry, who had visited the jail on other occasions, had long since mastered Timothy's signature head twitch and divined the secret of the jailer's humiliating nickname.

"Strawberry!" Chastity yelled. She grabbed the bars and yelled, "Strawberry, you need to listen to me!"

Strawberry raised a shoulder from his cot and looked without curiosity. Each cell had only one bed—Jerry had claimed the one in the boys' cell—so additional prisoners had to sleep on cots. "I'm listening," Strawberry said sullenly, but having his attention, Chastity didn't know what to do with it, and merely repeated, "Strawberry," in a warning tone.

"I'm going to need some help with this one," Timothy predicted, which turned out to be the case. He wrapped his arms around Chastity and pulled her nearly perpendicular to the bars, but she didn't let go. When he pried the fingers of one hand free, she grabbed tighter with the other. She screamed for Strawberry. "Adam," Timothy asked, "can you give me a hand here?"

One would not have imagined anything short of a squid could have had so many appendages to cling with. Addison, Adam, and Timothy wrested her hands loose, but Chastity got her foot between the bars and twisted so they had to release her hands to extract it. When they turned their attention back to her hands, she resorted to her feet again. At one point, although how this was possible none of them could have said, she seemed to be holding on with her chin. Then, just when Addison had begun to wonder if she might not have a prehensile tail, they detached her. Strawberry observed all this disinterestedly. Adam took charge of depositing her assorted squirming arms and legs in the girls' cell as Timothy held the door. Adam did not put Chastity down so much as peel her off and squeeze back through the door before she could follow.

Timothy closed the door, and Addison pushed the high heels Chastity had kicked off through the bars after her, but Chastity paid these no mind. She pressed to the wall and strained her arm to reach into the boys' cell, where she clung as if she were hanging from a ledge three stories up. "Strawberry, you need to listen to me. You ain't listened to my side of it."

Timothy led Adam and Addison to the boys' cell and said, "Well, this is you. Sorry, chief."

Addison took in his new accommodations. The jail, built thirty years ago and overdue for renovation, was a jail indeed. One could look far and wide without finding another to match its thoroughly jail-like quality, its utter and unmistakable jailness. Stains darkened the concrete walls, a lidless steel toilet squatted in the corner, and fat black palmetto bugs reconnoitered the ceiling. Even in winter, there being no window or air-conditioning, the fug was so thick, you could have stood a spoon upright.

"This is quite fine, Timothy," Adam said. "Do not give it another thought. 'Stone walls do not a prison make, nor iron bars a cage.'"

As Timothy digested this piece of architectural data, Jerry stuck his hand through the bars and said, "Shake, Officer Tiddler." This last was Jerry's idea of high hilarity. Timothy's right hand had never properly formed; it looked as if it had originally set out to be a foot, but had been talked into becoming a hand late in life by well-meaning friends. Timothy ducked his head, lost his smile, regained it, and said nothing. Jerry said with exaggerated contrition, "Sorry, Tiddler." Adam frowned. He did not relish sharing a cell with Jerry McIntyre.

"Move to the back of the cell and turn around," Timothy told the cellmates. Larry and Strawberry got off their creaking cots and complied.

"I'm sorry, Officer Moreland," Jerry said, sounding truly regretful this time, but Timothy knew this was part of the joke; even to acknowledge the apology was to give his tormentor power over him.

"Move to the back of the cell," Timothy repeated.

"Okay, if that's the way you want it." Jerry said in an aggrieved voice and joined his brothers at the far wall and turned his back.

"Goldurn idiot thinks I don't know I'm spastic," Timothy whispered to Adam as he took out a surprisingly small brass key to unlock the door and let them in. Timothy's entire body twitched, and his face turned from Adam's. "I know I'm spastic."

"I know you do. We all know you're spastic," Adam said sympathetically. "Durn idiot." He and Addison wheeled their cots inside, and the iron door clanked behind them.

"Hey, do you know Officer Tiddler?" Jerry asked, coming forward. Adam ignored him.

Unlike others who at one time or another had come to Timothy's defense, Adam had never used this as a pretext to bully him later in other ways. For this, Adam had Timothy's undying loyalty.

"It looks like me and Evelyn may be getting back together," Adam told Timothy. He thought the news would cheer the jailer up.

"But Lily?" Timothy asked.

"She doesn't understand me," Adam said resignedly. "Not like Evelyn. She's going to take me back as soon as I can wrap up some other business."

"Oh, really? Adam, I hope so. I keep praying for you two."

"Well, we haven't reaching anything definite yet. I've got some other business to wrap up first. I can't tell you about it. It's pretty confidential. You'll read about it in the papers when it comes out."

"Okay," Timothy said, nodding his head. Through his teeth he gave a soundless whistle of solemn respect.

As Timothy left, Jerry went into his routine again, "Good-bye, Officer Tiddler. Hey, Officer Tiddler, shake hands. Don't be that way! No hard feelings. I'm sorry, Officer Tiddler, I'm sorry."

"Sorry about fighting you at the Fish Camp, Mr. Newman," Strawberry said, his voice drained. "I shouldn't of done that." Up close, Strawberry's lackluster eyes were red-rimmed.

"It's okay," Adam said. "We all do things in the heat of the moment." Adam opened his cot and let it fold down. "Son, are you okay?"

Addison told himself he was not going to let himself cry, but of course as soon as he did that, the tears began. Addison wiped them from his face, and they just kept coming. At least Kathleen wasn't here to see this.

"It's okay, son." Adam put an arm around him. "It's going to be okay."

Larry joined them, standing beside Addison, and said, "It's all right, buddy. It's okay. Everybody takes it hard their first night in jail. I'm sorry, too, about wailing on you back in the Fish Camp."

"Don't mention it," Addison sniffled.

"Sorry about your shirt." Larry pointed at the ink stain. "I did that?"

Addison plucked his shirt away from his chest to inspect it. "It's not important," he said. "You got one too," he said, pointing at a matching stain on Larry's white blazer.

"Ahh, it don't matter," Larry said, twisting the sleeve and looking at the ink stain as if he'd acquired a new and not displeasing tattoo.

Addison found himself liking his former attacker. With five occupants, the quarters, while not so snug as an olive jar, were cramped. Such conditions tend to inspire a sort of rough-and-ready brotherhood, and they had done so here. Had there been Ritz crackers and Snack Mate on hand, Addison would have invited Larry to some.

"We'll be out of here before you know it," Adam said. "We'll get the—those things we were talking about—back, and you'll get your reward, and that girl you like will go to college, and everything will be just fine. You'll see."

"You got a girl? Someone you like?" Larry asked condolingly.

Addison nodded and dried his eyes, but he no longer had any faith in the existence of the diamonds; at best he found them only marginally more credible than, say, the story of the old man who broke-and-entered people's homes for the benevolent purpose of leaving presents under trees, or the sensate rabbit who, through some conflation of the animal kingdoms, went around depositing gaudily painted hard-boiled eggs.

Chastity's fingertips curled around the adjoining wall like pink worms, and her soft voice filled the air, "You know, Strawberry, it was partly your fault anyway. You shouldn't of gone to Gainesville without me. I don't see what you got to be so hard-headed for."

"What was that thing you said?" Larry asked Adam. "The thing about iron walls don't make a prison. It sounded like a poem."

"It is—'To Althea from Prison:' 'If I have freedom in my love, and in my soul am free, angels alone that soar above, enjoy such liberty.'" Adam thought of Evelyn and then, inexplicably, of Lily.

"Pretty," Larry said.

Jerry, deciding that Timothy was well and truly out of range, returned to his bed, laughing. "That Tiddler is all right."

"I'll have you know," Adam said sternly, "that when you insult Timothy, you have as good as insulted me." Obscurely he felt that in defending Timothy, he was also somehow defending Evelyn. He planted himself on his cot to dramatize this statement of principle, but instead of stopping, he continued sinking to the floor, and the walls drew in, muffling his ears with soft pressure and whiting out everything in his peripheral vision.

Larry and Jerry laughed. "Man, I never saw that happen before," Larry said. "You forgot to lock the cot so it won't fold up."

Addison helped his father extract himself from the cot, which had closed on him like a giant clam.

"That's better," Larry said. He showed Adam how to push the lever in place so the cot wouldn't fold up again.

"Well, if that's the way you want to be about it, good riddance," Chastity said. Her fingers still reached into their cell. "I'm damned if I'll beg. I'm better off without—" It was at this point that Chastity began to sob. It was an unearthly sound calculated to give anyone the all-overs: something between the baying of a beagle and a police siren, and yet somehow like a hymn; it rose and fell in volume and pitch like a velvety river. At the sound, Addison's blood chilled and the small hairs at the back of his neck stiffened. Strawberry's birthmark paled, and he defiantly pulled his coverlet to his ear, exposing his feet; a pink toe protruded from a hole in his white socks. Larry and Adam elected to act as if someone had farted during a sermon, pretending not to hear. Jerry was more decisive. He walked to the wall and slapped it with his hand, "Shut up! Shut up! He don't want you! He knows about you! He knows about you!" The sandy white boot print on his green plaid cap was a fresh scar in his memory.

"If you'd just married her sooner, none of this would of happened," Larry softly remonstrated.

Adam thought *some* of it might have happened, but was not inclined to be a naysayer now. If Adam had his druthers, he'd have just lain on his cot dwelling on his own catastrophes, and he had ample catastrophes on which to dwell. But something in the contour of Strawberry's unmoving shoulder told Adam that the big man wanted more than anything in the world to forgive Chastity and take her back, but he lacked the stuff to do it without help. Adam couldn't stand by and do nothing, could he? He went to Strawberry's side.

"She really is sorry," he said. He set a foot on Strawberry's cot in a gesture of manly sympathy, with his forearm on his thigh. "She told me so."

Instead of speaking, Strawberry rose and walked to the wall adjoining the girls' cell. Without Strawberry to anchor it, the cot upended and Adam found himself wrestling with the mattress. He managed to throw his foe to the ground but promptly stepped into the cot's empty metal frame, tumbling again, contending this time with an opponent of wire and aluminum.

"Man, you and cots just don't see eye to eye," Larry said in a tone almost like admiration. "Maybe you should just put your mattress on the floor and sleep on it that way."

Strawberry's progress across the room was something majestic. When he set his feet on the floor, he seemed to swell like a thunderhead breaking off a cloudbank and gliding silent across the sky. Jerry did not hear his brother approach, but turned when the shadow fell across the wall. Finding Strawberry looming there, his birthmark scarlet with rage, his shoulders seeming to brush the ceiling, Jerry looked like a bass that has just gulped a tasty-looking morsel and found a hook in it.

Strawberry, however, did not raise his hand, and Jerry sidled from his path like a paper scrap before a whirlwind. Strawberry stood, his forehead against the damp prison wall, a few inches from Chastity's whitened fingers, and let the sound well and swell around him.

"He don't want you," Jerry insisted from a safe distance. "He knows all about you!"

"Tell her you love her, you can't live without her," Adam repeated.

Strawberry lifted his head to look at them with liquid eyes.

It was exactly what he wanted to tell her, but the mother who'd christened him with his wondrously accurate name had also endowed him with a heart that though tender, was proud, and that though slow to anger, was unbending once moved. What Strawberry could not say, however, Chastity could, and she left off crying to say, "I love you, Strawberry. I don't deserve someone good as you, but I know I don't. That ought to count for something."

"She's right," Larry said. "It ought to count."

"It ought to. Tell her you love her," Adam advised again. He disengaged himself from his metallic adversary. His shins were bruised and one forearm abraised, but he was otherwise unhurt. "Tell her you love her."

"I," Strawberry's voice was soft thunder, "I love you, Chastity." He closed his palm over her reaching fingers.

A moment of tender silence, and then Chastity added, "It was partly your fault, anyway. You should of took me to Gainesville with you."

"I know, I know," Strawberry said miserably, tears flooding down his face. "I'm sorry. I'm sorry."

Chastity's silence said she forgave him.

Timothy returned. "What is all this noise?" he asked.

"These two are in love of each other," Larry said, even though the real source of the commotion had been the wrestling matches of Adam versus Cot.

"This is the time to tell her you will always love her," Adam advised. "Lay the world at her feet. Nothing is too good for her."

"I love you, Chastity," Strawberry said. "I'll always love you." Adam had good reason to feel satisfied with the turn events were taking, but then they went on an unscheduled detour. "I want to," Strawberry said, " I want to marry you, Chastity."

"I want to marry you too," Chastity said joyously. And then, "Mr. Newman can marry us. He's a minister. He told me."

Before Adam could respond to this astonishing statement, Jerry said in outraged tones, "He ain't a minister."

"Did you get ordained?" Timothy asked, as if he'd known for quite some time Adam had been studying for the ministry.

"Are you a minister?" Larry asked.

"Well, I—"

Adam felt like the rider falling off a galloping horse—hanging midtopple after leaving the stirrups, as if the sunlight between him and the saddle could offer enough traction to grip him there, allowing him a moment of serene quiescence before he plunged headfirst over the mane.

Addison felt a similar plummeting sensation, except instead of a horse, he felt like he'd fallen off a Ferris wheel. He shot his father a glance that said, *Why did you tell her you were a minister?*

Adam's glance in return said, *I never said I was a minister. Who knows how she got that idea?* Then it added sheepishly, *Maybe I did say something about being a minister, I don't remember.* As glances go, Adam's were very talkative.

"He ain't a minister," Jerry maintained.

"He don't have his own church yet," Chastity admitted, "but he's already a minister. He gives out counseling and everything. He told me."

"Will you marry us?" Strawberry asked, turning to Adam with pleading eyes.

"Well, I, well," Adam temporized. "I need a Bible."

"We got a Bible," Larry offered. He reached into the darkness under Jerry's bed to retrieve a cardboard-bound copy left by the Gideons.

Adam looked to Timothy, expecting him to dissuade the parties involved, but Timothy surprised him. "I can get some forms—the justice of the peace office is right here too. You and your son can come with me to make sure you got everything we need to make it legal."

"He ain't a minister," Jerry repeated stubbornly from his bed. No one is more outraged by dishonesty unpunished than a rightly imprisoned villain. He'd lain down with his face to the wall, determined not to have any part in this, but no one listened to him.

Adam asked himself, after all, why not? Did being in jail require him to forego doing a good deed? Who better to perform a marriage ceremony? Evelyn would be glad to learn he had helped a couple setting sail on the journey of love. She'd want him to do at least this much. Think how proud she'd been when he'd helped the neighbors with their taxes—right up to the moment that black sedan from the revenue department pulled up. Adam rubbed his stubbly jaw. He had gone many hours without shaving. His body odor rose above the assorted smells of urine and fug mingled with the faint bristly odor of iron bars, which, Richard Lovelace to the contrary, no prison is complete without.

Timothy had everyone but the Newmans move to the back of the cell, and then escorted Adam and Addison out of the jail and into the upper levels of the building, which housed the courthouse with its rabbit warren of various offices, including the justice of the peace.

"I got a key to all these doors," Timothy said, proudly displaying a ring of shiny brass keys.

In the semidarkness of a stairwell shortly after they left the cell, Addison took Timothy's sleeve. "He can't do this," he whispered. "My father's not a minister."

"He's right," Adam concurred, nodding vigorously, "I'm not."

"I know he's not," Timothy said. They stopped midway

on the steps, their faces half in shadow, half in light. "It don't matter. A marriage is mostly just making sure there's witnesses. The state of Florida says they're legally married if they live together five years. Hell, if they jump over a broomstick, they're married. Besides, Jerry McIntyre don't want them married, and I'd like to give him something to stick in his damn pipe and smoke."

"He has a point there," Adam said, and Addison had to admit that the thought of giving Jerry something to smoke in his damn pipe was an attractive one, so with a nod he consented to admit no impediment to the marriage of true minds, and they went up to the office of the justice of the peace.

"I want to make a phone call," Adam announced.

"You waived that," Timothy said.

"I wish to unwaive it," Adam said. Timothy shrugged. There was a phone in the justice of the peace office, and Timothy let him use it.

"Yes, 'That's Amore,'" Adam said into the receiver. "Send it out to Evelyn."

"I didn't expect you to call a radio station," Timothy said after Adam hung up.

"A phone call's a phone call," Adam replied with unanswerable logic.

Adam, who was an expert searcher, found the certificates in a manila folder in a file cabinet under *M* for "marriage." They took two copies in case they messed up the first one and returned to the cell.

"What should I say?" Adam stopped and asked Addison before they reached the cells. "As far as I can remember, I've never done a marriage before."

Addison paused to consider this. Unlike his father, he'd never even been in a wedding, but as a writer, he felt he could supply the requisite touch of verisimilitude. "Get them to join hands. Say something with God and love in it. It doesn't have to be long. In fact, the shorter, the better. In fact, that's the main thing. Keep it short. Then you do the vows. Ask them if they take each other in sickness and in health, and like that. Then pronounce them man and wife. Oh, and Strawberry should put a ring on her."

Adam ticked off Addison's prudent list on his fingers, "Hands. God. Love. Sickness. Health. Ring. Got it."

"And ask if there's any objections," Timothy added.

"Check," Adam said.

When they got to the cell, Adam told the couple to join hands, and by Strawberry reaching through the bars toward the girls' cell, and Chastity reaching toward the boys', they were able to do it.

Addison stood by observing his father's method. Jerry, lying on his cot, pretended to snore. Adam ignored him and turned pages in the Bible. Fortunately, his sojourn at Sisters of Mercy had left him with an enviable amount of scriptural knowledge. He recalled an apropos passage in First John he'd once incorporated into a love poem to Evelyn. At last he found it and declaimed triumphantly, "'Beloved, let us love one another; for love is of God, and everyone that loveth is born of God and knoweth God. He that loveth not, knoweth not God, for God is love.'"

There are times in a speaker's life when he knows he has brought home the bacon. There, he says to himself, that's the stuff; this is how Adam felt now. He exchanged a glance with Addison, and Addison gave an approving nod.

"It doesn't say God created love," Adam explained, "or wants love, or approves of love, or even that God loves us. It says God *is* love. God is made out of love in the same way a dog is made out of dog meat. So when we are in the presence of love, we are in the presence of God. Now think about that for a minute." They thought about it, and Adam searched his mind for something to add, and when he discovered he didn't have anything, said, "Now do you, Strawberry, take this woman to be your lawful wedded wife? To have and to hold, in sickness and in health, for richer or poorer, for better or worse, as long as you both shall live?"

Strawberry's cheek was pressed to the wall, but he managed to give a lopsided, "I do."

"And do you, Chastity, take this man to be your wedded husband? To have and to hold, in sickness and in health, for richer or poorer, as long as you both shall live?"

"I do."

"And for better or worse?" Adam realized he'd forgotten that part.

"I do."

"Strawberry, do you have a ring?"

"No, sir."

"Use my Masonic ring," Adam said, slipping it from his finger.

"Man, I always wanted to be a Mason," Timothy said. Adam was not really a Mason, either, although he had on occasion pretended to be. He had won the ring in a bet.

"Is there anyone," Adam asked, "who knows just cause why these two should not be wed?"

"I think that part is supposed to come earlier," Timothy said.

"I was wrong what I said before." Chastity added an unexpected ad lib to the service. "I think maybe your wife will take you back, Mr. Newman."

"Thank you, Chastity. I now pronounce you man and wife," Adam said.

"You are all as dumb as a' ox," Jerry grumbled. "He ain't no minister."

In the jail, following the immediate glamour of the wedding ceremony itself, a mood compounded from anxiety, boredom, and buyer's remorse settled upon Strawberry. He continued smiling, if anything he smiled more—the adamant smile of the bluffer who wants you to believe he has an excellent hand and is—yes!—supremely confident, but all along is hideously conscious that he holds only a pair of twos and suspects you know it also. Adam could not see into the adjoining cell, but he assumed that within it, Chastity was undergoing similar emotions.

"Don't worry, Strawberry," Adam consoled him. "I can see you're having second thoughts."

"I ain't having second thoughts," Strawberry lied. He sat on the edge of his cot with his hands between his knees like a truant boy waiting to see the Mother Superior. "I feel great. It's just this durn jail is all. I love you, honey!" he shouted. To the first few such shouts, Chastity had replied in kind, but more recently Strawberry had been answered only by his own echo.

"He's not a real minister, you know," Jerry's defiant voice filled the silence.

"Bless him," Adam said benignly, making a cross in the air that would have accommodated a six-legged Jesus.

"It's perfectly natural," Addison told Strawberry, "to get cold feet after the ceremony."

"You know what the Bible says?" Adam asked. "'He who finds a wife, finds a good thing.' Now, what do you think of that? And I fully endorse your tactic of reminding her you love her every ten minutes or so. Saying you love a woman is like voting; it should be done early and often. I always used to—" Adam realized he was speaking in the past tense and corrected himself, "I always tell my wife I love her first thing in the morning. That way I get it out of the way and have the rest of the day free to do as I like."

Adam sought words to paint Strawberry a picture of wedded joy: staying late in bed on Sunday amid breakfast remains with the unfinished coffee cooling in cups on the nightstand along with the residue of scrambled eggs and grits. But Adam didn't know how to convey the mingled sensations of warmth and pleasure with Charley the beagle or possibly spaniel curled in rumpled sheets between your legs, lying in your sweetheart's arms, finishing the last triangle of buttered toast as she softly blows on your bald spot, tickling and rousing the delicate hairs with her breath.

"Your mother's here for you," Timothy said, coming down the hallway.

Adam's eyes smarted and he patted his pocket, and taking a cigarette, he checked his watch, which he still had not wound. Adam decided that since Addison was leaving, he might as well call Lily to get him too. There were no windows in the cell, but feeling it was morning renewed hope. He laid a hand on Strawberry's shoulder. "Joy cometh in the morning," he said, quoting the Bible.

"Well, not in this case," said Deputy Dooley, who appeared at the cell door next to a shamefaced Timothy. "In this case what cometh in the morning is the judge. For you, anyway."

# TEN

# Adam Goes to a Hearing

The sun cast its light upon the just and the unjust alike. It lit up the formerly brick streets of the square, awoke the mourning doves in the cornices of buildings, who sang *too-too, too-too-too*, and the cardinals, who sang *pretty-pretty-pretty, sweet-sweet-sweet*, on fence rails. It sent palmetto bugs scuttling under the dried fronds and roused the Old Anchises Boar himself, who lolled on his side and blinked benignly with his one good eye at cumulous clouds rolling in. A marsh rabbit, as marsh rabbits sometimes do, took a few steps on its hind legs to peer over the cattails at something in the marsh.

Meanwhile in a three-bedroom, two-bath stucco on Ponce de Leon Place, the percolator, set on a timer, gurgled and coughed, the cue for the morning routine. Addison, home from jail, put on a pot of water for grits and laid six strips of bacon in a skillet. He planned on eggs, grits, bacon, and fresh orange juice. He also planned on some sliced hothouse tomatoes to go with it. He needed fuel for a busy day ahead.

Usually Addison fell asleep imagining scenarios that threw him and Kathleen together, making her see him in a new and favorable light. Some brutish Lothario forced unwelcome attentions, and Addison landed the punch that felled him. Addison asked no thanks, merely showed the tenderest concern as he took Kathleen's hand to lead her from the scene, her head on his chest as she gazed with melting gratitude into his eyes. At a key juncture, he would take her chin in his fingers and tip her head upward; he would lower his lips almost to hers; there would be a moment's pause, and they would kiss.

Even in Addison's fantasy, it was difficult imagining how she could contrive to hold his hand, rest her head on his chest, and gaze meltingly into his eyes as he simultaneously tipped her head up to meet his lips, but it seemed indispensable for these things to happen together. Or else Addison, now a famous author, would spot her among the admirers waiting to have books autographed, and he would thrill her with an inscription disclosing his feelings' unsuspected depths. Some nights he lay awake an hour or more redrafting exactly what he would write in her book should the chance arise.

Spending the night in the pokey, however, leaves little time for such pleasant imaginings.

Likewise, Addison had to forego his usual morning daydream of cinching a hemp rope securely around his throat, an ample length of heavy coil hanging loose behind his back to ensure a good neck-breaking drop when he kicked the step stool from under his feet. Instead, he thought only of his father's pending commitment hearing.

Kean entered, white gauze affixed to a shaven spot on the back of his head.

"Hey, kiddo," Kean said and put three eggs in the pot of

water Addison had intended for grits. Addison's lips tightened. For two brothers who had been virtually raised in a kitchen, as Addison and Kean had, cooking was like playing jazz: improvisation was welcome, but there were limits. If the trumpet led off with "Beale Street Blues," he did not expect the clarinet to jump in with Chopin's "Nocturne in E." Kean couldn't have overlooked the bacon already turning translucent in the skillet, so starting soft-boiled eggs was a deliberate affront. Bacon meant fried eggs. Now there wouldn't be grits. Or tomatoes. Who would eat a tomato with a soft-boiled egg?

Their mother came in wearing the dress she'd had on when she'd picked up Addison at the jail. She didn't acknowledge Addison and Kean except to look over their shoulders at the stove and begin buttering three slices of bread for the broiler. Then she went through her morning routine almost—*almost*—as if her sons weren't there. There was no mistaking that she might be making coffee with them or for them—she was definitely making it *at* them. Seldom had coffee been poured in a manner of such unspoken rebuke. She gave her reflection in the percolator a stare as stern as any stare ever was, and her pouring possessed an unspeakable vigor; had it been possible, she would have squeezed the coffee out by hand, crushing the percolator like a grapefruit. When she set the coffeepot on the counter, she did so with an audible thunk.

"Mother," Addison asked, "are you angry?"

Evelyn Newman always drank coffee black and without sugar—but today even the color and lack of sweetening seemed fraught with intent, and when she took a sip, it was a sip of fury, as if to say, *I don't care where you were last night or what you did, nothing's coming between me and enjoying my damn cup of coffee.*

Addison asked again, "Are you angry, Mother?"

Evelyn took another sip and got out oranges to squeeze for juice. She looked up from the juicer, however, before Kean had time to spoon the hot eggs into cups, evidently having reconsidered her policy of silence. "When you said you were taking your father to his jeep, it was with the understanding that you were headed straight home. Then at the hospital, you really should have stayed. You had a responsibility to make sure Kean was all right." She did not allude to picking Addison up at the jail.

Evelyn had suffered a series of unpleasant surprises, thanks to her ex-husband. Shortly after she'd gotten Addison home, the clock radio had come on with the maniacal strumming of mandolins, and a chorus singing, *In Napoli, where love is king*, before Dean Martin broke in with "That's Amore." In spite of herself, she'd smiled; that song had always made her feel better. Hearing the lyrics they had sung together so many times in the old restaurant, she momentarily forgot the jail, the divorce, Lily Manzana, and everything, and looked at the bed to see if Adam heard it too. Too late she remembered that her bed was Adam-less—and had been Adam-less for a long time and for very good reason. She felt disappointment at not finding him there, and then righteous indignation at the way he'd tricked her into wanting to find him there.

Evelyn breathed an irritated, "Well."

The orange rinds and coffee grounds were dropped in a bucket on the counter as a later repast for the worms, and Addison set out plates. Kean laid two strips of bacon, a slice of buttered toast cut into pirate hats, and an egg cup on each one. Evelyn set hers on a wicker tray along with her coffee and orange juice and commanded, "When you're done, put your eggshells in the worm bucket. I'm eating mine on the back porch." It was not an invitation to join her.

The brothers put their plates on the kitchen table, and Kean whacked off the top of his egg with a butter knife. "We were worried about you," he said. "Mother nearly called the police."

"I heard," Addison said. It seemed unfair to Addison that he should bear the brunt of his mother's anger, when it was his father who had been the efficient cause behind everything. For some reason, Adam Newman seemed to get a free ride for misdeeds.

"I had a mild concussion," Kean said in case Addison had not heard Kean's diagnosis confirmed. "I had to get three stitches." He ate a spoonful of egg white and pretended to read the front page of *The Sentinel* before he asked, "So what were you and Adam doing?" He didn't raise his eyes from the page.

"Well, to tell you the truth, we were chasing stolen diamonds."

This brought Kean's eyes up, but then he decided Addison was joking and looked back down, but then he decided he wasn't joking and looked up again, but then he decided not to show any interest and looked down again.

"And," Addison said after a sip of orange juice, "we were tracking down a Communist front."

This further revelation could not make Kean raise his eyes again. If Marilyn Monroe had stood on the table in a swimsuit and high heels hoarsely singing, "Happy Birthday, Mr. President," it would not have kept Kean from staring at the little weather box on the front page with its picture of a smiling sun wearing a knit cap and sunglasses. *Sunny and cold. High tide at 4:30.* Imagine that, four-thirty. He dipped the corner of his toast in the yellow and tasted it. "Later can you take me to get my motorcycle?" Kean asked, turning to page two.

Officer Dooley had set the wheels in motion for a commitment hearing. Adam's lawyer Bucky O'Leary met Lily and Adam in the old Greek Revival courthouse next to the new annex.

"I don't think it will amount to much," Bucky said. "From what I gather, this is an officious officer raising a big fuss about nothing. Your record didn't help matters, of course," Bucky flipped the pages inside a manila folder and read from a list of previous charges, "drunk, drunk and disorderly, drunk, driving under the influence, drunk."

Lily sat beside Adam and held his hand. Her expression was hard to read: bright-eyed concentration that might have been alarm or might have been something else. They sat at a scarred wooden table in a small and musty room—the sole window had been painted shut.

"But, thank the Lord," Bucky said, "the distance between being drunk and being certifiable is broad and spacious. Your previous visit to Chattahoochee is going to come out. We'll make sure the judge knows that was voluntary. Also a Dr. Dewberry is here from Chattahoochee—he was your—uh—doctor before, wasn't he, Adam?" Bucky tapped the folder's edge on the table, straightening the papers inside. "So how are you, Adam?"

"I have a hell of a headache," Adam said, "but other than that, not too bad. So what are the chances commitment will rear its ugly head?"

Bucky's eyes half closed and he shook his head. "Slim to none, I'd say." Bucky O'Leary cut a distinguished figure in a charcoal gray suit and with prematurely gray hair that he kept unparted and combed straight back. When he was feeling particularly lawyerly and confident, Bucky had a habit of twisting the white hairs of his left eyebrow between his thumb and forefinger. He twisted his eyebrow now. "Dooley is an officer of the law, but that hardly makes him a head-shrinker. Unfortunately," Bucky's voice became solemn, "Florida's still behind the times about this stuff. Other states, you'd have to endanger yourself or others to be committed, but here they only need three affidavits plus a judge's say-so. Right now there's an affidavit from Deputy Dooley, of course, and one from another doctor, Dr. Bateman—isn't he your GP, Adam? I have no idea how the court got hold of that one." Adam didn't have any idea either. He looked at Lily, but her attention was absorbed by a nick in her fingernail polish. "Anyhoo, they're still one short, but even if this Dr. Dewberry signs too, Judge Carmichael's pretty sure to swing our way, I think.

"You did bring him a change of clothes like I asked you?" Bucky asked, turning to Lily.

Lily held up a burgundy garment bag. "I brought his wing tips, his best pinstripe, a good white shirt, and a silk tie. I thought that would be most suitable."

"Suitable as all get-out." Bucky laughed. "You're going to look better than your lawyer," he joked with Adam. "Also some mouthwash, a razor, and shaving cream?"

"They are in a little compartment in the side. I put them in a separate zippered container so the contents wouldn't stain the clothes."

"Jim Dandy," Bucky said. Then he spoke to Adam again, "Hold out your hands." Adam did so. "A little shaky, huh?" Bucky snapped open his briefcase, and Adam's heart leapt up to behold a whiskey fifth in his hand. "I poured most of it out before I came," Bucky explained as he passed it to Adam with a moist pink hand. "I want you steady in there, not petrified, but you can have a little taste before you get dressed. You have time to change and freshen up a little in the men's room. The hearing is in room one-oh-five. We'll see you there in about ten minutes."

In the men's room, Adam downed the whiskey and dropped the empty in the trash, where it landed with an echoey thud. It was an old-fashioned restroom with a dark wooden door that had a porcelain knob and MEN stenciled on opaque glass. Slightly uneven black and white tiles covered the floor, and an invisible soap-smelling fog of decades of legal discussions and back-room bargains filled the air. Sanguine after a gratifying Jack-flavored belch, Adam stripped his shirt, ran hot water in a sink, and lathered his face. Good old Bucky will take care of everything, he told himself as he drew the razor down his cheek, leaving a swath of pink skin amid the foam. Soon he would be released. He would find the diamonds. Evelyn would take him back. He began to sing "That's Amore." The walls returned his baritone voice to him and he paused amid strokes of his razor to savor the notes, "that's ah-more-hore-ay!"

No friend is more loyal, true-blue, stalwart, trustworthy, or dependable than a man's lawyer, Adam reflected as he looked in the mirror.

After shaving, Adam stepped into a stall and locked the door to change his clothes. He had his pants on and was tucking his shirttail in his boxers when the bathroom door opened and two others came in. He had reached the part where "the stars make you drool just like pasta fazool," and dropped into silence.

"I tell you," a voice said, "I've reached the end of my last up-to-here with those dang Murchinsons."

"I know what you mean, brother," said another voice. "I

thought 'divorce case,' piece of cake. Huh! Well, that'll teach me."

Twin streams of urine sounded against porcelain, and Adam hummed softly. He pulled on his jacket and stepped into his shoes. One urinal flushed and then another. Adam put his dirty clothes into the garment bag and zipped it.

"You and me racked our brains to the bone ironing out every piece of property with a fine-toothed magnifying glass, but this damn custody thing is the last straw."

Adam stepped from the stall. The two men stood with their backs to him washing up. The bottoms of their jackets parted in upside-down V's over expansive butts. Adam joined them and began knotting his tie in the mirror.

"Hey, it's Adam!" said the short fat one.

"Adam!" said the tall fat one happily.

"Hello!" Adam said heartily, feigning recognition.

"Bob Rio," the short one said, "and this is Bob Hambrick. We met at the Twilight Room that time. You showed us that great magic trick." They smelled of cigar smoke and too much cologne, but Adam couldn't tell who smelled like which.

"Of course!" Adam snapped his fingers as if he recalled. "So y'all are on opposite sides of a divorce, I take it."

"It's this dang custody battle," Rio said.

"Snuffy!" Hambrick said in exasperation.

"Snuffy!" repeated Rio.

Adam could not forbear making comment. "Good Lord, what manner of parent would name a child Snuffy?"

"Snuffy isn't a child," explained Hambrick, turning toward Adam and flicking water from his fingers. "It's a dog."

"They are fighting over custody of a dog?"

"A golden retriever," Rio said in a disgusted voice. He shook his head like one who has looked to the depths of the human soul and not liked what he beheld. "It's just spite.

It's a case of monkey-see, monkey-doing the devil's workshop."

"That's exactly it," Hambrick agreed. "You know what we ought to do?" He turned to his colleague. "Go out and just get lunch. Leave them here and let them stew in their own prunes."

"By golly, you're right. I'm tired of wasting my time on this stupid settlement. We'll come back when we're good and ready. See how they like them chickens. Do you want to come with us, Adam?"

"I'd love to, fellas, but I've got a hearing of my own in a few minutes. I'll have to take a rain check."

The two lawyers exited, leaving Adam smelling of lawyerly cigar and cologne in their wake. Adam finished putting a voluptuously plump knot in his tie and rinsed his face a final time, then took a good mouthful of Listerine and swirled it around to get rid of his whiskey breath. He stepped back and examined himself in the mirror. He looked pretty sharp, if he said so himself. There was a slight swelling in his lip, and his eyes were red and baggy, but his pinstripe fell perfectly over his shoulders, and his shirt front was crisp with starch; he looked like a prosperous albeit somewhat overworked attorney. Having completed his ablutions, he stepped into the hallway.

Adam had more difficulty locating his room than he had anticipated. Had Bucky said 115 or 511? The courthouse was only four stories, so unless they were holding the hearing on the roof, it couldn't possibly be 511, Adam reasoned. The notion that they might be up in a belfry looking for bats made him chuckle. That was a good one; he'd have to share it with Bucky.

But in the meantime, where was Bucky? If it wasn't 511, it had to be 115, but the doors in the hallway only went as high as 110. Adam was sure the room number had a one or a zero in it somewhere. It didn't help matters that all the doors were identical: dark wood panels with a pane of frosted glass and a stenciled number. Adam tried the door of 110, but it was only a room similar to the one in which he'd met with Lily and Bucky. A couple looked from staring coldly at each other long enough to stare coldly at Adam.

"Excuse me," Adam said, and closed the door.

A young man came down the hallway, his shoe sounds reverberating from the dark-stained doors. "Pardon me," Adam began, but before he could ask where the commitment hearing was, the young man spoke.

"Are you Judge Crater?" Adam said he was not. "The guys told me to go find Judge Crater," the young man said miserably. "They said it was urgent." He stared at his shoes. "This is my first week, but I never heard of a Judge Crater in this building, have you?" Adam admitted he was a stranger there himself, and the young man said, "I thought you worked here. Yesterday they told me to bring back the Snipe files down from the fifth floor."

"There is no fifth floor," Adam said.

"I know that," the young man said morosely. "Now." And he was off to find his judge.

Adam reconsidered retrying room 110. Although he'd lived in fear for some time lest the dread weight of involuntary commitment descend upon him and compel him to give up his shoelaces and paint alligators, Adam had never actually attended such a hearing, either his own or anyone else's. He knew it wasn't held in a regular courtroom, but he had no idea how the setting would appear. Was it possible that room 110 was the right room and Adam had arrived before Bucky and Lily? Perhaps the young couple was finishing up some previous business. Perhaps they were court functionaries required to attend.

Adam cracked the door experimentally and asked, "Is anyone in here expecting me?"

"We're waiting for our lawyers to come back," said the man through gritted teeth.

"You must be the Murchinsons," Adam said.

"Do we know you?" asked Mrs. Murchinson.

"I've discussed your case with Bob," Adam said. "And Bob."

"You know our lawyers?" asked Mr. Murchinson.

"Well, in passing," Adam said, "from the bar." Adam mentally bit his tongue—it was indiscreet telling people their lawyers frequented the Twilight Room, but the couple showed no reaction. "I'm afraid your lawyers aren't returning anytime soon," he told them. "When I spoke to them, I believe they were heading to lunch."

"Perfect," said Mr. Murchinson, hitting the table with the flats of his hands.

"How do we wrap this thing up?" said Mrs. Murchinson. Then her head lifted at a thought, and she asked, "Have you ever handled a divorce?"

"Well, yes," Adam said, stroking his chin. Fresh from shaving, it was as smooth as glass. "A temporary one." Adam felt it odd that she said "handled" instead of "been through," and the Murchinsons were struck by the novelty of a *temporary* divorce, but nobody remarked.

"I don't suppose you could help us. Our own lawyers sure aren't doing us any good."

"Well," Adam temporized. Staying with this couple was not an appealing proposition; their mutual anger made the atmosphere as itchy as a wool blanket. What should Adam do? He couldn't just leave them here to—as their lawyers expressed it—stew in their own prunes, could he? Evelyn would want him to do something. "I've got to get to my own hearing in just a few minutes." He checked his watch and realized he still hadn't remembered to wind it. "Are you sure there's no hope of reconciliation?" Adam asked. Two pairs of frigid eyes gave him the answer to that one. Adam's mind hearkened back to the night of the french fries and his own temporary divorce from Evelyn; the sight of the decree had made his eyes burn, and putting his name to it had felt like signing a pact with the devil. He wished he could do something to save this romance, but of course he could not. The Murchinson's marriage was definitely on the rocks, a sad story, but a familiar one. Often it seemed the more lovey-dovey a couple were before a divorce, the more acrimonious they were during—as if every whispered *snookums-ookums* and *I wuv 'oo* required an equal and opposite quantity of slammed doors and thrown bric-a-brac. Adam shrugged. There was no sense beating a gift horse, he told himself, gratified to find he was thinking like a trained legal mind. "Perhaps I can do something to help out," he offered.

"Wait a minute," Mr. Murchinson said in a voice frosted with hostility. "What do you charge?"

"Why, nothing," Adam said, nonplussed that they'd expect him to want money.

"I don't know what you think he can accomplish," Mr. Murchinson told his ex.

"Will you just let him work?" retorted the woman.

Adam reflected sadly that if only he had met this couple earlier and taught them to say "Praise Jesus" while they were still married, all this might have been averted. But that was water under a burned bridge, and there was no point crying over it. "My name is Adam Newman." He reached across the table to shake hands.

"Robert," said the man.

"Sally," said the woman.

To preserve his impartiality, Adam elected not to sit beside either one, and instead paced the perimeter like Nigel Rathbone gathering clues as Sherlock Holmes. "So tell me the particulars of this case. When and under what circumstances did you acquire deed to the disputed canine?" At the end of the room Adam paused at the window. He pried the dusty blinds apart with his index and middle fingers and peered through the fly-specked panes. A blue Volkswagen that looked like Addison's pulled into a parking place.

"I bought it," Robert said.

"Ah!" said Adam, but before he could pronounce a summary judgment, the missus broke in.

"But I take care of him," Sally said. "I feed him, water him, bathe him, take him to the vet. I housebroke him."

"Ah!" said Adam again.

"What do you mean by that?" Robert asked suspiciously.

"Nothing, just 'ah!' "

"I bought it," Robert said.

"I love him," Sally said.

The Volkswagen parked askew, its rear bumper overlapping the white line. It was Addison! Adam pulled at the strings to raise the blinds so he could signal his son, but only succeeded in heaving up one side.

"I bought it," Robert repeated. This seemed his answer to everything. Adam was beginning to decide he did not care for Robert.

"How old is Snuffy?" Adam asked. He pulled the strings again, and this time both sides of the blinds went up, but when he let go, they dropped with a bang.

Robert's brow furrowed, and he seemed to be working out Snuffy's age in his head. "Seven years," Sally supplied.

"Interesting," said Adam. "The life expectancy of a golden retriever is fourteen years. Barring car accidents." Adam raised the blinds again and gave the strings a sideways jerk to lock them in place, but only succeeded in pulling the right side of the assembly off its bracket. Now the blinds hung lopsided in the window frame, unmoored at one corner.

"Excuse me," he said. He took the chair next to Sally and put it under the window. Unfortunately, while mounting the chair to replace the blinds in the bracket, he lost his balance. He seized the blinds on his way down, and there was a terrific crash as chair, blinds, and Adam hit the floor.

"I'm okay," his voice emerged from below. Adam rose with as much dignity as he could muster and wrapped the strings around the blinds. He set the whole mess on the windowsill and brushed bits of plaster and dust from his coat. He removed a fly's desiccated corpse from his ear. Addison was no longer in sight, no doubt on his way inside. Adam pulled up the chair and took a well-deserved seat after his ordeal.

In a moment he had collected himself again. He put his elbows on the table and steepled his fingers under the tip of his nose. "You, sir, are in the position of a property owner, having clear title to the canine without liens or quits." The smell of plaster on his fingertips elicited a noisy sneeze. "There is no mortgage on the dog, I presume?"

"What?"

"I didn't think so," said Adam. "Your wife has had full access and benefit of the dog's use, and has also maintained the dog and provided for reasonable upkeep and repair. Unless, ma'am, you have a lease or some sort of signed document, you are in the position of what we call a squatter."

"So Snuffy's mine," said Robert, beginning to feel satisfied with where this was heading.

"Well, not necessarily," Adam corrected. "A squatter assumes ownership of any property if he or she has occupied it for ten years without a challenge by the owner."

"But Snuffy's only seven years old," Robert pointed out triumphantly.

"This is true," Adam conceded, "but a single dog year is the equivalent of *seven* human years."

"Oh, this is stupid!" Robert said impatiently.

"You're just sore because he wants to give Snuffy to me," said Sally.

"Not so fast, not so fast," Adam said. He did want to give Snuffy to Sally, but he felt it impolitic of her to say so. He foresaw a perfectly good divorce heading off the rails unless he acted promptly. It was no good proposing a solution unless Sally and Robert both agreed. "This predicament is more glutinous than most, but I'm sure there's a solution. King Solomon would suggest cutting Snuffy in half, which might work here, except you both probably know that gag already and won't fall for it." Adam laced his fingers behind his head and stared at a rabbit-shaped crack in the ceiling. "What we'll do . . ." His voice trailed off as he realized he couldn't think of what to do. Lawyering was harder than he'd imagined, and he felt more respect than ever for his friend Bucky. Then it came to him. "What we'll do is switch."

"What do you mean 'switch?'" Sally asked suspiciously.

"For the last seven years you've owned the dog," he pointed to Robert, "and you, dear," he pointed to Sally, "took care of it. Well, for the next seven years," Adam was still talking to the woman, "*you'll* own the dog."

"That's crazy," Robert said. "I'm not giving up Snuffy."

"But there's something in it for you too," Adam said mildly as he began to see the elegance of his own plan. "For the last seven years your wife got full use of Snuffy. For the next seven years, you will. You'll get to feed him, water him, bathe him. Walk him, take him to the vet. The works."

"I'm not taking care of someone else's pet!"

"I'm talking unlimited access here," Adam pointed out. "You can comb out his fur, trim his toenails, feed him peanut butter, anything you like."

"I'm not doing it."

"Don't be hasty," Adam advised. "We all say things in the heat of the moment. I'm sure in the fullness of time when emotions cool, you'll see things differently."

"I won't."

"You absolutely don't want to take care of this dog? You're sure you're not going to change your mind?"

"Hell, no!" Robert was adamant.

"You're sure? You absolutely refuse to look after Snuffy?"

"I do."

"Well." Adam looked down at his hands a moment in consternation. "This is a real poser." He blew out air, vibrating his lips, then looked hopefully at the former Mrs. Murchinson. "Will you take care of Snuffy?"

"Of course," she said.

"Whew! Thank goodness," Adam said, pushing back his chair. "Of course that means he'll have to stay with you. I'm glad we settled that." He rolled his eyes as he shook Robert's hand, as if to say, *We dodged that bullet, didn't we?* And then Adam left the room, leaving Robert Murchinson with the perplexed sensation he had been rendered one dog the less without knowing exactly how.

As Adam closed the door behind him, he saw his son, Addison.

"Dad," Addison said. "I was just on my way to your hearing. Room one-oh-five."

"Ah," said Adam. "It's here, then." And he opened the

door for them just across the hallway from the Murchinsons.

The mills of justice grind exceeding slow as a general rule, but there are certain times and places when they can be made to grind a good deal more briskly. Adam's commitment hearing was conducted with a speedy efficiency to make central Florida the envy of judicial systems everywhere. A semiretired county judge with an empty docket was inveighed upon to look over the case, and various witnesses compliantly showed up.

Bucky had just a few moments to confer with Addison and Adam before the judge arrived. Everyone sat around one long table—the courthouse seemed to be filled with such tables—Adam, Addison, Lily, Bucky, Deputy Dooley, and a man with wispy brown hair and heavy-framed glasses whom Adam recognized as Dr. Dewberry from Chattahoochee's sixth floor.

The door opened and a man who looked like an elderly Don Ameche entered. Bucky and Deputy Dooley rose, and the others started to follow suit, but Judge Carmichael—for it was he—gestured them to sit.

"You don't have to do that," he said. The judge was dressed not in a robe, but a herringbone jacket and a black bow tie. Carmichael sat at the head of the table and looked over some papers. He blew a long, noisy exhale. "So we're here to determine whether to commit. Okay." He looked at Adam over the tops of his glasses. "Are you Adam Newman?"

"Yes, sir."

"Right. I knew your father. My first job. He was a very good man." The judge looked back at the papers. "Sorry I'm late. I had some trouble finding the right room." The judge read and the room waited for him to speak again. "I sure am thirsty," he said at last.

There was another silence, and finally Dooley said, "I'll go get you a glass of water."

"That'd be great," Carmichael said, giving him a stiff smile.

The sheriff's deputy rose, and Addison noted that the shirt button just above his belt buckle was not undone as he'd expected, but as the officer left, they could see the white elastic band of his briefs where his pants sagged slightly in the rear. Judge Carmichael sighed and gave his head a half shake as he returned his gaze to the papers. "Okay, I have the deposition here from Dr. Bateman." He looked at Dewberry. "Is that you?"

"No, I'm Dr. Dewberry."

"Hmm." The utterance communicated that the judge held MD's in no great awe. Adam began to feel increasingly confident. Bucky twisted the hairs of one eyebrow between his thumb and forefinger.

"Your Honor," Bucky said, "I was wondering if my client's son could go ahead and give his deposition now. He has a part-time job at *The Sentinel* and he has to be there to do the obituaries."

Judge Carmichael took his glasses off and gave Addison a cool gaze. "You write obituaries for *The Sentinel*?"

"Yes, sir," Addison said.

"I'm familiar with your work," Carmichael said. He put his glasses back on and looked at his papers. "My aunt passed away last month. Perhaps you remember her: Nadge Carmichael, mother of flour?" Addison's face heated. "Very well, you can give your statement. I'm actually looking forward to it."

Mortified, Addison explained his father had gotten somewhat tipsy, and they'd pulled to the shoulder of the road beside the prairie so he could sleep it off.

"You can talk to me," the judge said. Addison had been looking at his father for silent confirmation that he hadn't strayed into a forbidden topic during his statement. "So what were you and your father doing with Miss Spratt in that section of town in the first place?"

"She was just riding with us after the hospital," Addison said, and realized he might have spoken not wisely but too soon.

The judge's eyebrows went up. "Why were you at the hospital?"

Having said as much as he had, there was no help for it but to explain about the bar fight and his brother's concussion, so Addison did so.

"You two had a busy night," the judge said, understating the matter by a wide margin. At this point Dooley returned with a glass of water. Judge Carmichael took a sip and said, "And you had gone to the Fish Camp because—?"

Had Addison possessed a speck of mental telepathy, he would have kept silent. Adam was shooting a silent warning at his son like water from a spray nozzle: *Don't say anything. You don't need an explanation for going to a bar. Just admit we went and leave it at that.* The Newman men, however, for all their many virtues, have no mental telepathy whatsoever, and Addison blundered ahead, "We were looking for my father's . . ." He subsided, with the sensation that he'd just waded hip-deep into lukewarm perleu.

"You were looking for your father's—?" prompted the judge.

Addison looked down and muttered an answer. The judge asked him to repeat himself, and Addison said, "We were looking for my father's diamonds. He'd lost a bag of diamonds."

Dooley smirked. Bucky stopped twisting his eyebrow. Unexpectedly Lily came to the rescue.

"I can explain that," she said.

"And you are?"

"His fiancée. We're to be betrothed the Sunday following Christmas. He obtained the diamonds for me yesterday morning. It was intended as a surprise," she said, pouting playfully. "But I had no idea it was an entire *bag*ful. Sweetie." She coiled her arm around Adam's and snuggled up to him briefly. Adam managed a weak smile and kissed her forehead.

"So Deputy Dooley, have you anything to add?" the judge asked, turning his attention to the officer, who sank a little lower in his chair. Carmichael pronounced the name to rhyme with "dippity-doo-dah."

As Dooley stumbled through his testimony, his face seemed to deflate. At last, having narrated to the end of what seemed more and more like an ordinary if somewhat humiliating roadside stop—the lowlight of which was being slapped by a girl—Dooley trailed off meekly with a, "And then he acted like he thought I wasn't really a deputy."

"Well, we're all entitled to our doubts," the judge said dryly. "Is this your first amicus motion?" the judge asked. The officer nodded. He looked like someone who'd just downed a glassful of spoiled milk. The judge gave a tight-lipped smile. "Well, this is very educational for you, I suppose. Now you see how we do things. So." He looked at Dr. Dewberry. "Well, Doctor, I'm afraid we've made you come a rather long way for this. Do you have anything to share? I understand Mr. Newman was under your care at Chattahoochee."

"Yes. Alcoholism." Dewberry took off his glasses and polished them with a handkerchief.

"That was purely voluntary, Your Honor," Bucky put in. Adam nodded; he had gone out of love for Evelyn, that reason and no other.

The judge acknowledged this with a curt glance, and

Dewberry went on, "He would definitely benefit from coming back to us."

"So you could cure him?"

"There is no cure for alcohol addiction," Dr. Dewberry said, "but coming to Chattahoochee would be an excellent place to start his recovery."

Adam's jaw tightened at having to sit quietly while someone accused him of being a drunk. Between Dewberry and Lily he was feeling cornered, like somebody's property, somebody's fiancé, somebody's patient, somebody's little boy you could dress up in funny-looking shorts and put on a train to Savannah. He wasn't sure how much he could take.

"But with all that, would you sign an affidavit that Mr. Newman is incompetent?"

"No." Dewberry examined his fingernails. "No. He's competent. He knows who he is, and he's not likely to hurt anybody. He can't control his drinking, but he knows the difference between real and not real. Now, on the other hand, if he showed signs of delusional belief—well, that'd be different."

"Delusional such as?"

"Oh, delusions of grandeur, conspiracy, persecution," Dewberry ticked off the top three.

"And if he had delusions, he might be dangerous."

"Oh, definitely. Delusional people can become quite hostile if you challenge their worldview, their belief that some conspiracy is out to get them."

"But Adam Newman shows no signs of delusions."

"None."

"And there we have it," Judge Carmichael said. "Well, Mr. Newman, it seems you are careless, irresponsible, and drunk, but probably not certifiable." The judge looked at the papers. "In your own words, what happened? How did you give this officer the impression you were—"

"Koo-koo crazy?" Adam asked breezily. Judge Carmichael was not one given to indulgent smiles, but there was a ghost of one on his lips as he looked at Adam. "It was really just a misunderstanding," Adam explained. "In retrospect I can see that claiming that Chastity Spratt was my daughter was imprudent, nor did the topic of missing diamonds win favor in the deputy's eyes." Something like amusement ran around the table. Addison breathed more confidently. Deputy Dooley's face, which has already been described as deflated, appeared nearly flattened. Bucky twisted his eyebrow between his thumb and forefinger. "I can explain to you the rest of my behavior, but I really have to do so in private."

"I beg your pardon?" the judge asked.

"I can explain everything," Adam said, "but it needs to be just the two of us."

Bucky had stopped twisting his eyebrow. "Adam, I think you need your lawy—"

"No, it's okay, Bucky. The judge is a friend of the family. This is for his ears only."

A strained silence followed. The judge nodded, and the others filed from the room. When the door had closed, the judge asked, "So what is this about?"

"I'm telling you this because I know I can trust you," Adam said. The judge looked somewhat surprised and Adam began to explain. "It all started several years ago when I noticed someone was buying up these huge tracts of land for something called the Venezuela Project. Naturally I assumed it was the barge canal."

"For Venezuela?"

"No, Florida," Adam corrected. "The government was covering their tracks pretty well, and I guess you can't blame them, what with Fidel Castro and everything, but then, there was this other group, Compass East. This is where the Reds come in."

"The Reds?" At the mention of Reds, a glimmer of alarm appeared in Carmichael's eye.

"Yes, and here's the funny thing." Adam permitted himself a chuckle at the misconceptions one is apt to form sometimes, "When Deputy Dooley picked us up, at the time I thought we had been abducted by Communists. Of course I felt dreadfully silly about it afterwards," Adam hastened to add, "but if you put yourself in my shoes, you'll see it was a perfectly understandable mistake. It seemed too much of a coincidence. I mean, picking us up right when we were staking out their headquarters."

Adam would scarcely have credited the speed with which Carmichael's expression changed. A moment ago, he'd been listening with a judicial blend of alertness and calm; now, although Adam was speaking perfectly sensibly and saying nothing but the unvarnished truth, the judge looked as if Adam had stuck straw in his hair and started strumming his lips with a finger and going *dblb-dblb-dblb-dblb-dblb.*

"Of course," the judge said, rising from his chair, not taking his eyes from Adam's, "perfectly natural. You probably thought he was with the Venezuelans."

"There aren't any Venezuelans," Adam protested. "It's probably the Cubans."

"Just as you say, Mr. Newman," the judge said, sidling toward the wall. "Sidling" was the only word for it. "I'm going to step out in the hallway for just a second, and—"

"You can't tell them about it," Adam warned. "This is national security."

"Right, right, right, right," the judge said, holding a shaky finger to his lips. "Hush-hush. I just want to step out and get a glass of water."

"You already have a glass of water," Adam pointed out. The judge started and gave the water a look, as Macbeth might, seeing Banquo's ghost show up just as the haggis was being dished out. The judge continued his sidling, and sensing something was ganging terribly a-gley, Adam began speaking faster. "It's all tied together, you see? The canal, the interstate, the railroad . . ."

"Nevertheless," the judge said, easing past Adam toward the door, "I think I'll step into the hallway for just a sec—"

Adam grabbed Carmichael's sleeve, and the judge gave a little hop and a squeal. "But there's more. There's this thing called the Experimental Prototype."

There are moments upon which, even if one is unaware, the entire universe pivots: what is heading up turns down, good becomes bad, sweet goes sour—in short, everything gets bungled. One instant the air is so thick with bonhomie you could cut it with a knife, and the next instant the specter of doom lurks in and pulls a stinker. Such a moment took place in Adam's childhood when he stole into his father's study: the air outside heavy with a coming thunderstorm, the room smelling of pipe tobacco and leather, a mahogany gun case in the bottom drawer of the rolltop desk. Another moment had been when he was making himself french fries late one night: slicing potato wedges on the scarred wooden cutting board, a white iceberg of Crisco melting to clear liquid in a cast-iron skillet on the stove, crickets chirruping beyond the black panes of the kitchen window.

At the time these experiences had seemed unremarkable, but the details were to be etched vividly in Adam's memory ever after.

This was another such moment.

# ELEVEN

# Adam Goes to the Sixth Floor

If your only information source were TV shows and movies, you might imagine Chattahoochee's sixth floor would be full of patients mumbling throatily, picking invisible flowers from the wallpaper. This was not the case; except for one very old man, all the patients could have told you precisely who and where they were. If anything, they seemed on the whole healthier than patients on the other floors, although one had gauze bandages on his wrists; if you were observant, however, you might notice none of them had shaved recently or wore belts or shoelaces.

"What I regret most is the little things," Adam told a new friend in tones of one who too late learns a painful lesson. They painted alligators at a long white-papered table. Adam twirled the wet brush tip under his nose; the chalky smell was oddly reassuring.

"Ah," said Adam's friend understandingly. Adam's friend painted orange and green racing stripes on his alligator while Adam applied a checkerboard pattern to his. Michael, the youngest person on the floor, sat on a stool, his paintbrush dry and unused before him. That morning an angel of the Lord had informed him that alligators are an abomination.

"What I'd give to hear her tell me about her earthworms once more," Adam said. Now that his life was thoroughly and utterly bungled, he understood what was truly important. The first morning after their honeymoon when Evelyn had brought up the digestive habits of earthworms, Adam murmured politely and sipped his coffee to hide a repulsed grimace. As years rolled over the Newman household, however, it became evident that earthworms were of more than momentary interest to Adam's bride, and indeed formed the leitmotif of her breakfast-table conversation. Apart from issues surrounding the restaurant itself such as recipes for chili sauce and sweet relish, it was earthworms in their many aspects—earthworms in frolic, earthworms in repose, earthworms in sickness and health—that provided the bulk of Evelyn's conversational material. Throughout Adam stoically maintained a policy of feigned interest and concealed disgust; too late he understood the opportunity he'd lost.

When Evelyn talked about earthworms, she had been saying, *I love you.*

What else could it mean except *I love you, I love you, I love you?* What could be more private, more intimate, more tender, than to talk of earthworms to your darling? What spoke more sincerely of complete contentment and ease with another soul? Indeed, to whisper, "The number of earthworms in an untilled field ranges upward of ten per cubic foot," made ordinary pillow talk seem like tepid bus stop chitchat by comparison.

This is what Adam confided in his friend as they painted their alligators.

"Gee," said Adam's friend, stippling a five-o'clock shadow

on his alligator. Orange flecked an admirably bushy eyebrow; neither Evelyn nor Lily would have permitted his own to get that full, Adam thought wistfully. A beard concealed his friend's face like a gray and black bandanna, but his eyebrows had a repertoire of raising, lowering, pursing, and cocking to express an encyclopedic emotional range. Adam's friend said little, but he freighted every utterance with more genuine understanding than others squeezed into hours of sympathetic gab.

Adam began painting long lashes around his alligator's eyes.

Years ago someone had donated a veritable warehouse of unpainted ceramic alligators, so in addition to everything else, the sixth floor provided occupational therapy. A young lady named Beatrice who always smelled pleasingly of hand lotion came after breakfast to supervise the painting of the alligators, which she took away in a cardboard box and brought back the next day fired to a glossy sheen. Dr. Dewberry—who had never had a very good French teacher—thought of this as his "*piece of resistance.*" His patients returned to their families, not only mentally healthier, but bearing objects of ornamental art, for these items were theirs to keep. *See that lovely alligator on the mantel? My husband painted that for me at Chattahoochee.*

Donnie, one of the orderlies, brought in the box of alligators from the previous day's firing. He smiled shyly at Beatrice as he set them down, and Adam detected a light in Beatrice's eyes. He pondered this, then stared at Beatrice speculatively, his head tilted. She looked at him apprehensively, and Adam dropped his gaze. Then he looked up again and said softly, "I guess you do."

Beatrice looked suspiciously at Adam. "What?"

"Well," Adam said. "Just a second. Turn your head just slightly to the right. She does, doesn't she?" he asked his companion, who replied, "Gosh."

"When Donnie came for the breakfast trays, he said the alligator lady reminded him of Doris Day."

"What? Oh!" Beatrice shook her head disbelievingly, but blushed and grinned. Later Adam saw her puff a strand of hair from her forehead—Doris Day's trademark gesture.

The patients painted alligators until lunch.

There is a good reason why restaurants make claims such as *A taste of Little Italy in downtown Ocala!* or *Meals just like Mom used to make!* but never *Food so good, you'll think you're in a hospital!* Though he could do nothing to improve the entrées, Dr. Dewberry had wrestled with the powers that be to see to it that his patients got chocolate milk. No one imagined such luxuries on the other floors, but on the sixth floor they got to savor creamy chocolate milk as they spooned tuna salad at lunch or Salisbury steak at supper—for obvious reasons, knives and forks were not permitted.

"The irony is," Adam told his friend as they sat on vinyl chairs in the dayroom with trays on their laps, "I was just on the brink of reuniting with my wife." He showed how close he'd come with his thumb and forefinger. In the day since Adam had arrived, he'd already developed a slamming headache. "There were obstacles, of course, but I was setting things right, and now this." If he could have just one more chance he would read up on earthworms and provide fascinating tidbits of his own. *The bull male nematode can reach lengths of up to three inches,* he would say, and with those words he would be telling her, *I love you, I love you, I love you.* He looked glumly at his tray. Chocolate milk offered but little solace.

"Oh, dear," said his friend, one eyebrow raised and one lowered in a response too nuanced for words.

"'Yet each man kills the one he loves,'" Adam quoted. "'By each let this be heard. Some do it with a bitter look. Some with a flattering word. The coward does it with a kiss.'"

"I've noticed every time you see a picture of an angel," Michael interrupted them, "it's always a man with wings. Do you think when I die and turn into an angel, it'd be okay to be a wolf? I don't want to be a wolf man or anything like that. I don't want to be blasphemous. I'd just like to be a man and a wolf. With wings."

Adam dutifully finished his tuna and did not venture an opinion on this theological matter. "You know," Adam remarked to Donnie as he returned his empty tray to the cart, "you don't have to carry those boxes."

"What?"

"The alligators for Beatrice," Adam clarified, mildly indignant at how some people impose upon hospital orderlies. "She's perfectly capable of doing it herself." Adam carefully nestled his tray into the one below, as if his only concern in life were easing Donnie's lot. "She told me she only makes you do it so she can look at your muscles."

"I don't mind," Donnie said with shy astonishment. As Donnie wheeled the squeaking cart away, he touched his bicep tentatively.

After lunch they sat in a circle in one of the side rooms for therapy.

"I understand congratulations are in order," Dr. Dewberry said, addressing Adam. Adam held his pants up with one hand, even though seated as he was, there was scant risk they would drop. His belt and shoelaces were safely behind the front desk. "You're going to be married soon, I understand." Dr. Dewberry meant this as a kindly remark, but Adam felt like a mouse informed by a cat, *I'm afraid I'll have to go shortly, but I'll be leaving you in the capable paws of a colleague.* "Would you like to talk about it?" Dr. Dewberry pushed his glasses back up the bridge of his nose and prepared to listen.

Adam talked about it, what a wonderful woman Lily was,

how supportive, how his behavior had let her down, and how he wanted to get well again as quickly as possible—not just for her sake, but for his own—so he could be reunited with her and return to a productive life. Adam struggled against a sense of deep ugliness, a black whirlpool sucking him down inside.

"I want my book," Michael interrupted. It relieved Adam to have attention turned away from himself. "I can see it every time I go by the desk," Michael said.

Dewberry made a mental note to upbraid the desk nurse. *The Inferno*, still in its glossy cover, sat tantalizingly on the desk behind the nurse's chair. It should have been put in a box—leaving personal possessions in the open was unnecessary torment.

"All that stuff about boiling rivers of blood." Dewberry wrinkled his nose as if he'd recently visited that very river and couldn't clear the stench out of his nostrils. "Michael, that is not a healthy book for you to read right now."

After group therapy came visitation. Each patient was allowed a family member at a time. Visitors passed through two separate doors. First the patients could hear the faint buzz as the hall orderly opened the outer door, then a loud click when the desk nurse opened the inner.

Adam sat in the dayroom, hands on knees in anticipation and dread. Which would be worse, to have loved ones see him in this condition or to have no loved ones at all? Would Evelyn come? He imagined her browbeating the attendant on the other side of the door: *Only immediate family, ma'am—But I'm his wife, damn it.* There was no stopping her when her mind was made up. He remembered her negotiating with the rolypoly bow-tied field rep from Sunshine Mustard Company. *This mustard's too sweet and not hot enough—Do you want Chinese mustard?—No, that's too much hot and not enough sweet, and the yellow isn't right.* In the end, of course, they'd had to make their own mustard. It was the only way to get things perfect.

The outer door buzzed and the inner door clicked. Adam's heart beat at the thought that Evelyn might be on the other side. The door opened. Lily came in with a blue suitcase.

She waved at Adam, fingers rising and falling as if playing a scale on an invisible keyboard. "I brought you some articles of clothing," she informed him, and handed the suitcase to the desk nurse as if the most natural thing in the world were surrendering your fiancé's possessions to a total stranger. She took the chair in front of Adam, her knees almost touching his. A look of expectation on her face prompted him to rise and peck her on the lips, his hands resting lightly on her shoulders.

She smiled like a mother softening the news that a child's favorite pet had died by promising Sloppy Joes for dinner. *Won't that be nice?* "I put in that blue polo shirt you like so much and some nice slacks. I was going to put in your khaki shorts, but I was not certain what temperature they would maintain in here. Now I see I was right. It is quite cool. Do you think I should ask them to adjust the temperature?"

"No, it's fine."

"You are looking much improved, Adam. I think this will do you good."

"I'm sure it will," Adam said, wondering how much good he could stand. The Valium tablets Dewberry prescribed controlled his trembling and replaced grim foreboding with general grogginess, but did not relieve his headache. He gently touched his throbbing forehead.

"Oh, Adam," Lily said. She pulled a tissue from her purse and touched the corners of her eyes. Adam could think of nothing to do except take her free hand and hold it. He did that. “Oh, Adam, you are so brave. I know this will all . . .” She paused to recover herself and slipped back into her normal conversational gear. “. . . transpire for the best.”

“So who all is here to see me?” Adam asked. “Is anyone else here?” It was indelicate to ask about Evelyn, and so he didn’t, but he was hoping Lily would tell about her anyway.

“Addison,” she said. “But there’s lots of others who wanted to come but couldn’t. It’s a long drive.” She squeezed his hand. “You are a very popular man.” It was the playful voice people use when they say *naughty, naughty* without really meaning it. “So I can’t stay long.”

For a time Adam and his fiancée endeavored to sustain a normal conversation; finally Adam said, “Did you pick up my jeep? I left it on Hanover.”

“Yes, I retrieved it,” Lily said. “Bucky O’Leary transported me. We had a most interesting chat.”

“That’s nice,” Adam said. “Did you by any chance find a brown leather attaché in my jeep?”

“No,” Lily said. Having settled the attaché question, she returned to her topic. “Bucky said it has been too long—entirely too long—since the two of you have gone fishing together, and as soon as you’re completed here, you and he must get out to the lake, and he said something else very interesting too, now what was it?” She placed a polished fingernail on her chin.

“Are you sure about the attaché? It’s about this big.” He held his hands apart to show the size. “You couldn’t miss it.”

“I do remember,” Lily said triumphantly. “It was something called power of attorney. I told Bucky I let the men handle all the business matters because I simply have no grasp of them,” her hand fluttered in the air, a delicate butterfly marveling at an ocean liner’s giant anchor, “but I promised I’d mention it. He seemed to think it very crucial.”

"It might be in the backseat. Did you happen to look in the backseat?"

"You see, it's a matter of protecting your assets," explained Lily, who had a better grasp of these things than she gave herself credit for. "We have no way of knowing how long you'll be here, and in the meantime you need to empower someone to dispose of your business affairs until such time as you can do it for yourself. Now, I do not pretend to be an expert, but I could—"

"I don't think I'll be here long enough to need that."

"Those diamonds you mislaid have to be replaced, you know, and also, Sam Martin called, your broker?" Lily liked to deliver urgent news as if she were asking a question. "He mentioned something about a margin call? You will sign those power-of-attorney papers, won't you?" She patted his knee and stood. Cedary perfume filled his nostrils and waxy lips kissed his cheek. He sat motionless as a painted ship upon a painted ocean while she took out another Kleenex. She licked it to wipe the lipstick off his face. "Don't concern yourself needlessly over this. Just recover. I will bring the power-of-attorney papers tomorrow." She pressed her cheek to his. "Adam, get well. Please get well." She straightened and held him by the shoulders as if she were inspecting his appearance on the first day of school. She smiled, but her eyes shone. "Before I depart, is there anything you'd like me to bring you?" Adam could think of nothing. "Addison is waiting to see you."

Sitting across from Addison in this place was at once the greatest comfort and worst burden possible.

"So, Addison," Adam said sheepishly, "I guess with me in here, you at least finally have something to write about, eh?" Lord, his son was beautiful. Addison had smooth clear skin, a good straight nose, fine brown hair with a tendency to curl, and clear bright eyes. In fact, Addison looked a lot like

Adam—minus the blistered scalp, bloodshot eyes, smashed nose, and puffy skin—before time and a long history of bungles had ruined his looks. No matter what befell, Adam knew he had never bungled utterly as long as Addison was in the world. The ugly black pit inside him receded slightly.

"I'm too upset to write," Addison said. His father's tremulous voice had shocked him. "I thought you might want this." He handed Adam the newspaper's financial pages.

"Thank you," Adam said greedily, crumpling them under his shirt with a guilty look right and left. Newspapers were no more condoned on the sixth floor than Dante's *Inferno.* "You're not writing anything?" Adam had wanted so much to hear about some exciting new story his son was working on. "Is your mother coming to see me?" he asked.

"You're looking good, Dad," Addison said, dodging the question.

"Is your mother coming? I was really hoping to see her."

"No, Dad, she isn't." Adam wilted. "What we need to talk about right now," Addison said, "is how we're going to get you out of here."

"Right," Adam said. He took a steadying breath and planted his hands on the armrests decisively. He had lost Evelyn—he still had Addison. "You have to get in touch with General Potter. He's with Ayefour—the good guys. I don't have his card now, but you can get his number from Information. You got to tell him about Wrigley Adder and the Experimental Prototype."

Addison tactfully suggested that Experimental Prototypes were not a topic likely to secure Adam's release.

"But here's the thing," Adam said, "the reason the judge thinks my mentis is not quite compos is what I said during the hearing. I see that was unwise, but it's so big—what Compass East and Ayefour are up to—you can't imagine. And they've been at it for years. I have no idea how far their connections go. I overreacted, but it was an understandable mistake."

Addison's gaze dropped, and he put his hand over his face.

"If you'd seen half the things I'd seen, you'd realize it was a perfectly understandable mistake," Adam said, "but I'm afraid the damage is done. You have to prove the conspiracy and the Experimental Prototype really do exist." Addison's silence seemed ominous. "Addison, you do believe there's an Experimental Prototype? That there's a conspiracy?"

"I . . ." Addison said, and the pronoun hung between them as if someone had drawn it on the air in white chalk. After a moment it became clear he could think of nothing to add.

"But you've seen Exhibit A yourself." Addison stared blankly at the mention of Exhibit A. "The document," Adam clarified, "with the notations about the Experimental Prototype."

"Well." Addison's "well" was no more reassuring than his "I" had been.

"I showed it to you."

"Well, truthfully, you didn't show it to me. You showed me the briefcase it came in."

"But the diamonds—"

"As a matter of fact, I never saw those either, Dad." Although those were real, of course.

Adam wiped his brow. In spite of the coolness of the sixth floor, his forehead was damp. Making plans was hard when all he could think about was something to drink. "We can do this, Addison. First, we just have to turn Compass East over to the authorities. As soon as they're exposed, we'll get the diamonds back. That means I can break it off with Lily, and your mother and I can get back together. By the way, I lost track—is this Tuesday?"

"Wednesday."

"Sweet Jesus." Adam leaned back in his chair and bit a knuckle. "We're cutting it close. The rehearsal was supposed to be on Saturday. Look, once you get your ten percent for recovering the diamonds, you'll have more than enough to cover Kathleen's tuition." Another silence, and Adam felt himself sinking back into the blackness. "You believe me, don't you?"

"It doesn't matter anyway," Addison said. He did not bother asking how his father knew the money was for Kathleen. "Her committee's meeting day after Christmas. If they rescind her fellowship, and she says it's guaranteed they will, she's already made up her mind to go to Arkansas. She's got an aunt there who says there's a job at a bauxite mine." The air in the room seemed to solidify. "It's an office position," he finished weakly.

"Addison, we've got to do something. We can't let that happen. What about that professor of hers? The man who came up with that Tojo-a-go-go thing? Can't he help out?"

"Dr. Buskirk?" Addison said. "As a matter of fact, I believe that's him right there." Addison pointed to Adam's bushy-eyebrowed friend who sat contentedly studying the back cover of a *Reader's Digest.* After a moment, he turned it around in his hands and thoughtfully regarded it upside down. "I've got to go now, Dad."

Addison rose and placed his hand on Adam's shoulder. Adam didn't seize it and beg Addison to stay; instead Adam said, "Please call General Potter. Please do that for me. And ask your mother how the earthworms are. Tell her I asked."

Adam stood. He wanted to hug his son, but Addison was already at the front desk on his way to the door before Adam's arms had even closed around the empty air.

Afterward Dr. Dewberry spoke to Lily and Addison in his office. A framed photograph of a catamaran showed the psychiatrist was an avid sailor. The room smelled of lemon oil and old cigar smoke. A box of Kleenex stood ready for distraught families.

"I'm concerned he's showing signs of depression," Dr. Dewberry said. He half sat on the edge of his desk with one foot off the floor. He always adopted this medical-looking pose when talking to families. "It isn't surprising, of course. He's just had his autonomy, control over his own life, taken away. That's an upsetting event for anyone." Dr. Dewberry crossed his arms. "I have him on Valium for alcohol withdrawal, but I don't want to add clomipramine right away. It is something we'll have to keep an eye on. I understand his family has a history of depression. His father committed suicide."

"I think what concerns the two of us," Lily said with grave precision, making a gesture that included Addison and herself, "in addition of course, to his *drinking*, are these impersonations. What recourse do we have to ameliorate those?" Lily asked.

It took Dr. Dewberry a bit to parse Lily's question. "You mean what he told the judge?"

"That and the way he continuously goes around helping people. Sometimes he even says he's a doctor."

"Sounds like he'd make a good psychiatrist," Dr. Dewberry quipped. Nobody laughed. Virgil Dewberry went around all the time claiming to be a doctor.

"I feel . . ." Lily struggled for words as if she were on the brink of some grand insight that eluded articulation, "that subconsciously he is repressing something. If you could just unlock his subconscious, it might be the key to everything."

"Yes, well, that's what we're here for," Dewberry said with

a tight smile, repositioning himself on the desk. The corner dug into his left buttock, but getting up would destroy his look of professional ease. He pushed his comb-over back, silently cursing Alfred Hitchcock. Years ago if someone had told you, *So-and-so is developing a guilt complex from sublimating unresolved Oedipal impulses,* you could take those words to the bank, they meant something; but ever since *Spellbound* the subconscious had replaced baseball as America's favorite pastime. Amateurs hovered on every corner, tossing around "ego" and "id" to beat the band. They'd diagnose a neurosis as soon as look at you, and the only thing they liked better than a good neurosis was analyzing dreams. To them analyzing dreams was better than pot roast to a bulldog. They'd cross busy streets against traffic for a chance to analyze a dream. Everything symbolized something to them—for example, a wheel in a dream symbolized a revolver. (Oh, please!) Freud's once incisive lexicon was now gummy from overhandling and just another roadblock to therapy.

"We just want what is best for him," Lily said. "I am his fiancée. We were supposed to be married next week."

Dr. Dewberry held up the box of tissues, and she took one even though her eyes were dry.

"Dr. Dewberry," began Addison, and Dewberry waited for Adam's son to frame his question, but, though it burned on Addison's lips, he could not bring himself to ask it.

"Did you happen to find a tan leather attaché in Dad's car?" Addison asked Lily as they left.

Lily seemed to search her memory as if she were trying to recall a name from her childhood. "No, I can't say that I've seen it," Lily said. Then brightly, "Perhaps you should ask your father about it. The next time you see him."

After he got home, Addison went to Kean's room and sat on the edge of the bed. His brother stretched out on top of the covers reading his fat red and blue MCAT book. Kean dog-eared a page and laid the book on his chest while Addison told him about his visit.

"I think it's the best place for him," Kean said. "You're forgetting what Adam was like—you have a way of forgetting things you don't want to think about. It wasn't so bad when they were at the restaurant, but at home . . ." Kean shuddered. "On days off, they'd stay in bed until eleven or twelve o'clock in the afternoon, naked. They always expected me to bring them breakfast in bed. I think they were having *sex.*" The last word came out of Kean's mouth as if he'd dragged it across sandpaper. His mother had been a different person while she was married to Adam. "And then there were the dogs."

"The dogs?"

"You remember. We always had a dog, and we always named him Charley, but they weren't well cared for. They just ran around loose, and sooner or later they'd run in front of a car. Pow. No more dog. But then we'd get another and name him Charley too."

Addison recalled the ceremonies they arranged whenever a pet died. The family gathered beside a mound displaced by the volume of a basset or a dachshund. His father always said a few words. Once it was Ogden Nash: *I marvel that such small ribs as these can cage such vast desire to please.* Another time, Arthur Guiterman: *A pause for rest, a rest for paws, a place to moor my bark.* Yet another time, Bryant: *Yet not to thine eternal resting-place, shalt thou retire alone . . . Thou shalt lie down with patriarchs of the infant world—with kings, the powerful of the earth—the wise, the good, fair forms, and hoary seers of ages past.* Looking back on it, there seemed to be an awful lot of funerals.

"It was not a well-ordered house," Kean concluded.

Addison took a mica rock from the collection on Kean's bookcase. Dust had settled on the geodes and zirconiums. He peeled off a chip, transparent as a fingernail, studied it, and then peeled that chip in two. Addison didn't know much about rocks, but mica was his favorite. It seemed you could keep peeling off chips forever. "Kean, do you think Dad's delusional?"

Kean laced his fingers behind his head. "Well, in a way, I suppose. He may have confabulations."

Addison said he had never heard of such a thing.

"If Adam blacks out," Kean inhaled slowly through his nose before speaking, "even for a few seconds, he may create a false memory to fill in the gap. Like if he passed out or lost consciousness at the breakfast table, and later you asked him what he'd had for breakfast, he might say, 'Scrambled eggs and bacon.' He wouldn't be lying; he'd actually think that's what he had. It's sort of a delusion, I guess."

Addison held a chip of mica between his fingers. Someone had told him that in the old days they'd used mica for windows. "Thanks, Kean," he said.

"Don't mention it, kiddo."

Kean picked up his MCAT book again, and Addison closed the door.

After visiting time came Salisbury steak, corn nibblets, green beans, and chocolate milk. Dinner conversation did not sparkle. Dr. Buskirk offered only interjections, and Michael spoke of angels, wolves, and whether Salisbury steaks were biblical. Adam brought up Addison's writer's block.

"While I'm in here, he's too upset to get inspired, but I was thinking, why couldn't he?" It grieved Adam to think of

Addison not writing *at all.* "Just to keep his hand in, you understand, take someone else's story, swap all the names and places out, and, you know, just write that."

Michael looked up from the spoon he'd been using to herd a blob of jellied brown gravy over the tray dividers. "You can't do that," he said. "Everyone knows you can't do that."

"Why can't you do that?" Adam asked.

"Because every story has got to be a completely new thing, totally original." Michael trained his bright eyes on Adam's. "Everyone knows that. It's got to be unique. You're crazy if you don't know that."

Adam slumped in acquiescence with this diagnosis, but having read more than his fair share of Shakespeare at Sisters of Mercy, he recalled that in all his plays the Bard had only two endings: everyone either got married or buried. Shakespeare didn't seem to fret over making each play different from the others, and most of the plays he did write he cribbed from history books or other writers. Adam shared this information with Michael.

"Well," Michael said after considering this, "that may have been good enough for Shakespeare." Donnie took their supper things, flexing his biceps as if a ball and chain hung from the tray stack. "But it won't do now. We're more advanced than that."

For the first time Adam grasped the wonderful, terrible burden of his son's vocation: to write stories, each had to be a thing apart from all the others. Imagine if that had been the case making hot dogs; the first could be long and pink in a white bun, but once it had been made that way, it could never be duplicated. The next might be blue and square in a green bun, but then blue square hot dogs in green buns would be off limits forever. To have to reconceive the whole hot dog from the ground up each time you made one—that's what it meant to be a writer. Adam nearly wept for the sublime impossibility of such a task.

After dinner came shower time, when Adam snuck the financial pages behind a door—although he couldn't lock it—of a bathroom stall and perused them in relative privacy. The words "fraud" and "embezzlement" leapt at him from the page. It took several breaths to calm himself enough to read the news that the president of Moore Locks had absconded with company funds. Adam flipped to the stock market columns to discover that without even knowing it, he had lost a fortune overnight. He laid the gray pages on his knees like an apron and leaned his head against the cool metal wall. He was poor! Was it possible for anyone to lose so much money so quickly? Lines he'd learned as Macduff back at Sisters of Mercy came to him disjointed from his past: *All my pretty ones? Did you say all? Oh, hell-kite, all? . . . At one fell swoop?*

He pictured how he must look from above—on a toilet too big for his feet to reach the floor, his shoes dangling from his heels because they'd taken away his shoelaces, his pants around his ankles, his hairy white legs shaking in terror at how he'd bungled once again.

Why should it surprise him? It's what he always did sooner or later. Warn him and warn him not to say something, not to do something, not to touch something—but it did no good; sooner or later he always bungled.

*"Who started it?" Adam had held the earpiece and tried to speak into the receiver, but the words choked him. Sister Eglantina, a giantess in black, stood beside him. Adam knew his mother was on a party line, and the neighbors were listening in. "Aren't you ashamed," Sister Eglantina had asked, and he was. His face burned with drying tears and his ear stung from the punch it had gotten.*

*"Who started it?" The other boy started it, Adam wanted to say. He was looking at me funny. You started it by making me wear those funny-looking shorts on the train.*

Adam tore the newspaper into confetti and flushed it.

After shower time, the rooms were unlocked—patients were locked out of their rooms during the day and locked in at night. Outside, raindrops that sounded as big as pie plates pelted rooftops and treetops, but on the sixth floor, all was silent. Adam tried recalling how it felt to have Evelyn's weight on the other side of the mattress, or working side by side in the aprons she'd made, pulling sizzling red-hots from the grease. Instead, he kept remembering the one thing he tried never to remember: the Old Man's accident.

*Playing in the garden, Adam let the mimosa flower fall from his fingers at the sound. The hot fear rushing into his chest told him what that bang was even before he heard his mother's screams. They had told him not to touch that gun, but he'd been so giddy after eating swamp chicken and being like the Old Man, he'd snuck into the study and taken it out of the case to admire.*

*Adam hid amid the preserves in the little closet under the stairs for hours and hours, it seemed, until he heard unfamiliar voices, and curiosity got the better of him.*

*The sheriff was there. Was Adam going to be arrested? Mother's face was dry by that time but still had red blotches from crying. Her voice was calm as she told the sheriff, "He was cleaning it. It went off by accident." She shot Adam a look, though, that said, I told you not to touch that gun. I told you.*

Adam listened to the emptiness and finally fell asleep like a spanked child.

Adam dreamed he was in the dayroom with Michael and the Old Man. Michael was having trouble becoming a wolf. Sometimes he was a flamingo, sometimes a rabbit, sometimes an alligator with pink spots. Adam tried to hug the Old Man, but his arms went right through him; then he'd forget, and try again with the same result.

"You keep forgetting," the Old Man said. "You can't do that."

Adam woke and sat up in his bed. The Valium did not help him sleep again that night. He held his pounding head in his hands. If he didn't get out soon, he was sure he would die. Adam had to get out of Chattahoochee. Would Addison track down General Potter?

# TWELVE

# Addison Takes the Reins

Christmas Eve, Lily Manzana put on her satin slippers and the sheer pink robe that matched her nightie before going into her kitchen for breakfast.

Except for Lily's grapefruit, which came straight from the tree, her breakfast contained nothing unsanctified by modern chemistry. Sweeta was as sweet as sugar and had the astringent flavor of all things clean. The crystals of instant Sanka she rehydrated by stirring in hot water shared nothing in common with real coffee but the name, and the menthol cigarette she lit for her first smoke of the day was as far removed from the flavor of Cuban tobacco as you could get. As for her nondairy creamer, she had never seen a milk cow, but she had looked at enough goats' udders flecked with excrement and stray bristles to vow she would never knowingly drink anything squeezed out of some animal's glands.

She drove to Adam's house and let herself in. She had a great deal to do that day, but she lingered over another cigarette before starting. She began in the kitchen; she took beer from the refrigerator and vodka from the freezer. She upended all of it in the kitchen sink and let the contents gurgle out. She checked cabinets. Jack Daniel's, more vodka, and tucked next to the cabinet door where you could only find it by touch—a fifth of rum. These bottles joined the others in the sink. By now the beers were empty, and Lily threw the cans in the trash. Evelyn would have expected Adam to throw out his damn liquor bottles himself, but Lily loved Adam more than Evelyn did.

Lily stood on a footstool and checked the refrigerator top. Behind it? Unlikely, but better ascertain for certain. Lily was small but determined, and she shifted the heavy Kenmore from the wall to look behind it. She found a dust-bunny amalgamation as big as a welcome mat; she wouldn't be able to eat another thing from that refrigerator again knowing what was under it, so she got her broom and mop to clean up. She moved the stove and did likewise.

In the bedroom she stood with her hands on her hips. It was no use asking herself, *If I were a liquor bottle, where would I be?* Adam would hide things in precisely that last place she'd look. He was a sly one. Other words for "sly" are "crafty," "cunning," "devious," "wily," and "scheming." For example, no liquor bottle would think of hiding itself in the toilet tank, but Adam would think of it. Lily thought of it too, and was rewarded with a fifth. She moved on to go through his dresser drawers. Then she took the drawers out and looked behind them.

The phone rang; it was Bucky.

"Hello, Lily girl," he said. "When you weren't at your place, I figured you might be here. Just calling to see if you're coming by today to get those power-of-attorney papers like we mentioned."

She looked at the bedroom clock. She needed to drive to

Chattahoochee in time for visiting hours to see Adam, which meant she wouldn't be able to pick up the papers. "I'll have to obtain them tomorrow," she said.

On the other end of the line Bucky sighed. "Well, make sure you do. It's important for Adam's sake."

"I understand," she said. "First thing tomorrow." She could have postponed her search and gotten the documents, but Lily wanted this out of the way. She reached under the mattress, not expecting to find anything—too obvious—but her fingers touched the square-shouldered side of a fifth.

By the time she added the new bottles to the kitchen sink and had thrown the empties in the trash, the air already smelled woozily of alcohol, and she hadn't gotten to the other rooms yet. She lugged the clinking trash can out to the curb. Naturally it tipped over so Adam's neighbor Mrs. Sykes, who was watering her lawn, could get a look. Lily knelt, face burning, and gathered spilled bottles from the driveway.

Lily knew better than anyone the cost of being the other woman. Evelyn criticized, so Lily must never criticize. Evelyn gained weight, so Lily must stay slim. Evelyn talked about earthworms and unseemly things.

Lily lifted her chin and returned, fighting the urge to walk faster under Ms. Sykes's lemon-sucking gaze, to resume her search in Adam's office.

Lily must observe decorum; she couldn't let Adam see her pee or put on cold cream or fart. Lily would have to stay prettier than Evelyn, more admiring than Evelyn, be a better listener, and laugh louder at Adam's jokes. Lily would comply in the bedroom, protect Adam from drinking, curb him from straying, and forgive him when he did stray without mentioning it.

But Lily knew that regardless of what she did, she would never be to Adam what Evelyn was. Not if she lived to be a hundred. She would never wipe out that "other" from "the other woman."

Lily opened Adam's rolltop desk drawers. Adam would certainly have told *Evelyn* the meaning of the big map on the wall. She remembered the silly song about the moon and pizza pie Adam and Evelyn used to sing while they worked at the restaurant. Lily knew Adam would never sing with her. That was how Lily knew she loved Adam more than Evelyn did—because Evelyn only loved him in return for loving her, but Lily gave her entire self for the skinny slice of Adam Newman he let her have in return.

After taking his desk at *The Sentinel*, Addison hunched, forehead in his hands, and cussed himself out. "You are the biggest fool ever if you do this." A list of reasons why he shouldn't make the call would have run for pages—beginning with the Communist conspiracy, the Experimental Prototype, and the Venezuela Project all being confabulations of a disordered mind, and it wasn't as if Addison didn't have problems of his own to deal with, to wit, his imminent dismissal from his job and being in love with his brother's girlfriend. No, not in love with her, he reminded himself, just very, very—*I like her is all.*

Weighed against the reasons for not making the call was only one reason to make it: his father asked him.

With a leaden hand Addison lifted the phone. "I can't believe you're actually doing this." He dialed Information. "No, I can believe you're doing this. This is exactly the sort of thing you'd do. Stupid, stupid, stu—Hello, Information?" He got the number of Ayefour. A receptionist answered, and Addison said he was calling about some acreage he understood General Potter was interested in; she put him through, and Addison was mildly surprised there actually was a General Potter. At least his father wasn't making up that part.

"Yellow?" responded a man's voice.

Addison reminded Potter that Ayefour had made an offer on Adam Newman's land, and said that Wrigley Adder had approached him on behalf of Compass East for the same parcel. The mention of Compass East did not provoke the reaction naming a Communist front ought to. Potter didn't, for example, suck in his breath as if he'd been snake struck. Addison felt increasingly foolish, and the black phone grew heavy and clammy in his hand. He began stammering and speaking faster, barely managing to stumble to the end. "Anyway," he concluded, "my dad said he found some papers in Mr. Adder's briefcase. They said something about an experimental prototype." Having unburdened himself of his message, Addison started to hang up his trembling phone in embarrassment and relief, but something in Potter's silence stayed him. "General?" Addison asked. For a moment he thought he'd lost the connection.

"Yes, well," Potter said. "Perhaps you'd better come in, then."

Addison seemed to hear the sea's rush. The general betrayed no emotion, but the mention of "experimental prototype" accomplished what "Compass East" had not. "I'll be over right after work," Addison said, and Potter gave him the address.

Perhaps curiosity sped his hands, but in any case, while it would be untrue to say Addison's index fingers flew over the keyboard as if on magic wings, never had he typed an obituary with greater speed than that day, and seldom with greater accuracy. Writing "Pop Nish" for "Bob Nish," an error so slight that no one noticed it, was one of only two mistakes he made that day.

He discovered the nature of his other mistake after he arrived at the office of Ayefour.

Addison parked behind a green Pontiac and went up the flagstone path between bright puddles. The thunderclouds that had opened up the night before had moved on, and everything smelled rain-washed. Ayefour was headquartered in a blue and white frame house that had been someone's cottage before the street had gone commercial. Unruly scuppernong vines laced the arbor; green sandspurs filled muddy flower beds under the windows, but Addison guessed the original owners had planted them with red and white pansies.

He knocked, and getting no answer, let himself in. Two wet umbrellas stood in a brass umbrella stand in the foyer, and beyond that was another room. The receptionist Addison had spoken to was gone, her ladder-back chair pulled out behind her empty desk. The door behind it clearly led to the main office. Addison put his ear to the door and heard the voices of the general and another man discussing business. The other man said something and the general cut him short in a clipped, somewhat peremptory tone.

Addison didn't want to interrupt so he took a paper cone from a watercooler in the corner and poured himself a drink. He sat at a conference table that occupied the center of the room. Ayefour's decor was an amalgam of home and office furnishings. A Persian carpet was spread on the hardwood, and two armchairs upholstered in worn blue cloth, antimacassars draped over their headrests, sat in opposite corners. Lace curtains filtered the bright late-morning sunlight falling on the pink-and-yellow-striped wallpaper. Darker squares on the wallpaper showed where pictures had once hung.

Finally, Addison decided he might as well let Potter know

he was there, so he gave two polite knocks as he pulled the office door open, saying, "Excuse me, General, I'm Addison Newm—"

He pushed the door shut again as if he'd walked in on his mother taking a bath.

What on earth was General Potter doing with Wrigley Adder?

That he'd caught them together was the result of Addison's other mistake, although it took him some time later to piece together what had happened. When Addison told Potter that he'd come by after work, Potter assumed this meant after five, but an obituary writer—even one of excruciating slowness such as Addison—leaves work much earlier than that, so Addison had stepped into the middle of what the general and Wrigley had expected to be a private meeting.

Addison felt the knob turn as someone on the other side attempted to push the door open. Addison kept it closed.

"Mr. Newman?" Potter said. His voice was tainted with something akin to annoyance. "You're Adam Newman's son, right? We spoke on the phone."

Without thinking, Addison grabbed the receptionist's chair and propped it under the doorknob as he'd once seen James Garner do in *Maverick*. He stepped back in alarm at his own action and bumped the desk behind him. After you lock people in a room, typically there comes a moment of quiescence when you pause and think, So far, so good, but now what? These were Addison's thoughts at this juncture.

The doorknob rattled impatiently, but the chair held the door closed. "What are you doing?" Potter's voice had become, if anything, calmer in the emergency.

It was a pertinent question, but Addison had no idea himself what he was doing. There was an indistinct muttering as Wrigley and the general discussed their situation.

The door shook, and Wrigley warned, "If you don't let us out, Mr. Newman, we're going to call the police."

Addison lifted the phone from its hook and set it on a contract on the desk. The blue ink of some landowner's scrawl was still fresh. There was a soft click as someone picked up the extension in the office and attempted to dial. After a few seconds, Potter's voice came through the receiver, "Mr. Newman, please hang up on your end so I can call." Then after a little bit, there was another click as the general hung up, and the door resumed its fruitless rattling.

Addison's instinct was to get out while the getting was good, but something about the contract on the desk held him. He realized finally what it was; the name on the contract wasn't Ayefour, but Latin America Development.

Addison tried the desk drawer. It wouldn't budge, and Addison was again on the point of fleeing, but then he realized it was one of those ingeniously secure desks such as schoolteachers have, in which the top drawer absolutely will not open unless you open the bottom drawer first. He slid open the bottom drawer, and the top drawer opened easily. The rattling stopped, and from the mumbling that replaced it, Adam could imagine his adversaries in the other room plotting their next move. The door is useless, they realized, shall we try the window?

If Addison hoped for some massively incriminating piece of evidence—blueprints of the White House, for example, with a big red X and the words *put bomb here*—he was disappointed. There was nothing in the drawer but paper clips, one of those typewriter erasers that look like a pencil with a white eraser nub at one end and a white brush on the other, and General Potter's business cards.

Addison felt a faint vibration through the floorboards and heard an *oof* as someone pushed through a window and landed outside. Through the lace curtains he saw a man's silhouette dash to the front door. There was another thump and another, slightly higher pitched *oof.* The front door was already opening, but Addison didn't care. The business cards all bore the general's name, but the company names were different. Some said *Reedy Creek Development*, some *Ayefour*, others *Tomahawk Realty*. One even said—and if Addison's blood didn't actually freeze at the sight, it certainly cooled—*Compass East.*

Wrigley Adder came in the room, huffing from recent exertion. General Potter was not far behind. From the mud caking his hands and shirt cuffs, Addison guessed that Wrigley had emerged from the window headfirst. Potter had muddy feet, indicating he'd elected to go feetfirst, but the torn pants, missing shoe, and brown smear along his flank said he'd slipped on impact. It could not have been pleasant depositing themselves into the muddy and sandspur-choked beds, Addison decided, nor was the experience one they'd had time to forget.

"I don't know what the heck you're up to," Potter said, mustering as much dignity as an army officer can after falling from a window. "But you're getting out of here this instant." Wrigley came forward, his hands poised to seize Addison.

"Who do you work for?" Addison asked.

It was much the same query Adam had put to Deputy Dooley, but while the question did more harm than good dealing with law enforcement officers, it now froze the other two in their tracks. There was a stillness in the air as the three of them silently tried to sort out who had been caught red-handed and who had done the catching. Who among them should point the accusing finger with a triumphant "ah-HA!" and who should twist his toe in the carpet and look down in silent mortification? General Potter and Wrigley

Adder stared at Addison, and Addison stared back, nervously fingering the business cards. Addison expected at any moment one or both of them would pull a gun. Neither one did. Maybe they expected him to draw a gun himself, but of course he didn't. It was like a Wild West shootout in which no one remembered to bring the props.

"There are a lot of companies here," Addison said vaguely.

Potter regained his composure. "You're leaving here right this second."

Before Wrigley could come around the desk, Addison said, "I work for *The Sentinel.*"

Addison hadn't meant anything in particular by the comment; it was merely all he could think of to say. He might as easily have said, *My grandfather had a big white mustache*, but the words acted like a spell. Wrigley hesitated. Addison didn't elaborate on his employment situation; he didn't say, for example, that he was in the obituary department or that he faced almost certain termination for rotten spelling. Instead he said, "I don't know what you're up to. It really isn't any of my business. I'm sorry I broke into your office this way." Addison realized that technically he hadn't broken in; he'd come through the front door like a normal person, but what he had done was more difficult to describe and apologize for. In a gesture of goodwill, he belatedly removed the ladder-back chair from the doorknob and replaced the phone on its hook.

Wrigley took Addison's shoulder and said, "I think you just need to get out."

"But it's my father. There's some land of his you need. Except right now he's in the Chattahoochee psych ward. He can't sell it to you as long as he's in there." Addison allowed them time to gather the implications. Wrigley's hand left Addison's shoulder. "I don't know what y'all are up to, but I get a feeling you have some pretty powerful connections. A man named Judge Carmichael sent him there. Judge Carmichael," Addison repeated, to make sure they'd gotten the name.

"We don't have anything to do with that," Potter said. Some indefinable change had taken place, and he seemed almost sympathetic.

"I know," Addison said. "Maybe there are some strings you can pull. If there's a way you could get him out, then you'd get what you want, and I'd get what I want." Addison took a deep, unsteady breath. "He's there because he told them about the prototype, and now they think he's crazy. If the only way I can get him out is to explain he's not imagining things about the Experimental Prototype and Compass East, then that's what I'm going to do." His voice cracked humiliatingly, but Potter and Adder didn't seem to doubt his seriousness.

"You don't have to threaten us," Potter said.

"I know. I'm sorry. Excuse me." Addison allowed Wrigley Adder to guide him out. He dropped his gaze as he passed Potter. "I'm sorry about your office."

Addison could no longer control his shaking as he left the front door and walked down the wet flagstones to his car. He still half expected one of them to pull a gun after all and plug him in his back.

"We can't promise anything."

Addison turned and saw the two of them on the stoop. General Potter raised a muddy hand in a gesture of farewell. "We're not promising anything. We'll see what we can do. About your father."

Addison sat in his car until the all-overs passed, and then he began laughing. He twisted the mirror so he could see his face. "You're no James Bond," he said, "but you handled yourself pretty well. Dang, I wish Kathleen could have seen me back there."

Christmas morning on the sixth floor the patients were served eggnog instead of chocolate milk. According to the LP playing behind the front desk, the entire Mormon Tabernacle Choir planned to build a snowman in the meadow and pretend that it was Parson Brown. Santa himself showed up looking a lot like Dr. Dewberry in a red suit and acrylic beard, distributing presents to everyone from a cardboard box.

With unsteady hands Adam tore the paper off his, and stared at the ceramic plaque in puzzlement. "I don't get it," Adam said, not wishing to appear ungrateful. "Of course I'm somebody."

"No, you're saying it wrong," said Santa, pausing his ho-ho-ho's to explain, "It's supposed to be, I *am* somebody."

"You're not really Santa Claus," Michael informed Dr. Dewberry. "Nobody thinks you're really Santa Claus." He had also gotten a plaque reminding him that he was somebody. Everyone's plaque said the same thing.

Lily came at visiting time. After kissing him and saying how well he looked—he felt like hell—Lily spread out the power-of-attorney forms on a low table in the dayroom, and Adam regarded them with a fishy stare. "Now, Adam, I have all the necessary papers right here." She would have had them yesterday, she explained, but she'd been unable to pick them up from Bucky's office until late afternoon.

"Is there anyone else here to visit me?" Adam asked.

"Now, you'll need to sign here, here, and here. Bucky put *X*'s to indicate all the spots where you sign." Lily pointed at the lines in case the *X*'s didn't make it obvious enough.

"So no one else came," Adam said. The air seemed to squeeze him. Lily ignored his remark and handed him a blue ballpoint. "Okey-dokey, then." He uncapped the pen with a dull click.

Michael and his father knelt enjoying a nice round of father-and-son prayer, and Dr. Buskirk stared placidly into the middle distance with his hands folded across his belly and the unopened gift from Dr. Dewberry in his lap. At the front desk Dr. Dewberry carried on an unusually vociferous phone conversation, agreeing with whoever was on the other end, but in a voice that sounded far from agreeable. "Yes, I understand. Yes, well, if that's the way it is, that's the way it is. Right."

Normally Adam signed with a grand illegible flourish, but today he took greater care forming his letters than he had at any time since elementary school. He'd gotten as far as *Adam Newm* on the final line of the final page, when Dr. Dewberry interrupted him.

"It looks as if somebody has some friends," Dr. Dewberry said, as if friendship were an unaccountable breech of decorum. "Judge Carmichael has just called rescinding his order. We're checking you out today."

Adam's pen lifted just before forming the penultimate letter. Reprieve. The miracle had happened. "And that's," said Adam, quoting a poet whose name he could not recall, "what we call balling the jack." He tore the power of attorney in two with a voluptuous rip.

Adam collected his suitcase—the blue one Lily had brought with his favorite polo shirt—and packed his remaining belongings. He was also given his shoelaces and belt at the front desk. He shook Dr. Dewberry's hand. "Thank you, Doc, for everything. I really feel a lot better. Really." In spite of his throbbing head, Adam felt like a child getting to leave school early.

"I'm glad to hear that," Dr. Dewberry said with a dead smile, "but you know, there really hasn't been enough time. I know what you're feeling, Adam. Do you know what those sensations mean—the headache, the dizziness? See how your hands are shaking? That's alcohol withdrawal, Adam. Your body's angry with you—it's saying it needs a drink. I know it's hard to believe this, but that's a sign that this place is good for you. Now, if you would consider—" Adam met his gaze and nodded, but Dr. Dewberry could tell he wasn't hearing a word.

If one knows where they are, and how to pull them, there are strings to make the door of even Chattahoochee's sixth floor swing wide. Powerful individuals had found these strings and pulled them on Adam's behalf, but painting ceramic alligators isn't a miracle cure—it doesn't instantly restore the mind to its proper function, but requires time and patience to take effect. Adam's second alligator hadn't even come back from the kiln; there was no way he had received the full benefit of his treatment.

"My head is a lot clearer now, I can tell you. Clear as a bell," Adam reassured Dr. Dewberry, tapping his recently cleared head, although as it suddenly struck him, bells are not clear at all, but opaque. "If I had to put it down to one thing, I think it was the wonderful opportunity to express myself in group therapy," Adam said. "I think I achieved a genuine breakthrough." Silently Adam vowed that at the first opportunity, he'd wash the taste of chocolate milk from his mouth with a good stiff drink. This thought made him feel better.

Dr. Dewberry took longer shaking Adam's hand than was strictly required and seemed to have more to say, but Adam could spare no more time to allay his concerns; he was eager to leave. Besides, Michael was at the doctor's elbow wanting to know if he could eat his meals from a bowl on the floor, to practice being a wolf.

"So long," Adam told his friend Dr. Buskirk. "I don't think I mentioned it, but I know one of your protégées. Kathleen Something-or-Other. Anyway. So long. Don't let the bedbugs bite. Ah-ha-ha-ha-ha."

No one heard what Adam's friend, the good listener with the bushy eyebrows, said to this, because Adam and Lily had already been buzzed to the other side of the inner door, Dr. Dewberry was asking Michael if he really thought eating meals off the floor was a good idea, and the desk nurse was busy doing whatever desk nurses do, but had they been listening, they would have been astonished to hear Dr. Buskirk, who had not mumbled more than an interjection since his arrival, deliver a brief impassioned soliloquy behind his beard, his bushy eyebrows meeting in an angry crease in the middle of his forehead, a rumble like the approach of a line squall, "Kathleen Neligan, Kathleen Neligan, she always called it the Opoyo. It's the Opoy*ul*, Opoy*ul*!"

Addison was on the other side of the outer door. Adam dropped his suitcase to hug him. "You had something to do with this, didn't you? You were behind this?"

"Well," Addison said, his ears turning pink, "I talked to some people. I had some hopes."

"This is quite the Christmas present, isn't it?" Lily said. On tiptoe she gave Adam a kiss on his forehead. "The most desirable Christmas present we could receive."

Outside, the rain had dried and the clouds had fled. Sunlight scalded his eyes all the way to the backs of their sockets, but Adam was out. "'My heart leaps up,'" Adam quoted Wordsworth, "'when I behold a rainbow in the sky.'" At the moment there was no rainbow, but the air was washed so clean, he would've sworn he could have numbered the leaves on the moss-hung live oaks across the street. Following his dreary sojourn on the sixth floor, Adam's spirits rose like a rubber duck bouncing to the water's surface after being held submerged against the tub bottom.

In the parking lot Donnie and Beatrice broke hastily from an embrace. Donnie loaded the freshly painted alligators into Beatrice's trunk, not raising his eyes to Adam's, and forgetting in his embarrassment to stop flexing his muscles. Beatrice blew a strand of hair from her forehead like Doris Day, but by now this had become a nervous habit and had nothing to do with Donnie.

Adam jammed his suitcase in the trunk of Lily's Buick as Lily's mind turned to practical matters.

"Tomorrow, of course, we have the wedding rehearsal," Lily said happily. Although getting him into Chattahoochee had been her secret heart's desire, it had the drawback of requiring a postponement, but now that he was out, everything could come off as originally planned. Lily felt light as a feather.

"Oh, yes, right," Adam said. The reality of the wedding dawned on him like a Monday. Though the air was as bright and clean as ever, it no longer seemed so. If asked about the state of the atmosphere, in fact, Adam might have groused it left something to be desired in the cleanliness department. He covered the lower part of his face with his shaking hand. "It's a good thing I got out in time for that. Darling."

The drive home along the Orange Blossom Trail was a long and silent one. Adam rode with Lily, and Addison followed in his Volkswagen. Lily thought about the wedding, and Adam thought about Evelyn. His life was over, he knew that. He was bankrupt, and Evelyn would never take him back. When had things turned so rotten?

They arrived at the house, and as Adam walked with his suitcase to the front door, a stranger in a red-and-blue-striped polo shirt emerged from a black sedan and intercepted him. "Mr. Newman," the stranger said, "we need to talk."

Lily's and Addison's eyebrows went up, but Adam put down his suitcase and allowed the stranger to take his elbow.

"Is something the matter?" Lily came up to them.

"No, nothing's the matter," the stranger said loudly, "me and your husband just need to talk."

Lily followed them with a sharp-eyed, protective stare. "Is anything the matter?" she repeated.

"No, nothing's the matter," Adam lied. "Let's go inside." For some reason his knees were suddenly shaking. "Perhaps we can discuss whatever this is over a drink."

"What would you like?" Lily asked as they entered the foyer, "Fresca or Sanka?"

"Sanka," Adam said. Neither sounded any more appetizing than chocolate milk, but Sanka required Lily to boil water, and Adam wanted to talk to Addison and the stranger alone.

While Lily went into the kitchen, Adam took his suitcase and led the way to his office.

"My brother-in-law says you borrowed some diamonds from him," the stranger said in a soft voice.

"Oh, ah-ha-ha-ha, you must be Bert," Adam said.

"That's right," Bert said, with a smile so intense it was nearly a snarl. He put an arm around Adam's shoulders, and with his free hand held one of Adam's shirt buttons between his knuckles. Bert stood nearly a head taller than Adam; he appeared shorter than he was because of an astonishingly boxy frame. He was damn near to being a perfect square.

Now that he was in this bearlike embrace, Adam realized that in saying Bert was not someone you'd want to meet in a dark alley, Ernie was understating matters. Even in the most commodious and brightly lit of alleys you would not say to yourself, *Why, there's good old Bert. I'm glad to meet him here.*

"And now you don't know where they are," Bert said. Adam confirmed this part of the story too. Bert nodded and did not stop smiling; his smile did not crinkle the corners of his eyes or form dimples in his cheeks; it only bared his teeth.

"Dad, what's this about?" Addison asked. He felt a distinct sense of protectiveness toward his father.

"Is this your son?" Bert asked, still smiling, in a tone that was a little too interested, like a cannibal pointing his fork at the last slice of missionary and asking, *Are you going to finish that?*

"It's nothing, son. Don't worry about it."

"Ernie's an in-law of mine. And he owes me money. And now you owe him money. You see how that works?" Bert didn't wear a double-breasted suit with a boutonniere, speak with a Jersey accent, or carry a machine gun in a violin case—but he didn't need to. Those pale blue eyes of his had no more expression than varnished wood. "You know what I think, Mr. Newman?" Bert released Adam's button, and instead twisted his nipple between his knuckles. "I think if you thought about it, you might remember where those diamonds are. What do you think, Mr. Newman?"

"I promise you I'll get those diamonds back," Adam said. Ernie twisted his nipple again, and Adam added, "Or else pay Ernie every cent."

"Okay," Bert said, releasing Adam. "I'll let myself out. Tell your lady I didn't want coffee after all. Think about those diamonds." And Bert left.

Adam fell into his chair and sat motionless until the all-overs subsided. He slid out a drawer of his rolltop desk. Astonishingly, the fifth he kept there was missing. He sighed. He would get the diamonds back one way or the other. He was bound to.

He dumped a stack of colorful brochures for various tourist attractions on the desktop. Then he opened his suitcase and rummaged through it. "So update me," he said, after taking a deep breath. "You talked to General Potter about the prototype?"

At several points as Addison filled his father in about his remarkable encounter with General Potter and Wrigley Adder, Adam stopped what he was doing to gape in astonishment. Locking Potter and Wrigley in the room impressed him particularly. "Would that really work?" Adam asked. "Putting a chair under a doorknob that way?"

"Evidently," Addison said. "As long as the door swings out."

Adam shook his head in respect. "That's something I'll have to try out sometime. Very resourceful, son." Addison smiled at this compliment. He realized that while his father was in Chattahoochee, life had seemed rather tame. When Addison finished his narrative, Adam sat thoughtfully, holding a strip of cellophane tape poised above the plaque he was wrapping in a Silver Springs brochure.

"This is big, then, bigger than I thought. The Cross-Florida Barge Canal is the least of it." The air seemed to bristle with electricity. Beneath its perpetual sunburn, Adam's face was pale and clammy. "And I'll bet they've been keeping their eyes on us. If you know I'm out, then they know too. It won't be long, I bet, before they get in touch with us."

Addison studied his father's map. Amid the blue and red pushpins, two vacant spots represented by his father's tracts stared back like eyes. "Well, Dad," Addison said reasonably, "there's no point being paranoid. It's not like they're going to call us on Christmas D—"

The phone rang, and they both jumped.

"Hello, Mr. Newman," said a familiar voice on the other end. "We have to meet."

# THIRTEEN

## Adam Has a Meeting

After Lily poured the Sanka, Adam gave her a Christmas present.

"Oh, Adam, how considerate of you!" she said. First she read the card, on which Adam had appended his own name beneath that of the insurance company which originally sent it; then she tore the glossy Silver Springs brochure from her present. "Oh, I adore it. How superlative. I *am* somebody."

It struck Adam that she read the plaque exactly the way Dr. Dewberry read it. "And now, sweetheart," he said, "I regret to inform you that Addison and I must take our leave." Lily's eyebrows went up at this. "We have to get some tuxedoes for Addison and Kean. I, of course, possess my own tuxedo already, but the boys don't." After arranging to meet Potter and Wrigley within the hour, Adam and Addison had concocted this plausible lie to explain their departure.

"But, Adam," Lily protested, "the stores aren't going to be open on Christmas Day."

"We're not going to a store," Adam said with the nonchalant air of a magician remarking that if anyone in the audience needed a rabbit, he knew where to lay hands on one. Adam had anticipated this objection and was ready for it. "There isn't time for that. We'll go to Caleb—he'll whip some up for us. He'll work all night if he has to."

Lily pursed her lips and delicately lifted her cup from its saucer as she considered this. She took a sip of instant coffee and for once could think of nothing to say.

"We'll head out in just a second," Adam said as he went into the kitchen, "but first, I'm going to indulge myself in an unexpected luxury." The refrigerator held no beer. The bottle of vodka he usually kept in the freezer was also gone. Adam confirmed his mounting suspicions by looking in the cabinets under the sink: no Jack, no rum.

"Well," Adam said cheerily, "I don't think I'm thirsty after all, but now I need to put on some shoes with shoelaces."

He went in the back room and Lily set down her coffee on a glass-topped coffee table. She weighed this development; Addison had not demonstrated himself the most reliable of keepers for Adam, but this was Christmas; liquor stores and bars would be closed. Lily reached over the coffee table and patted Addison's hand. "I want you to know," she said, "I have no intention of taking your mother's place." Addison, who had always felt awkward having his hand patted, disliked Lily's assumption she had even been considered for the part. "I know you love your mother. You should. And I will never, never attempt to interlope between that."

"Well, thank you. I appreciate that," Addison said.

Lily raised her cup and saucer again, extending one crooked pinky finger, and took another sip, her eyes raised above the cup to study the framed seascape on the wall. She had something more to say, but it was hard to steel herself to say it.

"Do you know where my blue windbreaker is?" came Adam's voice from the bedroom.

"You gave it to those people," Lily reminded him. Now she said it. She leaned forward and said in an intense but quiet voice, "I know some people think they're superior to I." Addison started to protest, but Lily stopped him. "It does not perturb me, I am not concerned about that." Tears clouded her vision, but she would not permit herself to cry. She held Addison's wrist. "I know I don't have other people's," her hand fluttered out of her lap as she sought the words, "intellectual acumen. But. I will take care of your father. I will take care of him. I will take care of him. I will take care of him. I depend upon you to help me."

Addison recalled something his mother had said when he'd told her scornfully that Lily was only marrying his dad for his money. His mother had paused thoughtfully before saying, *Probably. But if she is, she's going to earn every penny.* His mother's tone had sounded not only resigned to Lily Manzana, but *grateful.*

Addison could think of nothing else to say to Lily but, "Yes, ma'am."

She held his wrist and did not let go. "I will take care of him. I am depending on you. You and I are going to be close friends, I think."

"Here I am, ready to go," Adam said, making his entrance.

In his jeep, Adam found Wrigley's attaché under the seat. "Look what we have here," he said with grim triumph. "We'll just put this puppy back for safekeeping." He slid it back into place. At least there had been one happy discovery that day.

Even the bottle he kept in the toilet tank had disappeared—whatever made her think to look there? "So, what's the news on Kathleen?" he asked. "Has she had the meeting about her fellowship yet?"

"That's tomorrow," Addison said. Being with his father had unexpectedly brightened his mood, but thinking of Kathleen darkened it again. "There's a special meeting at eleven o'clock with her professors in the conference room of the Humanities Building. It's not good. She's already made up her mind to go to Arkansas and work at her aunt's bauxite mine." The cotton padding a neighbor had laid along his roof in a misguided imitation of snow was dark and sodden with rainwater. "There's no way," Addison hesitated to even ask, "you could give her the money even if we don't get the diamonds back?"

Adam removed a cigarette from his pocket and lit it with his trusty Zippo. "I would if I could, son. At the moment, though, it looks like I'm headed straight for El Casa de Pobre. Do you know what a margin call is?" Addison shook his head. "In a nutshell, my broker is about to sell off all my holdings to pay off my losses. I had already sunk a considerable pile in a high-flier called eLoye, which I sold at a loss. I invested the proceeds—unwisely as it turns out—in a company named Moore Locks. A couple of days ago, the president of Moore Locks ran off."

"Good Lord, where?"

"That is a question much on the minds of the Securities Exchange Commission," Adam said and blew a stream of smoke. "Presumably somewhere tropical, a place still unspoiled by the rat race or extradition treaties. He took only such provisions as required for an extended trip: his personal secretary and a suitcase of bearer bonds." Adam's jaw tightened as he imagined Moore Locks' president reclining under a palm tree in swim trunks and flip-flops enjoying a frosty pineapple-and-parasol-bedecked beverage. *Adam* would have enjoyed a frosty beverage. "Anyway, I had just enough reserve on hand to make good on the diamonds," Adam said, "but with this thing too, I'm kaput." Adam decided not to get depressed just because he faced a future of crushing poverty and perhaps something worse than that from Bert; it was a beautiful Christmas Day, he was with his son, and they were hot on the trail of Compass East. If only he didn't have this headache. He really needed a drink. He changed the subject to a brighter one. "How's your job at the newspaper going?"

"I'm quitting."

"No!" Adam exclaimed, letting go of the steering wheel in dismay.

"Yes," Addison said. "I'm just sick of it. Beasley hates my guts, and I don't blame him."

"But you have so much talent." Adam, who had never extended himself creatively beyond painting the odd alligator, hung all his personal artistic aspirations on Addison's shoulders. He imagined that starting out as an obituary writer, Addison could rise through the ranks of the literary profession by hard work and determination, earning promotion after promotion, until one day—taking a ferry somewhere, perhaps—he would rescue the drowning infant of a famous publisher who would say, *We have an opening just now for a Pulitzer prize–winning novelist. Are you interested?* The thought that his son might abandon the path to literary glory smote him as he'd seldom been smote before. "What did they say when you quit?"

"They didn't. I'm supposed to go in tomorrow, but I'm just not going to. Ever."

Adam meditated glumly on his son's decision. His own

disasters he could face with equanimity, but he must do something to help Addison.

"I'll sign these papers on one condition and one condition only." Adam filled a paper cone from the watercooler and took a sip. He had silently rehearsed this very line on the way to Ayefour's office, and he was pleased it came off so well when he finally got to use it. The others sat at the conference table in the front office—Wrigley Adder and General Potter on one side, Addison on the other. A fountain pen lay crosswise on a fresh contract. Someone had hopefully and helpfully made little *X*'s on the spots where Adam was to sign. "I must know what this land is for. I have to meet your employer." He crushed the paper cone in a decisive gesture.

"Do you need a paper towel, Mr. Newman?" Potter offered.

"That isn't necessary." Adam wiped water from his eyes and looked at his wet shirtfront. The dramatic intensity he'd aimed for had been somewhat marred because he'd crushed the cup while it was still two-thirds full. "I need to see your employer," he repeated.

"That's not possible," Wrigley said. "He insists on staying in the background."

"Ah!" said Adam.

"What do you mean 'ah'?"

"Nothing, just ah!"

"Mr. Newman—Adam, Addison," Potter said, "I thought we were going to do business today. You got us out here on Christmas Day away from our families—"

"I thought you people didn't believe in Christmas," Adam said.

"What 'you people'?" Potter asked.

"Communists."

"We're not Communists, Mr. Newman," Potter said patiently.

"Then what are you doing here on *Christmas*?" Adam asked with unanswerable logic, stabbing the tabletop with his finger.

"I've been looking at my father's map," Addison interjected. "My father has a map," he stumbled on, answering Wrigley's and Potter's perplexed stares. "It's hard to explain. But anyway, I can tell you're buying up everything all around Dad's land. His property leaves two holes right in the middle of yours." Addison made a gesture of punching two holes in the air with his index and middle fingers. "You can't do without his land, and you know it. He's not selling it until he knows what it's for. He has to meet your boss. He deserves that much."

"That's right," Adam said. "We deserve to know. Who are you working for? The CIA, the AEC?"

"It's the MIC," Potter said. There was a teasing glint in his eyes, and he pursed his lips as if he were sucking a sweet.

"What?" Adam said. "What? What?"

"The KEY," he went on. It was clear he found himself amusing.

Wrigley was not amused. "Stop joking around," he said. "You'll say too much."

"Give us a little time to talk, Mr. Newman," Potter said. He and Wrigley went into the back office and shut the door behind them.

Adam pondered the general's cryptic remarks. "The KEY. The key? The key?" Giving it up, he looked at Addison and waggled his eyebrows like Groucho Marx. "You were magnificent, son. Cool as a cucumber." Addison exhaled slowly, releasing a little of the tension, and nodded without speaking. He was glad he'd made his father proud.

Potter and Wrigley came back a few minutes later and sat at the table. Potter spoke, "You have some property of Mr. Adder's, a briefcase."

"When we meet your employer," Adam said.

General Potter and Wrigley exchanged a look.

"Let us see what we can do," Potter said.

"Does that mean we're meeting your boss?" Addison asked.

"What it means is we will see what we can do. He may be here tomorrow. He may not. And in any case, he probably will not agree to see you. We will see what we can do."

"When do you want us to come by?" said Adam.

"We will get in touch with you."

"Well, I'm going to be pretty busy the next couple of days," Adam said, leaning back in his chair and waving his hand. "I'm supposed to get married and—other errands."

"We will get in touch with you," Potter said with no more emphasis than the first time, a voice like plugging a cork in a bottle. So that was that.

They pushed their chairs back before rising and shaking hands across the table, and Adam said, "I'll agree to meet your boss on one condition and one condition only." Since Adam had already used the one-condition-and-one-condition-only line before, this did not make imminent good sense now, but Potter and Wrigley seemed prepared to listen patiently. "You have to give back the diamonds."

"The diamonds," Potter said.

"I've come up short a couple of hundred thousand dollars' worth of diamonds. I believe you have them in your possession."

"I swear to you," General Potter said, raising one hand and placing the other lightly on the unsigned contract as if it were a Bible, "we don't know anything about any diamonds."

When they returned to the jeep, even with his personal finances sunk beyond salvation, and his head pounding like his brain had grown three sizes too big, Adam managed a smile for his son. "I don't think I ever said thank you, son," Adam said. "For getting me out. For believing me." Adam started the jeep. "You were superlative back there, son." He imitated Addison, " 'You can't do without my father's land, and you know it.' " Adam sighed. He had his foot on the clutch, but hadn't put the jeep in gear. He turned to look at Addison. "Promise me, son, you won't take up drinking."

Addison, nonplussed by this request, could only mumble, "Yes, sir."

"No telling how much harm drinking's done me," Adam said. He touched his throbbing forehead, and changed the subject. "Want to hear a joke?" Addison said he wouldn't mind, so Adam told his joke, and when he got to the punch line, "No one else stood up," Addison laughed out loud. He completely got it. "Now we have to get the tuxedos," Adam said. "Lily's going to be expecting us to get some tuxedos." Adam had long experience in establishing alibis. "You've never worn a tuxedo, have you, son?" They pulled from the curb. On the sidewalk two brothers, happy to be gallant on Christmas Day, were guiding their little sister on her wobbly new two-wheeler. Everyone's face was bright and pink with pleasure and the brisk air. "You'll be amazed at what a tuxedo will do for you," Adam said. "You'll look astonishingly good."

Kean was not eager to go along when Adam showed up and said he was taking him and Addison to get fitted for tuxedos, but Evelyn gave a look with an arched eyebrow that said he'd better not refuse—she would not let him admit any impediment to this marriage of true minds—so they got into Adam's jeep and drove to an area locally referred to as Colored Town.

Florida was the last Confederate state to surrender; they weren't tougher fighters particularly, it just hadn't occurred to the Union to get around to them sooner, but slavery itself was long since abolished; instead of slaves, Florida had tenant farmers and maids. And there were no more slave quarters, just Colored Town. As far as the white citizens were concerned, this was a big improvement.

After they crossed the tracks, Adam turned on a narrow dirt road and parked at a blue-shingled house half hidden in a profusion of tall privet bushes and twirling whirligigs. Adam opened the gate of the chain link fence. "There's nothing like the sound of rain on a tin roof," he said appreciatively, pointing at the roof, as if the owners had installed it for that specific purpose. A fluffy calico cat darted across the paving stones in front of them and into some marigolds.

"Hey, Caleb," Adam called, knocking on the door. "Hey, Caleb!"

Caleb Jones came to the door, smiled, and said, "Ernestine, it's Mr. Newman!"

"Why, hello, Mr. Newman!" called a woman's voice from the back. "Merry Christmas."

"Merry Christmas," Caleb said as he ushered them in. "Dig any wells lately, Mr. Newman?"

"Well, you know, Caleb," Adam said vaguely, "here and there." As far as Caleb knew, Adam was an expert well digger. The day Caleb moved in—they'd brought the house on rollers from another street—there'd been a ponderous neighborhood discussion over where to sink the well. Luckily an expert happened by. Adam cut a forked branch from a sassafras tree—"Some folks try doing this with a stick off the ground," he said. "That's a big mistake, I can tell you"—and walked around without any fuss or hullabaloo until he stopped and said, "Here's the spot." They dug where he told them, and the well came in like gangbusters.

"We need two tuxedos for my sons," Adam said. He laid a hand on Addison's shoulder. "Do you think you could make us some by Sunday morning?"

Caleb bared his teeth as he considered this deadline. He did not object to working on Christmas; his life consisted of little more than work, eat, and sleep—but time was short. "For you, Mr. Newman, I expect I can," he said at last. "I'll stay up all night if I have to."

"Is these your babies?" Ernestine came into the front room as Kean and Addison entered. "Ooh, look at them. They so pretty and fat." She pinched Kean's cheek.

"I'm Adam's stepson," Kean clarified.

"You just missed our daughter," Ernestine said. "She drove all the way down from Detroit with our grandbabies. She's a registered nurse." Ernestine was simultaneously explaining their daughter's absence and bragging. "We was just finishing supper," she said. "Do y'all want some cake and coffee?"

"I wouldn't mind some coffee," Adam admitted, "if it had a little . . ." With his thumb and fist, he pantomimed drinking from a fifth.

Caleb caught Ernestine's look. "No, sir, I'm sorry. We don't have none of that," he said. "Now, you stand here, and we'll take your measurements." Caleb posed Addison on a footstool and got a yellow measuring tape, a notepad, and a pencil stub from the sewing machine in the corner by the Christmas tree. He held the pad and pencil in his teeth while he measured from Addison's shoulder to his elbow. Then he licked the pencil tip and recorded the result.

"Caleb is the smartest man I know," Adam said. Ernestine brought in a tray with slabs of cake on rose-patterned china.

"And your daddy is the smartest man I know," Caleb said.

They were both telling the truth, but it had to be admitted, Caleb didn't know that many people. Neither Caleb nor Ernestine could read or write, but Caleb could cipher and had become the most respected tailor at Goldstein's Department Store. He also took in business of his own on the side. Ernestine, whose father had been born a slave, had made herself indispensable to a doctor's wife, cooking and cleaning and making out shopping lists—painstakingly copying labels of empty cans and bottles: *Comet*, *Coca-Cola*, *Maxwell House*.

By dint of excruciating hard work and fanatical economizing, Caleb and Ernestine Jones, with nothing but glad hearts and determination on their side, had scaled a tall and rickety ladder that the world seemed always determined to snatch out from under them. The Joneses had saved enough not only to buy their own house, but the two houses on either side of theirs. Now their neighbors didn't rent from a white landlord, but the Joneses. As far as the Joneses were concerned, this was a big improvement.

"Your daddy is a good man. The Lord is with him." Caleb raised Addison's arms as if they were wings and stretched the tape across his shoulders. "It's kind of like Jerry Lewis. I was watching a Jerry Lewis the other day at the Paramount." Downtown had two theaters: the Paramount, which allowed blacks only in the balcony, and the Bijou, which did not allow blacks at all. "And it was the funniest—! That man, the more he tries to set things straight, the worse they get. He always trying to set things straight, and they just got worse and worse. And just when I was thinking they can't get no worse, what? Everything sort of flips around at the end and it all turns out all right. And you know why that is?" Caleb pointed to Adam with the eraser end of his pencil stub. "Because the Lord was with him. Can't do nothing without the Lord."

"People don't like stories like that," Addison said softly.

"What's that?" Caleb asked.

"People don't like stories like that." Addison wished he hadn't said anything.

"Why is that?" Caleb asked. "Well, I'm finished with you, young man." He gestured for Kean to take Addison's place.

"It's a deus ex machina. Addison's going to be a famous writer," Adam informed the room, his mouth full of Ernestine's lemon pound cake.

"You don't say," Caleb said, stretching tape from Kean's elbow to wrist. "So why don't they like that sort of story?"

"Well, it's just," Addison felt miserable telling Caleb what sort of story he should and shouldn't like, "stories where everything gets worse and worse and then at the very end turn out happy. Life isn't like that. Reading stories like that is like being lied to."

"Well, if people don't want to be lied to," Caleb asked reasonably, "why'd they pick up a story in the first place?" He wrote down one of Kean's measurements and said, "Now, do you want me to run you up some cummerbunds to go with these? Or vests?"

# FOURTEEN

# Adam Sets Things Straight

Adam surprised Lily by getting up early Saturday. She had indulged him in the rare privilege of spending the night with him; humiliating to let Mrs. Sykes know they were shacking up, but Lily had no intention of letting Adam out of her sight. However, he got up while it was still dark and went to the bathroom. She figured he was relieving himself and went back to sleep. By the time she got out of bed, Adam and his jeep were gone.

Adam's head hurt, and he felt simultaneously fatigued and jittery when he started up the engine and backed down the driveway. What he wanted more than anything in the world was a drink, but that would have to wait. His own life was bungled past repair; he knew that and was prepared to face it; however, he must do what little he could to save his son's job and Kathleen's fellowship. Evelyn would want that. So preoccupied was Adam with his mission, he didn't notice that as he turned out of the neighborhood, a long black limousine turned in. After Adam's jeep passed, the limousine stopped, executed a laborious three-point turn, and followed.

Adam turned onto Livingston where gold tinsel still hung over the street and then onto Magnolia. The signs proclaiming the number of shopping days left were gone, but not replaced by announcements of after-Christmas sales. Store windows glared like empty eye sockets. He parked behind *The Sentinel* and puffed his cheeks as he sat behind the wheel. The air was cold yet his face was moist. Alternating chills and sweats had filled his past twenty-four hours.

Since he had no knowledge of the newspaper game outside of what he'd seen in movies, Adam's curiosity was understandably piqued as he walked through the doors of Addison's job. He half expected to catch sight of the pressman, his face dark with ink stains and long-suffering, holding a freshly printed page, as the gray-templed publisher pounded a table, waving his other hand magisterially, bellowing, "I don't care, make over the whole thing!" Maybe a blond cub reporter would run in shouting, "We got a break in the Presky-Vanderhoot Murder Case!" Or else the cartoonist would be just then adding the finishing touches: a famous politician strolling hand in hand with a notorious hooligan and carrying a bulging bag with a big dollar sign on it, while another figure looked on—who? Weeping Lady Liberty? Scornful Uncle Sam? Above it, the sardonic caption, *The People's Trust.* In any case there was bound to be a feisty girl reporter—all newspapers have a feisty girl reporter—with ginger hair and a sailor's vocabulary, swiping a match from a colleague's shirt pocket and striking it on her hip to light her cigarette, saying out of the corner of her mouth, "I tell you, this time I'll get that no-good alderman dead to rights, see if I don't." Telephones would jangle everywhere, and cigarette smoke rising from reporters' desks would make the newsroom resemble Pittsburgh from a distance, and everyone, even the feisty girl reporter, would wear a fedora with a big white card in the headband that said *Press.*

There was none of that.

It was very quiet. Adam let himself in a room where he saw rows of tables with newspaper layouts in various stages of completion. A chemical smell like photographic developer made his stomach flip-flop. This is not the place I'm looking for, Adam decided. A side door led him to a more promising-looking area with desks and typewriters and telephones, but if he expected the feisty girl reporter to notice him over her shoulder with a contemptuous, "Get a load of this lug," so he could ask for directions, he was mistaken. He stared pensively at the empty desks wondering where everyone had gone and if perhaps a mob boss, irked by the blond cub reporter's getting just a little too wise, hadn't tied everyone up in a back room.

His apprehension was allayed when a young man materialized at his elbow. "Can I help you?"

Adam felt disappointed it wasn't the feisty girl reporter; although he'd never met her, he was already half in love with her, but, he told himself, any port in a storm. The young man had a narrow black tie, black hair, and heavy black glasses. Even though he had never seen a rodent of any description in either tie or glasses, something about this person gave Adam the uneasy impression of being addressed by a large two-legged rat.

"Where is everybody?"

"Most of them aren't here yet. The others are in a meeting. I'm Mortimer Patton."

"I see. Well, Morty, can you direct me to Mr. Addison Newman's office?"

"The desk Addison works at is over there," Mortimer said, giving the word "desk" just a little extra push out of his mouth as he spoke. He pointed to the spot. "What do you want?"

"If you must know, Morty," Adam responded in the sweetest, politest voice you can possibly imagine, "I am filling in for Addison today. I am the Addison Newman du jour."

Adam took a seat, and Mortimer Patton shrugged with a huff, pushed his glasses back up his nose, and scuttled off.

"Don't bruise yourself getting back under your rock," Adam cautioned him under his breath as he examined his surroundings. There was a typewriter, a telephone, and an index card taped to the desk with the name Rhonda Peterson and a phone number. Following the silent instructions implied by this arrangement, Adam rolled a piece of paper into the typewriter and dialed the number.

After two rings there came a smacking of gum on the other end, and a woman's voice said, "Hello?"

"Hello," Adam said. "Do I have the pleasure of addressing Rhonda Peterson?"

"That's me. Who's this?"

"I am Addison Newman's understudy. His anamenueusis."

"His which?"

"I am taking Addison's place today. Feel free to divulge anything to me that you would have said to him."

"You're doing the obituaries?" Two smacks as she considered this. "Okey-doke. You ready, dearie? *Smack smack*?"

"Ready as rain."

"*Smack smack*. Are we going to get it right today?"

"Right is what we shall get it, and we shall not settle for one iota less. This obituary shall be all a good obituary should be if not more."

"Okey-doke. Double-you."

Adam made two keystrokes. "Okay."

"Okay. Eye."

Adam made three keystrokes. "All right."

As he drove to the university, Adam tried to distract attention from his throbbing head by reflecting on what a fascinating job his son had. The people one came across writing obituaries must be a constant source of inspiration for a writer. Take Mr. Uuokilsom, for instance, or the mysterious Miss Ajrolbfom; what strange sad fate had drawn them to this country's distant shores, only for them to die like moths beating against a windowpane?

With these thoughts Adam sped up the long highway to Gainesville. He took the Orange Blossom Trail to 441. A water tower painted to look like a giant orange with a gargantuan green leaf brooded over the horizon. By this time the stores were open, and Adam could have, had he chosen, pulled off and gotten something to drink, but he didn't. He had another opportunity at Wildwood, where he picked up the southernmost junction of 75, but even with his every corpuscle screaming, *Stop for beer! Stop for beer!*—he didn't. A drink would wait.

It would normally have been a two-hour drive, but traffic was light the day after Christmas, and Adam kept his foot to the floorboard, weaving in and out of lanes as required. Shortly after Micanopy, he left the Interstate and got back on 441 up to Gainesville. He should just be able to make it in time for Kathleen's meeting. He gritted his teeth against the woozy feeling of carsickness creeping up his gut. Immediately after setting things straight for Kathleen, he would stop at a convenience store and get a couple of beers.

He never noticed the limousine in his rearview struggling to keep up. It had lost track of him when he turned into the parking lot of *The Sentinel*, and circled the streets hoping to catch sight of him again, only doing so when he left the parking lot.

Kathleen left the conference room mentally squaring her shoulders to embark on a new life in the bauxite line. Through the slimy muck of academic Opoyo, the slimiest and muckiest variety of all, Kathleen had managed to extract a single clear answer: *no*. The actual word had never been said, of course, because given the gelatinous concentration of Opoyo in the room, great gooey gobs pooling on the tabletop and drooling to the floor in viscous cables, puddling up to her calves, the only sure way to communicate anything was *not* to say it.

Her reverie was interrupted by the sight of Adam Newman entering the hall as she was leaving.

"Mr. Newman?"

"I'll see you at the wedding rehearsal," he said, playfully aiming his finger at her like a gun. He pulled the trigger back and made a clicking noise with his tongue. "Is this the way to the conference room?"

"It's there," Kathleen said. Meeting Adam Newman on the way to a meeting she had left was like coming upon a missing pair of socks in the refrigerator's crisper drawer—she didn't know whether to be pleased or vaguely uneasy. His face looked molded out of bread dough. She'd had another surprise that day: stopping by Kean's house, she had seen Addison climb into a magnificent black limousine. The Newman men were certainly full of . . . surprises.

Three men rose from the table as Adam entered. Of them, only one looked distinctly professorial—bald with a trim gray beard. Another looked like a bank president, and the third—who had a habit of eyeing the walls as if looking for an escape route—seemed painfully conscious of not belonging in the room at all. The oak-paneled walls exhaled silent contempt for all things unlearned, and heavy leather-bound tomes glared dismissively at Adam through the glass doors of their bookcase. Although Adam could not have explained it, the air seemed to have an indefinable glutinous quality, as if an invisible, slightly congealed substance permeated the room.

"May we help you?"

"Is this—where they're discussing Kathleen—uh, Kathleen's," Adam realized he did not know Kathleen's last name, "Kathleen's scholarship? I've come to speak on her behalf."

The three men exchanged glances.

"You mean Kathleen Neligan?" said the one Adam had taken for a banker. "This is the place. I'm Dr. Joseph, and this is Dr. Holman," he said, nodding to the professorial one, "and Dr. Russell," indicating the young man who looked grateful for once to find someone more out of place than he.

"I'm Dr. Newman," Adam said, extending his hand. He hadn't planned on granting himself a Ph.D.—hadn't planned on anything, if it came to that, except exerting his considerable powers of persuasion on Kathleen's behalf—but when everyone in the room was Dr. *Something*, being a doctor yourself came as automatically as yawning after three people in a row have yawned.

Adam took a seat. Chairs scraped and squeaked as the others reluctantly followed suit.

"Are you from Tampa?" Dr. Holman asked.

"No—not Tampa," Adam said vaguely.

"So where are you from?"

Adam coughed into his fist. "That really isn't important now."

Looks were passed among the three professors. "I don't think I'm familiar with a Dr. Newman," Dr. Joseph said. Suspicion glinted in his banker's eyes. "Have you published?"

"Nowhere you would have seen," Adam said. He coughed again to conceal his agitation. "It's sort of privately circulated stuff. It's not just for anybody."

Dr. Joseph could not restrain a well-bred snort. "So we're not good enough to read your articles."

Adam said nothing and an uncomfortable silence as heavy as a thunder rumble oppressed the room.

"I don't want you to think that where I come from we look down on you or anything like that," Adam said at last. "We don't think you're *stupid*." He'd meant to be placating, but he'd had the opposite effect. It was as if he'd told a woman, "I don't think you're *fat*." "In fact," Adam said, "they speak very highly of—" The university's name slipped his mind, and he finished unconvincingly, "your institution." Adam smeared sweat off his neck, which did little good; his palms were equally damp. Under the table, his knee was bouncing. "Just the other day someone was saying some very nice things. Very nice." Adam tried smiling as if still savoring the memory of the nice things someone had said about them.

"You came here to talk about Kathleen Neligan," Dr. Joseph reminded him coldly.

Adam was doing his dead-level best to ingratiate himself, but everything he said seemed to work against him.

"Yes. Yes. Yes. Yes," Adam said. "Is there anything to drink in here? Some white wine? Sherry? Ahem. No? At any rate, we are very interested in Miss Neligan—very interested. In her publications. About Lobomo."

"Moloko?" repeated Dr. Russell.

"That esoteric mumbo-jumbo she and Merle were always on about," explained Dr. Joseph frostily. He leaned back in his chair, and it gave a contemptuous squeak.

"I wasn't aware she had any publications about Akoyo," Dr. Holman said.

"That's just the part we find so dad-blame interesting," Adam said. Their raised eyebrows told him they were perplexed. "You see, it's not so much what you write, as what you don't write."

"She doesn't write anything."

"And more of it than anyone," Adam confirmed. Another dangerous silence. "Are you sure you don't have anything to drink? At this point I'd even settle for water. Just about anything, in fact, besides chocolate milk. Ah-ha-ha-ha-ha-ha."

Dr. Joseph took out a pipe, tamped tobacco into the bowl, and lit it, filling the air with the scent of Copenhagen. It was a profoundly effective gesture. I should have brought along a pipe of my own, Adam mused regretfully, even though the aroma made him slightly ill. "Could I suggest," said Dr. Joseph, who seemed to do most of the talking in the department, "that if—your institution—is so interested in Miss Neligan, that you recruit her yourself?"

"We don't, uh, we don't do that sort of thing," Adam said. "That's not our line. Besides, we feel Miss Neligan makes an excellent contribution right where she is, to the—very nice work you all are doing."

"I'm afraid, Dr. Newman, that we must consider the fiscal position of the university," Dr. Joseph said. "The Reese Fellowship needs to go to someone whose efforts might prove financially valuable to the University of Florida at some point in the future. Whereas Miss Neligan's work on Arozzo, while very intriguing, I'm sure, seems of negligible benefit in that way. Of course, she's perfectly free to pursue her studies on her own, and if in the future—"

"Bauxite," Adam said. Bauxite is one of those words, which if spoken out of the blue, has the effect of silencing conversation. It did so now. "If Kathleen Neligan doesn't get her fellowship, she'll have to go straight to work in the bauxite mine. Are you familiar with bauxite, gentlemen?" Their looks said they were not. Adam was unfamiliar with bauxite himself, but he imagined Kathleen in a miner's hat and a pick over one shoulder. He perched his trembling hands lightly on the tabletop as if it were a keyboard and surveyed them impressively. "How it saps the intellectual faculties? What it does to the soul? Short of painting ceramic alligators for a living, it is the most spirit-deadening profession on the planet. If you consign her there, you will lose forever the valuable, valuable contributions she will make. Think of that, gentlemen."

Dr. Joseph drew a long, impatient sigh. "Thank you for your time, Dr. Newman," he said, and rose to shake Adam's hand. "I'm sure you must be very busy."

No one looked in the least bit persuaded—if anything, they actually seemed to mistrust that Adam was a professor at all.

"I'd hate to see the university make a mistake which it would later regret," Adam said impatiently as he shook Dr. Joseph's hand. God, this headache. He should have stopped for something to drink after all. He shook Dr. Holman's hand and Dr. Russell's as well.

"I'm sure all of us appreciate your concern," Dr. Joseph said.

"Well, good day, gentlemen," Adam said.

When the door had closed behind Adam, Dr. Holman raised his eyebrows and let out a long exhale of disbelief through pursed lips. "Whoo-eee."

Dr. Russell went to the window and peered through the venetian blinds, hoping to catch sight of the peculiar Dr. Newman as he left the building; his attention was arrested, however, by the unexpected novelty of a long black limousine on a college campus.

"Well, if we were going to take away Kathleen Neligan's

fellowship before, we certainly aren't going to let her keep it now. Imagine sending that lunatic to threaten us." Dr. Joseph's mood had already been testy, having to convene a meeting during winter break on the day after Christmas, and his introduction to Adam Newman, Ph.D. had not improved it any. He went on in a mincing voice, "'I don't publish in any journals you've heard of. You're not smart enough to read anything I've written. I'm too important for that.' Sweet Jesus Christ, give me a break."

"Lookee here," said Dr. Russell, forgetting to avoid slang in the presence of his colleagues, "a limo's pulled up to get Dr. Newman." The sight drew the other two to look. The rear window of the limousine rolled down, and a face peered out. "Great Scott! Is that who I think it is?"

What Adam chiefly needed was a good strong drink to clear his head while he pondered his next move. He tried to tell himself as he left the Humanities Building that there was no reason to think that his presence had merely ensured Kathleen would never get her fellowship. After all, the committee had not actually declared its decision one way or the other. Phrases such as "esoteric mumbo-jumbo" and "negligible benefit" might be open to any number of interpretations. He wished he had Evelyn there so he could get her opinion on the subject.

In spite of these cheering thoughts, Adam couldn't help feeling he had bungled on a monumental scale. So profound was his mood of self-doubt, he even began to worry if he might have mistyped Addison's obituaries. Was it really possible that the indefatigable Miss Ajrolbfom had taught third grade for *eighty* years, or had Rhonda said *eighteen*?

Apart from his mounting headache, these sad reflections

occupied his head when the limousine pulled up to the curb in front of him. The rear window lowered smoothly and an elfin, mustached face said, "Mr. Newman, I presume? I believe you've stumbled across a little secret of mine." A spasm of rattly coughing interrupted the speaker, and then he resumed, "Why don't you step in so we can have a talk?"

"Yes, sir," Adam said. The door opened, and Adam climbed into the cavernous backseat of the limousine.

Addison, who was already inside, said quietly, "Hi, Dad." General Potter was there as well.

"I'm forgetting my manners," said Adam's host, "I haven't introduced myself."

"Everyone knows who you are, sir," Adam said.

# FIFTEEN

## Adam Has Lunch

"Since you already know who I am," Walt Disney said, "let me introduce my brother Roy. He's the president and chairman of the board of Disney Enterprises. He does all the hard work. You might say I really work for him. Ha-ha. The general you already know." Adam shook hands all around. Roy Disney was a somewhat paunchier version of his brother.

Walt Disney stubbed out a cigarette in an ashtray, coughed, and said, "Nasty cold, I've been going nonstop lately and can't seem to shake it." He smiled at Adam. "You know what? I am absolutely famished." He looked at his watch and exclaimed in mock surprise, "No wonder, look at the time. Why don't you give General Potter here your key, so he can follow us in the jeep? If you don't mind going on a little drive and having a late lunch with me, Mr. Newman, I have something to show you and your son that you might find very interesting." His twinkling eyes made refusal impossible. "You and I can talk on the way." General Potter already had a hand outstretched to receive Adam's key.

"That would be stupendous, Mr. Disney, but please call me Adam."

Walt Disney said, "And you must call me Walt."

Adam gave the general his key and Walt pushed a button next to a little silver speaker. A voice said, "Yes, Mr. Disney?"

"Donald, we're going to HQ now," Walt said with a wink for Adam and Addison, sharing his childlike delight in getting to use the phrase "*HQ*." "You're tough to keep up with, Mr. Newman. I thought we could get you at home, but you were already leaving when we got there. Then we spent the rest of the day catching up with you." He reached in his pocket for a pack of cigarettes, but before he could get it out, Adam offered one of his own, first pretending to put it in his mouth and extract it from his ear. Walt laughed and accepted it, making it disappear into his own ear and pulling it from his mouth before taking a light from Adam's trusty Zippo. "I can see you and I have much in common, Adam," Walt said. Adam lit a cigarette for himself, and Walt leaned back into the soft black leather upholstery and exhaled a thin plume of blue mentholated smoke. His cuffs shot precisely one inch from under his jacket sleeves no matter how he moved, his pants broke perfectly over wingtips that gleamed like black water, and his pocket handkerchief was folded so crispy, it looked like a white name badge next to his lapel.

The limousine had started up smoothly and was even now gliding toward 441.

"Would you like something to drink, Adam?" Walt asked.

"Would I?" It was more of an exclamation than a question.

"Well, we have Coca-Cola, Fresca—I believe we even have chocolate milk."

"On second thought, nothing for me."

Walt regarded Adam and Addison seriously and said to Addison, "Son, what would you say is the single greatest problem facing the American city today?" Unprepared for this question, Addison looked at his father for help, but Adam was equally at a loss for an answer. After a moment Walt nominated some possibilities. "Crime? Unemployment? Mediocre schools? Traffic? Air pollution? All-around general squalor?"

"Those are all pretty bad, sir," Addison managed.

"Yes," Walt said, "they are all bad." He knocked ash from his cigarette and stared at the armrest ashtray as if it held the future of the American city. "I bet you're wondering why an animator—a mere cartoonist, heh-heh—cares about urban planning. Well, do you know what the developer of the new town of Columbia told the Urban Design Conference at Harvard?" Adam and Addison admitted they could not recall offhand. "The greatest piece of urban design in the United States is," Walt leaned forward and tapped Adam's knee, "Disneyland."

"Sixty million people have visited Disneyland," Roy said, "from every state in the union, and just about every country on earth. At the New York World's Fair, four of the most popular attractions were Disney shows and exhibits." Roy smacked his lips as if he were thinking about lemon meringue pie. "We entertained more than a hundred fifty thousand people a day."

"So that's what this is," Addison said, "another Disneyland."

"Not land," Roy corrected, "Disney *World*."

It was the first time Adam had ever heard those words put together, and the sound made his heart beat faster. "But why do you call it the Venezuela Project?"

"This is big, Adam," Walt said. "Bigger than you realize. We have to be secretive." For a while Walt stared out the window at the orange groves rolling past. "The Orange Blossom Trail," he mused aloud. He turned and looked Adam in the eye; the great cartoonist's face was sad. "People know Disneyland is their land," Walt said; somehow it seemed he should be singing it. "Disneyland is dedicated to the ideals, the dreams, and the hard facts which have created America, with the hope that it will be a source of joy and inspiration to all the world, but after we built it, almost overnight—cheap, garish, tacky," he said, as if each word had a unique and unpleasant taste, "hotels and restaurants sprang up all around. It was a disgrace."

"They were cashing in on us," Roy said. "Our work."

Walt acknowledged his brother with a grateful nod. "This time will be different. Florida has a blessing we never had in California—size. There's enough land to hold all the plans and dreams we could ever imagine." He spread his arms as far as the limousine's confines allowed. "And no one will have to drive through . . . ," he made a rolling motion with his hand to come up with the words he wanted, "through gimcrack and tasteless junk to get here. Every approach will be a thing of beauty."

"You're going to unbungle it," Adam said.

"Yes, that's it exactly." Walt laughed. "We're finally going to unbungle it. We're going to unbungle it," he murmured again. "Did you know, my parents were married here?" Outside orange groves gave way to a lake, and behind it a row of cypress, their crowns joining and curtained with Spanish moss as if they formed the colonnade of a gnome's palace. As the limo passed, a white kestrel tucked its wings and dropped to the water to retrieve a fat fish. Walt looked on this and folded his hands on his stomach and closed his eyes as he thought of all the improvements he would make, and in a moment he was sleeping. Roy delicately removed the burning cigarette from Walt's fingers and put it out in the ashtray. Then he spread a blanket over Walt's lap.

"He's so tired," Roy said. "You can't even imagine how tired, jetting back and forth across the country." Roy rested his hands on his thighs and looked at Walt's sleeping face with tender admiration. "This is the biggest thing we've ever done, he's ever done."

Two hours later, the limousine pulled off the highway and onto a side road. Adam realized they were driving through the property represented by red and blue pushpins on the map in his office.

Roy gently shook his brother's shoulder. "Walter, we're almost there."

Walt blinked and sat up, pinched the sleep from his eyes, and smiled at Adam. "You're going to see something we think is quite remarkable. And I hope you have an appetite."

Although he had skipped breakfast, the thought of putting anything in his stomach made Adam queasy, but he smiled sickly and nodded.

They turned off the blacktop and onto a rutted sand and gravel road. Orange trees moved past either window in shifting perspective.

"We're pulling up now, Mr. Disney," came Donald's voice over the speaker.

"Thank you, Donald," Walt said.

They stopped in front of a dilapidated two-story farmhouse. General Potter was behind them in the jeep. Donald opened the door for Roy and Walt, and Adam and Addison let themselves out the other side. They stood blinking in the bright December sunlight in a sandy yard.

Cars and trucks were parked in front of the porch rail, but there was no other sign of life. A coop, now silent and forlorn of chickens, stood behind them. In a shed door the nose of a rusty green tractor leaned its wheel-less axle on a stack of cinder blocks. Torn hogwire, partly detached from poles and sagging like a pregnant belly, fenced what must have been a garden but was now overgrown with onion grass and pokeweed. The front porch rails of the farmhouse were splintered or missing. A dust devil started up at their ankles but then thought better of it and desisted. Had there been tumbleweeds in central Florida, this would have been the perfect occasion for one to roll by.

"Not very prepossessing, is it?" Walt asked with a laugh.

General Potter joined them. "Lookee what I found," he said. In his hands was Wrigley's attaché.

"Good boy!" Walt said, taking it from him. He opened it and withdrew Exhibit A. "It's really my fault this fell into your hands," he told Adam. "I couldn't resist sharing some of my preliminary jottings with Mr. Adder. Good work, General," he said. "Tell Donald he may take you home." Potter's smile wavered at being dismissed this way, but Walt was too preoccupied by Exhibit A to notice. "And now," he said. He handed Roy the attaché. "Both of you must swear you will breathe no word to anyone of what you see here."

Adam jokingly raised his right hand and said, "I solemnly swear," but Walt and Roy nodded seriously and then stared at Addison until he did the same.

They walked up squeaky loose steps to the porch, and Walt opened the door.

Addison was so astonished, he not only gasped; he actually said the word "gasp."

It was like a cross between Santa's workshop and Frankenstein's laboratory.

Men in lab coats, business suits, and artist's smocks worked at tables covered with pneumatic tubes, hunks of modeling clay, oscilloscopes, and drawings. People around a table with a human head on it examined an array of glass eyes of all different colors glued to a white board. Boards with similar arrays of hair, teeth, and patches of skin rested against a table leg. Part of the ceiling had been cut away on the far wall, and an enormous map stretched from the floor to out of sight on the second story. Sheets of paper covered the map with notations and changes, which had smaller pieces of paper posted to them, which were posted with even smaller pieces of paper. There was a steady background hubbub of hammers, drills, and muted but excited conversation. From the rear of the house came delicious smells.

"The main office, of course, is back in Burbank," Walt explained, "but I wanted to have a satellite operation on-site." He put a hand on Roy's shoulder. "Roy doesn't always approve of WED Enterprises, doesn't see the money in it. But this is where the magic begins."

Three employees came up as Walt entered. The first showed him several pages of a script. Walt's lips moved silently as he read. His eyes turned to the ceiling and he mumbled a phrase to himself, tasting the words. "I think it's very good," Walt said, handing the pages back to the writer and pointing at one section, "but see if you can find a synonym for this one word. I mean, *I* know what it means, and *you* know what it means, but . . . You have to remember we're just talking to plain folks here. We're not giving them an IQ test."

"Yes, sir," the writer said, and hurried off for a revision.

The second unrolled a broad sheet of stiff paper to show Walt resort plans. "Yes, yes, I think it's much improved," Walt said, "but what if we—" He held his hand out, and Roy supplied a ballpoint. "Here. And here. And then we can put this here." With a few scrawls, loops, and lines, Walt uprooted and transplanted a golf course, changed the shoreline of a lake, and shifted a handful of high-rise hotels. "See if that doesn't work better."

"Yes, sir," the designer said and headed back to his drawing board.

The third showed Walt a drawing on which lines chased each other across an electric schematic. "I came up with something for the Sleeping Beauty Suite," he said. "We can hide the electronics in the wall, see, behind the mirror. And the mirror's one-way glass. When you turn on a switch, the mirror changes into a TV, just like—"

"Just like the magic mirror in Sleeping Beauty!" Walt exclaimed as he took the plans from the engineer. "This is stupendous—the very thing! And you know what else we need," Walt looked up, his eyes sparkling, "a glass slipper!"

"Sleeping Beauty's glass slipper," the engineer breathed in a hushed tone.

"We'll put it on a pillow or a pedestal. We'll put it on a pillow and put the *pillow* on a pedestal. Who are those people who make that fancy glass?"

"Steuben?"

"That's the folks! Get them on the phone and see what they can work up for us."

The engineer set off.

Walt rubbed his hands together. "Now, let's see what Marie and Anatole have whipped up for us. You're in for a treat, I think, gentlemen."

All morning a sensation of déjà vu had afflicted Addison; Disney reminded him of someone, but for the life of him, he couldn't think who until now. Disney and his father looked nothing alike, of course, except for the manic gleam in the eye, the irresistible quality that pulled everything toward them, like a bar magnet yanking paper clips and loose staples off a desk. What made them almost identical was this belief they shared, a belief that in their presence you couldn't help sharing yourself: although the world was a torn place and a sour one, it could yet be set to rights—and they were just the ones to do it.

On the way to the kitchen, Walt couldn't resist stopping by the long table and examining the workings of the human head, which Addison now saw was President Johnson. "We've built a talking, moving Abraham Lincoln," Walt told them. "We've put together the best parts from all his speeches. He's going to address a roomful of all the presidents. It'll be as if down through the ages our leaders are heeding his wisdom."

"As Lyndon listens to the speech," an engineer explained, "he's going to nod his head thoughtfully and blink his eyes." As one engineer held the head by the temples, his younger assistant reached inside LBJ's neck and worked some controls to make him do just that.

"Very nice," Walt said. "But don't overdo it. We don't want him to be distracting."

"So this is the Experimental Prototype," Adam said.

The engineers regarded Adam with amused smiles.

"Not even close, Adam." Walt chuckled. "This is a mere . . . taste, and speaking of tastes, let's see what's cooking for lunch."

In the kitchen, fragrant steam filled the air, and gleaming stockpots simmered on an enormous commercial stove. A white-aproned woman ladled sauce on a glistening bird in the oven. Cakes lay in profusion on a butcher-block counter. One was castle-shaped; white icing drizzled over its turrets like fallen snow, a red and white banner on a tower froze midflap.

A man in a pastry chef's hat came up as Walt broke a piece off the banner, which looked as supple as ribbon, but actually was brittle as a mica chip. Walt put it in his mouth and nodded with a smile. "Mmm. Peppermint. Gentlemen, this is our pastry chef, Anatole, the artist responsible for all this." He waved his hand over the display of desserts. "*Bonjour*, Anatole."

"*Bonjour*, Monsieur Disney."

"And Marie—come here, there's someone I want you to meet. *Bonjour*, Marie."

The woman who had been glazing the meat closed the oven and came over with a demure smile. She also wore a chef's hat, but hers was much taller than Anatole's.

"*Bonjour, messieurs*," Marie said.

They shook hands. Marie and Anatole had the deceptively strong, calloused hands of professional chefs.

"*Bonjour*," Adam said.

"Hello," Addison said.

"*Bonjour*," Marie said to Addison as if she were correcting him for speaking English. Addison suspected that Marie and Anatole would have never said *bonjour* in the States, except not doing so would have disappointed their employer.

"We hired Marie and Anatole at great expense from two of the finest establishments in Paris, didn't we, Roy? They're going to supervise the menus for some of our restaurants."

"I have something for you," Marie said.

"Ah, is it—?" Walt asked.

Marie sawed three crusty slices from a French loaf and spread them with brown paste.

"The pâté," Walt said, accepting his slice. "Pâté de fois gras," he told Adam with a wink, "just like they eat in Gay Paree."

The four of them took a bite. Adam, with his weak stomach, could do no more than nibble, but Addison recognized the rich flavor of goose liver as heaven smeared on bread. Roy grimaced as if he'd just bitten into dog turd while Walt chewed thoughtfully and stared at the ceiling. "I should have warned you, Marie," Walt said, "Adam here is a former restaurateur, aren't you, Adam? He knows a thing or two about food himself."

"The pâté is wonderful," Addison said. Adam nodded, although he could not bear to eat it; Evelyn would have loved it.

Walt discreetly cleaned a bit from his back molars with a finger. "You know what I think this needs," he said. "More bacon flavor."

"There is no bacon in pâté, Monsieur," Marie said.

"I know," Walt said. "But people like bacon. I like bacon. You like bacon, don't you, Roy?"

Roy nodded that he also liked bacon, and then said in a conciliatory way, taking a pinch of bread and tasting it, "The bread is great, though."

"Oh, yes," Walt said. "The bread is superb, can't improve upon the bread. But try some more bacon flavor in the pâté and see if that doesn't improve it any."

Anatole seated them at a table spread with a white tablecloth and set with china and crystal for two. Anatole brought two additional settings for Adam and Addison. "This is my favorite part of the job," Walt said with a smile. He took the elegantly folded stiff linen napkin from his crystal goblet and snapped it open with a flourish of his wrist. "Trying out our restaurants' bill of fare. As you can see, Adam," Walt waved a hand over the table, "we intend for the guests of Disney World to have only the best of everything."

"Yes," Adam said. "It was the same way with Paradise Dogs. The best of everything." Adam hardly dared to ask, "Does that include cocktails?"

"Well, of course, Adam," Walt said. "One of the wait staff here is a qualified bartender. What would you care for?"

Jack and Coke was what Adam would care for, and one was fetched without delay. Walt and Roy watched anxiously for Adam's verdict as he tasted it. "It's good, it's good," Adam said. "It's not bad. Actually," he finished it off, "I think it could use just a little less Coke and a little more Jack." A look from Walt communicated that another cocktail was to be brought more to Adam's liking. The second one arrived, and Adam drank it as well. Under the table, his knee stopped its bouncing. Then the world seemed not so bad, and he himself a sterling lad.

"By the way, we ordered some Châteauneuf du Pape to go with this meal," Walt said. Adam felt the day was taking a distinct upward turn. "Unfortunately the bottles were broken in transit." Walt shook his head regretfully.

"It was insured, though," Roy said. "The trucking company will have to cover it." As their waiter brought their drinks—Fresca for Walt and Roy, sweet tea for Addison, and another Jack and Coke for Adam—another waiter arrived with the first course, shrimp cocktail. Walt tasted one and pronounced it delicious.

"So if the prototype isn't the robot," Adam said, "what is it?"

Walt did not answer directly, but asked instead, "If you could design a city starting from scratch, from the ground up, how would it look?" Walt was interrupted by a spate of coughing and broke off.

Adam confessed he had no ideas on the subject. "Different, I guess, from the way cities are now." Walt nodded and pressed a napkin to his lips. Clearly whatever the Experimental Prototype was, he was not prepared to divulge it yet.

One waiter removed the remains of the shrimp cocktail as another brought the second course, bouillabaisse, and for a time the table was silent except for soft slurps and the clacking of soup spoons against bowls. When the third course came, duck a l'orange and asparagus tips in a cream sauce, Addison began to feel clotted with food. Adam set the edge of his cocktail in the cream sauce and, trying to wipe off the bottom of the glass with his napkin, managed to knock Walt's Fresca into the duck.

"I'm sorry," Adam said.

Addison reached to mop up his father's spill and his elbow struck Roy's unguarded glass, knocking it over as well. At this new catastrophe, Adam leaned over the table without looking where he put his hand. He yelped and jumped backward as only a man who feels warm cream and orange sauces oozing between his fingers can do. He kicked the table, and everything on it cleared the linen cloth a full inch before landing with a stupendous racket.

After the last clattering saucer had come to rest, silence reigned. Everything that could be knocked over that hadn't been knocked over already, was knocked over now. To be truthful, the additional tally wasn't much: Addison's and Adam's glasses, the salt and pepper shakers, and a cut-glass flower vase that poured a small lake onto the tablecloth.

"Is it all clear? Is it safe to sit down now?" Roy asked the Newmans with an aplomb that did him credit under the circumstances. He stood back, eluding the mixture of liquids that had chosen his side of the table as the best location from which to cascade.

"Don't worry about it, Adam," Walt said. From amid ice cubes and diet soda Walt salvaged one bite of duck in its sweet sauce, chewed it thoughtfully, then leaned back from the wreckage and patted his stomach. "I'm really full anyway. Whew! It's hard to believe the French eat like this every day!" He lit a cigarette.

Two servers came to clear the damage and replace the table linens and settings. "You're going to miss the crêpes suzette," one waiter said.

Roy looked up with interest. It was evident he was enjoying the rest of the meal more than he had the pâté.

"I am so sorry," Walt said. "Tell Anatole perhaps next time. I think our guests are replete as well." Adam and Addison both said they couldn't touch another bite, to Roy's evident relief. "You'll let us know how the crêpes were, won't you, Roy?" Walt asked. "I have something I want to show the Newmans."

Adam rose, somewhat woozily, feeling as if he'd ingested a glass paperweight, and he and Addison followed Walt back into the front room.

"Actually," Adam said thickly, "I think I need to see a man about a dog. Is there a—"

"A washroom?" Walt asked. "Of course. Right through there."

Adam stepped into the bathroom and had a nice refreshing vomit before rinsing his face and rejoining Walt. Thankfully, enough alcohol had already entered his system that his hands were reasonably steady.

The men and women were still hard at work at their various projects. Some of them were eating sandwiches or drinking from thermoses.

"I insist they stop for lunch," Walt said, trying to sound displeased, "but they just can't help themselves. Everyone is so excited about this project. When I built Disneyland, I had no specifications, no standards to follow. I created a design organization called WED Enterprises. Designers, engineers, artists, old-world craftsmen and people skilled in the latest space-age technology came together," Walt laced his fingers to demonstrate, "all working in cooperation in the Disney way. What we do is called imagineering: anything that works becomes the code, anything that doesn't is scrapped," he snapped his fingers, "replaced by a better idea." They stopped at a table to watch a white-smocked woman paint a replica of the fairy-tale castle on *Disney's Wonderful World of Color.*

"This is just a scale model. The real one will be visible from every spot in the park," Walt said, "and at night, Tinkerbell will fly from the tower . . . but come here, this is what I really wanted to show you."

Beside the enormous map that reached through the hole in the ceiling, Walt picked up a pointer such as college professors use, only longer. "You have been curious, gentlemen, about the Experimental Prototype. Again, you have to promise that everything you are about to hear and see will remain strictly confidential until the time comes for me to reveal it myself."

"Yes, sir."

"Of course."

Walt smiled. "I trust you. Adam. Addison." He tapped the map two times. "The Experimental Prototype."

"I don't—what?" Adam was nonplused.

"The Experimental Prototype Community of Tomorrow. For short, EPCOT." Walt pointed to something on the map that looked like a single-celled organism undergoing mitosis. "A whole town, twenty thousand residents, completely planned, controlled, and self-contained for workers to live in. Low, affordable rents. A showcase for industry, education, culture, and research. Since there won't be any landowners, there won't be any voting control. There aren't going to be any slums," he said with the finality of a restaurant patron sending back the oysters, "because I won't allow them. And no retirees. Everyone in my city has to *work*. I want them to keep my city *alive*.

"It's all designed as a circle. The businesses and commercial buildings will be at the center, then schools and community centers in the middle, and residential areas on the perimeter. People will get around on monorails and peoplemovers like at Disneyland. Autos will be routed through underground tunnels, so pedestrians will be safe aboveground." Walt unzipped a large black portfolio and showed them architects' conceptions of walkways and green parks radiating out from magnificent gleaming skyscrapers, cars whizzing through brightly lit underground transportation hubs, smartly dressed pedestrians admiring the old-world architecture of an Italian villa. Someone brought Adam another Jack and Coke, and as Walt continued describing his Community of Tomorrow, Adam realized it was a scheme so grand it made a roomful of robotic presidents trivial by comparison: there would no traffic, because all cars and trucks would travel in tunnels beneath the city; there would be no humidity or rain because the entire city would be enclosed in a transparent dome—the air inside would be climate controlled to an ideal seventy-five degrees year-round; all houses would be outfitted with the latest technology, students would be educated with the most up-to-date methods. "EPCOT will be in a constant state of becoming," Walt said.

"Imagineering," Adam murmured, staring at a marker drawing of passersby pausing under a vine-draped balcony to enjoy a bagpipe concert as a monorail glided silently overhead on an elevated track. Seeing artists' renderings of Walt's vision brought back a memory of standing before the empty storefront that would become Paradise Dogs. *We're not going to make barbecue*, Adam said, *or biscuits, or bagels. Just hot dogs.*

*But the very best hot dogs*, Evelyn had promised, nestling her head against his neck.

"The theme park and its hotels are also going to be a highlight of the development," said Roy, who had joined them, evidently having finished his crêpes. In one hand he held a contract, in the other a fountain pen. "We're developing an area between Bonnet Creek Swamp and Reedy Creek Swamp."

"So one thing we won't have to worry about is trespassing," Walt said with a wink.

"Oh, Mr. Disney," Adam said. In his enthusiasm he forgot to call him Walt. "This is the most wonderful thing I've ever heard." Impulsively he put his arms around the great man, dribbling a little diluted Jack and Coke down his back.

"I can see you're a visionary like myself, Adam," Walt said. He extracted himself from Adam's embrace. "Now you understand why I need this land. So under the circumstances," Walt said, taking the contract from Roy and presenting it to Adam, "shall we say a hundred and ten dollars an acre?"

"Under the circumstances . . ." Adam said, pulling out a handkerchief to wipe his teary eyes and blow his nose. He raised his glass and sucked the last remaining flavor from the ice cubes, ". . . let's say a hundred and twenty five."

"I think the rehearsal transpired quite satisfactorily," Lily said when she and Adam came home that evening from St. George's.

"Yes," Adam said. He set his keys on the counter. In truth, he had been less than impressed by Father Peel's handling of the rehearsal. The fact Adam had no ring put the priest at a loss. Father Peel, Adam thought, was not flexible—he had no ability to improvise. Adam himself had been known to conduct marriages in jail cells with far less fuss and bother, but his mind was on another matter. "Tomorrow I have to get up early to pick up the tuxedos."

"We will go together." Lily gave him a kiss on the cheek and filled his nostrils with her cedar-smelling perfume. "The photographer will be there early, so we can get pictures. You were such a sly boots this morning, slipping out of the house before I knew you were up. Heh-heh."

For some reason, her employment of the phrase "sly boots" struck Lily as risible. Adam shrugged. "I may watch a little television."

"You go right ahead," Lily said. "I am going to take care of some things in the kitchen." She kissed him on the head, and as soon as his attention was absorbed by *Daily Business Roundup*, Lily slid Adam's keys off the counter into her palm, careful not to let them make a noise. In the cabinet? Too obvious. Under the toaster? He'd see it there.

Adam sank into his chair and stared at the gray image of an announcer reading news bulletins. Adam's attention wasn't really directed to the program, although it shared some very gloom-inducing revelations about the personal life of Moore Lock's president. He was thinking that tomorrow he would definitely break it off with Lily, but would wait until the photographer was done so at least she could have the pictures. He was also thinking that he still had one last chance to help out Addison. Kathleen was bound for the bauxite mines in the wilds of Arkansas; there was no way to prevent that, but Adam was certain that if she could just spend some time with Addison alone, she would recognize his hidden but unmistakable qualities of character, and at least know what she had missed.

But how to handle Kean? Chloroform under the window? Knockout drops in his orange juice?

As Lily looked for a place to hide Adam's keys, she was very pleased, and she had reason to be. Earlier, at the church, she had already begun to fabricate an alibi for the priest when Adam and Addison came through the church door. Adam was not only on time for the rehearsal, but only mildly drunk. It had been a miracle; there was no other word for it, but there was no point hoping for two miracles. Adam had slipped out of Lily's supervision once without provoking utter calamity, but she did not believe in pushing her luck.

Anywhere inside the house, she decided, was too risky. She quietly slid open the glass door and stepped onto the back patio. A terra-cotta flowerpot tethered to the wall by a dusty cobweb sat overturned beside the spigot. Careful not to disturb the web, Lily tilted the dusty pot back just enough to slide two sets of keys—hers and Adam's—underneath. She came inside and rinsed her hands. Tomorrow, he would not leave the house without her, she was sure.

No doubt sleep came slowly to Don Quixote when he was looking forward to dealing with a tricky batch of windmills in the morning; thus it was with Adam. That night in bed, Adam was still tumbling in his mind what to do about Kean. He would have to be free to operate without Lily around—that went without saying, so he'd have to make sure to leave the house without her. Sunk into the pillow, facing the wall, stratagems and tactics for the dawn filled his head, swirling and colliding like free-falling pieces of a jigsaw puzzle. Suddenly he smiled as he realized that he was doing just what Walt Disney himself did all the time. "I'm imagineering," he murmured, pleased with himself. "Imagineering."

Lily thought he said, "Imagine earrings," and was glad she had hidden the keys.

That night Adam dreamed the Old Man was showing him the lawnmower and explaining, "You see here, this lever." He pushed down a little steel handle on the side of the engine. "You have to be very, very careful with it, because if you accidentally leave it up, it goes off by itself." The Old Man was angry because only moments ago, the lawnmower had started up while he was cleaning it. A wheel had gone off and grazed his ear and somehow left a hole in the ceiling. Adam had been playing in the garden when he heard the lawnmower's backfire, and then somehow he was in the closet under the stairs, among the dusty glass jars. He had come out to see the Old Man waiting for him. Adam's mother had overreacted and called the sheriff. "He was cleaning it," she lied, "and it went off by itself." There had been a big to-do getting everything calmed down again, but in spite of being in serious trouble for ignoring their warnings not to touch it, Adam felt lighthearted, and in his sleep, tears of relief filled his eyes.

# SIXTEEN

# Adam Fetches the Tuxes

"Caleb is still finishing up Kean's pants," Adam explained. "He's going to bring them by in just a bit." Adam stood in the doorway, already dressed in his own tuxedo. He had arrived with everything but the aforementioned pants before Evelyn and her sons had scraped egg yolk from the breakfast dishes into the compost bucket. Evelyn was in her robe, and Kean was wearing his striped pajamas.

Adam presented Addison's tuxedo to him. "Why don't you go ahead and change?" Addison toddled off to do as his father suggested. "What I think we ought to do," Adam said in lower tones to Evelyn and Kean, who regarded him with suspicion born of long familiarity, "in the meantime is that, Evelyn, you go ahead and pick up Kathleen and get her to St. George's. The photographer will be there shortly and they can go ahead and get in their shots. As soon as Kean's pants arrive, we'll join up with you. Kean probably needs to take a quick shower anyway."

Adam had woken that morning with a tremendous thirst

and searched his house thoroughly for a restorative, but of course, as he'd observed earlier, the cabinets, refrigerator, and toilet tank were bare of the necessaries. He seemed to recall, however, having once placed a cocktail out of harm's way under a flowerpot when he was mowing the backyard. He couldn't remember how long ago he had done it, but there was a slim chance some residue might remain. When he looked, however, instead of a partially evaporated Jack and Coke, there was his car keys, which, while an unexpected discovery, was really just as good because the Little General would open at ten, and in the meantime he could deliver the tuxedos and carry out his plan.

"Really," Adam persisted, answering their silent stares, which were as cold as the refreshing malt beverage that no one had thought to offer him. He looked at the Christmas tree to avoid their eyes, only to meet the placid, all-knowing gaze of a disturbingly effeminate Yogi Bear. "The photographer's got to get in as many pictures as he can before the ceremony. People will start arriving at the church in another hour or so. We don't want to push things behind." He looked at his watch to emphasize the point. " 'The bird of time has but a little way to flutter, and lo! The bird is on the wing!' I really advise you to giddy-up."

Evelyn bit her lip and behind her languid eyes pondered the dilemma; she was deeply torn between the desire to make sure this wedding came off without a hitch, and the very sensible reluctance to leave Adam without a keeper. Adam seemed sober, always an unexpected plus, but she had the definite impression that he was not to be trusted.

"I don't see why you can't just go with Mom and Addison while I wait for my pants," Kean protested.

"Surely you're not suggesting you come to the wedding on your motorcycle," Adam said reasonably.

"This is silly, Adam," Evelyn said. "Addison can just take Kean to the church in his Volkswagen."

Adam's knee began bobbing. What would Don Quixote do in such a situation—when windmills stubbornly refused to cooperate with the plan? What would Walt Disney do?

"That's a good idea," Adam said with all the coolness he could muster. He avoided Boo-boo's eerily staring eyes. "You and I can go to the church alone, Evelyn. There's something I wanted to tell you on the way."

Evelyn reacted as if a palmetto bug had gone down her neck. That settled it. Evelyn got dressed, half hoping Kean's pants would arrive before she was ready to leave. They did not arrive, however, and in spite of grave misgivings, she went to collect Kathleen. She gave Kean a look as if to say, *You look after him.*

When they were gone, stepson and stepfather stared at each other like deer heads mounted on opposite walls. Adam drummed his fingers lightly on the arm of the couch. "You'd like to take a shower before your pants arrive, I expect," Adam said.

"I took a shower last night."

"That long ago? Then you definitely do need a shower. I expect you've already been doing your—whatchamacallit—your karate practice. You're rather sweaty, I can see."

"I'm not sweaty. I won't do my dojo until after the wedding."

Adam exhaled through tightened lips and said, "I didn't want to tell you this, Kean, but frankly, you stink. Body odor. It's nothing personal—it's just what comes from having a muscular physique. I didn't want to say it in front of the others, but you really need a shower." A terrible stillness fell over the room. Time stretched between the ticks of the wall clock like telephone poles along a state road. "In fact, don't tell her

I told you this, but when you weren't looking, your mother told me, 'Please make sure Kean takes a shower before you let him put on that tuxedo.'" An angry furrow appeared between Kean's eyebrows and his face reddened, but he made no move. "You should have just enough time to shower before the pants arrive."

Kean stood up with a huff. "Okay! Okay!" And left the room.

Adam waited a few minutes and then stole quietly to the back of the house. Sure enough, as he passed the hall bathroom, he heard water running. Next, Adam went into Kean's room. The striped pajamas Kean had been wearing were draped over the foot of the bed, and the tuxedo coat Adam had brought was hanging in the closet. Satisfied, Adam took the wooden chair from behind Kean's desk. The clatter when he knocked over Kean's karate trophy nearly made him jump out of his skin, but a moment's silence calmed him. When Adam righted the trophy, he saw that in its fall the little karate fighter that topped it had broken off. Adam carefully leaned the figure against the gilt laurel wreath that adorned the middle tier.

He took the chair into the hallway and propped it under the bathroom doorknob. He pounded on the door. "Kean! Kean!" He pounded again. "Kean, turn off the shower!"

The shower noise ceased, and Adam imagined Kean stepping dripping onto the bathmat into soap-fragrant steam.

"Are the pants here?" Kean asked from the other side of the door.

"No. Actually I had the pants all along," Adam replied. "It was subterfuge."

"What?"

"Subterfuge. Kean, I've locked you in the bathroom." There was a pause as Kean absorbed this, then a storm of rattling as he tried to open the door.

"Adam, what the devil are you up to?"

"Look, Kean," Adam said patiently. He was pleased to find Addison's stratagem had worked as advertised. "There's no point letting yourself get irrational about this. You could, if you really wanted to, squeeze through the bathroom window, I suppose, but I seem to recall there being some holly bushes under that particular window, so your landing would be far from pleasant. And then what? I'm going to make sure all the doors are locked when I leave, so you'd have to figure out a way to break in, in the meantime scampering around dressed, at best, in a bath towel."

Loud pounding on the door commenced, and Kean shouted, "Goddamn it, Adam, goddamn it!"

"Kean, please, you're getting irrational," Adam said. He didn't like raising his voice, but he had to make himself heard. It was so hard dealing with people when they didn't act reasonable. "On the other hand—on the other hand—listen, Kean, listen—on the other hand—there's another hand. Are you listening?" The pounding stopped. "You could just make yourself comfortable and wait until the others get home. The wedding won't last more than an hour on the outside. You can take a relaxing bath, study for the MCAT—unless I miss my guess, you have a study guide in there with you right now, am I right?—and generally just relax. When you think about it, you really won't be that disappointed to miss my wedding, will you?" No answer. "Will you, Kean?"

"Addison," Kean shouted. "Addison, come here!"

"He can't hear you," Adam said, not believing this himself.

The phone rang and rang again, then stopped. Somehow the knowledge that elsewhere in the house Addison was conducting an ordinary phone conversation took the wind out of Kean's protests. There were three more pounds on the door, but Adam could tell Kean's heart wasn't in them. They were the pounds of a man who no longer expects to be released but who feels obligated to demonstrate his resentment. "For the love of God, Adam," Kean said at last.

"Yes, Fortunato, for the love of God," Adam replied, but if Kean appreciated the allusion to Poe, he didn't show it.

Adam made a quick tour of the house to make sure all the doors were locked.

Addison had been admiring himself in the full-length mirror on the back of his mother's bedroom door. A heavily starched shirt fresh from the dry cleaner's and a clip-on bow tie completed his ensemble. He had turned right profile and left, seeing the figure he cut from each side and full-on. He had posed his arms in suspended gestures of casual conversation, like the models in the Sears catalog. The black elegance had made him look slim and smart.

He became aware of a loud commotion of pounding mixed with his brother's voice. He heard his own name and was just about to see what the matter was, after allowing himself just one more three-quarter turn in the mirror, when the phone rang; it was Mr. Beasley. Addison anticipated a discussion of just what the heck he'd meant by not showing up for work yesterday, but as it turned out Beasley had quite a different topic in mind. "This is awful, Addison, the worst, even for you." Although it is impossible that Beasley's candid critique of his latest obituary should have blown from the receiver in a hot wind, Addison felt it did, and as he held the phone from his ear during this inexplicable conversation, he passed a hand over his hair as if it had been mussed in a gale. "Clearly you aren't fit for writing obituaries," Beasley said, and Addison waited for the hammer blow to fall, *you're fired*, but instead, Beasley went on, "I'm putting you on features. I mean, what the hell. You can't do any more damage there, I reckon."

Beasley hung up, and Addison replaced the phone numbly. The noises from the other end of the house had ceased, and Addison idly wondered what it had been about. Before he could ponder this or his employer's mysterious phone call further, his father came in the room.

"Well, Addison, let's go ahead and get in the jeep and we'll go to the wedding."

"What about Kean?"

"Plan B," Adam said cryptically. "Go ahead and get in the jeep."

"So is Kean coming later?"

"Something like that. There's a couple of stops we have to make on the way."

They drove to an exclusive neighborhood and turned between two stone gates surmounted by lions. A winding drive of blindingly white concrete led them between overhanging palms past a birdbath with the Venus de Milo and another featuring a Greek discus thrower. The driveway came to a circle around a three-tiered fountain topped by Rodin's "Thinker" in front of a white stuccoed mansion with Corinthian columns and terra-cotta roof tiles.

Adam got out and raised the heavy knocker on the massive oaken door before noticing and pressing the door chime. A few moments later a man opened the door wearing a blue terry-cloth robe and bedroom slippers. In spite of the lavishness of his surroundings, the mansion's owner did not look as if he'd known a moment's peace. A girl, somewhat younger than Addison, appeared in the door behind him, eating a bowl of Froot Loops with a sullen expression.

"Adam!" the man said. "You have the diamonds?"

"No," Adam said. "But something just as good. For you, anyway. The money to pay for them." Adam took his checkbook out of his jacket pocket and held it on his thigh as he made it out. The sight of the sum staggered even him. It was every penny he had on earth.

"Is it any good?" the girl asked. Milk dribbled down her chin.

"Of course it's good," Adam said. " "I have to ask you not to cash it until Tuesday, but it's good. I've got a deal that went through, and then I have to transfer some funds around." He tore off the check and gave it to his friend. Addison surmised correctly this was Ernie Costa.

"Thanks, Adam," Ernie said solemnly. "So you don't think the diamonds will show up?"

"'Fraid not," Adam said almost cheerfully. "Will you be able to keep Bert off till Tuesday?" Adam's left nipple twinged at the memory of meeting Ernie's brother-in-law.

"Sure," Ernie said. "And if the diamonds show up in the meantime—"

"And if the diamonds show up in the meantime, you'll be the first to know," Adam said. "Well, I have a wedding to get to."

Ernie gave Adam a hug. "Good luck, boss," he said.

Adam and Addison walked back to the jeep. "That pretty much cleans me out. It'll wipe out what I made from the land sale plus whatever dregs are left after Sam liquidates my portfolio." Adam snapped his fingers. "But, as Longfellow had it, 'Into each life some rain must fall.'" Adam shook his head, and they climbed back into the jeep and started off. "I have the strangest sense of déjà vu."

"Didn't you just say that?"

"What?"

"Nothing."

By the time they pulled into the parking lot of the Little General, Adam's hands were shaking quite violently from the release of adrenaline and the sheer intestinal fortitude it had taken dealing with Kean and writing a check that represented all his earthly riches. Heretofore, Adam had always imagined his stepson a very calm and rational sort of person, but Kean's extreme reaction to being locked in the bathroom showed just how far wrong he had been.

Adam parked the jeep in front of the store and took the key from the ignition. "At the church you're going to have some time alone with Kathleen before she's off to the bauxite mines," Adam remarked, seemingly apropos of nothing. "Best man and maid of honor." Adam sighed and rested his hands on the steering wheel. "I'm going inside and get myself a ginger ale. I'm a mite parched." But he didn't get out of the jeep right away. Instead, he turned to Addison and said, "My own life is pretty much bungled beyond repair. Even with the profit from Walt Disney, I've got to pay off the mortgage on the property, and then there's that bloody margin call to cover. If only we'd found the diamonds, or even half of them, I could rebuild my finances—I'd like to invest in Disney Enterprises, I can tell you that—but it's too late for me. I've bungled, like I said. I'm not feeling sorry for myself." Adam put a trembling hand on Addison's shoulder and said, "I only told you that so I could tell you this." And then Adam made a speech, if you could call anything so concise and to-the-point a speech. In any case it moved Addison profoundly. Adam began with a line of poetry—it might have been something from the St. Crispin's Eve speech in *Henry V*—and then he spoke of the past, and how it had been ruined, and the future, and how it might yet be redeemed. Addison felt that the mantle of the Newman family had been laid upon his shoulders, and that his father felt fully confident that he would rise and fill it magnificently.

While Adam was inside, Addison pondered his father's words, and repeated them to himself to be sure that he would never forget them. He could not recall later, however, exactly what his father said because the unexpected sight of Adam dashing from the convenience store as if it had caught fire scattered Addison's thoughts like blackbirds.

Stepping into the store had overwhelmed Adam with déjà vu: first from the cashier who told him he couldn't buy beer on Sunday, then from the display of inflatable Xmas palms marked down for after-Christmas clearance. It was when the cashier told him she had been there when he'd delivered the baby that Adam recalled. It was she who had brought the bag of ice, she said, proudly taking a drag on her Lucky Strike and popping her gum.

"The baby, yes, of course," Adam had said, pointing to the spot where the incident had taken place. They had mistaken him for Dr. Bateman, and he hadn't had the heart to let them down. He'd let them have his blue windbreaker to wrap the baby in. He'd been on his way to give Evelyn one last chance. "And that couple, they live nearby, don't they?"

The cashier told him they lived across the street in Cypress Trailer Park.

Of course they couldn't find the trailer.

"Things like this never happened to the shoeshine boy," Adam said.

"What?"

"In the books I read as a child," Adam explained, craning his neck as he searched for the rusty two-tone Belaire, "they were always about a shoeshine boy. But he never had to stop for directions in an emergency, or if he did, the author didn't mention it." This was only one of many aspects in which literature was superior to real life, Adam reflected as they anxiously circled the trailer park a second time without spotting the young couple's car. He slowed to a stop beside a portly bald man walking two standard poodles, and rolled down the window. "Excuse me. By any chance do you know where a young couple live who recently had a baby? Their names are Johnny and Jane."

The man, who managed to look simultaneously astonished and bored, turned his back without speaking. Adam and Addison exchanged a look. Had he heard the question? Was he looking around for someone else to answer it? Was he demented?

The dog owner turned back and spoke in a ludicrous British accent, rolling each word off his protruding lower lip like a licorice toffee. "They live in the trailer behind me."

The shoeshine boy's creator would have excised such a scene without hesitation; it was undignified to make someone in a crisis depend for information on such a preposterous character.

They parked beside the trailer and for a time did nothing else.

"Dad?" Addison asked. He waited for his father to get out, but Adam just sat there. Adam's shoulders sank. He stared heartsick at the dented trash cans chained to a rusty metal post. At last he opened the jeep's door and swung his feet to the ground. Unaccountably, Adam realized he had felt better when he'd given up finding the diamonds for good. A horrible weight returned to his stomach at the thought that the diamonds actually might be somewhere inside that trailer.

Adam looked at his watch; it was ten-twenty. The bird of time had but a little way to flutter and the bird was on the wing. He had to wrap this up for good or ill and get to the church before the wedding to break it off with Lily.

He mounted the overturned plastic drum that served as a front stoop, but a thought stayed him as he raised his hand to knock: in the world of fiction, shoeshine boys hold all the cards and culprits hold none. The thief who takes the shoeshine boy's passbook always trips himself up in clumsy lies and contradictions as the shoeshine boy from his place of concealment looks on almost as much in pity as blame, but Adam's situation was different—how exactly did he hope this little drama would play out?

INT. DAY.

Johnny and Jane sit at ease reading the Sunday papers snug in their little trailer, little imagining their misdeeds are soon to catch up to them.

SOUND: Knocking on door.

JOHNNY

Goodness. I wonder who that could be at this time of the morning?

ADAM

(Entering with Addison, in tuxedos) Excuse me, I believe you have some stolen property of mine. May I search your trailer?

JANE

(In stunned alarm) Don't search the closet!

And of course that would be the very *first* place Adam would search, and having recovered the diamonds, would depart in frosty dignity. But Adam knew that the far more likely outcome—and by likely, Adam meant positively certain—would be their stout denials of having ever seen the diamonds, perhaps even truthful denials at that, and Adam would slink away shamefaced and not one diamond the better for his ordeal.

"Since we're here, Dad," Addison said, seeming to read his thoughts, "we need to go through with it. We'll always wonder and regret it if we don't."

Adam nodded, but without conviction. Really, there was no point even knocking, but Adam watched his knuckles tap on the doorframe as if they belonged to someone else. A two-beat pause, and he knocked again.

Frantic high-pitched barking greeted them, and Adam thought, This really is overdoing things. There'd just been a scene in which a man had appeared with two standard poodles, and now, here was another dog. The shoeshine boy's creator would never have employed such a feeble device twice in such a short space.

The door opened, but instead of Jane or Johnny, there was a compact woman with thundercloud-colored hair who by sweet talk and deftly aimed backward kicks interposed herself between the door and a yipping Jack Russell that seemed eager to tear Adam and Addison to shreds. "Stay back, sweetie." Kick. "The nice men won't hurt you." Kick. Kick. "Are y'all Mormons, or y'all here about the TV?"

"We aren't Mormons," Addison said.

"Are Johnny and Jane here?" Adam asked.

"Come on in," said the woman. "Y'all're going to fall off that bucket." Adam entered and the woman tried fruitlessly to scoop the dog from the floor, but it eluded her flabby arms and seized Adam's cuff in its sharp teeth. "Sweetie, leave that man alone."

"Who is it?" asked a man with close-cut red hair and a two-day growth of beard sitting at a rickety dinette table. His body looked as if fat and muscle were vying to see which would predominate.

"It's the men about the TV," said the woman, who evidently believed that on Sundays TV repairmen made house calls dressed in tuxedoes.

"I think we may be in the wrong place," Adam said apologetically. He was unwilling to kick Sweetie, but he shook his leg vigorously to make the dog untooth his cuff; if anything, however, Sweetie seemed to relish being hefted from the floor and hanging by his mouth. *Hey*, Sweetie's happy snarl seemed to say, *This is fun! Let's do it some more!* Addison knelt and tried to prize the dog's jaws open. "We're looking for Jane and Johnny."

"You're in the right place," the woman said. "I'm Jane's mama. I'm baby-sitting while they're at the early service." A bassinet sat under a curtainless window.

"Is that little Bateman?" Adam asked.

As soon as Addison succeeded in freeing his father's cuff, Sweetie twisted her head and nipped his hand. Addison dropped her, but she no longer harried Adam, devoting her full attention to Addison's ankle instead.

"I don't think they're calling it that anymore," Jane's mother said, peering over the edge of the basinet as if the child might have a name tag. "They're calling it Sally now. Anyway, my son-in-law says he knows he's behind in the payments, but he ain't sending y'all another dollar because the TV don't work."

The trailer was sparsely furnished, and what furniture there was seemed to have been found on the roadside. The dinette, already mentioned, was tucked near the kitchen end and filled up the greater part of the room. A piece of cardboard under one leg, folded triple to reach the desired thickness, did an inadequate job of steadying it. A kit-kat clock, grinning hopefully, but with forlorn eyes and pendulum tail unmoving, adorned a wall. Two lawn chairs, their woven plastic straps beginning to fray, faced a wooden spool once used for a power line, now turned on end as a coffee table, and a TV sat on a fragile-looking aluminum stand.

Formerly Addison would have balked at being taken for a TV repairman, but abetting a bogus jail-cell wedding and barricading suspected Communists in an office had brazed him for anything; the woman could have mistaken him for a dozen TV repairmen, and he wouldn't have batted an eyelash. Adam experimentally pulled the button. The screen lit up, but showed only hissing snow. Adam turned the knob; every channel was the same. Addison twisted the aluminum-foil rabbit ears that augmented the antennae. This did not improve the reception.

Adam knew that the world as he lived in it dictated that some like Ernie Costa should have fancy, transistorized TV's while others should pay exorbitant rent for obsolete lemons like this one, but somehow knowing that the girl who'd briefly named her daughter after him belonged in the second category struck him as monstrously unjust.

Adam tilted the TV forward. "Look in the back," he told Addison. "Maybe there's a wire loose somewhere." Sweetie continued to worry at Addison's pants cuff.

"Anyway," said the man at the dinette, continuing a conversation their arrival had interrupted, "speaking in tongues"—he paused, collecting his opinions on this important subject as if he were gathering detritus into a pile prior to sweeping it into the dustpan—"is a gift." He spoke in the ponderous way of an expert who must choose his words carefully for fear of being misunderstood by a layman. "There's speaking in tongues, and there's interpreting. Now without interpreting—"

*WHAM!*

The trailer shook, and the snarling and tugging at Addison's ankle ceased. For a moment Addison feared that he would discover Sweetie's flattened corpse under the fallen TV, but no; the dog huddled trembling under the lady's chair. Sweetie had fled the instant the falling set's shadow descended over her. There was a mewling whimper as the baby woke.

Adam and Addison hefted the TV back on its too-small stand, and Adam pulled the knob. The black screen came to life with Charlie Brown offering Linus a thousand dollars if he could name any car as beautiful and economical as a Ford Falcon. On another channel, a cartoon showed a frustrated Chinese baby trying fruitlessly to eat Jell-O with a pair of chopsticks.

Adam turned off the TV.

"We should have tried that ourself," said the woman in frank admiration.

"It's you," said a voice with soft, feminine hostility. Jane stood in the open door. She said louder, so Johnny, who was just stepping onto the bucket behind her could hear, "It's him." Jane lifted the baby from the basinet. "I told you, Mama," she said sternly, jiggling her fretful daughter on her shoulder, "don't put Sally under the window. You know there's a draft there."

"Well, sugar," Jane's mother said, beginning what sounded like a lengthy explanation, "if I put her in the bedroom, then I can't—"

"Thank you, Mama Price," Johnny interrupted. "We sure appreciate you looking after Sally for us. But Jane and me need to talk to this fellow alone."

"They fixed the TV for you," Jane's mother said defensively. She sensed by Johnny's and Jane's reactions that she had done something wrong letting Adam into the house. She picked up Sweetie, who this time allowed himself to be carried, and she and the expert on speaking in tongues stepped from the door onto the bucket and were gone.

Johnny and Jane regarded Addison and Adam silently. Against Jane's shoulder, Sally continued to whimper, working her way up to a full-scale squall. Jane sat at the dinette and draped a faded blanket over her shoulders, so she could discreetly unbutton her blouse and nurse.

"Who are you?" Johnny asked. Jane's piercing look asked the same question.

"Yes, I can fully understand your curiosity on that score." Adam coughed. "Let us say, in the words of Popeye the Sailor, I am what I am. I have never believed, however, in letting that fact stand in my way. Do you have the diamonds here?"

Johnny stared with resigned fury as if Adam were a granite outcropping that had unexpectedly obtruded through the kitchen floor and could not under any circumstances be removed. Johnny left the table and headed to what Addison imagined was the bedroom.

"And how's little Bateman?" Adam asked.

"We're changing her name to Sally," Jane said sullenly. Her eyes were bright with unshed tears. "I wish we'd never met you. Me and Johnny thought we was happy. We never even thought about how poor we was until we found them diamonds." Jane seemed to ponder this new and unwelcome discovery. "I wish we never met you."

Johnny returned and tossed the purple bag on the table. "Here they are. I didn't tell Jane about them until just yesterday."

"Good," Adam said. Addison couldn't help a noisy intake

of air when his father poured a dozen diamonds onto the table. "By now I suppose you've learned that diamonds aren't so easy to unload. It's not like finding a bag of jelly beans. Each diamond is individual—itemized and recorded meticulously. You can't just show up somewhere and say, 'Does anybody want to buy a bag of diamonds?' "

"We don't sell stolen goods," Johnny said, his chin thrust forward.

"No, no, of course not," Adam backpedaled. Why had he said that? Why did he have to sound supercilious just as he was on the verge of snatching away more riches than these people had ever dreamed of? In spite of his poverty, the shoeshine boy never stole because stealing was mean, but then bags of diamonds never fell into the shoeshine boy's lap, and the Shoeshine Boy didn't have a baby to care for. He and Evelyn had been poor once—not quite as poor as this—but they had been young like this and in love like this. "I wasn't suggesting—It's just something you would have naturally found out in the course of . . . looking after them. They were in my windbreaker pocket, I suppose, when I gave it to you after . . ." Delicacy prevented him from reminding them what he'd been doing when he gave them the windbreaker.

"We just couldn't figure what any honest man was doing with all them diamonds. Especially a *doctor*," Johnny explained unconvincingly. He sat at the table and stared angrily at the shiny pebbles that had cost him so much sleep.

Adam never imagined recovering his diamonds would be so joyless. He held open the mouth of the purple bag and dutifully began to gather the stones into a pile. Jane bit her lip and turned her head so she wouldn't see.

"Dad," Addison said, "what about the reward?"

Adam looked up gratefully. "Oh, that's right! There's a

reward—ten percent." He reached for the checkbook in his coat pocket. "And also, Jane, why don't you pick out one for yourself?" Jane looked up, disbelieving, first at Adam, then at the sparkling stones on the Formica. She reached shyly for the one nearest her.

"The one next to it is bigger," Addison suggested.

Adam said, "And this one has a better color." After she selected, Adam began to make out the check. "I'll put in a little extra," he said, "so you can have it set into a ring, and some to set up a little college fund for little . . ." He trailed off.

"Her name is Bateman," Jane said decisively.

## SEVENTEEN

# And So to Wed

They arrived at the church, and Adam told Addison, "Go on inside and let them get some pictures of you. I'll be there shortly."

"When is Kean coming?"

"I really couldn't say," Adam said ambiguously.

Adam did not go into the chapel, but into a side door that opened into the hall leading to Father Peel's office. Between his excitement over discovering the diamonds and the urgency of halting the impending marriage he imagined ticking like a time bomb, he needed to call in some reinforcements and no mistake. The office door was locked, but Adam recognized the knob as an inferior model, easily popped open by a tight jerk. Adam gave it one, and sure enough the lock gave way and he was inside. Moore Locks, for all its president's peccadilloes, produced a vastly superior product to this one.

Instinct told Adam that the wooden cabinet behind the priest's desk would have what he needed, and it did. Two little cut-glass pitchers—one filled with communion wine and one with water—were stored there until shortly before the service, when they would be placed in a niche near the altar. A silver chalice also waited and a paten full of communion wafers.

Adam poured himself a good chalice-full and quaffed it unmixed with water. Under other circumstances, he would have found the sacramental wine hideously sweet, but after nearly twenty four hours of drought, it came as a refreshing aperitif. He stuffed his cheeks with communion wafers to rid his breath of the smell, and finding they expanded in his mouth like so much wet cardboard, filled the chalice with water—it was really ordinary tap water; it wasn't actually holy water until a priest blessed it—and rinsed away the gummy residue of unleavened bread. He removed the last gooey bits from his back gums with his finger.

Now, he thought, for Lily. She would no doubt have something to say about this, and would probably say it at length and in a loud voice. It was not unlikely she would throw things.

Adam dried the chalice with a cloth reserved for the purpose and replaced it in the cabinet. He shook himself all over, coughed into his fist, rubbed the corners of his eyes to check for any matter there, and exited the priest's office, thoughtfully pulling the door closed after himself.

He returned to the chapel. Wedding guests were starting to fill the pews. There was Lily's appalling Aunt Esperanza in an even more appalling hat. He didn't see Lily, but Evelyn was waiting in a pew. He sat beside her. She looked alarmed to see Adam there without Kean, but did not comment.

"Well, so this is the big day," Evelyn said.

Adam hunched forward and clasped his hands between his knees. "Yes. Yes, I suppose it is." He could smell the polished wooden pew in front of him. He had always liked that smell. He sighed. "We were happy, weren't we?"

"We were very happy."

"Do you remember that day after the article came out?"

"Oh, yes."

Paradise Dogs opened to such a prolonged drought of customers that it scared them lest all their hard work, not to mention their pooled savings, would—in the words of Robert Burns—gang a-gley. But then someone wrote a review in *The Sentinel.* The day after that it seemed all of Orange County discovered them. They drafted Kean into ferrying food to tables while Adam and Evelyn shoveled hot dogs and onion rings across the counter as fast as they could and took in so much money they couldn't stop to count it. The till was too jam-full to close, and crumpled bills fell to the floor to be trodden on as the Newmans ran back and forth filling orders. Baby Addison slept through the whole thing, lulled to sleep by the pleasant cacophony of hectic commerce. All Adam kept thinking was that soon they would run out of food, and he could lock up with the brass key on the hook by the fry cooker, so they could sweep up and count their profits.

"We didn't make chicken, or hamburgers, or pizza, or tacos," Adam said. "Just hot dogs."

"But the very best hot dogs," she said.

Lily came in the chapel and posed near the rail in her wedding gown, looking over one shoulder at a stained glass window as if she expected St. George to step out of it and speak to her. The fat photographer knelt in front of her, his face behind a camera. An arsenal of additional cameras, lenses, flashbulbs, and leather cases hung from him like baby possums.

"Adam, you must never do anything to hurt her," Evelyn said. "Do you understand? I don't want you ever to hurt her. She'll take care of you. You need taking care of."

Adam rose and went to Lily. "Adam," Lily said. "It is bad

luck to see the bride before the wedding." In spite of this, Lily risked further misfortune by lifting the gown's skirt with simple pride to display its drape.

"We need to talk a little."

"Are you prepared for the ceremony? We must expedite this."

Luminous silk cinched her waist and came up caressingly over her bosom. A high lace collar rose up her graceful neck. She really was beautiful, Adam thought sadly. Slim but curvaceous with dark lustrous hair and a good jawline. Most people would have thought her prettier than Evelyn. She wouldn't have difficulty finding someone else. A verse went through his head: *Each man kills the thing he loves, by each let this be heard. Some do it with a bitter look, some with a flattering word, the coward does it with a kiss . . .*

"Yes, well, but give me just a moment. There's something I—" His voice faltered and failed, like that of a child who can't bear admitting some shameful thing. *I was the one—I know you warned me.* He beckoned her with a gesture.

Lily was not an easy woman to beckon, but she finally left the window when it became clear Adam was not budging until she did. He led her into Fellowship Hall. He pulled out a chair from one of the tables. "Let's sit here," he said.

"Please inform me what this concerns," Lily said. "Adam, we are on a schedule here."

"You need to sit for this," Adam said. She sat in a folding chair, and he sat also. He took her hand in his and patted it. It surprised him how tiny it was. Her skin was smooth and cool. Perfect fingernails gleamed with clear polish. A stiff lace cuff covered her delicate wrist. Her expression said she was bracing for whatever surprise he had in store, but that she wasn't anticipating it to be a pleasant surprise. "Lily, I'm not going to marry you." He waited for the thunderbolt—for her to curse him because he'd broken his promises, wasted the best years of her life, humiliated her, ruined her, et cetera, et cetera. And the people who were waiting to see a marriage—what were they going to tell them? "I'm very, very sorry," he said, "I can't tell you how sorry I am. But I wouldn't be able to make you happy, and you deserve better. Lily?"

It was like watching shaved ice on a stovetop.

Lily's face didn't just crumple, it toppled. Her mouth dropped into a rectangle of grief, and tears ran from her eyes. The sob worked its way slowly down her body; she filled her lungs and wailed, and hid her face in her hands.

Adam had not anticipated this. Stamping of feet, slamming of doors, shouts, projectiles aimed at his head, yes, but not this.

"You—could—make—me—happy," she gasped between sobs. "You—make—me—happy." His arms were around her at once. She clutched his sleeves and her surprisingly delicate shoulders heaved. "I—love—you—can't—live—without you."

Adam stroked her hair and found himself kissing it tenderly.

What was Adam to do? He couldn't let another human being suffer so, could he? In spite of everything, even Evelyn had said she did not want Lily to suffer. In the past few days he had been a minister, a doctor, and a TV repairman. How hard could it be to act like a husband? He was an expert husband. Tell them you love them once a day, do the occasional odd job, and that was all there was to it. "There, there," he said and kissed her perfumed hair. He'd always liked her perfume, he realized. "I didn't mean it. I'm sorry. I don't know what I was thinking. I love you. Of course, I'll marry you."

"Oh, boo-hoo," she said. "Boo-hoo." It was the most astonishing thing; when Lily cried, she actually said *boo-hoo.*

Probably it was something she'd picked up from *Reader's Digest.* When she sneezed, she also said *ker-choo.*

"Are you sure?" she said, lifting her head from his shoulder slightly. "I don't want to make you marry me if you don't love me. I couldn't bear it."

"I'm sure, I'm sure," Adam said. "I love you. I don't know why I said it. I was just afraid that you didn't love me, I guess."

"You know I love you. I've always loved you." The sobs subsided to sniffles. "I can't live without you. You're the most wonderful thing that ever happened to me." Her arms were around his neck, and her wet face was against his skin. "Are you sure you want to marry me, are you sure?"

"Of course, I'm sure," Adam said. He gently lifted her away from him by her shoulders and took the purple bag from his jacket pocket. Careful to conceal the Akron Marbles label, he poured the loose diamonds into her lap, where they sparkled against the white satin like crystals on a snowy field. "Take your pick, darling, any one you want."

The fat photographer interrupted Kathleen in the midst of explaining to a woman in a big hat, "No, that's *arroz con pollo,*" so he could take pictures, of the best man and maid of honor: in front of the altar, in front of the chapel doors, beside the bird fountain in the garden, beneath various stained glass windows. When he told them they made a cute couple, they did not trouble to correct him. In every pose he had Addison and Kathleen link arms or hold hands until it became second nature to do so. When, having exhausted the possibilities of the best man/maid of honor motif, the photographer finally waddled inside to take pictures of the bride, Addison released Kathleen's hand.

"I wonder where Kean is," Kathleen said.

"I don't think he's coming," Addison said.

"I'd be just as happy if he didn't," Kathleen said. They studied the stained glass above the vestibule door—a graphic explanation of the Holy Trinity that resembled a uterus. In the center was the word *Deus* connected by banners reading *est, est, est* to a dove, a lamb, and a thundercloud, each of which was connected to the others with banners reading *non est, non est, non est.* It was a perfect visual representation of the Opoyo: no doubt intended to illuminate some tricky theological point, it only succeeded in being completely opaque. From her childhood, she remembered something from the Bible that in the beginning was the Word, and the Word was with God and the Word was God; a notion began to take form in her mind like a droplet trembling at the lip of a leaky faucet.

"So when do you leave for Arkansas?" Addison asked.

"I'm not," Kathleen said. Addison looked at her in surprise. "Dr. Joseph called me yesterday afternoon and said they were letting me keep the fellowship after all." She shook her head in disbelief. "It's the strangest thing, but I think your father had something to with it. I didn't tell you, but he showed up at my meeting. Dr. Joseph kept asking me who 'Dr. Newman' was. He seemed to think your father was some sort of a big shot."

Addison recognized uncanny forces at work. He shivered as if a rabbit had run over his grave, as if an entire herd of rabbits were running over it in unrelenting relays. "It's the damnedest thing," Addison said and told Kathleen about Mr. Beasley's remarkable phone call. "But it doesn't make sense because I didn't *go* to work yesterday," Addison said, remembering that when he was trailing his father in the limousine the other day, Adam's jeep had disappeared for a lengthy period, and finally hove back into sight not far from *The Sentinel.* In Addison's imagination he seemed to hear the grinding of gears of a deus ex machina lowering Zeus onto the stage to tidy up all the loose ends: unsatisfactory in fiction, perhaps, but extraordinarily gratifying when it occurs in real life.

Addison shook his head. By some inexplicable power, his father had made things turn out all right in spite of overwhelming odds. The Amazing Adam Newman.

"So all this, my fellowship, you and the limousine—it had to do with what you were doing in the Fish Camp and after?"

"Yes," Addison said.

"And you left Kean in the hospital because of this?"

"Yes," Addison said. "We didn't want to, but it was something we had to do."

"So what was it all—? What exactly went on? What all did you do?"

"I'm not at liberty to tell you everything," Addison said, thinking of the promise they'd made Walt Disney. It pleased him that her eyes widened. "Can I kiss you?" he asked.

"Don't. It would be a mistake," Kathleen warned.

He took her chin in his fingers, and she allowed him to tilt her head up. Addison's stomach flipped and he began to shake at the step he was taking. It would definitely be a mistake, no doubt a catastrophic one, to kiss his brother's girlfriend, but then, Addison was a man who'd faced down Communist agents and recovered stolen diamonds, why should he hesitate now? She closed her eyes, and her delicate brown lashes lay against her cheek. I'm also going to kiss the tip of her delectably crooked nose and that too-high forehead, he told himself. He leaned in.

Then it came to him, the story title he'd been searching for, "The Vaguely Whispering Dusk." He froze, scant millimeters from Kathleen's lips, and tried it several times in his mind's ear, finding it more gratifyingly perfect each time: "The Vaguely Whispering Dusk," "The Vaguely Whispering

Dusk," and with the title, like Athena springing full-grown from the brow of Zeus, came the story entire, and Addison knew exactly what he would write. It would open with a young man who lives with his wife, daughter, mother, *and* a puppy.

Kathleen sensed some thrill run through Addison and it passed into her like electricity. An enchanted frog might not be so bad after all, she reflected, and she might even forgive him for writing that letter—which she had never thrown away—telling his true feelings for her only after she'd started dating his brother. Enchanted princes, after all, are princes nonetheless and worth the risk of maintaining certain recidivist froglike tendencies. For a moment they were poised that way, lips almost touching, the breath from his nostrils stirring the invisible hairs along her cheek, and saying nothing.

# Epilogue

Walt never saw Disney World become a reality. Ten days before Christmas 1966 he died of lung cancer, the result of a long-standing smoking habit. The family had kept his condition a secret from him, but by then he'd already lost a lung, so he must have suspected time was drawing short. Roy sat with Walt in his Burbank hospital room the night before he died, and the two brothers discussed plans for EPCOT. Roy was the last person to see Walt alive. After Walt's death, *The Miami Herald* ran a cartoon picturing Mickey Mouse and other beloved Disney characters weeping.

The Experimental Prototype Community of Tomorrow didn't live up to Walt Disney's dreams for it. The glass-domed model city with its carefully planned green spaces and underground transportation hub was never built; instead, EPCOT functions as a permanent world's fair, exhibiting future technology alongside cuisines, customs, and merchandise from around the world. EPCOT plays host to millions of visitors each year.

Johnny and Jane used their reward money to open a restaurant in Fort Walton called Paradise Burgers. Because Adam's name was on the check, they would have known the identity of their benefactor, so this may not have been the long stretch of coincidence it appears at first. Bateman got an MBA and plans to franchise.

# Disclaimers, Acknowledgments, and Apologies

Although Compass East and Ayefour are real entities, the description of their Florida offices is wholly imaginary, as is my depiction of the headquarters of WED Enterprises; plot requirements forced me to transplant the latter to Florida, but I wanted to convey the excitement and bustle surrounding the development of the Experimental Prototype. Frankly, I describe WED HQ as I wish it appeared. Knowledge of the massive land purchases involved was much more widespread than portrayed here, and occasioned much speculation about the agents involved.

The concept of Opoyul was given to me by Stephanie "J. S." Buskirk, she of the short-lived but justly renowned "Info Demo" series in Atlanta.

Thanks above all to my patient readers and fellow writers Jamie Iredell and Chris Bundy, and my own sweet wife, Nancy.